DARE YOU
TO LIE

DARE YOU TO LIE

AMBER LYNN NATUSCH

TOR
TEEN

A TOM DOHERTY ASSOCIATES BOOK
NEW YORK

DARE YOU TO LIE

Copyright © 2018 by Amber Lynn Natusch

A Tor Teen Book
Published by Tom Doherty Associates
175 Fifth Avenue
New York, NY 10010

www.tor-forge.com

Tor® is a registered trademark of Macmillan Publishing Group, LLC.

The Library of Congress Cataloging-in-Publication Data is available upon request.

ISBN 978-0-7653-9767-6 (hardcover)
ISBN 978-0-7653-9769-0 (ebook)

Our books may be purchased in bulk for promotional, educational, or business use. Please contact your local bookseller or the Macmillan Corporate and Premium Sales Department at 1-800-221-7945, extension 5442, or by email at MacmillanSpecialMarkets@macmillan.com.

First Edition: September 2018

Printed in the United States of America

0 9 8 7 6 5 4 3 2 1

To my agent, Jess
We did it

ACKNOWLEDGMENTS

Flowery thank-you notes are not my specialty, but I'm going to do my best because these people deserve it.

First and foremost, I need to thank my agent, Jess Watterson. You took a chance on a self-published author. You were with me before I even had something for you to sell. At every turn, you've proven to be one of the best decisions I've ever made in my writing career.

Behind every great story is an amazing editor. Mine is Amy Stapp. Yes, I might have been traumatized by your suggestion to gut my book and rewrite most of it, but it was for the better. That's what a great editor does: takes your work and elevates it. I'm so grateful that you chose to work with me, and I think we have some amazing stories yet to tell.

To my beta-reading team, Kristen Bronner, Kristi Massaro, and Courtney DeLollis. You guys do more for me than you could possibly know.

Shannon Morton . . . what can I say? I'm lost without your brain to balance mine. This story in particular would have been much harder to bring to life without your input. Thanks for the early morning messages (should read "rants") and talking me off ledges. Ky and I both appreciate it.

Truth be told, I'd never get anything done without my amazing assistant, Jena Gregoire. Thanks isn't enough for all you do for me (which is probably why I pay you . . .). We make a good team.

To Megan O'Brien, Lindsey Flaherty, and Jonathan Blanton, thank you so much for your professional expertise and your patience dealing with my tedious hypotheticals. I feel like, at times, they were never-ending.

Three years ago, I wandered into Baan Muay Thai to try out one of their classes. At the time, I was really struggling with my identity as a has-been athlete and dancer. After I became a mother, I couldn't seem to find a sport/fitness routine that I really wanted to commit to. Then I discovered Muay Thai. Thanks to Kru Mark Klemm and Maria Kritikos (and the Baan Muay Thai family), I've finally found not only a great outlet for my frustrations in life but also a sport I love and a main character I adore. I'm so grateful to you all.

I want to thank Zohra Ashpari for doing a stellar job filling in for my editor during her leave, as well as the rest of the Tor Teen team. I may not have worked with you all directly, but I appreciate your hard work nonetheless.

Lastly, I want to thank my husband, who never bats an eyelash when I randomly rattle off a new scene idea (or act it out), or lock myself in the bathroom to jot down some notes (because it's the only place to hide from my kids for more than five minutes), or have to work on weekends (because writing hours don't always fall between Monday and Friday). I know it isn't easy, but you weather it (and me) like a champ. *Ich liebe dich*.

DARE YOU
TO LIE

ONE

Guilty . . .

That single word unraveled my entire life.

From the time of my father's arrest until his verdict was delivered, nothing else mattered to me. Not school. Not my friends. Nothing. I was consumed by the trial—the lies and scandal surrounding it. There was no doubt in my mind that he was innocent, but the evidence said otherwise.

And there was plenty of that.

The prosecution had paraded witness after witness up to take the stand and testify against my father. Colleagues. Friends. No one was off-limits.

Even me.

I'd cried that morning, knowing that I had no choice but to stand before the court and swear on a Bible that I had seen my father, FBI detective Bruce Danners, on the night in question. The night when his alleged criminal activities came to a head. I was the one who placed him with the victim.

I was the nail in his judicial coffin.

I knew I'd never forget the look on his face as he stared at me while I sat on the witness stand. There was pride in his eyes when I told the truth. There was also relief. I'd said I'd lie under oath if it meant keeping him out of prison. I mean, what juror wouldn't believe a sob story from a poor seventeen-year-old girl who had been coerced and leveraged into testifying against her own father? If I'd poured on the tears and played my cards right, surely at least one of them would have found my story plausible. And if they did, the jury would have been split and unable to convict him. That whole "beyond a shadow of a doubt" thing would have gotten in the way.

My father would have been home free.

But I couldn't do it. The integrity that I'd inherited from my father was the reason why. And that integrity was also the reason I knew my father couldn't possibly have done what he was accused of.

The sound of a gavel echoed through the room, branding my father a cop killer. That slap of reality yanked me from my mind's downward spiral. I looked up through bleary eyes to see my father being led away by the bailiff. My heart pounded wildly in my chest. "Daddy!" I screamed before realizing the word had left my mouth. He looked back over his shoulder to me and forced a sad smile.

"It'll be okay, Kylene. The truth can't stay buried forever."

Tears fell freely down my cheeks.

The commotion surrounding me died off not long after my father disappeared. The reporters scattered to interview the winning team. The witnesses dispersed to go on with their daily lives. The jury was taken back to their private area to un-doubtedly be thanked for fulfilling their civic duty. I, how-ever, sat and pondered my father's final words as they ran over and over again through my mind. By the time the courtroom was empty, two things were abundantly clear: my father would never stop proclaiming his innocence.

And I would never stop trying to prove it.

TWO

I stood outside the massive red brick building, eyeing it as if it were an enemy. As far as I was concerned, it was. Almost two and a half years ago, the end of my freshman year at Jasperville High, had been torture. I didn't think I'd survive the next. So, the day my father came home and told me he'd been promoted and we'd be moving to Columbus, I was elated. I squealed so loudly he actually had to cover his ears. But that elation was short-lived.

Fast-forward to my senior year, and I once again found myself standing just outside the gates of hell, knowing exactly what that spiteful place had in store for me. This time, however, I was ready for it. Nobody within those walls could make my life any worse than it already was.

My father's conviction had made certain of that.

With that unwelcome thought in mind, I took a deep breath and climbed the wide concrete steps that led to the main doors. On the pole to my right, the American flag flew high and proud above me—our country's symbol of freedom.

"'Liberty and justice for all,' my ass."

A group of younger girls—probably freshmen—overheard me talking to myself and giggled, whispering conspiratorially to one another as I passed. I sighed heavily. It was going to be a long day.

I hadn't wanted to move back to Jasperville. In fact, I might have died a little inside the day my mother announced that she was getting a divorce and moving out west to live with her new boyfriend. I could either go with her or move into her childhood home with her father. Though I loved Gramps with a passion, I loathed where he lived—or at least which school district his home fell within. The only positive I could see at the time was that Logan Hill Prison was only thirty minutes from his house.

And that was my father's new home for the next twenty-five to life.

Through the entire move, I did my best not to let Gramps see just how dismayed I was by my homecoming. With no other outlet for my anxiety—no one to turn to—in the quiet of the night, I'd lie on the cot Gramps had set up in his tiny den, and let the pent-up tears roll down my cheeks. Tears full of hurt and betrayal. Tears fueled not only by my father's incarceration and my mother's all but abandoning him and me both, but also by the wrong I had escaped when we moved to Columbus.

A wrong I had wanted to keep in my past.

One I would now be constantly reminded of.

I stopped at the top of the school stairs to stare down the cluster of would-be mean girls, to let them know I didn't care about what they thought. That their ridicule didn't bother me. It was amazing how well a glare could silence others, especially when paired with a raging case of resting bitch face. It took only seven seconds to do just that—a personal record. That particular group of wannabes was going to have to find some other poor kid to gang up on.

My skin was far too thick for their low level of skill.

Once inside the building, I made my way up the half flight of stairs to the front office to pick up my class schedule.

Mrs. Baber sat behind her wall of aged dark wood, as always, assuming her post as the gatekeeper to the principal and all other high-level administrative staff. With her glasses perched near the end of her nose, she looked up at me and exhaled heavily.

"Ms. Danners."

"Mrs. Baber. You look lovely this morning. Did you get a new hairdo?" I asked, knowing full well that her helmet of silver curls hadn't seen a new style in at least a decade. Maybe two. Ignoring my obvious attempt at sucking up, she slapped a piece of paper down on the counter between us and slid it toward me.

"You're late for first period. Not the best way to make a good impression. You have physics with Mr. Callahan. I suggest you get up there as fast as those skinny legs will carry you. He's not known for being gracious about tardiness."

"An excellent and helpful observation, Mrs. Baber. Consider it duly noted." I threw her an exaggerated wink before snatching the class schedule off the counter and turning to leave. In my hurry to escape, I slammed into someone entering Mrs. Baber's chamber of doom.

"I'm so sorry!" I exclaimed, staggering back from the wall of distressed black clothing I'd just collided with. As my eyes scanned up toward his face, Mrs. Baber started in.

"Mr. Higgins. Don't you have somewhere to be right now?"

It was then that my gaze reached his face. It was a welcome sight indeed.

"Garrett?"

"Well, I'll be damned," he said, the distinct curl at the corner of his mouth upturning.

"Language, young man!" Mrs. Baber shouted.

"Sorry, ma'am. I just thought I saw a ghost."

"Shut up," I said with a smile.

"Kylene Danners, what in the hell are you doing here?"

"Long story, and since I'm late for physics, not one I can share at the moment."

"Callahan?"

"Yep."

His smile spread wider.

"Then allow me to show you the way. We can be delinquent together."

"Some things never change," Mrs. Baber mumbled to herself.

Garrett made a sweeping gesture with his arm, complete with a bow, and I curtsied in return before heading out of the office. He followed right behind me. Whatever he'd come down to the office for was no longer a priority.

I seemed to have taken its place.

"You sure are all grown up now, Ky. They put something in the water up there in the big city? Because, damn, girl . . ."

I shook my head. Garrett had always been incorrigible. Even after my absence, it appeared that hadn't changed.

"Hey, eyes up here, big guy." I pointed to my face, which earned me a hardy laugh from the boy I'd grown up with. The best friend I'd left behind. "And since you feel it necessary to comment on my appearance, I think it's only fair for me to inquire about this rather interesting new look you have going. Burglar chic or daddy-never-loved-me bad boy? I can't decide."

He frowned at me, his big brown eyes covered by a mess of black hair that slipped out from behind his ear.

"You don't like it? It doesn't scream, 'Bring me home to meet your parents'?"

I laughed.

"It screams something, all right." My sarcastic tone was hardly lost on him. Garrett and I had known each other since we were four. There was little to nothing he didn't know about me. At least until my family left. I hadn't really spoken to him since then, but he knew why. By the look of things, he didn't hold that against me. Maybe he was just being nice. Maybe he knew that coming back to Jasperville High couldn't be easy for me. Or maybe there were some people in your life that you would always just be friends with regardless of what happened between you.

I hoped that was true.

I really needed an ally.

We crested the final stairs to the third floor and made our way to room 333. The hallway was empty, affording the two of us as much privacy as we were likely to get in that building. Garrett stopped me right before I could reach the doorknob to the physics room.

"Ky," he started, giving me his super-serious Garrett stare. The one that reminded me of his father, the sheriff. "About your dad . . . I just wanted to tell you—"

"Please," I interrupted him, putting my palm up to deflect his pity. "The entire state of Ohio and the better part of the country know all about what my father was convicted of. I can't rehash this right now. It's all I can do not to run from here screaming. I wanted to homeschool myself instead of come back here, but Mom—before she bailed on me—wouldn't sign off on it. She said it was unhealthy for me to hole up in the house all day—and she'd know a thing or two about that."

"Listen, I wasn't trying to pry, I was just—"

The door to room 333 swung open, revealing a rather perturbed-looking Mr. Callahan in all his middle-aged glory, complete with pleated khaki pants and coffee-stained oxford shirt.

"Mr. Higgins, I thought I—" He stopped short and his eyes fell on me. It seemed to take a second for him to realize who

I was, but once he did, that realization was written all over his face. "Ms. Danners. How nice of you to join us this morning."

"It's nice to be here, sir," I replied with a hundred-watt smile plastered on my face.

"Perhaps you two will find it easier to learn about Newton if you actually enter the classroom."

"I was just telling Garrett that, Mr. Callahan, but you know how those cops' kids are. They think the rules don't apply to them."

"Says the daughter of an imprisoned ex–FBI detective," Mr. Callahan muttered under his breath, though he did little to hide the contempt for my father's crime from his expression. A jolt of hurt and surprise shot through me. I'd mentally prepared for snide remarks from the student body at JHS, but not from the staff. I felt my expression fall for a second, before a spark ignited within me. I narrowed my eyes at him and did my best to rein in the anger that raged inside.

"Detectives' kids are an entirely different breed."

"I'm sure they are, Ms. Danners."

He stepped back from the doorway to allow us to enter. Garrett went first, casting a sympathetic glance back at me. He knew that Callahan's remark was only the first of many that would be thrown my way that day. He also knew that I wouldn't take any of them lightly. I was a pit bull when people came after someone I loved. If they crossed me, they didn't just burn a bridge—they doused that thing in gasoline, laced it with TNT, lit a match, and blew that bitch sky-high.

Garrett knew that Mr. Callahan had just made himself an enemy.

I wondered how many more Jasperville Fighting Badgers would find themselves on my shit list by the end of the week.

THREE

Because of the move and the different school calendar Jasperville had, my peers were two weeks into the first semester when I started my senior year. The bad news was I had two weeks' worth of crap to get caught up on—starting with physics. The good news was that would keep me busy during my second period study hall. Busy enough to ignore the stares and pithy comments that always echoed through the room no matter how quiet you thought you were being.

I knew all too well about that.

Garrett had English next, so that left me alone to brave second period. I'd forgotten how amazing he had been amid all the chaos surrounding both my departure from town and settling into a new life. A pang of guilt tugged at my heart. He didn't deserve the way I had shut him out. I needed to right that wrong.

With that in mind, I sat down at a vacant table, sprawling my books out everywhere to deter anyone from taking up residence near me—not that anyone was dying for that privilege. I quickly slipped my earbuds in and turned up my music in an attempt to drown out the gossiping around me. I had high hopes that I could make it through the period.

But those hopes were crapped on in a hurry.

I dared to look up from my textbook just long enough to

see a gazelle walking amid lions. A tall, lanky, freckle-faced ginger came striding into the room, her books clutched to her chest. I didn't recognize her. And judging by the uncomfortable look on her face, I could tell she was new enough to the school to still have the expected amount of uncertainty when it came to where to sit. I could see her scanning the tables, none of which were empty any longer. My best guess was that she got derailed on her way here, something she'd made a point before that day never to do, but was now stuck in "Where do I go?" hell.

Her gaze darted over to a nearby kid, who was clearly talking to her. Her nose scrunched up like she'd just smelled something awful, and she walked away from him in a hurry.

I pulled my earbuds out.

"Aw, c'mon, Tabby. I just want to know if the carpet matches the drapes."

Her faced flushed so red that it almost blended in with her curly chin-length-bob haircut. Captain Curious laughed with all his asshat friends, thinking they were clearly the shit for picking on the new girl. If they wanted a new girl to pick on, I'd give them one.

"So, you're interested in interior decorating?" I shouted across the room at him. He and his group of jackasses turned to face me. "I'm going to let you in on a little secret." I leaned forward over the table as if I were going to tell them something juicy. The new girl hovered nearby, her eyes darting back and forth between me and the guys. "You know what she is? She's the room in your parents' house that you're not allowed in. The one with the nice couches and fancy tables and knickknacks and crap that you're too clumsy to be around because God knows you'd break them." He looked at me with confusion that quickly bled to anger. "It doesn't matter if the drapes and carpet match in that room," I said. "You know why? Because you're never going in there. Understand?"

He scoffed at me, looking to his friends for support.

"Shouldn't you be trying to get your dad out of jail or something?"

"Or dying of embarrassment?" his unhelpful friend added.

"But if I died, I wouldn't get to enjoy this special time with you fine gentlemen."

"That's okay, A-cup. I've seen your goods. We all have. We don't need to spend any special time with you."

They all laughed heartily.

I could feel the blood leave my face even when I tried to force it to stay. I was used to people saying things about my father. I was less prepared to have the internet scandal of my past thrown in my face.

While I tried to collect myself and throw something back his way, the new girl stepped in.

"Hey," she snapped, drawing their attention. "Yes, my curtains match the drapes, you idiot. And from what I've heard in the few weeks I've been here, the only thing I'd get if I let you near either is a healthy case of crabs." She placed her hands on my table and leaned forward at them like a CEO talking to her minions. "Those are lice that live down there," she whispered, pointing down toward their nether regions.

"Shut up, you stupid immigrant! Why don't you go back to your third-world country? Stop mooching off our tax dollars."

"I'm from Canada, you moron. And I'm here legally. My dad runs the plant that your dad works for. We pay taxes." She shot me a bewildered expression. "Are all Americans this ignorant?"

I looked up at her, wondering where in the hell this burst of confidence had come from, then realized it didn't matter. It was funny as hell, so I laughed. Hard.

The target of her insults and his befuddled companions were stumped for the first time since class started, and they chose to tuck tail and run rather than tangle with the spirited red-head. She, however, just smiled down at me before joining in with my hysterics. With an inelegant motion, she flopped down at my table two seats over and laughed until tears formed in the corners of her eyes.

And that was how the new girl and I became outcast allies.

It turned out that the new girl, Tabby, was a whiz at school—one of those book-smart, socially awkward types. Apparently wherever she'd attended before moving to the United States was way ahead of Jasperville's curriculum, so she'd already learned everything we had planned for the year. By the end of study hall, I was already halfway caught up on physics. Sticking up for Tabby was going to give me a stellar GPA.

The bell rang, and I started shoving my books into my bag. When I got up to leave, Tabby stood beside me smiling, her books once again clutched to her chest.

"What class do you have now?"

"Gym." The way I groaned my reply let her know just how excited I was.

"Great! Me too. Let's go. Ms. Davies can get pissy if you aren't dressed and in the gym in a timely fashion."

"Yeah. Seems everyone around here is a stickler for punctuality. It's like they're trying not to let the patients run the asylum. So weird . . ."

She looked at me strangely for a second, then laughed.

"You're funny. Are you always this funny? Are you actively trying to be? Or do things just come out that way?"

"It's a reflex. I can't control it. I've been afflicted with a terrible case of sarcasm for which there is no cure." I sighed in my most put-upon way. "It is my burden to bear, but bear it I shall."

"With grace, no doubt," she replied with a smile.

"Is there any other way?"

"I'm sure if there was, you'd have found it by now."

I looked up at her, feigning awe.

"It's like you truly know me."

"You know, I feel like I already do. Is that weird?" She shied away, looking uncomfortable that she'd just told me that. There was an innocent charm to Tabby that couldn't be denied. A childlike quality that was endearing, and coming from me, that said a lot. I didn't usually find anything endearing, especially not people. "Is your dad really in jail?" she asked before her eyes went wide and she slapped her hand over her mouth. "Sorry! I shouldn't have asked that. I don't have much of a filter. It's just that . . . once I'm comfortable around someone, ideas just pop into my head, and then, *whoa* . . . there they go out of my mouth. It gets me in trouble sometimes."

"Don't I know what that's like. I'd trade mine for yours any day of the week." We walked in silence for a beat before I decided there was no point in evading her question. She was going to find out sooner or later. It was probably for the best that it came from me. "Yes, my dad is in prison. His name is Bruce Danners. Google will happily answer all your other questions. It's not my favorite topic of discussion."

"I'm sorry," she said. Whether she was sorry for his situation or for asking the question, I didn't know.

"Not your fault."

Tabby pushed the heavy wooden door open, and I followed her into the changing room. It was already filled with the other girls in our gym class. I always thought too many girls in one place was a special kind of hell. The inherent pack mentality in them was undeniable. The second they smelled blood, these seemingly lovely high school seniors would turn feral, jumping on their prey and tearing it to shreds, all without even breaking a sweat—or a nail.

With a sigh, I opened a locker at the end of the center row and threw my bag in. Tabby took the one next to me and started to get changed. Her pale, freckled skin was washed out by the white T-shirt she slipped on, and the black gym shorts she stepped into did little to flatter her lanky legs. She was gawky at best. Her saving grace was her huge boobs. It seemed unfair for someone so skinny to have a rack like that.

I looked down at my modest chest—the girls just chilling in my bra—and frowned.

"They look great," she said, glancing down at them. "And they're clearly not As. Bs, right?"

"Are you like a bra-size savant or something?"

She shrugged.

"We all have gifts."

"It's uncanny. . . ."

I pulled my white T on and unbuttoned my jeans while Tabby leaned against her locker waiting for me. Until then, she'd proved a welcome distraction from the others in the room, but I suddenly became all too aware of them, as was their intention. I looked over to find a group of them huddled together just beyond Tabby.

"You know, there's a much easier way to get a good look at Ky's tits," one girl said before breaking out into mocking laughter.

"Looks like yours finally came in," I replied without skipping a beat. I did little to hide the bitchiness in my voice. Why bother? She wasn't exactly hiding hers.

Meet fire with fire, Dad always said.

"I only suggested it since you two seemed to be having such a great time checking each other out."

"She has nice boobs," Tabby said with a shrug, as if that were going to settle the matter—or be helpful in any way. The new girl was right about her lack of filter. We were going to have to work on that.

"Yeah, well, try that with me, new kid, and I'll slam your face in a locker."

Tabby's expression went slack for a moment. I don't think she was expecting such a violent response. It was clear she wasn't from Jasperville. Adults seemed to think it was always the boys who resolved matters with their fists, but in this school, you were far more likely to find two girls going at it in the hallways or the bathrooms. On any given day, you could find tufts of ripped-out hair blowing down the hall like tumbleweeds. It was lowbrow at best, Neanderthalish at worst, but any way you sliced it, it was reality. Plain and simple.

"Girls!" a gruff, disembodied voice shouted at us. Seconds later, Ms. Davies, in all her clichéd female-gym-teacher glory, rounded the corner and pounded her fist on the lockers. "Let's go! Don't make me start handing out extra laps to run this early in the school year, even though some of you look like you could use them."

Without replying, we all filed out into the gym. The mean girl walked past Tabby and me, glaring the whole way. I just smiled and waved. Tabby looked rattled. The two of us were the last to leave, followed by Ms. Davies, who pulled me gently aside before entering the gym.

"Kylene," she started, her voice quiet, "I know what happened with your father. I just wanted to tell you that I knew him. I'd worked with him on two different occasions—projects for the community—and I just don't believe he is capable of doing what they accused him of."

I forced a tight smile in return while I choked back my rising emotions.

"Thanks, Ms. Davies."

"And if anyone is giving you crap about him, you come to me. Understand? I know how things are in this school. But not in my class."

My smile softened into a genuine one.

"I appreciate that. Really."

"Good. Now get your ass in there. You're doing a lap for being the last one to class."

She shot me a mischievous look before pushing the gym door open and walking in, blowing her whistle to announce her entrance.

Note to self: Ms. Davies is all right.

FOUR

By the time lunch period rolled around, I realized that there would be no shaking Tabby, even if I'd wanted to. Thankfully that wasn't the case. She was a breath of fresh air in a stale place—a very necessary distraction.

We made our way down to the cafeteria. The whole way there, she asked a million questions about me, the school, the town, and the United States in general. I was thankful to get a small reprieve when we entered the à la carte section of the food line. I grabbed a bag of chips and an apple, then made my way over to the register to pay. Tabby wasn't far behind.

Once we'd paid, we made our way outside to the terrace. Upperclassmen were allowed to eat out there, weather permitting. Having never had the privilege to use it before, I was excited that for the first time at a school I could bask in the sun while eating my lunch.

I was even more excited when I saw Garrett leave his table to come join us where we sat.

"You survived the morning, I see," he said, straddling the end of my bench seat.

"I did. So did everyone around me, which is even more surprising."

He stole one of my chips.

"Very true. I can see that your time away from here didn't improve your sunny disposition."

"I mean . . . it did, but there's just something about this place that brings out my finer qualities."

"Mine too," Tabby chimed in.

Garrett looked over at her, then back to me. His eyebrow quirked with curiosity.

"Garrett, this is Tabby, Jasperville's latest import, fresh from north of the border. Tabby, this is Garrett, the sheriff's kid."

His expression soured.

"That's it? The sheriff's kid? That's all I get?"

I shrugged before shoving a handful of chips in my mouth and chewing them dramatically. "You're losing your edge, Ky." Garrett then turned his attention to Tabby, who smiled at him like a giddy schoolgirl. "Nice to meet you, Tabby."

"You too, Sheriff's Kid."

She shot me glance that screamed *Did you see what I did there?*

"Turning another innocent mind to the dark side, I see," Garrett drawled, grabbing another chip from my bag.

"Don't you have a lunch to eat? Wanna save some calories for me? I don't want to fall asleep in English lit this afternoon."

He laughed.

"Good luck with that. We're reading James Fenimore Cooper. If that isn't coma-inducing, I don't know what is. . . ."

"You don't like his writing?" Tabby asked, looking wounded. "I loved *The Last of the Mohicans*. It was so powerful. So haunting."

I stared at her blankly, waiting for her to break out into laughter, but it never came. Instead, her wide blue eyes just darted back and forth between Garrett and me, hoping one of us would see the wisdom in her words. When we didn't, her shoulders slumped forward in a huff. "Nobody appreciates the classics anymore."

"I have a 'fifty-eight Corvette I'm fixing up," Garrett said. "Does that count?"

Judging by her expression, it didn't.

"So Garrett," I said, changing the subject. "I think we really need to talk about all this black. What's going on here? Is this a phase or the new you?"

"Well, it's not really either. I just didn't have anything else clean, but the days of preppy Garrett are long gone. You don't know anything about that because I haven't seen or talked to you in over two years."

Though he tried to make that statement playful, there was a clear undercurrent of hurt that couldn't be denied. I lowered my chip-wielding hand from my mouth and frowned.

"I sent you text messages," I said softly, averting my eyes.

"At first. Then they stopped."

"Garrett—"

"Listen, Ky. I know that things were beyond rough for you when you left, but, c'mon . . . this is me we're talking about."

"Why did you leave?" Tabby asked.

"I think that's a story for another time, North of the Border," Garrett replied.

"I know I hurt you, Garrett. I need you to understand that that wasn't my intention. I can't tell you how good it felt to be somewhere where nobody knew me. Where they had no idea what happened."

"I get it, Ky. I do. I just wished you hadn't shut me out; that's all I'm saying."

I held up my chip to him, grinning.

"Nothing says I'm sorry like salt-and-vinegar chips," I said. He pulled it from my fingers, then took it down with one big chomp. "Good. Now that that's settled, can we get back to this look you have going on? It's very Kylo Ren. I like it and all, I'm just trying to figure it out. It doesn't scream quarterback."

"It doesn't need to."

"Has your cool status reached a level that societal cues no longer apply to you?"

"Nope. I quit the team."

I stared at him for a moment, my mouth nearly hanging agape.

"You *what*?"

"I quit."

"When? Why? You love football, Garrett. You used to make me play with you all the time. Hell, I can still throw a perfect spiral because of you."

"How can you not know why I quit, Kylene? Or when? Seriously . . . did you think I could spend time with the people that did that to you? After how you suffered?"

I swallowed hard. I'd never really thought about it that way. When the topless pictures of me surfaced, I was so caught up in being mortified that I never considered how it affected my friend. They were taken at a football party—with one of the players' phones. Garrett had integrity, like my father; I should have known he wouldn't have been able to stomach being around the people who did that to me.

"I never considered it."

"Yeah, well, you know me. You should have."

"I'm sorry."

His grip on the water bottle in his hands tightened until it practically begged him to let go. Garrett wasn't your run-of-the-mill outsider—the nerdy, wimpy guy that you always see on TV. In fact, he couldn't have been more the opposite. He was tall and built and really good-looking. More importantly, he was one of the most popular kids in school. At least he had been. I guess he relinquished that position when he abandoned football and took up his new look.

It made me wonder just how isolated from everyone at JHS he'd become.

"And for your information, I don't look like Kylo Ren. I look like a tortured artist. A misunderstood rocker."

"Who doesn't play an instrument, unless you took one up in all your post-football downtime," I countered.

"Chicks love rockers."

"Yep. That is true. How's that working out for you?"

He smiled.

"Better than you'd think."

"Well, I really like the black," Tabby added cheerfully. "You have the complexion for it."

"He's the dark cloud to your sunshine!" I exclaimed, a little too proud of myself for coming up with that one. Neither of my companions looked overly amused. I snatched Garrett's water bottle and tapped on the lid before blowing on it a few times. "Check, check . . . Is this thing on?"

"Very funny, Ky. Hilarious in fact," Garrett said.

"I do what I can," I said, bowing my head.

"Ladies, it's been a treat, but I've got to stop by the front office, since I got derailed there this morning." He shot me a pointed look, then stood up from the bench and reached his hand out for his water bottle. I tossed it to him and he caught it with ease. "I'll see you later. Nice to meet you, Tabby."

She and I waved goodbye to our would-be rocker companion, then cleaned up our table. We only had a couple of minutes left before next period, and I needed to run to my car to drop off the books I'd been given that morning.

"Wanna run with me to my car really quick?"

Tabby nodded enthusiastically and was soon at my side,

walking off the terrace and through the side gate of the school. Across the street was the parking lot where students could park. In it was my less-than-glamorous ride.

"That's so cool that you have a car. My dad won't let me have one yet, but I get to drive his sometimes."

"You won't think it's so cool when you see it." We reached the row where my baby was parked, in all her rusty glory. I walked up to the 1988 Honda Accord and gave her a pat. "Tabby, meet Heidi. She doesn't look like much, but she's family."

Tabby did little to hide her dismay at the sight of poor Heidi. Apparently, she didn't have a filter for her facial expressions, either.

"Does it actually run?"

"At least fifty percent of the time," I told her, yanking the sticky driver's side door open. When I slammed it shut, it sounded like the whole thing was going to fall off in one spectacular thud. I looked over to find Tabby's nose scrunched up with mild disgust. "Aw, c'mon, Tabby. I'll let you drive it. Does that make it look better?"

"Marginally."

"She'll grow on you. I promise."

I smiled and started back through the parking lot toward the school with Tabby at my side. But something made me pause for a moment. A muffled cry made my hair stand on end.

I looked back beyond where I was parked to find a group of football players hanging out in the far side of the lot by their massive pickup trucks—the kind designed to make up for certain shortcomings, if you know what I mean. It was their usual hangout spot. The one I used to find myself in my freshman year.

They were all scattered about, leaning on two of their vehicles, eating lunch. I recognized every single one of them.

They were all part of the crew accused of taking those pictures of me at the end of our freshman year—The Six, as I liked to call them. Mark Sinclair, Scott (aka Scooter) Brown, Eric Stanton, and Jaime Chavez all stared at me with a mix of expressions ranging from surprise to amusement and everything in between. Only two were missing from the crowd that had been there that night.

I couldn't move. Seeing them there, staring at me, paralyzed me for a moment. A wave of unresolved feelings broke through the dam that I'd shored up against them and crashed down on me. I was suffocating in the past as I looked at them in all their carefree glory. They'd taken that from me. That and so much more.

"Ky?" Tabby said, tugging on my arm.

"I . . . I thought I heard something."

Right on cue, that same sound echoed toward us from one of the trucks. I sheltered my eyes from the sun so I could better see who was in it. It was still hard to make him out from a distance, but once I focused long enough, I saw him. A mountain of a boy taking up more space in the cab of his truck than he should have hovered over someone in it, shouting at her. Apparently, the guys eating their lunches weren't too concerned.

Without thinking, I bolted toward the black pickup. I ran past the others and yanked open the passenger door when I reached it. A waif of a girl practically fell out when I did. She must have been pressed up against it like her life depended on it.

And judging by the look of fear in her eyes, it might have.

"Are you okay? I thought I heard a scream." Her wide eyes darted from me to the hulk in the truck, then back to me. It was then I saw the day-old bruises on her forearms where her long-sleeve shirt had been pushed up in the chaos. She quickly slid the sleeves back down before folding her arms across her stomach.

Blood hammered in my ears as my rage built.

"Mind your own business, bitch," the hulk yelled, making his way out of the truck through the open door. He reached for the girl as if to snatch her up and throw her back in the vehicle, but I scooped her behind me with one sweep of my arm and put myself between him and her.

"You like hitting girls, do you? You should give me a try. Not sure you'll like it as much, though. I hit back."

His sneer told me he would be more than happy to take me up on my offer. It was only then that I realized I knew him. What was now an overmuscled bully used to be the average-built kid that lived down the street from me. Donovan Shipman had been an okay guy for the most part. Even-tempered and athletic. He'd been on the football team our freshman year.

He'd also been one of The Six.

Without pause, he came to tower over me, all six foot six of him and the 250 pounds plus he carried on that frame. I braced myself, sliding my right foot out and back just enough to steady myself—just like Kru Tyson had trained me to. I'd grown up in his Muay Thai gym since I was four. My dad had a great appreciation for martial arts in general and always wanted his only child able to protect herself.

In that moment, I was immensely grateful for his line of thinking.

Donovan just loomed there silently, assuming that he could cow me with a menacing stare. Man, did he have another reality headed his way. Truth be told, the last thing I wanted to do was try to go mano a mano with him, but I would not be shut down just because he wanted me to be.

"You do know there are witnesses out here, right?" I pointed toward the group of players that had slowly come around the truck to see what was going on. Though I was relieved that they were there, I soon realized that their presence didn't mean a whole lot. Not given how they'd all covered for each other before. Not one of them lifted a finger to help me or said a word.

Fucking cowards.

"You think they'll say anything? You're dumber than I remember, Danners. You and your dad both, I guess." He leaned down, thrusting his face in mine. I could feel my heart start to race, but I did what I could to calm it, taking a big breath through my nose and out my mouth. Fighting required control, and I needed to regain mine over the situation—and fast. Usually abusers pick their victims carefully, knowing that they won't fight back or don't have a support system in place to leave. I fit neither of those categories, and yet there I was, five seconds away from likely getting my ass kicked.

"C'mon, Donovan," Mark Sinclair said, stepping forward from the others. "She's not worth it."

Donovan looked over at his friend, undoubtedly glaring at him to shut him up. He turned back to me and grabbed the front of my shirt to pull me up onto my toes. Out of reflex, I drew my arm back, ready to slice him with an elbow.

"Say 'cheese,'" Tabby shouted, startling us both. I saw her holding her phone up, taking either a video or pictures of what was happening. Whichever it was, I didn't care. That clever little Canuck was getting evidence of Donovan's attack on me. One that he and his band of asshats couldn't refute this time.

The new girl was clutch.

"Give me that," Donovan roared, letting go of me to lunge toward Tabby. I used his momentum and a well-placed leg sweep to drop him to the ground.

"Run!" I shouted to her, grabbing Donovan's girlfriend by the hand to drag her away.

"No need," Tabby said calmly. "I already emailed it to myself. It's just sitting there, ready to be sent out if he lays a hand on any of us."

Donovan was already scrambling to get up, ready to tear us apart like a bull seeing red.

"Yeah, I'd still run," I said, grabbing her with my other hand as I hauled ass back to the school. Along the way, I made a point to slam my bag into a fancy silver car—one that would surely have an alarm of some kind. Just as I expected, a siren started blaring. Seconds later, the windows on that side of the building were filled with witnesses. The three of us were well past the car, leaving Donovan and his hostility standing next to the BMW with the flashing lights.

He stopped his pursuit, but we kept on running until we reached the school. As my adrenaline rush started to subside, I realized just how close I'd come to fighting Donovan.

Tabby shot me a sideward glance as we entered the building. I nodded at her once to say *thank you*, and she smiled. She continued up to the stairs to her classroom, and I took Donovan's girlfriend into the bathroom with me just as the bell rang.

"You have no idea what you've done," she said, pacing the floor.

I ignored her comment, already pretty clear on what I'd just started with Donovan.

"My name is Kylene," I said, forcing myself to look calm and kind, when really I was more shaken up than I would have liked to admit.

"Amy," she said softly, folding her arms over her stomach again.

"You want to tell me what I broke up out there?" I asked, doing all I could to contain my anger at what I already knew was going on. Her bruises spoke volumes.

"It was nothing. I said something I shouldn't have and he got mad."

"I have a feeling you must do that fairly often." I let my gaze fall to her arms, then back to her face. She said nothing in response. "You don't really think it's your fault, do you?"

"I guess not. I mean, I know he doesn't like it when I talk to other guys."

Red flag number two.

"Talking isn't flirting."

"He's just a little jealous, that's all."

"That looked like a lot more than petty jealousy. How long has this been going on?" I asked her bluntly, pointing at her arms.

"Not long," she said, unable to hold my gaze. "He wasn't always this way. He used to be sweet. But now—"

"Yes?"

"He's just on edge a lot. He's stressed with the pressure of football and training. He doesn't mean to take it out on me. . . ."

Strike three.

"Whatever the reason, it doesn't excuse what he's done to you."

Her arms cinched in tighter.

"You just don't understand." That, we could agree on. "He was fine at the beginning of the summer, but it's just getting worse. The first week of school he picked up this sweet kid from my math class and threw him halfway across the hall just for picking up the pencil I dropped."

"Did anyone see him do it?" She nodded. "Who? Who saw?"

"A few students. A couple teachers."

"Did he get suspended?" She shook her head. "You're telling me that he physically assaulted a kid in front of witnesses and nothing came of it?" She nodded. "Amy, none of this is okay. You need to tell someone who can help."

Tears welled in her eyes.

"I know . . . but I love him."

My hackles raised at her words. He'd really done a number on her. She was young—probably a freshman. She was pretty, but not pretty enough for her to get by on her looks. Judging by her clothes, she wasn't well off. And if I'd been a betting girl, I'd have put a lot of money on her coming from a father-less family. She was so desperate for the love of a man that it was painful to see.

She was the perfect victim for someone like Donovan to prey on.

"He's really not a bad guy, Kylene. . . . He's just—"

"An abusive asshole?" She shied away from my question, and I knew I'd gone too far with that one. Then someone walked into the bathroom and entered a stall behind me. "We should go."

Amy looked up at me, wiped the tears from her eyes, and straightened her spine. Without another word, she made her way out of the bathroom, leaving me with a moment to think. I collapsed my hands onto the sink's edge and hung my head, taking a few deep cleansing breaths. When I felt more to-gether, I looked up into the mirror, wondering how in the hell I'd gotten myself into this mess. Then I realized the answer. It was written all over my face.

I was every bit my father's daughter.

And it was likely to get me into just as much trouble.

FIVE

The end of the day couldn't come soon enough. There was an undeniable knot in my stomach, knowing that Donovan wasn't going to be happier with me when he found out I'd spoken to his little punching bag. I hoped for Amy's sake she didn't mention it. If she did, he'd freak out for sure.

I walked into final period, bummed to be without Garrett or Tabby. Mrs. Stewart, the new Spanish teacher, who knew nothing of my past at the school, smiled widely at me and told me (*en Español*) to take a seat in the back of the class. The seat next to Jaime Chavez.

Why the child born of two Mexican immigrants needed to take Spanish was beyond me.

My disapproval of my seat assignment must have been written all over my face when I sat down beside him. He shrunk down in his seat and trained his gaze on the front of the room.

"Fancy meeting you here, Chavez. Isn't there some other language you should be broadening your horizons with right now, or are you just in it for the easy A?" He rattled off his response in Spanish and far too quickly for me to catch it all. I did, however, pick up on some choice phrasing that I was pretty sure Mrs. Stewart hadn't taught him. "I'll assume that meant the latter."

As the fiftysomething teacher explained our assignment for

the day, I stared at Jaime. He'd always been so quiet, even when we were friends back in the day. He'd moved to town our freshman year—along with his parents and twin sister, Maribel. In fairness to him, moving to Jasperville had to have been one hell of a shock, having lived in California his entire life. To say that our school was whitewashed was an understatement. The week he and Maribel showed up, I heard more racial slurs than I could even count. Garrett and a few of the other football players were the first ones to befriend Jaime. After that, it got easier for the twins.

Maribel and I became close, and we'd all hang out at parties together. Until the night everything went to shit. The next day, when my boobs were plastered all over social media and texted to basically anyone in the county with a cell phone, and it became clear who had been last seen near the hot tub where I'd passed out, our friendships ended. Maribel stood by her brother, turning her back on me. Jaime never said a word to me about it at all. Even if he wasn't the one who took the pictures or shared them, I always thought he'd try to help me—not tighten the ranks with his buddies against my story.

"So, still not talking to me after all this time, Jaime?"

He shot me a sideward glance and exhaled.

"Not much to talk about."

"Well, that sure is one way to look at it. I feel like betraying your friend is kind of a big deal, but really . . . I shouldn't be surprised you wouldn't see it that way."

"It's been over two years, Ky. Being bitter about it doesn't make it better—it makes you a target."

"A target? What the hell does that mean?"

"Nothing . . . Can't you just let it go?"

I felt my blood pressure rising.

"Is that your approach to all major problems you face? You just let them go, no matter how unjust?" He didn't reply, but

I could see his features tighten in frustration. "Tell me something, Jaime," I said, leaning closer to him. "Is that why you were fine standing by while Donovan beat up his girlfriend? Why you're okay with someone taking naked pics of me?" I pulled away, but his warm brown eyes were boring holes in me, his hand clutching the desk so hard his knuckles turned white. I'd hit a nerve with that question for sure. "Oh! Follow-up question: How would you feel if somebody roughed Maribel up like that? Would that be cool? Would you just let that go? Maybe you'd be cool with them taking some topless pics of her, too?"

"Shut up!" he snapped. Judging by how his head snapped toward Mrs. Stewart right afterward, he hadn't meant to say it quite so loudly.

"Is there a problem?" she asked, her previously jovial expression replaced by a no-nonsense glare.

"I just asked if he was willing to help me get caught up on the assignments I missed," I said, feigning shock.

"Jaime! I think you should go pay a visit to Principal Thompson. Now."

He shot me an angry look before he collected his things and walked out of class.

Mrs. Stewart, thinking all was now well, turned her back on the class so she could start pointing something out on the screen at the front of the room. Unfortunately, very few kids were paying attention. At least half of them were staring at me, accusation in their eyes. Yeah, I'd lied and gotten Jaime in trouble, but his temper was his own problem. I didn't make him yell at me. His guilt at my mini interrogation was plain. Jaime seemed too easily rattled by our conversation—like he was trying to hide something about what had happened that night at the party.

And if he was, I had every intention of finding out what.

SIX

I bolted from Spanish the second the bell rang and wove my way through the bodies in the hallway until I reached the front entrance. I caught a glimpse of Donovan escorting Amy out to the truck I'd dragged her from earlier that day, and I knew what that meant. Either Amy was humoring him for the time being to stay safe, or the clichéd apology had happened and she bought it. My guess was it wouldn't have been the first time, either. With a sigh of frustration, I made my way out of the school to my car, where a little present was waiting for me.

Shattered glass was strewn all around the ground surrounding poor Heidi.

"Who needs windows?" I muttered to myself before carefully walking over what had once been my driver's side window.

I yanked the door open and cleaned up what I could of the glass that was sprinkled all over the interior of my car. While I did, I weighed my options. I could file a report with Garrett's dad, but I had no proof of who actually broke the windows, only a possible suspect—maybe six. But the last time I'd gone to the sheriff without ironclad proof of who had committed the crime, it didn't end so well for me. Garrett Higgins was an amazing human being. His father, not so much. He was gruff and cold at times, and extremely old-school. His knee-jerk reaction to girls having half-naked pictures taken of them seemed to be that "boys would be boys" and all that jazz.

My dad was nearly arrested showing Sheriff Higgins exactly what he thought of that rationale.

So, knowing I wouldn't likely get far with the police, I decided to eat shit with a smile and drive home with my new air-conditioning system. Heidi's had been broken for years, so it wasn't all bad. At least it wouldn't be . . . until winter hit. Hopefully by then I'd have scraped together enough money to pay the deductible on my car insurance and get the windows replaced.

But first I'd have to find a job.

I drove through Jasperville, memories floating through my mind. Not all of them were bad. There was Mr. Matthew's Ice Cream Shop, which my parents used to take me to after my youth league soccer games. The park where Garrett and I always played until it got dark. The vintage movie theater where I'd had my first kiss with Troy Jenkins in the back row. Each place put a smile on my face as I passed it. I hadn't always resented the town. It had some redeeming qualities, though they seemed to dwindle as I aged.

Then I drove by an all-too-familiar house, and my stroll down memory lane turned sour. The Millers' house was a big Victorian on one of the original main streets in town. It was stunningly kept and was equally beautiful inside. I knew because I spent the greater part of my freshman year there. Their son had a thing for petite, feisty, blue-eyed blondes, and I seemed drawn to their prodigy football player, who was so good that he was on the starting varsity squad as a freshman. He was tall and gorgeous, with piercing green eyes framed by long black lashes and shaggy dark hair that never appeared to be "done" but always looked amazing. He was a dream come true.

Until the day he wasn't.

Before my mind could wander too far down that dark path, I gathered that particular memory up, crumpled it into a tight ball, and stuffed it away in my brain where it wouldn't easily be found again. After two and a half years, it still hurt too much to think about what he'd done. The knowledge that I would eventually cross paths with him at school was almost more than I could bear. Thankfully for me, I hadn't seen him that day.

But I knew that luck wouldn't last forever.

As if the universe wanted to remind me that I didn't have any luck to start with, the gas light in my car came on. With a heavy sigh, I continued down the street to one of only three gas stations in town. When it had first opened, it was a small convenience store. Now it was an absolute monstrosity that boasted a fast-food chain inside. Just what Jasperville needed.

I pulled into the lot and rolled up to the only open pump. Once I located my wallet inside my bag, I found I only had twenty-three dollars. I frowned, knowing that was all I had to get me through the week. My lunchtime options were going to get iffy by Friday.

I took fifteen bucks out before tucking my wallet back into my bag. Food was optional. Taking the bus to school, however, was not; Gramps had been adamant about that. He knew it was just a sunny-colored mobile prison and could be equally brutal. I was all too amenable to his no-bus demands. Money spent on gas was a damn good investment, as far as I was concerned.

Once I finished pumping the gas, I walked over to the mammoth building to pay for it. When I opened the door to enter, I almost slammed into a woman hurrying out. She looked up at me only seconds before we would have collided, and she startled to a halt.

"I'm so sorry!" she said before her sharp eyes focused on pre-cisely whom she'd almost barreled over. As soon as she real-ized who I was, she smiled. It was a huge, toothy smile that I'd known for the better part of my life. Meg was my mother's best friend, and probably the only person in Jasperville County that still cared about her, other than Gramps and me.

"Geez, lady! How about you pull your head out of your tight ass and watch where you're going," I said, returning her smile.

"Because I like my head up my ass. It's a better view than the one I have now."

With that snappy retort, she threw her arms around me and pulled me tight against her. Meg had never had any kids—never married, for that matter, either. She'd been the crazy aunt I'd never had by blood, and some of my most outrageous memories involved her.

Ones I would never tell my mother about.

"How are you, Ky?" she asked, ushering me back outside the building so we could talk. "I'm working on a crazy case right now and haven't had a chance to come by and see you. Have you settled in?"

"Yeah. As much as I can."

"And your mom?"

I cringed at the question, not really knowing where to be-gin. How to tell her that my mom and dad fell apart during his trial—that her desperate need to be the center of attention had driven her into the arms of someone else. Someone in Cali-fornia. Meg didn't want to know that my mom totally bailed one week after my father's sentence was handed down. But it turned out that I didn't have to say anything at all. Her law-yerly instincts took over, and she filtered my answer to find out what I hadn't said.

"Where is she, Ky?"

"California . . . with Frank the engineer."

She muttered a string of swears under her breath before composing herself.

"How long has that been going on?"

"Longer than I'd like to know, I imagine."

Meg nodded, her expression tight.

"Does Gramps know?"

"Yes, but he doesn't talk about it. He still tries to shelter me from it as best he can."

She looked thoughtful for a moment before replying. "Gramps is the best."

"He really is."

"So, tell me about school. How's it going?" My lack of immediate response told her all she needed to know. "You're miserable, aren't you?" I nodded. "Ugh. I'm so sorry, Ky."

"My dismay at being in this town isn't your honor to claim, I'm afraid. No need to be sorry."

"Damn, girl . . . that smart mouth of yours has only gotten worse, hasn't it?"

"'Fraid so."

Her eyes twinkled with delight.

"I couldn't be prouder." She glanced down at her watch and frowned. "I'm sorry to do this, Ky, but I have to run. I have a meeting in twenty minutes. Are you doing all right otherwise? Do you need anything?"

"Other than a transfer to another high school and a job, no. I'm good."

She laughed—a knowing, bitter laugh that let me know that maybe Meg hadn't enjoyed high school any more than I did.

"I can't help with the school BS, but I might be able to help with the job. We need a part-time assistant at the office. You'd be a glorified gopher, but if you don't mind coffee runs and filing, it would be a great gig. Pays a hell of a lot better than working at a place like this." She jerked her thumb to the massive building behind me and laughed.

"That'd be really great, Meg. Thanks."

"Sure thing, kid. Come by some time this week and I'll show you around. We can get the paperwork started then."

"I really appreciate it. I'll see you soon."

She looked me over once more, then gave me a goodbye hug. I could see the tears welling in her eyes as she let me go and walked away without a word. Meg was more worried about my mom and me than she wanted to let on.

After I gassed up, instead of heading straight down Church Street, I veered off onto the exit ramp and headed east to Logan Hill Prison. I hadn't had a chance to actually see my dad since he was incarcerated—we only talked a couple of times on the phone—so I was excited to finally get the chance. And terrified, too.

The thirty-minute drive went by quickly, and my anticipation grew with every mile. I was familiar with the prison because Gramps had worked there as a correctional officer as long as I could remember. Now past his prime, he worked in a less stressful part of the facility, but he was still dealing with convicts on a daily basis. Gramps was the kind of guy that everyone just liked. I assumed the people imprisoned in Logan Hill weren't any different in that regard. For whatever reason, they never seemed to give him any trouble—or at least none that he ever let on about.

I parked in visitor parking and went through all the necessary steps to gain access not only to the building but also, eventually, my father. Security took a while to get through. By the time they had things all sorted to their liking, I was brought—sans backpack—to the visiting area. It was just like I'd seen in movies: a long line of cubbies, each separated by a thick piece of Plexiglas, and phones hanging on the wall of each cubicle. An officer escorted me to a chair, and a minute later my father was brought in.

The initial shock of seeing him was hard to get past. It was also hard to mask my expression. Wearing his orange jumpsuit, with two guards leading him toward me, reality set in. He was really in prison.

He wasn't coming home.

Under the circumstances, I expected to see a change in him. A tiredness. Resignation. But none of those things had tarnished him yet. Instead, he stood tall and proud, his sturdy frame still holding strong against his situation. Even the black ring around his eye didn't faze him. But it sure as hell worried me.

When he sat down across from me, he gave me the smile he always did. The one that begged mischief to find us. Judging by the size of that shiner and the way my day had gone, mischief already had. I picked up the phone beside me, and he mirrored the gesture, putting the receiver to his ear.

"Hi, Daddy."

"How's my girl? How was school? Was today your first day back?" I nodded. "That good, huh?" His expression darkened. "I guess two and a half years away wasn't long enough. I'm so sorry, baby girl. I wish there was a way to fix this for you."

"As if I need your help," I said, feigning annoyance. "I owned that place from the second I walked in."

"Kinda like I did?" he countered. His sarcasm was duly noted.

"With less punching, yes. Probably a lot like that. But I did manage to come out of it with only two threats of bodily harm and no front windows in my car, so I think I won."

Without skipping a beat, his interrogation began.

"Who threatened you?"

"Some girl in my gym class who was just being a bitch. Technically she threatened the girl next to me, but I took it personally."

"Who else?" he asked. I sighed, not really wanting to tell him who it was. That would only lead to deeper questions I didn't feel like answering. I should have kept my damn mouth shut about it in the first place.

"Donovan Shipman. You remember him?"

My dad's face flushed with anger.

"Threatened how?"

"Long story short, he wants to kick my ass because I wouldn't let him kick his girlfriend's."

His eyes widened as he exhaled heavily, leaning back in his chair.

"Kylene, that's serious stuff. I don't want you messing around with him directly. You need to go to Principal Thompson. If you know for a fact that's going on, someone needs to protect that girl. Her parents need to be brought in. His too. Possibly Sheriff Higgins, if there's physical proof—not that he'd know what to do with it. . . ."

"There is proof. I saw four striped bruises on her arms. But she's in love. It's a classic case of emotional abuse, low self-esteem—the total package."

"I want you to listen to me, Kylene. This girl needs help, but she needs an army of it, not an army of *you*, understand? I don't want you confronting him again."

"No problem there. You should see him now—he is jacked. Like *huge*."

"Then what were you thinking, going after someone like that, Ky?"

"I couldn't just watch him go after her, Dad. He had her pinned in the cab of his truck. I heard her cry out even with the windows shut. She's small and weak and scared. What was I supposed to do?"

"Call for help?"

"There were four other football players standing around doing nothing. I was the only cavalry."

"You were in over your head, kiddo."

"Right, but at least I'm trained, thanks to you and Kru Tyson."

"Not for a fight with someone that big." He leaned forward to rest his elbows on the counter, his eyes practically burning holes in the glass between us. "I think it's best if you just steer clear of him, okay?"

"Okay, Dad."

"That's my girl. Now tell me something far less frightening about your day."

I grimaced dramatically, forcing a laugh from my father.

"I made a new friend. I did it in the most unconventional way possible, but I did it. She's new—Canadian, witty, a bit socially awkward—and a whiz with the academic stuff."

"An asset."

"Exactly. And she helped save my ass from Donovan by taking a photo or video of him as he was threatening me. She emailed it to herself before he could get to her phone."

"Quick on her feet," my father mused. "She's a keeper."

"Yep. Totally."

"Well, that's good. Anything else?"

"I saw Garrett. . . ."

My father's expression became instantly sympathetic. It was clear that he didn't quite know what to say to that. He'd known how close we were. He didn't understand why we'd drifted apart. Obviously he was aware that I wanted to distance my-self from all things that reminded me of Jasperville, but he knew how much I loved Garrett. I think he assumed Garrett would be the exception.

"How is young Mr. Higgins?"

I smiled.

"Amazing. It was so great to see him, Dad. It's like we were never apart."

"Just fell back into your old roles?"

"Exactly!"

"Those are the good ones, Kylene. Friends like those are the kind you have for life."

"I literally ran into him leaving the front office."

"Tell me he isn't getting sent to Principal Thompson this early in the year."

"I have no clue," I said, and laughed. "He was so derailed when he saw me that he just walked out."

"Well, I'm glad you have a couple friendly faces at school to count on."

"I do. No worries there." My laughter died off as I wondered about my dad's situation—if he had any friendlies to count on yet. "How about you? How are you making out?"

"Pretty well."

I wanted to believe him. Wanted to hold tight to the notion that we didn't have to talk about what was so plainly going on. That we wouldn't have to talk about his trial, or the fact that Mom was gone, or that the bruise on his face meant that he had been put in with the general population. Because if we did talk about those things, it made them more real. And I needed to pretend they weren't, sometimes. All the time, if I could muster that level of denial.

I took a deep breath, then faced reality. "Your shiner says otherwise, Dad. Let's not pretend I can't see it."

He leaned back away from the window again, as if the extra few feet would somehow minimize the mark on his face or the danger it represented.

"It seems as though there's been a mix-up with my paper-work. Until it's resolved, I'll be in with the general population."

Gen pop . . . I swallowed hard at the thought.

"Mix-up, my ass, Dad! Someone is trying to get to you!"

"Kylene, now is not the time for an overactive imagination."

"Don't patronize me. I'm not being ridiculous right now, and you know it!"

"It's a clerical error. They happen all the time. I should be good to go in a day or so."

My heart hammered against my chest. He was putting up a good front—a great one, in fact—but I knew it was all an act for my benefit. He didn't believe the words coming out of his mouth any more than I did. He was worried. I wanted so much in that moment to be brave, to live the lie right along with him, but my fear wouldn't let me. Instead, it penetrated my defenses, letting my terror bleed through to the surface. If my pale, slack expression hadn't been enough to alert my father to my state, the tears forming in my eyes were.

"It's my fault, Daddy. I should have lied. It's all my fault—"

"Kylene Marie Danners, you listen to me right now," he said, standing to lean forward until his face nearly pressed the glass. "None of this is your fault, do you understand? None of it. Whatever happens from here on out, I need you to know that."

"Sit down, Danners!" a guard shouted from the far side of the room. When my father didn't comply, too all consumed with getting through to me, the officer approached. "I said, sit down!"

"Daddy," I cried. "Sit down. Please."

"Say you understand."

"I understand! I understand! Now sit down!"

My father sat just before the guard reached him and put his baton back into his belt. I exhaled heavily, wiping the tears from my face.

"Time's up, Danners," the guard said, hauling my father up from the seat he'd just sat down in.

"I'll come see you tomorrow, if I can. After school."

"I'd like that," he replied with a smile.

The guard grabbed the phone from my father, slamming it down in the cradle.

"I love you!" I yelled, hoping that maybe he'd understand. When he mouthed the words back, I knew he did.

I watched as he disappeared, my heart in my throat. I wondered what shape he would be in when I came to visit him the next day. I wondered if his paperwork would be found and filed. Then I wondered if it would matter at all.

There was no need to separate him from the real criminals in Logan Hill if he was dead.

With that grim truth firmly planted in my mind, I made my way out of Logan Hill Prison and back to my car. Heidi looked like I felt. Shattered and broken.

Losing my dad wasn't an option. Not by a long shot. In light of that knowledge, I made a call on my phone, then sped down the road. I needed to meet with someone who could help me get started with my investigation. I needed my dad's old partner.

SEVEN

Striker agreed to meet me, so I jumped on the highway and headed toward Columbus. The drive took about an hour and a half, and I tried to enjoy the changing landscape as I worked my way north. The rolling hills flattened out to farmland, then turned to a city skyline in the distance. Columbus wasn't huge by any means, but it was definitely a city. It was also centrally located in the state, which made it the perfect hub for the FBI.

I wove my way around the outskirts of the Ohio State University campus to finally reach my destination right in the middle of downtown. After parking my car on the street, I walked into the coffee shop Striker had said to meet in and looked around for my father's ex-partner. It didn't take long before I found him sitting in the back corner of the tiny mom-and-pop establishment. In fairness, Striker was kind of hard to miss. He had deep brown skin, a shaved head, and was built like a linebacker. Even sitting down, he seemed to take up more space than he should. I used to laugh at him when he'd stop by the house with my father and practically had to pry himself out of Dad's sedan. He was exactly the kind of guy you wanted to have your back.

And he did.

"Hey, little lady. Fancy meeting you here." He smiled as I approached his table and stood to greet me, opening his arms wide to hug me. I gladly let him. Striker had quickly become a second father figure in my life while we lived in Columbus. He was the same age as my father and had a daughter a year older than me. Our families spent a lot of time together—even after the investigation into my father began. Through everything that happened, Striker's confidence in my father's innocence never wavered. He was a stand-up guy, and I had a ton of respect for him.

"I really appreciate this, Striker."

"The hug? Anytime, kid."

I laughed and pulled away from his embrace.

"That, too, but I meant that," I said, pointing to the massive stack of transcript files on the table.

He looked down at me, his dark brown eyes assessing me like one would expect a detective to. He was as intense as he was funny and could switch from one to the other at the drop of a hat. It reminded me that I never wanted to be on his bad side. Ever.

"Of course. You said you wanted to review it all, so I got you all the copies I could." He indicated that I should have a seat, then called out to the young woman working behind the counter and ordered me a banana muffin and coffee. Two of my favorites. Once she placed them down in front of me, the interrogation began. "So, how was the return home?"

With Striker, there was zero point in lying.

"Shitty."

"Just like you expected. Anything in particular, or just a general level of shittiness?"

"It's pretty general, but it's clear that I'm still seen as the girl who cried wolf about those pictures."

Striker's face went grim—more so than I'd ever seen. He knew about why we'd left Jasperville. My father had told him the whole story. Striker took it about as well as my dad had when it happened. He had a teenage girl at home. He could clearly relate.

"Only one way to solve that problem," he said before taking a big sip of his coffee. He stared at me over the rim of the mug as he did, willing me to see the answer.

I sighed when it came to me.

"Figure out what happened that night and expose the guilty party—or parties."

He nodded.

"You know your father would have—"

"But I didn't let him."

Another nod.

"He understood why you needed to just get away from that town, Kylene, but maybe now—maybe now it's time for you to get yourself a little slice of justice."

"I don't think that works out so well for people in my family."

He looked down at the stack of files, then back to me.

"Maybe it just hasn't worked out yet."

I tore into my muffin and coffee like I hadn't had anything to eat or drink for weeks. Hardly ladylike, but Striker didn't care. He seemed to find it rather amusing.

"So," I said, mouth still full of muffin, "what are you up to tonight? Just heading home?"

He gave his watch a look, then took a big swig of coffee.

"Actually, no. I have to work late tonight. I just stepped out so I could meet up with you, but now I have to head back. I'm going to go take care of the bill, then I'll walk you out."

I nodded, taking what was left of the muffin and wrapping it up so I could stuff it in my bag. Then I collected the armful of files, putting as many as I could in a different pocket of my bag. I still ended up carrying a few of them under my arm as I followed Striker outside.

We stepped out onto the sidewalk together, and he saw my

car sitting there, looking sad and beat up. "Am I to assume that your windows fell victim to Jasperville's warm welcome?"

"That would be some keen detective work there, Agent Striker."

His laughter boomed through the street.

"Be careful driving home, and text me when you get there."

"Will do."

I smiled at him and turned to walk to my car. As I did, a man approached us. He was young, in his early twenties at best. His short brown hair was clean-cut and neat but still had a style to it that was modern. It greatly contrasted the shirt and tie he was wearing. He looked like a hipster wearing his dad's clothes.

A very hot hipster wearing his dad's clothes.

"Agent Dawson," Striker called out from behind me. "You want to work late and do some grunt work for me?"

"If you'll have me."

I looked over my shoulder at Striker. His face gave nothing away.

"If you pick up coffee for everyone, then, yes, you can help out."

"Excellent, sir. I'll see you there."

"You've got fifteen minutes. And don't be late. You know I hate that shit." He looked down at me, an apologetic expression on his face.

"What? I'm pretty sure I swore first tonight. You're good."

"That's right," he replied with a smile. "You did. You should probably go wash your mouth out with soap."

"If she's giving you lip, sir, I'd be happy to take her in," the young fed said, giving me a playful look.

"Agent Dawson, this is Kylene Danners."

"Hi," I said, reaching my hand out to shake his. He took it but didn't say anything at first. All the warmth from his expression disappeared. He just stood and stared.

"Apparently your beauty has charmed yet another one, Kylene," Striker said with a laugh. Then his face went deadly serious. "She's only seventeen, Dawson, so keep that in mind. I'll kill you if you lay a hand on her." Dawson flashed a smile at Striker and quickly withdrew his hand from mine. "Fifteen minutes, Dawson. Better quit flirting with the teenager and get your ass movin'."

"Will do, sir."

With a brisk nod, Striker started down the street to FBI headquarters, leaving me with the selectively mute agent.

"It was nice to meet you," I said, heading for my car.

"You're Bruce Danners' kid, aren't you?"

I turned to find eyes as cold as ice staring at me.

"Yeah. I am." He scoffed at my reply. I took a step closer. "You got a problem with that?"

"No. No problem at all. I love traitors. I'm sure their progeny are fabulous."

"Listen, asshole. You barely look old enough to even be in the FBI, which makes you a new graduate. You're a glorified gopher until someone in that building over there decides otherwise. So I'd climb my ass down from that high horse real quick before you get bucked. Got it? And as for my father, you should hope to be half the agent he was."

"That's cute. Defending Daddy. So sweet. So juvenile. Maybe when you grow up one day, you'll actually understand the ramifications of what your father did."

"*Allegedly* did."

"There's nothing alleged about it. He shot an agent. He was tried and convicted. He's guilty."

"For now."

"Wrong. Forever."

"He may have shot him," I argued, "but the circumstances leading to that event aren't clear."

"Clear enough for a jury of twelve of his peers to convict him."

I took a deep breath to calm myself before I did something I regretted.

"Well, this sure has been a slice and all, but I gotta go. Try not to be late for your ass-kissing—I mean briefing. Striker really does hate that shit."

I'd almost made it into my car without saying anything else to that dickhead. Then his next words stopped me dead in my tracks.

"Did you know Agent Reider?"

I turned to find him staring at me, unadulterated rage in his eyes.

"No."

"He's the reason I went to the academy. He's the reason I wanted to be an agent. He's the reason I busted my ass to be top of my class. I wanted to be just like him when I got out. And now he's dead. He's dead because of your father."

There was no way to deny the pain and anger in his hateful stare. No way to ignore how awful that loss had been. Dawson hated my father for taking someone he cared for from him forever.

I felt the blood drain from my face.

"My dad did not kill him in cold blood. There has to be a reason why," I said, though there was no fire in my voice. I sounded weak and sad and rattled.

"Keep telling yourself that, little girl. Your dad nearly brought down the entire agency and killed the man amassing evidence against him. You think on that for a bit while you pine away for the justice you think your father was denied. Better yet, maybe you should go visit Agent Reider's grave, then talk to me about justice. Your dad should be six feet under. Not him."

That particular sentiment cleared the fog of sadness that had settled over me.

"Talk shit about my dad some more, and I'll put you six feet under myself."

"Are you threatening a federal agent?"

"No, I'm threatening some hotshot punk who's begging for me to bury an elbow in his face."

His expression was stone. His eyes raged with fire. "Time for you to go, Kylene Danners."

"Gladly, Agent Douchecanoe."

I hopped in my car and slammed the door. It took an extra few seconds for Heidi to spring to life, but when she did, she did it with a puff of black exhaust that was aimed right at Agent Dawson. I could see him coughing in the rearview mirror. The sight made me smile.

With my middle finger flying out my permanently open window, I drove off and headed for the interstate that would take me home. Anywhere far away from Agent Hotshot was fine with me. To say our encounter had left me enraged would have been an understatement.

I never wanted to see that bastard again.

EIGHT

I woke up with paper stuck to my face, glued firmly in place with crusted drool. My alarm hadn't gone off, leaving me only about fifteen minutes to change, throw my hair up in a top-knot, grab a bagel, and go to JHS. Gramps was up and at 'em as usual, making a full breakfast in the kitchen. He was old-school like that.

"That's not enough to eat," he said with a scowl. To humor him, I broke a banana off the bunch lying on the counter and held it up to him for approval. "Better," he said. I stopped to give him a peck on the cheek as I passed him on my way to the front door. "You wanna tell me what happened to your car, or do we not have enough time for that right now?"

"No time now. You home for dinner tonight?" He nodded. "Perfect. I'll give you all the gory details then."

"Every last one," he said sternly.

I chuckled to myself as I ran out the door. He sounded just like my father would have. No wonder Mom married my dad. She loved what she knew.

I hopped in the car and sped my way to school, hoping I wasn't headed for yet another lecture from Mrs. Baber and Mr. Callahan on tardiness. Two for two would have been an impressive record, even for me. Thankfully, I narrowly avoided one, squeaking through the door to physics just as the final bell rang. Garrett shot me an amused look from his seat two rows over. I gave him one in return.

Forty-five minutes of torture later, the bell rang, and I bolted from the room. Anything was better than enduring Mr. Callahan's pompous, overinflated ego. Anything. At least that was what I'd thought. But the second I laid eyes on Donovan and Amy walking toward me from the far end of the hallway, I reconsidered my stance.

His arm was draped over her shoulders like the curtain of ownership it was. The vision made me gag. I instinctively looked to her, searching her face for any sign of what she was feeling, and was mind-blown with what I found. Glaring at me with hateful eyes was the petite girl I'd rescued only one day earlier. I'd have been lying if I said her reaction to me wasn't a surprise. In truth, it shocked the hell out of me. As if it wasn't enough that her penetrating stare all but said *Leave me the hell alone*, she wound her arm around the small of Donovan's back for good measure. If I'd been in an alternate universe—somewhere in which the day before hadn't taken place—I'd have thought she was jealous of me and letting me know that he was as much hers as she was his.

But I wasn't in the twilight zone, and the previous day *had* transpired.

As they neared me while I stood unmoving in the middle of the hallway, I finally managed to get past my shock and walk to the far staircase, which would take me down to the cafeteria. It would also take me right past Amy and her gorilla of a boyfriend. She looked over at me right as our shoulders brushed one another's, and she mouthed the words "Back off" to me.

Message received loud and clear.

Whatever had gone on between them after I'd intervened seemed to have made everything right as rain, and my concern was no longer appreciated. Maybe I didn't understand it. Maybe

I didn't like it. But that changed nothing. At least her one-eighty with Donovan would keep him off my back. He'd gotten what he wanted.

I reached study hall just before the bell rang. Tabby was sitting at the same table that we had shared the day before, wearing a smile from ear to ear. The second she saw me, she patted the table, beckoning me to her.

"Cutting it close today, eh?" she asked as I threw my bag down on the table.

"I like to live on the edge—makes me feel alive."

I pulled out a chair and quickly sat down before the teacher made a fuss.

"After what I saw you do yesterday, I'd say that's an understatement."

"Speaking of . . . guess who I just saw all cozy-cute in the hallway outside Mr. Callahan's room?"

She stared at me blankly for a second, then her eyes went wide with realization.

"Noooooooooooo! No way. I don't believe it."

"And yet it's still true. The two of them were clinging to one another, parading their sick love through the halls."

"That's totally messed up."

"Agreed."

I started to rummage around through my bag for my Spanish assignment, while Tabby told me all about what happened in her first-period class. By the time I had dumped all my belongings on the table, I realized I'd left my homework in my locker the day before.

". . . You should have seen the look on Ms. Bevins' face," she said as I tuned back in.

"Shit! I forgot my Spanish."

I raised my hand, and Mrs. Summers started over toward us.

"Oh! That reminds me. I have to tell you something. I saw—" Tabby started before the teacher cut her off.

"Ms. Newberry," she said as she approached. "Do I need to reiterate the purpose of study hall to you again?"

"Sorry, Mrs. Summers," Tabby replied, slouching into her seat. "I'll be quiet."

"See that you are." Mrs. Summers turned her eyes to me. "What is it that you want, Ms. Danners?"

"I forgot my Spanish. Can I have a hall pass to go get it?"

She reached into the pocket of her oversized sweater and handed it over.

"Five minutes."

"Thanks!" I replied, jumping out of my seat.

I was out of the room in no time, rushing up to my third-floor locker. I rounded the final corner to find that someone else was there. Someone like Donovan Shipman. He hadn't seen me, so I jumped back around the corner and tried to spy on him. He was crouched down at the foot of his locker, fishing through a pile of something. He looked flustered, slamming his stuff around. Then, when he found what he was looking for, he stopped. I saw him pull an orange prescription bottle out and open it up.

"Pretty sure those should be in the nurse's office with Mrs. Henry," I muttered to myself. The school policy was that all prescriptions be locked up in the nurse's office. That under no circumstances were you to carry them on you. If Donovan had a legit script for those drugs, I couldn't help but wonder why he didn't want Mrs. Henry to have them.

I watched as he dumped what looked like a handful of pills into his palm, then tossed them into his mouth, swallowing them easily without water.

"I guess that's why. . . ."

He stuffed the bottle into a pocket of his backpack before

he stood up to leave, and the sound of his locker slamming shut echoed through the hall. Thankfully for me, he headed the opposite direction and disappeared down the stairs. He never saw me.

Knowing I'd just wasted four minutes watching Donovan's shadiness, I quickly got what I'd gone up there for and ran back down to study hall, handing the hall pass back to Mrs. Summers before sliding back into my seat. Tabby took one look at how hard I was breathing and cocked her head.

"What happened?" she whispered, trying to hide her face behind a raised textbook.

I put my head down to stare blankly at my homework. "I saw Donovan at his locker. He took a fistful of pills, then went back to class," I said.

"What kind?" Tabby asked, leaning closer to me.

"No clue."

"Do you think that maybe it's something to do with—"

"Ms. Newberry!" Mrs. Summers shouted. "Collect your things. You'll be sitting with me this period."

Tabby flashed me an apologetic look, then did as she was told. She walked away, leaving me in silence. I tried to chip away at my Spanish homework, but I couldn't focus. My mind was a mess of random thoughts about Donovan, Amy, and whatever was in that pill container. If his behavior went south about the time he started taking the drug, then surely there was a connection there—one that could be easily addressed with a doctor's intervention and a change in meds. It made me wonder about what exactly he'd been prescribed and why. Two questions I wasn't likely to get answers to anytime soon.

By the time I looked up at the clock, my mind tired from running in circles, I realized that study hall was almost over. I hazarded a glance over at Tabby, who seemed to have been waiting for me to do just that. With frantic hand gestures and

overly mouthed words, she tried to tell me something that I
hadn't a hope in hell of understanding. The girl looked like she
was going to explode any second. It was all I could do to keep
from bursting out into hysterics.

Tabby's pale face flushed with frustration as she continually
tried to convey whatever message she had for me without drawing Mrs. Summers' attention. Not surprisingly, she failed. Just
as the bell rang, I heard Mrs. Summers summon her.

"Ms. Newberry, a word."

Tabby's cheeks turned crimson red.

"Of course."

Tabby stayed behind with the middle-aged woman to receive her lecture. Knowing she'd likely be a while, I headed
off to the girls' locker room and got changed without her. I
figured it might be best after the confrontation we'd encountered there the day before.

By the time I was dressed and locking my locker, Tabby still
hadn't arrived, so I decided to join the rest of the class in the
gym, hoping she'd pop in sooner than later. If she didn't, she'd
be running laps. A lot of them.

I pushed the door open and walked into the gym to find an
unpleasant surprise waiting. Donovan stood on the far side of
the room, smiling wickedly at me with his stare. While I tried
to figure out why he was suddenly in my class when he hadn't
been the previous day, I heard one of the doors to the gym fly
open, crashing into the wall. I looked over my shoulder to find
a skinny redhead running toward me.

Moments later, Tabby was at my side, whispering in my ear.

"He dropped a class, and they had to switch his schedule
around. That's what I was trying to warn you about in study
hall."

I looked up at my friend, who was proving more and more
to be a surprising wealth of knowledge.

"Yeah, I never would have gotten that from the routine you were doing." I smiled at her and earned myself a scowl in return. "How do you even know that, Tabby?"

"I was in the office when he asked to drop it. He was given two different options for gym class, and he was very quick to choose this one. Convenient, don't you think?"

"I sure do. If I thought he had a brain in that massive head of his, I'd have thought he was trying to get to me. And just when things seemed to be all settled."

"Sure doesn't feel that way, judging by the look on his face and the way he hasn't so much as glanced at anything other than you since I walked in."

"I'm inclined to agree."

"This is bad, Ky."

"Quite possibly. I hope for our sakes he's on our volleyball team. I don't want to be returning whatever rockets he spikes at me."

I looked at Donovan across the room and realized that what had gone down yesterday had very little to do with Amy. He didn't like that I'd made him look bad, look like anything other than the mountain of muscle he saw himself as. I'd challenged that reality in front of his friends. And that was an injustice he had zero intentions of leaving alone. Donovan would keep coming after me until he felt he'd gotten his pound of flesh. That meant I needed whatever leverage I could find to make sure he didn't get it.

"All right, kids, listen up," Ms. Davies announced, interrupting Tabby. "I know you're all thrilled about today's sport, especially those of you with some pent-up aggression, but remember, there are rules. No crossing the center line under the net. Call the ball so we don't have any collisions and the school board decides to ban yet another sport from the curriculum. And remember that spiking the ball is not a show of brute force. It's not how hard you hit it that's important. It's where you place it." She looked at us as we all stared at her, completely mute. "All right then. Let's divide up into teams." She started assigning people to one side of the net or the other, and students began to disperse, assuming a position on the court.

Tabby was on the other team, finding a spot in the back row. I took up a place by the net in front of the server on our team—who just happened to be Donovan. As Ms. Davies threw him the ball to serve, I couldn't bring myself to fully turn my back to him. I had a strong feeling the ball was about to be rifled right at my head.

Surprisingly, it went over, and the game began. Gym-class volleyball was a shit show at best. Watching a bunch of non–volleyball players flounder around the court was amusing, but the chaos somehow came together on Tabby's end, and one of the skinny kids next to her spiked the ball back at me. I called it, stepping back away from the net so I could get a solid bump in. Then I heard Donovan shout something behind me. Before I could puzzle together what was going on, he dove into me, driving me face-first into the floor. My forehead cracked against the hardwood, then his massive body held me down. I could hardly breathe with that much weight pressing against my ribs.

"Shipman!" Ms. Davies shouted, running up to us. She must have helped to haul him off of me, because I could finally breathe again. I coughed wildly as I gasped for air. Tabby rushed over to help me up, and I swayed on my feet, feeling light-headed.

"Are you okay, Danners?" Ms. Davies asked, walking over to assess me.

"Yep. Shipshape."

"You've got quite a goose egg on your forehead there. You need some ice. Tabby, I want you to go back to the locker room with Kylene, then go get some ice from the nurse."

"Okay."

"As for you, Shipman. Was I not clear about calling the ball?"

"Yes, ma'am, you were, and I did."

"Yep, you sure did. Right after Danners did. I think maybe you and your overeager need to go for the ball can sit out the rest of class."

Donovan turned to walk over to the bleachers, but not without flashing me a grin over his shoulder.

"What a jerk," Tabby whispered.

"Yeah. I think we firmly established that yesterday."

Ms. Davies pointed toward the door to the girls' locker room, and Tabby put her arm around my waist, ushering me toward it.

"Just keep an eye on her, Tabby. Let me know if anything changes. And remember, friends don't let friends die of head traumas." Tabby's face went pale for a second at the thought.

"Yes, Ms. Davies."

We walked across the gym floor to the locker room, and once we were there, she sat me down on the bench and looked me over with narrowed eyes.

"Are you going to be okay here while I go get the ice?"

I nodded, stopping the second my head went all swimmy.

"I'll be fine. Just go."

She hesitated for a second, then walked out, muttering to herself as she tried to remember where the nurse's office was. Apparently, she wouldn't be back too soon.

While sitting alone in the locker room, my head pounding, a thought occurred to me. If ever I'd wanted to find out what Donovan's prescription was for, now was the time. It was in his backpack, which was in the boys' locker room—where no one would be.

I stood up slowly, making sure I was steady on my feet before sneaking out into the hallway. A quick glance showed it was clear, so I hurried the few feet down to the boys' locker-room door. I stuck my head in, listening to see if anyone was in there. That area of the school had the bathroom in the locker room, so people would use the facilities in there rather than traipse halfway across the school to pee. Luckily, it was empty, so I slipped in and made a beeline for the rows of lockers. I tried to be quiet, but that was nearly impossible; my adrenaline was racing, giving me jittery hands. It made it hard to close them around the locker latches with any amount of grace.

Some lockers were actually locked up, which was immensely frustrating, but several were not. I had a feeling Donovan's wouldn't be, because, really, who would dare steal from him? Someone with a death wish, that's who. That made me question my sanity for a second.

Finally, at the end of one of the rows, I found an occupied locker. One containing a bag with a JHS football patch on it. I ripped the backpack open and pulled out a book. Shipman was written on it in black Sharpie.

"Gotcha," I said to myself.

I rifled through all the pockets, looking for the evidence. Inside the bag, in a zippered compartment, was the orange prescription bottle. I pulled it out and read the label.

It had been recently filled, but I didn't recognize the proper name of the drug. I repeated it over in my mind to commit it to memory so I could look it up later. I also memorized the name of the prescribing doctor, just in case. Then I opened the lid.

"Seems pretty empty," I said before closing it up and putting it back in the bag. Knowing Tabby would soon be back, I quickly zipped it shut and shoved it back in the way I'd found it and closed the door. I turned to hurry down the row of lockers, but something—or more accurately some*one*—was in my way.

"Something I can help you with, Danners?" he asked, reaching an arm out to lean on a nearby locker, caging me in. My heart thundered in my chest.

"I think that blow to the head is making me confused. Why are you in the girls' locker room, Donovan?"

"I think the question you meant to ask is why are *you* in the boys' locker room?"

"Am I?" I did my best to sound bewildered. "How did that happen?"

"I'm more interested in why it happened."

"I got sacked by a buffalo and hit my head, Donovan. I probably have a concussion."

His expression turned from darkly amused to predatory.

"See, now, I'd like to think that's true, but in light of recent events and your inability to keep your nose out of places it doesn't belong, I don't think it's that simple. It looked a lot more like you were rifling through my bag for something."

He took a step forward.

I took one in retreat.

"Tabby is probably looking for me. She'll be worried if I'm not there. Probably go get Ms. Davies to help her search."

"I don't think that'll be a problem. They won't start that search in here."

He continued to advance on me slowly, and I matched him step for step. It probably looked like an elegant dance of sorts— like something from the Renaissance era—but it was far more sinister than that. Donovan's narrowed eyes told me as much. He planned to let me know what happened to people that messed with him.

If I was going to go down in flames, then I'd do so fighting.

"I'm not sure you've really thought this through, Donovan. An arrest for assault is hardly going to get you a full ride to college."

He stopped short and smiled at me. The contorted set of his features was as ugly as it was scary. There was no joy in that smile—only malice.

"That won't be an issue."

"Oh, really? You weren't too careful with Amy. I could see those bruises from a mile away."

"Yeah, well," he said with a shrug, "I don't plan to bruise you where it can be easily seen."

My blood ran cold. Nothing about that statement was good.

"Or you could let me go and know I won't say a word about how you like to beat up on your girlfriend. No harm. No foul."

"Aw, but you see, Danners, it's too late for that now. You can't be trusted, and you need to learn your place. Someone needs to knock you off that pedestal you've put yourself on," he scoffed. "Amazing that your daddy going to prison wasn't enough to do that. Maybe this will."

He lunged for me and I dodged it, trying to push his momentum to the side, but there wasn't enough room to navigate in the narrow passage between the rows of lockers. It was only a matter of seconds before I found myself slammed against one of the red metal doors, the handle digging painfully into my back. Before I could scream for help, he clasped his hand over my mouth, cutting off my chance.

I was waist high in deep shit, and I knew it.

"I'm going to enjoy breaking you, tough girl," he whispered, his face only inches from mine. "All bitches can be made to heel. Even you."

"Donovan!" someone shouted. I couldn't see past the large frame holding me in place, to see who it was, but I knew. I'd have known that voice anywhere. "Let her go. Now."

Donovan's head turned to face the person who dared to interrupt him. The motion was slow and eerie and alien. If I hadn't already been scared out of my mind, that single movement would have pushed me over the edge.

"AJ," he said casually, as though he wasn't standing there, holding me captive. As if it were just any normal day.

"I won't say it again."

"You need to leave," Donovan replied, his tone now full of warning.

"Or what? You'll slam me against a locker, too?"

"Something like that." Donovan's gaze drifted back to me, dismissing the boy behind him. Seconds later, I saw strong arms wrap around Donovan's chest and yank him away from me. My assailant tripped over the bench in the center of the aisle and crashed against the adjacent wall of lockers. "I'm going to beat the shit out of you," Donovan said, his voice more of a growl than anything. He barely sounded human.

"I don't think so," the boy replied, stepping between me and Donovan. "You need me. If I get hurt, we don't win. And you need a winning record on your résumé, don't you? There are recruiters coming to the game on Friday. It'd be a shame for the starting quarterback to be out injured. Especially when our backup is nursing tendinitis in his throwing arm."

"I'm on the defensive line. Maybe if I was a wide receiver I'd give a shit."

"But without me, there won't be a state championship. And you know how those big schools like those."

Donovan huffed like a cornered bull getting ready to charge, but he remained still, his eyes darting from the hero to me and back again. After a minute or so, I could see the realization dawn on him. He couldn't afford to have a losing season.

"This isn't over, Danners," he snarled, pushing away from the lockers to leave.

"I think it is, Donovan. If anything happens to her, I'll start throwing games left and right. I'll bury our team so far in the ranking that those schools you're looking at won't even see us on their radar. You feel me?"

Donovan's jaw flexed so hard that I was pretty sure his teeth were going to break under all that pressure.

"I feel you. Just tell your bitch to keep her mouth shut."

With that final thought, he exited through the door that led back to the gym, leaving me behind with my adrenaline, my fear, and the boy who had crushed my heart.

NINE

AJ goddamned Miller.

Of all the people in that school, he was the last person I wanted to see—or second to last if I counted Donovan. It was like the universe had a personal vendetta against me. If AJ Miller saving my ass wasn't irony at its finest, I didn't know what was.

I should have run out of that locker room the minute Donovan left, but for whatever unfathomable reason, I didn't. Instead, I stood there, staring into the face of the person who stole a part of my innocence, and said nothing.

"Are you okay?" AJ asked, his green eyes intense but warm. He reached his hand toward me, and I shrugged away from him, revolted by the thought of his touch.

His arm fell limp at his side, the familiar look of dejection plain in his expression.

"I need to go." I did little to try to hide just how much I wanted to get away from him. He sidestepped in front of me, blocking my path, though not in an intimidating way. Apparently, it wasn't going to be that easy to escape my past.

"I just want to know that you're all right, Ky. That's all." I nodded silently in response. "He didn't hurt you?" I shook my head. "Will you please say something to me? Anything?"

I looked up at him with cold eyes.

AJ Miller had been my first real love. From the moment we'd started dating, we were inseparable. He was best friends with Garrett, which made things easier. Both of the boys I loved were always around. My life couldn't have been any better.

And then everything went wrong.

AJ was at the football party the night the scandalous pictures of me were taken. The photos had been captured with his phone. And though I'd been drunk at that party, having caved to peer pressure for what would be the first and final time in my life, I knew I didn't consent to what had been done.

He'd betrayed me. He was boy number six.

"I have lots of things I could say, AJ, but none of them would be worth my time. You're not worth my time." With that, I slinked past him, careful not to touch him. He moved out of the way.

"How about you tell me why I just walked in on whatever was about to happen in here, Kylene?" he called after me.

"Because Donovan is an aggressive freak who likes to beat on his girlfriend, and he knows that I know it. I know his dirty little secret."

"Kylene," AJ said, following me to the door. "He's dangerous. Like really, really dangerous. You need to drop this. I mean it."

I wheeled on him just before I opened the door to exit the boys' locker room, letting out some of my fear and adrenaline on him.

"Just like I dropped the picture scandal? You want me to bend over and take it again, is that it? Well, that ain't gonna happen, AJ. I let you get away with that, and I've hated myself for it ever since. I'm so tired of the football players in this town being above the law. It's bullshit. And speaking of bullshit, don't stand here in front of me and pretend to be concerned. You don't get to do that, understand? Those days are so long gone it's laughable."

"Kylene, I—"

"No, AJ, I don't want to hear it. Yeah, you just saved my ass, and I'm quasi-grateful for that, but it hardly makes up for what you did freshman year." He flinched at my words, his bright eyes full of pain. "Now leave me alone."

I shoved the door open, not caring if anyone was in the hall. Jerking the door to the girls' locker room open, I slipped in and pressed my back against the wall, trying to breathe. That moment—facing AJ—was the one I had dreaded most upon returning to Jasperville High. Up until then, I had been able to distract myself. But the minute I walked up those steps to the school, reality started to bleed to the forefront, leaving a knot of anxiety firmly planted in my chest. I was great at denying it. Pretending it wasn't there. But when forced to stand face-to-face with him, I couldn't pretend anymore.

My past had finally caught up with me.

And though I thought I'd made it pretty clear that I hated him and wanted nothing to do with him, I wasn't so certain he'd gotten the message. In all the scenarios I'd played over in my head about what it would be like when our paths eventually crossed, none of them involved him saving me. That act— that one single act—wreaked havoc on my mind. That was the AJ I had known before he'd done what he did, before he'd proven to be someone else entirely. Unable to reconcile the two versions of him, my head started to ache.

Or maybe that was the concussion Donovan had given me.

I managed my way deeper into the room where my locker was, clutching my head and rubbing my chest. The pain in both was fierce and sharp. I wanted to sit down and rest and try to forget about what had just happened, but I knew that wasn't likely. The lack of resolution from my encounter with AJ was destined to play over and over in my mind all day long.

When I rounded the wall of lockers, I found Tabby sitting

on a bench, fidgeting with the hem of her shirt. Her face was full of worry.

"Holy crap, Kylene. Where have you been? I came back and you weren't here. I thought maybe you were still in the bathroom, but I checked and all the stalls were empty. Did you wander off? Is your head okay?"

"My head is fine." I snapped those words out with more heat than was warranted, and judging by Tabby's expression, she felt their sting. "I'm sorry," I said with a cleansing breath. "I just needed to do something really quick."

"This is about Donovan, isn't it?"

"Maybe."

"Don't lie to me, Ky. I almost went to get Ms. Davies because I was worried about you, but I didn't. But I was more worried I'd get you in trouble if you were up to no good."

"Yeah . . . that might have been problematic."

"Where did you go?"

I sighed.

"The boys' locker room."

"Are you *high*?"

"Unfortunately not."

"Why would you do that?"

"To find out what drugs he's on."

"Holy crap, Ky! Did you find anything?"

"I did. And then Donovan found me finding it. . . ."

Her face paled. "What'd he do?"

"Well, as it turns out, he didn't do anything really, but it was damn close."

"How'd you get away?"

Another heavy sigh.

"The quarterback came in and found Donovan pinning me against a locker. Said he'd throw the season if Donovan laid a hand on me." Her expression turned dreamy. "Do *not* romanticize this, Tabby."

"Are you talking about AJ Miller? AJ Miller is your hero? I have Spanish with him. He seems really nice and he's so hot. This *is* romantic, Kylene."

"Under normal circumstances, I might be inclined to agree."

I cut myself off, not really wanting to rehash that part of my life when I was still all hopped up and shaky from my recent encounter. My hesitation seemed to pique her curiosity, and she leaned forward, taking my hand in hers. She looked at me as though she were trying to read my mind.

"Did something happen between you two before? You have some history with AJ, don't you?"

"You could say that."

Before she could ask me about it, Ms. Davies and the girls from class entered the locker room.

"How are we feeling, Danners? Gonna live to fight another day?"

I smiled and nodded.

"Sure thing, Coach."

"Atta girl."

She patted me on the back, then left so we could change for next period. Tabby dropped the AJ thing for the time being, but it was clear in the set of her brow that my reprieve wouldn't last long. She wanted answers. And, frankly, I owed them to her.

TEN

At lunch, I grabbed a slice of pizza and made my way outside. I wanted a chance to look up the name of that drug I found in Donovan's bag before I forgot what it was. I found an empty table and sat down, whipping my phone out so I could search for Deca-Durabolin. Article upon article came up, outlining how the anabolic steroid could be used to bulk up. It also listed a ton of side effects that could be seen when it was abused.

It read like a profile on Donovan.

"And the plot thickens. . . ." I said to myself, scrolling through my Google search. Interestingly, I found a headline stating that the drug could be used for various types of anemia. I deflated a bit in my seat, thinking that Donovan could be taking the drugs for legitimate reasons. But surely his doctor would have noticed the obvious signs of him abusing them? The acne. The mood swings. The aggression. Maybe even shrunken balls. I shuddered at that thought and continued scrolling.

"Whatcha doin'?" Garrett asked, plopping down next to me.

"Researching anabolic steroids. I'm thinking of beefing up a bit."

"Ooooh, that'll be sexy. Can't wait to hear your man voice and play with your beard."

"Right? I think it will really improve my standing in the school's social hierarchy."

He laughed. "It certainly can't hurt it."

"Don't you have other friends to annoy during lunch?"

"I do, but they've been put on hold . . . at least until I get bored of you."

I slugged him in the arm for that jab, then took a dramatic bite of my food. His playful expression slowly faded from his face when he picked up my phone and realized I wasn't joking. I hadn't told him about the Donovan run-ins yet. I was hoping not to have to. But I knew that look he wore—the one that said he wasn't going to let up until he knew what was up.

"Kylene, you wanna tell me why you're actually looking up steroids, or do I need to tickle it out of you?"

Dammit. He went right to fighting dirty. I could take a punch and not spill the beans, but tickling undid me every time.

"Listen, I don't want you to go all Neanderthal about this, okay?"

"No knuckle-dragging. Got it. So what's up? Why the 'roid curiosity?"

I took a deep breath.

"One of the guys on the football team is taking them, and I think they're affecting him mentally. He's abusing his girlfriend as a result."

His eyes narrowed.

"Who?"

"The who isn't super important, I just—"

"Tell me who it is."

The hard set of his jaw made it clear that there would be no evading Garrett.

"Donovan Shipman."

"I knew it!" he shouted before lowering his voice. "He blew up over the summer. I've heard of late growth spurts, but, c'mon . . . he's a *beast*."

"Yeah, well, he acts like one, too. The thing I can't make sense of is that he's getting them from a doctor. It's all on the up-and-up."

Garrett's expression turned incredulous.

"Ky, just because he has a prescription for it doesn't mean anything. He could be taking double the amount he's supposed to. Maybe more."

"Which means he'd run out before he was supposed to," I said, more to myself than Garrett. "His doctor would notice that, I think."

"Right, but you can get those things other ways. There's an entire market around illegal steroids."

"Interesting . . . I didn't know that was a thing."

"Why would you? You're not looking to put on pounds and pounds of lean mass."

"Were you? Is that why you're an expert?"

He scoffed. "Hardly. My dad pulled me aside freshman year, when it was clear that football was going to take me some-where, and he gave me a long-winded lecture on them."

"In a 'Here's how you get them' kinda way, or . . . ?"

"Um, no," he said with a laugh. "It was more of a 'Here's how I'll kill you if you take them' kinda thing."

"Gotcha. Well, thanks for clearing that up for me."

"Glad I could help."

"Hey, guys!" Tabby called as she approached our table. "Are you filling Garrett in on gym class, because I don't want to miss this explanation!" Her tone was cheery but her expression was not. She wanted her answers. And her timing couldn't have been worse.

Garrett was going to lose it when he put the pieces of the Donovan puzzle together.

"What happened in gym class?" Garrett asked, turning toward Tabby, who sat down across from us. Tabby shot me a look that said *I can't believe you haven't told him yet.* I shot one back that said *Don't you dare.*

She ignored my warning completely.

"Ky got tackled in gym class, courtesy of one Donovan Shipman," she explained. "Note the growing bruise by her hairline."

Garrett shot me an irritated look.

"Well, isn't that interesting. Ky and I were just talking about him. . . ."

"Ooooh boy. Here we go," I muttered under my breath.

"That is interesting," Tabby said. "Did she mention the part where she was sent with me to the girls' locker room but wandered off when I went to get her an ice pack?"

"Nope. Please do fill me in."

"The poor thing was so confused that she wandered right into the boys' locker room."

"I wonder what made her do that."

Garrett turned angry eyes to me, the kind that said *What in the hell did you do, Kylene?* I'd seen that expression more times than I could count.

"Okay, listen, I'll tell you. I went there to look for pills in Donovan's backpack because I'd seen him gobbling them down in the hallway earlier. That's where I found his stash of 'roids and why I'm Googling them right now."

"Steroids?" she asked. I nodded in response. "Well that makes a ton of sense. But . . . aren't you forgetting something?" she prompted.

When I didn't answer, Tabby proceeded to tell him everything she knew about what I'd done and what had happened because of it. Once she finished, Garrett turned wide eyes to me.

"Are you telling me that you were alone in the boys' locker room with someone hopped up on steroids?"

"Yes," Tabby answered before I had the chance to speak. "And since he was already angry with her from the incident yesterday—"

If Garrett had had some freakish superpower, I'm pretty sure it would have been laser vision, because I could practically feel him burning me alive with his glare. I quickly filled him in, then I waited for him to lose it.

"I—" Garrett started, too angry to get his thoughts together. "Do you have any idea how badly he could have hurt you?"

"Which time?" I asked.

"Not helping, Ky."

"I do, in fact. I have another pretty nasty bruise growing where the handle of the locker he slammed me against bit into—"

"I'm SERIOUS!" The volume of his voice seemed to silence the tables around us, drawing a whole lot of unwanted attention our way. The three of us sat quietly, waiting for the show to be over. After a minute or so, the others became disinterested and went back to their conversations.

"Listen, Garrett, I need you to take a breath and calm down for a minute."

"I'll calm down once you make me understand why you'd do something so reckless."

I hesitated for a second.

"You do know me, right?"

"You're impossible right now."

"I'm sorry, okay? I don't fully know why I did it, but if you'd seen his poor girlfriend all bruised and pitiful, don't tell me you wouldn't have done something, too!"

"I am six foot two and weigh almost two hundred pounds. You are five foot five and on a good day weigh one hundred and fifteen. Do you see the distinction here? Are you following the clear and present logic I'm laying out for ya?"

"Yes, Dad. I'm following."

"If it makes you feel better, Garrett," Tabby interrupted, "AJ Miller happened upon the whole thing and saved Ky."

"He did not *save* me. You don't need to be melodramatic about it."

"This just keeps getting better!" Garrett exclaimed, throwing his hands in the air like he'd given up.

"I don't get it." Tabby's features twisted with confusion. "Isn't that a good thing? That he intervened?"

"I'm not sure. Was it, Ky?"

To Garrett's credit, he softened his tone when he asked me that question. Mad though he was, he knew that encounter had to have dredged up some buried feelings. Feelings I didn't want to deal with. Feelings I'd wished were as locked up as my father.

"He got Donovan to leave me alone. I don't think either of them are going to be an issue anymore," I said quietly. "But it wasn't a good thing. Far from it, in fact."

"Will someone please fill me in on what I'm clearly missing here? What happened between you two?" Tabby asked.

"That might be a story for another time, Tabby," Garrett said, unwilling to take his eyes off me. "One that involves a late night and some tequila."

"AJ did something unforgivable. You won't approve of him so much once you hear everything."

"I'm so sorry, Ky—"

"Of course you are, Tabby, because you're a good person."

Her brows furrowed for a moment as she mulled something over in her mind.

"I know that, and I really am sorry, it's just—" She cut herself off, looking uncertain about whether or not she should say what was on her mind. Tabby seemed to have miraculously found a filter.

"What's going on in there, Tabs? You look like you're going to blow a gasket or something. Just spit it out."

"I can't seem to make sense of why someone who could do something so unforgivable to you would turn around and do something so heroic."

"Penance? Karma? Who knows? Better yet, who cares? I know I don't."

"Me either," Garrett chimed in. "He doesn't get off that easy. Not by a long shot."

"You're mad at him, too?" Tabby asked. "You were friends?" Garrett nodded.

"They were football buddies. The tightest duo on the squad."

"You chose Kylene over AJ." Her sentiment was not a question. She was weaving together the story of Garrett's and my past until she had something tangible to hold on to. Something to make sense of it all.

"Long story short, Garrett didn't take what happened well. He apparently quit the team because of it."

"And now yesterday's conversation is making much more sense."

"See? You're all caught up now. Well, mostly, but . . ."

"This is such a weird town," she noted. I couldn't help but agree.

"It'll grow on you eventually. Like a fungus."

"Listen, I'd love to keep this uplifting trip down memory lane going, but the bell's going to be ringing soon, and I have to haul ass to the far end of the school so . . ." Garrett stood up and gave a small but gallant bow to us, then picked up his garbage and walked away.

"I really like him," Tabby said absentmindedly. "He's a great guy."

I smiled. "The best. I don't know why I ever let things get so awkward and fade between us."

"I'm sure you had your reasons at the time. And he seems to have let that go." She got up from her bench and cleaned up her trash. With that, we made our way back into the school. I hoped the rest of my day would pan out differently than the morning had. The threat of bodily harm was getting old.

ELEVEN

One place I could guarantee I'd be safe was the law offices of Stenson, Marcus, and Clark. Meg had offered me a cushy job with solid pay, so, like a good little soon-to-be-employee, I stopped by, just as she requested.

The historic brick building sat facing one of the oldest streets in town, still paved in cobblestones. The former home was quaint and charming—an excellent disguise for a law office. My experience with lawyers—aside from Meg—hadn't been too stellar. I hoped that this job might prove me wrong about them.

I opened the vintage wooden double doors and walked in to find a middle-aged receptionist looking at me. She smiled and cocked her head to the side curiously before checking her computer, presumably to try to figure out who I was and why I was there.

"I don't have an appointment," I explained as I approached. "I'm here to see Meg—I mean Ms. Marcus. She offered me a job the other day—"

"Oh! You must be Kylene!" she said. I nodded. "Please, come with me. I'll show you to her office."

"Thanks."

I fell into line behind her as she walked down a long hall with doors along the left. To the right was a large room, most likely the original dining area, which was set up as a meeting space.

"She should be available right now, but wait here while I check."

I stopped a few feet short of the door at the end of the hall while the nameless receptionist knocked, then entered Meg's office. Moments later she stepped out into the hall and waved me in.

"Hey, kiddo! You ready to sell your soul to come work here?"

I scoffed.

"Like I have one to sell. . . ."

"Perfect!" she replied without skipping a beat. "Then we won't have to worry about that pesky detail, now will we?"

"Nope. Let's get right to the devilish deeds."

She laughed as she pulled out some paperwork and put it down in front of me.

"Soul or not, you still have some forms to fill out to be hired." Feigning a pout, I reached for a pen sitting on her desk. "You don't have to do it right now, Kylene. You can take them home. There's no rush."

"Perfect. I'm still not caught up in school, so if it's okay, I might have to be part-part-time until I am."

"That's not an issue. Now, since you're here, let me show you around a bit. Introduce you to some of the staff and familiarize you with what you'll actually be doing."

"Sounds good. Lead the way, boss lady."

She shook her head at me, managing to curb her undoubtedly snappy comeback. It appeared that she knew as well as I did that we'd never get anything done if she didn't. Meg and I were capable of epic verbal banter on occasion. Unfortunately, her place of employment wasn't really the best setting for a showdown.

We walked back down the hall toward the front office while

Meg pointed out the various lawyers' offices and explained what type of law they practiced. Given that Jasperville County wasn't huge, it made sense that they would try to offer various services. Meg was a litigator, but not the ambulance-chasing sort—more like Erin Brockovich. She fought for the little guy, something I'd long admired about her. The founding partner in the firm was Mr. Stenson, who practiced family law, though very part-time. She said I'd rarely if ever see him in the office. Luke Clark was a defense attorney and the newest partner. Meg made a point of saying how sharp and focused he was—how little to nothing seemed to get by him. High praise indeed, coming from her.

I met a couple of the paralegals, all of whom were young single mothers, judging by the pictures on their desks of them with children but no fathers to be seen. Lastly, I met the first person I'd encountered when I'd entered the building that day. Marcy, the receptionist, smiled again as we approached.

"Will you be joining us, Kylene?"

I shot a glance to Meg.

"I think so." I made a point to return her smile. The attorneys might have owned the business, but it was common knowledge that the receptionists ran the show. If I got on her bad side, my life would be miserable for sure. No, Marcy and I needed to be tight as tight could be.

"Who's joining us where?" a male called out from down the hall. I turned to see a guy in his early- to midthirties, dressed in a full suit, heading toward us. Since I knew Mr. Stenson was older than dirt and rarely ever there, that left one option.

"Luke," Meg said, stepping to the side a bit so he could come join our little group. "This is Kylene. She's going to be coming to work here part-time."

"Ah, the new gopher," he replied with a wide smile.

"Technically, I'm a badger, but . . ."

"I see . . . a Jasperville girl. My rival team."

I groaned.

"*Et tu*, Brute? Meg, I'm not sure I can work with a football lover."

Both Luke and Meg laughed heartily.

"Not your sport, I take it?" he asked.

"I prefer to avoid Satan's favorite pastime at all costs."

"How will you manage to rise above such prejudices to work here?"

"Honestly, I'm not sure, but I don't have a choice."

"Did you lose a bet or something?"

"Yes." I shot a playful glance at Meg. "Looks like I doubled down when I should have walked away."

"Rookie mistake. It happens."

"I've known Kylene since she was little," Meg said, interrupting us. "You'd better watch out for this one, Luke. If you think I'm a handful, you're in for a real treat."

The twinkle in his eyes was hard to ignore.

"If Meg thinks a teenager is a formidable opponent for me, you must really be something. I can't imagine what you'll be like when you're my age."

"Old," I said with a quirk of my brow. "I'll be old."

His booming laughter filled the room.

"This one's a keeper. Can't wait to see how much trouble you cause around here, Kylene."

"Me too."

"I'm about to be late for court, so if you ladies will please excuse me." He gave us a small nod, then headed for the front entrance. As he walked out the door, he looked back over his shoulder and smiled. "Pleasure to meet you, Kylene."

"You too."

As the heavy wooden door closed, Meg turned her attention back to me.

"I have to get a few things done now, too, I'm afraid, though this has been a lot of fun. Just bring the paperwork back once you get it filled out, and Marcy will take care of everything else for you, okay?"

"Sounds great. Thanks again for this, Meg. I . . . I really need it."

Her gaze softened.

"We all need a break sometimes, kiddo. Happy to give it to you." She gave me a quick hug before releasing me. "Now get out of here before Marcy starts thinking I'm a softie."

"Can't have that," I said, walking toward the door.

"See you later."

"Absolutely. You can't get rid of me that easily."

I pulled the door open and walked out into the crisp fall air. My day really had taken a turn for the better. Working with Meg and her crew promised to be as entertaining as it would be educational. Working at a law firm surely had its perks, especially with a defense attorney like Luke to consult with about my dad's case—unofficially, of course.

He might have been the best thing to happen to me in a really long time.

TWELVE

On my way home, I drove by another part of my past—one I needed to get reacquainted with. Kru Tyson's Muay Thai gym sat on the corner of two main roads, in what had once been a used-car shop. With large windows along the front, I could clearly see when I passed by that he was open. I yanked Heidi into a spot not far down the street and climbed out.

I didn't have my gloves or shin guards with me, but I had shorts and a T-shirt in my gym bag, which would have to suffice. Tyson always had extra gloves kicking around somewhere that I could borrow. I doubted that had changed in the past two years.

After my day with Donovan, I had an uncontrollable desire to hit things.

Muay Thai had always been a safe (and legal) outlet for my frustrations. I'd been out of the gym for far too long: I could feel it in my bones. I needed a date with a heavy bag. Badly.

The door squeaked loudly as I pushed it open, drawing attention from some of the guys training. They all looked at me for a moment like I was lost, then went back to what they were doing. I searched the room for Tyson, wondering if he was there. Then I heard a voice that fell on my ears in the most welcome way.

"You're late, Danners."

I couldn't help but smile. I finally located him holding a

heavy bag for someone, his familiar tattoos winding up his arms until they disappeared behind the leather bag. I had a sneaking suspicion he was hiding his amusement behind it.

"Like that's anything new," I replied, kicking off my shoes to enter the gym. He stepped out from behind the heavy bag and walked toward me, doing his best to look intimidating. It was pointless, though—he'd always had a soft spot for me, ever since I was little. In a town full of girls who aspired to be pageant queens and cheerleaders, I trained to be a fighter. He'd always appreciated that.

He secretly appreciated my smart mouth, too.

"You here to train?" he asked, wiping his brow with the hem of his shirt.

"I didn't come for your sunny disposition, that's for damn sure."

"Where's your gear?"

"I was hoping to borrow some gloves. . . ."

He jerked his head toward the desk in the corner.

"Still in the bottom drawer. Now go change. You can't kick in skinny jeans."

"I beg to differ," I replied, heading to go get the gloves. Then I stopped, realizing that I'd forgotten something. Something rather important. "Hey, Tyson?" He stopped and looked over his shoulder. "Any chance I have a credit left here?"

He nodded.

"Yeah. You've still got one."

"Any clue how much?"

"Enough."

"Enough for tonight?"

"Enough for as long as you want to be here."

With that, he turned and went back to the bag he'd been holding for the heavyweight whaling on it. I opened my mouth to thank him, then stopped myself. He wouldn't have wanted me to make a big deal about the fact that he was letting me train for free. He knew why my family left, and he had to have known why I was back—or at least part of the reason. He was trying to help me out. The best way I could thank him was to work hard and not embarrass him.

"By the way, Danners. You owe me a hundred and fifty skip knees on the bag. Twenty-five for each minute you were late."

I looked at the clock and my smile widened.

"Class started five minutes ago. That's only a hundred and twenty-five."

He peeked out from behind the cracked black leather cylinder hanging from the ceiling.

"Never was good at math." Then his dark, narrowed eyes drifted to that same clock. "But since you can't ever stop running that mouth of yours, it looks like you're six minutes late now. Guess it's still a hundred and fifty skip knees."

I ran to the bathroom to change and came right out, dropping my bag at the front door. I started jogging around the perimeter of the modest-size space to warm up before doing my penance. While I did, I watched the others in the gym, some sparring, others training on the bag or holding pads for one another—about fifteen people in total—making note of their techniques. Their strengths. Their weaknesses. I filed it all away, knowing damn well that Kru Tyson would be pairing me up before I left that day just to see what I still had in me after all that time away. Little did he know I'd been practicing in my basement in Columbus. My shit was on point.

Then I realized that Mark Sinclair was among them. One of The Six. The one who'd tried to call Donovan off the day before—however weakly. He saw me staring him down and shook his head, turning back to the guy holding pads for him. I couldn't wait to spar with him.

After my legs were warm, I stepped up to the only empty

heavy bag left and gripped it between my forearms. I smiled at the insignia on it—my favorite bag in the gym, perfectly worn in from years of being battered—and drew back my leg before slamming it forward, extending through my hip at the last second for a bit more force. I repeated this on the other side, going back and forth. It created a dance of sorts with the bag—a dance that would have been really painful for my partner. I pictured Mark's face on it and kneed the bag harder—right at man-junk level.

By the time I finished, I was sweating like crazy. Half the gym seemed to be watching me out of the corners of their eyes. When I leveled a steady gaze on them all, they turned their focus back to what they were doing. Douchebags.

I made my way over to grab a quick drink from the cooler, but Kru Tyson stepped in front of me, taking his fighting stance in the middle of the room. He said nothing, only raised his hands to his face for cover before he started circling me. Apparently, he really did want to see what I still had in me.

Technical sparring wasn't about doing damage. It was about combining your skills against an opponent in a controlled fashion. A fight without the brutality. I looked down at my hands, which were still bare, then back to him. He only smiled in response.

"What happened to safety first?" I asked, mimicking his stance.

"I'm not too worried about you, Danners."

Without so much as flinching, I hauled my right leg up and arced it toward his head, pivoting on my foot while swinging my hip around. The motion felt great. So did landing the kick square on his arm that sheltered the side of his head from my shin.

The familiar sound of cracking pads in the background went silent.

We officially had an audience.

Kru Tyson was quick to return my kick with one of his own. I blocked it when I should have caught it, but I followed it up with a fake front kick that I snapped back into a Superman punch. I pulled up at the last second, knowing I would have made contact with my bare hand if I hadn't. He merely laughed in response.

Then he hugged me.

"There's my little tiger." I wrapped my arms around his back and gave him a squeeze. He and I had so much in common, including a tough exterior that camouflaged our gooey insides. Until that moment, I hadn't realized just how much I'd missed him. So much of my life had been cast aside when my family had left Jasperville that it was easy for people to be cast aside, too. Tyson had been one of those people.

And he hadn't deserved it.

"I'd heard you were back in town. I wondered how long it would take before you showed up at my door."

"Longer than it should have, but . . . I had things to do. Trouble to cause. You know the drill."

And he really did.

Kru Tyson had been a bit of a rebellious kid growing up. Minor run-ins with the law, but nothing major. He'd enlisted in the U.S. Marines right out of high school and served his four years and then some. My dad had always respected him for that—for cleaning up his life. Going straight. Tyson had opened the gym when he was in his midtwenties after leaving the reserves. He'd moved away from where he'd grown up on the East Coast, wanting to start over. He, like my dad, had followed a girl here. She eventually left. He stayed.

And my life was better for it.

"Yo, everybody, listen up," he said, demanding the attention of everyone there—the attention we'd already garnered the second we'd started sparring. "This here is my girl, Kylene, otherwise known as Danners. She knows her shit. Treat her accordingly. And if any of you disrespects her in any way, I'll let her go bare knuckles on your face. Got it?"

A flurry of mumbled responses echoed off the cinder-block walls.

"Aw, don't scare them like that, Tyson. I'll wear gloves. Maybe six-ouncers."

I turned to see him fighting back his laughter. He lost miserably, but I admired his effort.

"Get your ass over to that bag and practice your kicks. You're not bringing your leg all the way back. And move faster. Don't be so lazy."

"Yes, sir!" I shouted before jogging over to the heavy bag I'd just kneed the crap out of. The one I'd pretended was Mark. As I took my stance, ready to unleash on the worn leather again, I heard Kru Tyson tell someone to come hold the bag for me. Imagine my surprise when Mark brushed past me to stand behind it, looking at me through the chains it hung from.

"Is this why you think you can step to guys like Donovan? Because you've got a little skill in the gym?" he asked, leaning his chest and pelvis against the bag. I stared at him for a second before switching my stance in a flash and uncorking a left body kick on the bag. He hadn't expected it to have so much force, and he stepped back, having been caught unprepared.

"Before you start mansplaining how training isn't the same as fighting, let me stop you. I've been in fights—both in and out of the ring. I'm well aware. And if you'd prefer not to find out firsthand, just hold the bag like you mean it and shut your mouth." After his surprise faded, he sneered at me. Maybe he needed a good front kick to knock a bit more of his hubris away.

"I was trying to help you yesterday, but if you're so tough, I guess you don't need it."

"If that was your idea of helping me, then we're just not on the same page at all."

"What did you want me to do, Kylene? Tackle him?"

"No, but I thought maybe one of you spineless shits might not have just stood by with your mouth full of PB&J while Donovan beat on Amy or me. But, then again, why am I surprised. None of you did a thing to stop AJ, so . . ."

I smashed the bag with a front kick that knocked Mark in the nuts. He let out a painful exhale and bent forward to grab his boys. Tyson, hearing the ruckus, came over.

"You all right, Sinclair?"

"Yes, sir."

"Good. Then stop being a pussy and hold the bag for her. I told you she knows her shit. Start acting like it."

Mark didn't say another word to me for the rest of our training. When it was over, he grabbed his bag and bailed without saying goodbye. I could see the unasked questions in Tyson's stare, but I just thanked him for borrowing his gloves and left. Unlike me, the identities of the boys had been better withheld from the public. Yes, people either figured out who they were or assumed, but they were usually referred to as "those nice boys." I, however, was called a barrage of names, none of which were very flattering. I wondered if Tyson was slowly piecing together that Mark and I had beef, and that maybe it had something to do with the scandal that drove me from town.

If he ever did, Sinclair would be in a world of hurt.

THIRTEEN

Striker sent me a text while I was training, telling me that he'd forgotten a file and that someone working down in my area would be dropping it off at Gramps' house in an hour. Since he'd sent it forty-five minutes earlier, I didn't have long to get home in time to receive it.

I raced through town and into Gramps' neighborhood. When I got to the house, there was a generic-looking sedan, not unlike the one my father used to drive, parked outside. I hadn't even pulled all the way into the driveway before Agent Douchecanoe was out of his vehicle and headed my way, file in hand.

"So you're the errand boy," I said to him as he scowled at me.

"You know you can hear that environmental hazard coming from a mile away, right?"

"Weird . . . kinda like your hostility and hubris."

His frown deepened as he extended the file in his hand toward me. I reached for it, but he pulled it back at the last second.

"Striker said to make sure you got this."

"Hence the errand boy comment—"

"Do you know what's in here?"

"Do *you* know what's in there?" I countered, knowing damn

well he would have looked. The suspense would have killed him.

"They're copies of evidence from you father's trial."

"Ding, ding, ding!" I exclaimed, snatching the file from his hand. "Consider your errand complete. I'd tip you, but . . . I don't get paid until next week."

"Why did Striker want you to have those?" he asked, totally unfazed by my jab.

"Because I asked for them."

He shook his head.

"That's adorable. You think you can find something that a defense lawyer and a team of FBI agents couldn't find."

"They weren't really looking, though, were they? They approached his investigation as if he was already guilty. Hard to be objective when your singular focus is to bring down the fall guy."

"Says the girl with the singular focus of freeing her daddy," he replied. "What a sad day it's going to be for you when all you find in those files is the truth of your father's guilt."

"We'll see about that."

I turned to walk away from him, dismissing him entirely.

"Striker also asked me to see how you're doing, so I'll ask. How are you doing?"

"Fine, before you showed up. Be sure to tell him that. It'll do your career wonders."

I didn't give him a chance to get in the final word. Instead, I opened the front door and slammed it shut. Gramps shot me a look from the kitchen, so I put on a smile and crossed the room to greet him with a little pep in my step. Despite Agent Douchecanoe's return, the afternoon had gone off without a hitch and I was still riding my post-workout endorphin high. Throw in my new job, and it was a total trifecta. "Did my door offend ya on the way in?" he asked, turning his attention back to whatever he was poking around at in the Crock-Pot. It smelled like heaven. I joined him and grabbed a fork from the drawer, ready to pillage the ceramic dish and abscond with its contents. Unfortunately for me, Gramps was still pretty quick for his age. He caught my wrist as I reached for the pot. "Nope. Got at least an hour left to cook. No liftin' the lid, you hear me?"

"Loud and clear, sir," I said with a nod.

"Well, all right then. How's about you doin' your homework until it's done, then we can have dinner together tonight?"

"Great idea. I'll be in my room if you need me."

I walked down the hall to my room and pulled my homework out of my bag. Sitting at Gramps' desk, I started to sort through the backlog of work I still needed to get caught up on. Though I was making some headway with it, study hall just wasn't long enough to put a dent in every subject. I had a lot of long nights ahead of me. Staying focused on the work would prove challenging, indeed, especially with everything going on.

An hour later, Gramps popped his head into my room with a smile on his face.

"Dinner's all set. You wanna join me on the porch?"

"Sure thing!"

He gave a quick nod, then disappeared into the hallway.

I closed up my books and made my way to the kitchen, where a plate of food was already waiting for me. I couldn't help but smile at the sight of it. Gramps was filling my parental void in an epic way.

The screen door creaked as I pushed it open. Balancing my plate in my hand and a cup of water in the other, I made my way to the porch railing and popped a hip half onto it. It was wide enough to precariously place my plate and cup on, so I did, giving me a chance to hoist myself all the way up to sit with legs dangling.

"There's a perfectly good chair right there," Gramps said, indicating Gram's old rocking chair. The one that matched his. The perfect pair.

She'd been gone since I was little, but something always seemed wrong to me about sitting in that chair. Like I was invading one of the only memories I had of her. The one where she used to rock with me in her lap and read me stories until I couldn't keep my eyes open any longer.

"I can see you better from here," I lied.

"Well, that's good then, since you're 'bout to tell me about your broken windows. I wouldn't want to miss the expression on your face while you try to find a way outta tellin' the truth."

"Now, Gramps," I replied before taking a big bite of his famous pot roast. "Would I do that?"

"Don't talk with your mouth full. Lord, your Gram would have a fit if she saw you doin' that."

"She's probably rolling in her grave at the thought."

"God rest her soul, I'm sure she is." The two of us shared a quick laugh. "Now. The windows?"

"Someone smashed them at school. Kind of a welcome-back present, I imagine."

"Rolled out the red carpet for ya, did they?"

"Apparently. Just think of what would have happened if they *really* didn't like me." I winked at him before taking another bite. That pot roast was the best damn thing I'd eaten in ages.

Gramps dropped the subject, knowing that I hadn't exactly left JHS under great terms. He knew I'd have some enemies upon my return. He also knew that if I wasn't pushing the issue, it was probably best left alone.

We ate in silence for a bit, Gramps enjoying the gradual sunset, and me running my various issues over in my head. Amy and Donovan, The Six, and my dad's case—the one I didn't even know how to begin solving.

"Somethin' botherin' you, Ky?" Gramps asked, still rocking in his worn-out chair. The sun hung low in the sky, casting a warm light on his weathered old face. A face that held an edge of knowing in its expression. He knew I was upset. He saw right through me. "I know I ain't your father, but—"

"I've just got a lot on my mind."

"Why don't you let some of it out, then? Maybe I can help. . . ."

I took a deep breath, placing my plate down carefully on the railing.

"I thought that maybe after all this time that the backlash of those pictures would have faded, but it hasn't. I can't escape it, Gramps. Everywhere I turn there's a reminder of it, whether it's a glare from some judgmental prick or the leer of some perv. The girls aren't much better. Most just look at me like I'm a whore, which is highly ironic given some of their sexual histories," I said, looking past him. I couldn't meet his gaze. "I just—I just don't think anyone will ever let it go unless I can prove that I had no part in it."

"Junebug—"

Junebug. Gramps only called me that when he was worried or wanted me to feel better about something—when he wanted me to feel safe and secure like I did as a kid. I don't think he even realized he did it. But I'd had a lot of Junebugs over the past two and a half years. The pattern was undeniable.

Junebug, your daddy's gonna to be okay.

Junebug, your mama's just stressed 'bout the trial.

Junebug, don't worry, your mama will come to her senses.

Gramps didn't realize that he couldn't Junebug everything into being okay, but he sure did try.

I took a deep breath and tried to calm my rising unease.

"I know I should learn to let it go. I tried to. It was easy to in Columbus. But here? It's just too hard. I need to put this to rest."

I finally let my eyes drift over to him. He was staring at me, brow furrowed.

"If that's what you need, then put it to rest, girl."

I smiled.

"Consider it done."

"Good, now, what else is going on over at that school that I need to know about?"

"Well, one of the football players is taking steroids and has all the side effects that go along with it."

The crease in his brow deepened.

"Like what?"

"Like beating on his girlfriend and trying to beat on me." Gramps shot from his chair like a threat had snuck up on us both. "Don't panic," I said, trying to calm him. "The day a man lays his hands on me is the day he'll find himself taking one long-ass dirt nap."

Gramps sat down. "Damn right."

"She stays with him, too. . . . I think that's the part I'm struggling the most with. How you could let someone treat you that way and still stay. I mean, I get that our culture breeds a certain amount of this, but I don't feel any pressure to tolerate it. How does it get so bad for someone that they'd rather live in fear than leave?"

He looked thoughtful for a moment, scratching the stubble on his chin.

"Because sometimes the leavin' is far more dangerous than the stayin'." I let that thought sink in while he continued. "I've seen a lot in my years workin' at Logan Hill. People always ask me about the prisoners, but I tell you, it's the visitors that are always the most interesting people in that building. I've seen women so cowed by their men that even with them locked away, those girls are too scared to start a new life for themselves. I've put a lot of thought over the years into why. Tried to sort out why a person would choose that life."

"Did you come up with any answers?"

"Too many to count." He reached over and took my hand, holding on to it while he spoke. "Kylene, you can never assume that people got it as good as you do, and that says somethin', given what happened to you and your father's current situation. But even if they do, that don't mean it can't happen to them too. Some of these girls—they've never known love at all, let alone from a man. Hell, half of them probably don't even know who their daddies are. It's damn shameful, creatin' a life and then walkin' away from it like it ain't nothin'. You think about that long and hard, Kylene. You think about what that would be like. What your life would have been without your daddy around teachin' you like he did. Takin' care of you when your mama couldn't."

Wasn't that the truth. If any parent was absent in my life, it was her, not him.

"And if they were 'round in the beginning, God knows they left when those girls were too young to understand—and they blamed themselves."

"But can't you change that? I mean, there are tons of girls in single-parent homes that aren't this way."

"Well, now, that's true, but you see, that's how it often starts. If not that, then somebody ain't done right by those girls. I can't tell you the things I've heard from inmates—vile things that I will take with me to my grave. Girls aren't kids anymore. They're women in smaller bodies. It sickens me to think that it's true, but I've heard hundreds of stories that tell me it is. And then you throw the TV and that damned internet into the mix, and it only gets worse."

"I know you don't think girls dressing a certain way means they're asking for unwanted attention, Gramps. Otherwise, you'd think those pictures were my fault."

"Hell no, Kylene. I don't care how a girl dresses; it ain't an invitation for someone to treat them like they ain't a person with rights. I'm sayin' that sometimes these girls with low self-esteem don't know any other way to get attention, so they try to get any they can. It's sad and it's wrong, but that don't make it any less true. They don't think they're worth nothin', so they let people treat 'em that way."

"Geez . . ."

"I know this is hard for you to wrap your head around, 'specially because you're a fixer, just like your daddy. And you crave a sense of justice that few these days still do. I don't know that you'll ever really be able to understand the why in this, Kylene, any more than you understood the why in this town turning its back on you after those damn pictures were taken."

"What if I could prove what Donovan is doing? Just like I'm going to prove what happened the night those pictures were taken."

Gramps looked thoughtful for a moment.

"I see where you're goin' with this, but I'm not sure it'll help her in the way you think it should. And if it means stickin' your nose in a dangerous place, I don't want you doin' it." His eyes narrowed and he shifted forward in his seat. "You need to mind yourself where this boy and girl are concerned. It ain't your fight. Your daddy's in jail and your mama's off living her new life. I can't have nothin' happen to you, you hear me?"

I did. I forced a soft smile as I got up and closed the distance between us to hug him.

"Nothing's going to happen, Gramps. I promise."

"I love you, Junebug, but don't you make me promises you ain't got no way of keepin'."

"I'm not. I swear."

"On your daddy's life?"

"On my daddy's life."

When Gramps finally released me, I gave him a kiss on the cheek and headed for the door. I stopped short, holding the knob for a second while I got control of my rising emotions. Swearing on my father's life seemed a grim reminder of where he was and the danger he was in—at least until his paperwork went through.

"He's going to be okay, right, Gramps?"

I couldn't look at him. I just held on to that knob and prayed for an answer I could cling to.

"I'm not allowed to work in his section of the prison, but my friends are keeping me posted. They're watching out for him as much as they can. He's gonna be fine, Junebug."

My grip on the door tightened.

"Thanks, Gramps," I said before heading inside.

I made my way to my makeshift room and plopped down on my cot, bouncing a few times before it finally stilled. I stared at the wall of photos in front of me, zoning them out until they were just a big messy blur.

I was too busy thinking to process anything else.

Gramps had tried to reassure me about my dad, but the truth was he couldn't, and deep down, I knew that before I asked. Maybe the little girl in me just needed to hear it—needed to believe it would be all right, even if the jaded teen knew it was a lie. Until I could find evidence worthy of reopening his case, I had to hope his paperwork went through sooner than later.

Or that Gramps' friends really could help keep him safe.

I closed my eyes and took a breath, trying to force my mind to focus on something other than my father. Distraction was often the only way to derail its train of thought. So I thought about what Gramps had said about Donovan—that going after him would only get me in trouble, more trouble than I was already in. And judging by how quickly things had escalated, another encounter with him wouldn't end favorably for me. But then I wondered if there was an easier solution: one that didn't involve going directly after him. What if I could just get enough leverage to keep him off my back—maybe off Amy's, too?

I lay back on the cot and folded my hands behind my head. A plan was brewing in my mind—one that could put an end to Donovan's behavior. In the morning I'd schedule an appointment at the Appalachian Valley Medical Center. Dr. Carle, prescriber of questionably legitimate medications, and I were going to have a little chat.

FOURTEEN

"Appalachian Valley Med Center; this is Sheila. How can I help you?"

"Good morning, Sheila. I would like to schedule a new-patient appointment."

"Excellent. I'm happy to help you with that. I just need to get some information from you first."

"Of course."

"Is there a particular doctor you would like to schedule with?"

I smiled. "Dr. Carle, please."

"Oh, I'm sorry. Dr. Carle only works part-time and rarely takes on new patients."

"Really?" I replied, sounding as disappointed as I felt. For once, I didn't have to put on an act.

"Our other physicians are just as wonderful."

"Oh, I'm sure they are; it's just that some of my friends at school rave about Dr. Carle."

"I'm sorry, but he's by referral only."

Interesting . . .

"I had a cancellation for later this afternoon with Dr. Frye. She's new here but an excellent doctor. Would that work for you?"

"No, that's okay. Thanks anyway."

I hung up, wondering exactly how one could get a referral to Dr. Carle. I had little doubt it was something sketchy.

School went by that day without too much of a hitch. Mr. Callahan continued to be a douche. Donovan sneered at me all through gym class. And Tabby and Garrett made me laugh at lunch. Everything was going great until my afternoon English class.

Ms. McManus started the class off with a discussion about classics with semicontroversial subject matter. It wasn't long before *The Scarlet Letter* came up and I found Eric Stanton and Scooter Brown whispering to themselves and staring at me like a couple of gossipy girls. It didn't take a genius to figure out why. The second Ms. McManus opened the floor for commentary, it was game on.

"I don't get what the big deal is with this book," Scooter said, not waiting to be called on. "I mean, she did what she was accused of. Why should we feel sorry for her?"

He made a point of staring at me.

"I think the question you need to ask yourself is whether or not it was an injustice to be publicly vilified for a private matter," Ms. McManus said. "Should she have been forced to wear the mark of her crime for all in town to see?"

Scooter shrugged.

Eric chimed in on his behalf. "That was the punishment at the time—an accepted practice. I don't see what the problem is."

My hand shot up in the air.

"Yes, Kylene?"

"So the letter was essentially an olden-times way of slut-shaming, right?"

"Well, yes. That's one way to look at it. . . ."

"She cheated. She was branded a cheater. It didn't matter the consequences surrounding her situation; it was boiled down to logistics. She had sex with someone else while married. She was an adulterer. End of story."

"I guess. . . ."

"So, my question is: Did men ever have to wear the letters, or just the women? I mean, if they did the same, shouldn't they be viewed the same way in the public's eyes? As cheating whores?"

"No," Scooter said with a laugh—like I'd said the most ridiculous thing ever.

"Why not?" I asked, turning in my seat to face him.

"Because they're dudes, that's why."

"Mr. Brown, if you could please raise your hand if you have something to add. Preferably something well thought out and not the first thing that pops into your head."

Scooter deflated a little at Ms. McManus' jab.

"Men didn't have to wear them because that behavior was expected of them. It's a woman's responsibility to maintain her virtue," Eric said, staring at me. The double entendre in his words was so thick I wanted to choke on it. A dolled-up version of "boys will be boys" rationale. How fitting.

"Really?" I countered, not even giving Ms. McManus a chance to respond. "So men aren't in control of their own actions? They can't help themselves because their hormones overtake their brains, and therefore they shouldn't be held responsible?"

He cocked his head at me. "Maybe if Hester Prynne didn't want to end up wearing that letter, she should have acted differently. If you can't handle the consequences, don't do the crime."

"Wow, that's enlightened. . . . So the entire town gets to judge her based on only what they perceive to be true? When they only have partial facts?"

"I think it was pretty obvious she was pregnant, don't you?"

"And if she'd been raped? If the child had resulted from a crime she had no control over? Should she be punished by the court of public opinion for that?"

Eric leaned back in his chair. "I guess it's a good thing that wasn't the case then, huh?"

While my blood boiled inside me, he winked from across the room. It was all I could do to stay in my seat. I wanted to launch myself over those desks and pound his smug, shitty face in. His attempt to get under my skin was wildly successful.

It only fueled my need to prove what happened that night.

"I think we're getting a bit off track here," Ms. McManus said, sensing the tension in the room. "Let's switch gears for a second and discuss *Of Mice and Men*. . . ."

I could hear her talking in the background, but I couldn't make out the words over the pounding of blood in my ears and the blinding rage I felt every time Eric looked over at me and smiled. I had to stare at the window and focus on my breathing, like Tyson had taught me long ago. I couldn't let my emotions cloud my judgment. That wouldn't lead to anything but a trip to Principal Thompson's office and Eric's enjoyment. He'd had enough at my expense. I didn't plan to give him any more.

When the bell rang, I hurried out of the room, the grating sound of Scooter's laughter chasing me. I walked to the nearest bathroom and locked myself in a stall. I needed a chance to breathe, to get over the emotional flashback I was having. Eric Stanton couldn't have looked less sympathetic if he'd tried to. In fact, he looked calm, cool, and collected. Too collected.

Like *sociopath* collected. For a moment, I wondered if maybe AJ hadn't been the one to take those pictures of me.

Then I wondered if learning the truth about that night would only make me feel worse.

As I made my way to my car after school, ready to go visit my dad, I heard Garrett calling me from the far side of the parking lot.

"Ky! Wait up!"

I hovered by my open car door as he ran toward me.

"What's up?"

"Are you going to be home later?"

"Nope. I have a hot date." My deadpan response wasn't lost on him. He grinned like the boy I grew up with. The one that always got me into trouble.

"Can I stop by?"

"Garrett," I started, feigning a patronizing tone. "Listen. I know you're totally into me and want me to be your girlfriend, but . . . I just don't love you like that. I hope you understand."

He rolled his eyes as he laughed.

"Don't flatter yourself, Danners. You know I don't like blondes."

"I do know, and I've hated myself for years because of that fact."

He roared with laughter. "Trying to have a serious conversation with you is like herding cats."

"Highly entertaining and a great workout?"

"I was thinking aggravating and damn near impossible."

"Huh."

"Exactly. Anyway, are you going to be there or not?"

"Yeah. I'll be there. I'm going to go see Dad now, but I'll be home after that."

"Cool. Message me when you get back and I'll head over."

"Sounds like a plan." I went to get into my car, then realized that Garrett was still lingering. "Something else you want to talk about?"

"Any problems today?"

"I nearly pummeled Eric Stanton in English, but other than that, nope. No issues."

"Good."

Garrett looked tense and his tone held an edge to it. It was clear that something was bothering him. If I hadn't known him better, I'd have said he was worried. But Garrett Higgins didn't do worrying.

He did fixing.

He caught my assessing stare and flashed me a smile that said everything was all right. I didn't buy it for a second, but I played along and mimicked his expression.

"So I'll see you tonight?" I said.

"Yeah. Tonight. See you then."

He turned and walked back the way he'd come, headed toward his truck. I watched for a moment, then slipped into my car. I wanted to get to Logan Hill. I needed to talk to my dad so badly it hurt. He'd know how to start picking apart The Six. He'd also understand why I wanted to.

FIFTEEN

The shock of being inside Logan Hill Prison to visit Dad was much less the second time around. I was already getting the hang of things. It didn't take long before I was in the visiting room, stationed behind the thick pane of glass yet again. When my dad walked in, I pulled the phone off the wall and held it to my ear.

The bruises on his face were turning an awful yellow color as they faded, but there were no new ones, so I saw that as a win. The cast on my father's arm, however, was not. I stared at it openly, wondering if whoever was after him planned to take him apart piece by piece or if they just kept getting interrupted. I shuddered at both potential scenarios.

Dad's paperwork clearly hadn't gone through yet.

He sat down across from me and picked up the phone.

"It's not as bad as you think," he offered without me asking. In fairness, I hadn't taken my eyes off the cast since I saw it. "I fell down the stairs."

"My ass you did."

"I thought a trip to the infirmary would keep me out of gen pop for a while."

"Wait, you did it on purpose?" He shrugged off my incredulous tone. "Well did it work? Tell me you didn't do it for nothing."

"I haven't been back since."

"That's a plus," I mumbled to myself.

"My paperwork should go through before I would be put back into gen pop, so everything is going to be fine, Kylene."

I breathed a sigh of relief. One bullet dodged for the time being.

Silence fell between us for a moment. I wanted to tell him so much—about Eric Stanton and *The Scarlet Letter*, about Donovan with his steroids and the mysterious Dr. Carle—but there was something else I needed to talk to him about. Something I knew he wouldn't take well at all.

"So I got a job working at Meg's law office," I said, thinking it might be best to just blurt it out. My dad was a proud man. Knowing he couldn't provide for me was likely eating him up inside. But I was out of cash from my summer job, and I hated leaning more on Gramps than I already was. He'd understand that.

The resigned look in his eyes told me he did.

"I'm sorry, Ky."

"It'll be fine, Dad." My father stared at me silently, his features slack, his face pale. The stress of everything was getting to him, and it was completely unnerving. All throughout his trial, I'd never seen him falter—never saw his confidence shaken. But seeing him through that thick pane of glass, looking like he was giving up, if only a little, was more than I could handle. "Dad? Dad, listen to me! It's going to be okay. It's just a part-time job. No biggie. I promise!"

"You shouldn't have to work and go to school, Ky. You should be out with your friends, enjoying what's left of your high school career." His voice was thin and hollow, and it scared the shit out of me.

"I shouldn't have to put up with Callahan's crap or eat that stuff they try to pass off as food at school, either, but I do. We both knew that me going to Jasperville was going to take a huge dump on what was left of my high school years. But sometimes you have to woman up and get it done. You taught me that, Dad. Trust that I can handle this."

He smiled weakly and shook his head.

"Where did that sweet little towheaded girl I remember disappear to?"

"She was upgraded to a stubborn, sassy pain in the ass who adores you. Can you deal with that?"

His smile widened.

"I guess I have to."

"Good. Now that that's settled, let's move on to something else."

"Kylene," my dad said, his eyes serious again. "Tell Meg thank you for me."

"Of course. I think the job will be great for me. I met one of the other attorneys the other day when I stopped in. He seems pretty cool. I guess he's the new partner there. Luke Clark."

My dad's eyes narrowed.

"He's a defense attorney?"

"Yeah. Why?"

"Because he was brought in by a couple of the families back when the boys were questioned."

My face went slack. "Oh . . ."

"I guess he didn't mention that."

"No, but I don't think he knew exactly who I am. And really, is he even at liberty to discuss that?"

Dad let out a harsh exhale before leaning back in his seat.

"No. He wouldn't be."

"Surely Meg knows this," I said, trying to work through things in my mind. "Doesn't the nature of being a defense attorney mean you're going to have to represent guilty people? Just like prosecutors have to let guilty ones go free sometimes?"

"Yes, but I don't have to like it." His angry expression slowly softened. "So what else do you want to talk about? The clock's ticking. . . ."

"I don't know . . . asshole football players? Sketchy medical doctors? Whatever that meat was at lunch today?"

"Pass on the last option. My detective skills aren't that good." He leaned forward to prop his elbows on the counter. "So who is this doctor, and why do you think he's dirty?" I took a minute to fill Dad in on everything I'd learned, intentionally leaving out the gory details about the locker room and AJ. By the time I finished, I could see his wheels were spinning. "Interesting."

"I did some research and found that with a controlled substance like that, he shouldn't have an auto refill with the pharmacy—that he'd need to be seen again to get a new script. But from what I saw, I think he must have an open-ended prescription. His bottle was half empty and it had only been filled a week or so ago."

"But if he was taking too much, he'd be out way too soon, and the doctor would know this."

I smiled. "Precisely."

"That is suspicious." He looked thoughtful for a moment before continuing. "When do you think he started taking this steroid?"

"This summer, according to his girlfriend. I can't remember which pharmacy had filled it, but there're only two in town. With the right information, I can track down his prescription and find out if he has refills on file. If he does, I'll have enough to report it—anonymously, of course."

"Not too shabby, Kylene, but I want you to come to me before you do anything like that. And I want you to lay low. Stay off of Donovan's radar, okay?"

"Already done. Someone took care of that for me. He shouldn't be a problem anymore."

"Who did that? Garrett?"

I swallowed hard. The last person my father wanted to hear about was AJ Miller.

"The who isn't really important, Dad. Just know it's been taken care of."

His gaze hardened, fine lines forming at the corners of his eyes.

"Who, Kylene?"

I exhaled heavily. "AJ. He threatened to throw the season if Donovan didn't leave me alone."

My father's expression was murderous. Thank God he was already in jail. If he hadn't been, I was pretty certain he'd have done something in that moment that would have landed him there. "Dad, it's fine. Really. Don't have an aneurysm about it."

"That little asshole! How dare he try to act the hero after what he did."

"Dad. Dad, you're turning really red. Purple, actually. It's not good for your heart. You need to calm down."

"I'm going to strangle that little fu—"

"Dad! Chill out. Please. I think your head is going to explode if you don't."

He took a couple of calming breaths before speaking.

"I don't want you anywhere near that boy, do you understand me?"

"Hey, no objections here. I didn't ask for his help. He just happened to be around when Donovan was being a dick, and he got him to step down."

"Well, next time he comes near you, I want you to kick him in the balls, then pull him into a clinch and knee his face until it bleeds. Got it?"

"I don't think Principal Thompson will be pleased you sanctioned that behavior, but . . . could you write me a note or something? Maybe that'll help my case when I wind up in his office."

"I don't care if you get suspended. That little bastard has it coming. He deserves that and so much more."

"Dad," I said, taking a softer tone. "It was fine. I told him that he could never make up for what he did, and I told him to leave me alone. It's fine. Really. I've got better things to worry about than AJ Miller—like proving how he and his friends got away with doing what they did."

"Now *that* I can get on board with."

I told him about my interactions with all of The Six, and he advised me on where to start. My working for Meg was already going to come in handy.

"She needs to get her hands on the sheriff's file. She'll let you look it over, I'm sure of that. Once you go through it, I want you to come see me so we can discuss it, okay?"

"For sure. I'll call her tonight and let her know." I looked up at the clock on the wall and realized that I needed to head home. "Dad, I should get going."

"Of course. See you soon? Once you get a look at that file?"

"Sure. I'll probably come by Friday night, if I can."

"No football game for you."

I rolled my eyes.

"I think my days cheering for the Fighting Badgers are over, Dad."

"Understandable. Maybe you, Garrett, and the new girl can find some trouble to get into instead. Trouble that doesn't involve Donovan or AJ or any of the rest of them, for that matter."

"Always."

"Love you, kiddo."

I smiled tightly at him, unable to reply. I couldn't bring myself to tell him I loved him, because I could feel the tension in my throat growing: I knew my voice would crack. I didn't want my dad to feel any worse about his situation, so I blew him a kiss and hung up the phone. I looked back at him as I made my way out of the room, and a guard escorted me back through security to the building's entrance.

I hurried to my car and sat in the parking lot, leaving a message on Meg's cell about the sheriff's file on my case. I hoped she'd be up for the off-book investigation. Hopefully bending a few rules to make it happen wasn't beneath her.

When I hung up, I hesitated for a moment before running a quick search on Donovan. It didn't take long to find what I needed. Idiots like him put way too much information on social media. Once I had his birth date, I dialed up the first of two town pharmacies and took a deep breath. If my plan didn't work, I'd be right back to square one again.

"How can I help you today?"

"Yes, I'm calling to see if my son still has a refill on his prescription. The name is Donovan Jason Shipman."

"Date of birth and medication?" I gave her both without hesitation. "Okay, let me see. It looks like he has three more refills left on this prescription, Mrs. Shipman."

"Well, that's a relief. I think he misplaced his meds, and I don't have time to take him into the pediatrician for a checkup. Thank you so much for your help."

"Of course. Is there anything else I can do for you?'

I hesitated for a second.

"Yes. Could you confirm for me when he last picked up his medication?"

"Looks like that was about two weeks ago."

"Two weeks. Okay. Great. Thanks again. Have a great day."

I hung up the phone and immediately did a Google search about controlled substances. Two minutes later, I knew there was a problem. He shouldn't have had a refill for that medication, and given that pharmacists knew more about drugs and their regulations than any other type of health care practitioner, they would know whether a prescription written by an MD was bogus or dangerous—or illegal. Furthermore, it was their responsibility to report suspicious prescriptions to the state board. And that clearly hadn't happened.

I filed that detail away for later and started home. With the warm, glowing sun hanging low in the sky, I pulled up to Gramps' house and found an unfamiliar red pickup truck parked in the street by our mailbox. I drove past it to pull into the single-car driveway. As I got out, a voice stopped me in my tracks.

"Ky. I need to talk to you," AJ said as he jogged across the front yard toward me.

"Oh, no you don't."

I quickened my pace, trying to escape inside before he reached me. I didn't want to cause a scene for Gramps' neighbors. He'd already gotten a lot of unwanted attention during the trial. Even more when he took me in. Cussing out my ex in his front yard didn't seem like a great way to pay him back.

"I just want another chance to explain—"

"AJ," I said, wheeling around on the front porch as he crested the bottom step. "There is nothing to explain. I didn't want to hear it two and a half years ago. I don't want to hear it now. What about that do you not understand?"

He had the nerve to look wounded.

It was then that I really saw him. Saw a shadow of the boy I'd once known in the face of the soon-to-be-man before me. He was taller than I'd remembered, and bigger, too—more muscular. His hair had lightened with the summer sun, undoubtedly from doing two-a-days for football. I hadn't really had the time or space in the locker room to notice these things, because my head had been ringing and I was scared out of my mind—not that I wanted to notice them now. But as he stood on Gramps' front step, staring up at me with hopeful eyes, it was impossible not to. I could feel my gaze drifting over his body, and immediately I focused my attention elsewhere.

AJ Miller didn't get to know that I still found him attractive.

That's because AJ Miller was as good as dead to me.

"Kylene," he started, "I understood why you shut me out when it all happened. I didn't push the issue at all because I knew you were hurting and embarrassed. Maybe I didn't handle things well in the aftermath. Maybe I should have tried to talk to you right away—"

"Your lawyer would have shit a brick if you had."

Though it was true, it still sounded like a dig when I said it.

Those hopeful eyes turned to the ground at his feet, as if it would help him find a way to refute what I'd said.

"Yes, he would have, but if it would have made a difference to you, I'd have told him to suck it and been at your side seconds later. I hated that I couldn't be there for you. I still hate it now. . . ."

I choked on a bitter laugh.

"Jesus . . . it's like you have a pornographic form of Munchausen or something. You don't get to create a shit storm and then be there to nurse my mental wounds afterward."

"But I didn't do it! I told you I wasn't the one who took those pictures, because I didn't, Kylene. C'mon. . . . We've been friends since fourth grade—ever since I realized that you and Garrett came as a package deal. How could you think I would do that to you?"

My irritation and anger boiled over once again. "Because you were drunk? Because it wasn't fourth grade anymore? Because people change. . . ."

He shook his head. "We were in love, Ky—"

"So who did it then, AJ? If it wasn't you, then who? Because I can assure you that I didn't whip up my shirt and start snapping pics of my boobs with your camera, and I sure as hell didn't post them on the internet. So I'm super curious to see what your thoughts are on the matter, since you're so innocent and all." He opened his mouth to reply, then thought better of it, snapping it shut again. "Yeah," I scoffed. "That's what I thought. You and all your buddies were the ones seen near the hot tub that night, and not one of you seemed to have the foggiest idea how my girls ended up on your camera."

"Kylene—"

"No!" I shouted, then lowered my voice. "Don't you dare act like you all didn't circle the wagons and tell the same bullshit story to the sheriff. I know you did. My dad was there, AJ. You're lucky you guys got out of the station alive."

"My story wasn't bullshit," he said calmly, taking a step toward me. "It was the truth."

"Yes, yes," I replied with a dismissive wave of my hand. "Right hand to God and the whole nine, I'm sure. You didn't do it. You didn't see who did. You weren't there when it happened. Yada yada. You all got off scot-free. The end. Meanwhile, I was left to pick up the pieces of my life, which was all but ruined, thanks to you guys, and you all got to start spring training for the next football season. I think that seems fair, don't you? Maybe that's the price I pay for having a couple of drinks at a high school party. Maybe I brought it all on myself—"

"You didn't bring it on yourself," he said, taking another step closer. There was anger in his tone, but it wasn't for me. Maybe it was for himself.

"And yet it happened, thanks to you."

He exhaled heavily before scrubbing his face with his hand, his frustration showing through. Then he lifted those piercing green eyes to me, pinning them on mine with an intensity I'd never seen from him.

"Tell me something, Kylene: Do you think your dad is guilty?"

"Go. Away." I bit the words out through a clenched jaw, my fists curled at my side. AJ Miller was seconds away from swallowing teeth. I had a nasty right cross and an even nastier left elbow. One more word about my dad, and he'd have been introduced to both.

"I know you don't think he is. I don't think so, either. I followed his case, and something about it never added up. Your father was always amazing to me—especially after mine left. And his reaction to what happened to you when those pictures surfaced was exactly what it should have been—pure rage."

"Do you have a point, AJ, or are you trying to see how far you can push me before I get stabby?"

"My point is that despite the mountain of evidence proving otherwise, you still believe your dad is innocent, because you know him. You know his character. And you know he would never have done what they accused him of." He paused for a second, looking at me with wide, mournful eyes. "Neither did I, Kylene. What I don't understand is how you can't even entertain that idea for a fraction of a second. That you can't see the parallels between your father and me."

Sweet baby Jesus, I wanted to throttle him.

"You and my father have nothing in common," I replied, my words twisting to a snarl.

"Why do you think I'm here?"

"To get punched?"

"Do you see any of the other guys that were accused standing on your front step, trying to earn back your trust?" he asked, his tone growing harsher.

"No, because they're clearly smarter than you are. They're not trying to die."

"They're not here because they don't give a shit."

"And you do?"

"Would I have done what I did in the locker room yesterday if I didn't?"

"Well, let's be honest, if you'd stood by and watched Donovan beat the shit out of me, you'd be even lower than I thought."

"I was willing to throw down with that big gorilla if I had to."

"I'd be lying if I said I didn't want to see him whale on you. . . ."

"If I thought it would help things between us, I would have. Gladly."

I hesitated for a second, my witty comeback dying on my tongue. He'd meant what he said. I could see it in his eyes— the fire. The conviction. It was enough to give me a moment of pause, however brief.

"AJ, I have a lot on my plate right now, and making me relive that night isn't helping. I don't understand why you can't just drop it or why you're still trying to convince me that you didn't have anything to do with those pictures. But if my forgiveness will make you go away, then fine, I absolve you of your sins. Now go away. I have bigger problems to deal with than you and your guilt."

"Do you think I don't know that? That I'm oblivious to the fact that your whole world has been turned on its ass? That you being back in this town isn't a form of daily torture? I know you, Kylene Danners. I always have. I always will. And right now, all I want is to help you. You may think that you're hiding it well, but I can see that you're hurting."

"Yeah, well. I'm not sure you're going to be the best candidate to help me out with that."

He inched closer to me, his eyes locked on mine.

"I could be," he said softly.

"I don't trust you, AJ," I said, shutting him down. "I never will. Hell, I don't even like you."

"Because, to you, I was guilty before proven innocent! You never even gave me a chance."

I opened my mouth to argue, then shut it just as fast. Though I was loath to admit it, he was right. I hadn't given him a chance to tell me his side. But I sure as hell wasn't about to in that moment. As far as I was concerned, that issue was dead and buried. And even if I'd wanted to dig it back up, I could see Garrett's truck coming down the street. He definitely wasn't going to let me entertain forgiving his ex–best friend.

"Garrett's here," I said with a little less heat in my tone.

AJ scoffed and shook his head.

"Of course he is." He backed down off the bottom step. "Come to save the day, no doubt." He walked toward his truck as Garrett approached, and my heart rate sped up. Clearly things between them weren't good, but maybe they were worse than I imagined. Maybe I was going to have that scene in Gramps' front yard whether I wanted one or not. "I wonder if you ever asked him where he was that night . . . if you would have turned on him, too."

AJ jumped into his truck and turned it on as Garrett threw his in park and jumped out, storming toward AJ's driver's side door. The truck sped off just before he reached it. I let out the breath I didn't realize I was holding.

"Why the hell was he here?" Garrett asked as he approached.

"Pleading his case while throwing a little shade."

Garrett shook his head.

"Like he has any room to do that."

"Right? And at you, no less."

"Me?" he said, sounding as shocked as I was. I simply nodded in response. "Unbelievable."

"Yeah, well. He's really pushing this whole 'Forgive me because I didn't do it' thing. Maybe he thought making someone else look bad would help? I don't know. All I do know is that he was surprisingly convincing."

"Not convincing enough."

"Yeah," I said absentmindedly, looking off in the direction AJ had fled. "I guess not." I let my gaze drift back to Garrett, who was standing next to me on the porch. "So, what's so important that you had to come over and talk to me about it?"

"Oh, it's nothing crazy. I was just hoping we could hang out. Maybe get a bit caught up on the past two years. You know. Basic small talk kinda stuff."

"How are you at math? Still good?"

"Total nerd. Why?"

"Then welcome to *casa de* Gramps. Feel free to stay as long as you prove yourself useful in the completion of my catch-up homework."

He laughed as he opened the screen door for me.

"I accept your terms."

"I really am sorry that I ditched you when we moved," I said softly.

Garrett straightened up in his chair and put his pencil down on the kitchen table. He took a deep breath, then lifted his eyes to mine. They were sad and warm, and full of things he wanted to say but never would. One of Garrett's greatest gifts was his ability to forgive, if he deemed you worthy of it. But even better than that was his ability to forget.

"Water under the bridge, Ky."

"I know it is. I just wanted to say that."

He smiled.

"And I appreciate it. I'm just glad to have you back. Life in Jasperville is way less entertaining without you around to help get me in trouble."

"You mean you couldn't find someone to TP your neighbor's car with? Or change the letters on the drive-in sign to say some highly questionable things?"

"Oh, my God," he laughed. "I totally forgot about that."

"How could you forget? I took that movie title and elevated it significantly."

"Or made it as offensive as possible."

I rolled my eyes.

"What about you? I'm pretty sure I got my fair share of groundings because of you."

"I still maintain that it was not my idea to cling-wrap that deputy's cruiser shut."

"You bet me twenty bucks I wouldn't do it!" I screamed, chucking my empty backpack at his head.

"Nobody said you had to take me up on it."

"You manipulated me into doing it because you know I can't say no to a dare."

"Clearly. Our dads were so pissed at us," he said, looking off in the distance and smiling. "I missed having my partner in crime." He returned his gaze to me. Instead of the hint of sadness I expected to see, I found a nervousness in his expression. He looked like he had something he wanted to tell me—something I probably didn't want to hear. But if it had to do with how things were in my absence, I'd hear it anyway. I owed him that much.

"Do you want to say something? Tell me something?"

"Because caring and sharing is suddenly your thing?"

"It could be if you needed it to."

"Thanks," he replied with a laugh. "But what I really want from you is to finish this homework here so we can watch a movie or something before my eyes start to bleed or I die of boredom."

"Deal."

We spent the next hour or so flying through my makeup assignments for math class. Once we finished, Garrett sprang out of his seat and made a beeline for the couch, jumping over the back of it to land perfectly on the other side. He snatched up the remote and turned it on, pulling up the guide so he could scroll through it. He'd already stretched out, taking up the entire sofa.

"Make yourself at home," I said, rounding the couch to sit in the well-worn armchair next to it.

"Okay, so our choices are horror flick or something that looks sci-fi–ish."

"Sci-fi. I'm actually trying to sleep tonight."

"Agreed."

He changed the channel to the movie that had started fifteen minutes earlier, leaving us to try to sort out what we'd already missed. Within minutes I was totally engrossed, but Garrett seemed distracted. He kept checking the time on his phone, and his gaze would occasionally fall to the far side of the room where the window to the front yard was.

"Do you need to go?" I finally asked. "You seem anxious about something."

"I'm good. Just don't want to get home too late on a school night."

There was a lack of conviction to his answer that didn't sit well with me. I leaned forward in my chair toward him, wanting to better assess his expression in the darkened room, but the deep growl of a diesel engine speeding down the road distracted me. So did Garrett's reaction to it.

He shot up off the couch and darted to the window, threw back the curtains, and stared in the direction of its approach. I could see the tension in his body, the moonlight illuminating the muscles in his forearms. His hands gripped the fabric a little too tightly.

"Get down!" he shouted, then launched himself at me, knocking me over. A second later I was sprawled out on the floor with Garrett's arm still wrapped around me.

"What the fu—?"

The sound of glass shattering shut me up in a flash. It rained down around us, tinkling like bells as it hit the hardwood floor. The brick responsible for breaking the window landed only inches from my head.

When Garrett deemed it safe to move, he jumped up and ran for the front door. He tore it open and darted out into the front yard. I wasn't far behind. The two of us stood there in the darkness, staring at the red glow of taillights disappearing around the corner at the end of the street. I couldn't make out the vehicle model, but I had a feeling it didn't matter.

My guess was that Garrett was all too aware of who had paid Gramps' house a visit that night.

"Are you okay?" he asked, his eyes still wide and wild with adrenaline.

"I'm great. Now, do you want to tell me what the hell that just was?"

His features tightened.

"My guess? Donovan Shipman."

Even though I half expected to hear it, that name said aloud was a healthy wake-up call.

"You knew he was going to do something, didn't you? That's why you wanted to come over tonight. Why you were so antsy."

"I overheard him talking to his boys in the hall today. Something about paying someone a little visit tonight. At first, I didn't really believe him—I thought he was just running his mouth—but the more I thought about it, the more I got worried. So I came over to make sure you would be okay. I thought maybe my truck out front would deter him, if he planned to actually follow through."

"Why didn't you just tell me? Or tell your dad for that matter?" Garrett's expression darkened further. I knew that he and his dad hadn't been close for a long time—that their opposite natures often made it hard for them to maintain a good relationship—but despite their differences, Garrett still loved his dad. At least I thought he did. However, standing there in Gramps' front lawn, his vandalized house behind us, I started to second-guess that. "What? Why are you making that face, Garrett? What aren't you telling me?"

"I'm not sure it would have mattered if I'd told my dad," he said, his voice empty. For whatever reason, he couldn't bear to look at me. Instead, he stared over his shoulder at the gaping hole in the front window, awaiting my reaction.

"Garrett, your dad is the *sheriff*. He's kind of a big deal. Of course it would matter if he knew."

"Maybe." When he finally turned to face me, there was a mess of emotions swirling in his gaze. Too many to count. Too many to name. "We should go inside," he said, leading the way to the front door.

"What do you mean 'maybe'?" I grabbed his arm to stop him before he reached the house. His face was cast in shadow, but what I could see in it scared me. I knew that face. I'd seen it once before. He wore it the night he got the call that his mother had been in a head-on collision with a drunk driver and was being flown to Columbus Regional Hospital. The disbelief and fear marred his expression.

I saw it again that night on Gramps' front steps.

"Donovan's going to hurt you, Kylene. I know it. And I can't let that happen."

"It's just a window, Garrett. He seems to have a thing for breaking them—"

"This isn't funny!" he shouted, grabbing my arms and shaking me lightly. "He's going to keep messing with you because you have a big target on your back now. He'll hurt you because he can, do you understand me? Because he *knows* he can." He paused for a moment to let the gravity of that statement sink in. He knew I was stubborn to a fault—that I had a thick skull. If I didn't want to hear the truth, I could easily play things off so that I didn't have to. But Garrett was having none of that. I was going to hear him that night, whether I liked it or not. "I don't care what AJ told you, Ky. How under control he thinks he has the situation. He's a liar and a prick. And he doesn't know what I know. He didn't hear what I heard."

Garrett was coming more and more unraveled by the second. His wild eyes were unnerving at best, and a bad omen at worst. Whatever it was that he knew or heard or thought he'd figured out had rocked him to his core.

"What do you know, Garrett?' I asked, my words barely a whisper.

"That Donovan Shipman is above the law in this town. . . ."

Silence.

"Come again?"

"I said, he's untouchable."

I thought back to the conversation Donovan and I had shared in the boys' locker room. He'd said something to that effect about assaulting me. Something that, in retrospect, seemed like 'roid-induced bravado. Hearing that very same sentiment from Garrett, however, altered my perception of his words significantly. "There's something else, isn't there? Something you're not telling me?"

His jaw tensed as he led the way into the house, closing the door behind us.

"When I overheard him in the hallway, he was talking about paying back some bitch tonight. That he was going to screw with her for a while before really sticking it to her. One of his buddies asked what the plan was, and Donovan told him not to worry—that nobody could do anything about it. He sounded as though he knew that for fact. That he had diplomatic immunity as far as Jasperville County was concerned."

"That can't be true," I replied as I flopped down into the armchair not covered in glass and tried to steady my breathing.

He simply shrugged, unsure what to say.

"Listen, I want you to sit tight for a minute," Garrett said. "I need to go find something to board this hole up with and then I'm going to call my dad and have him send someone out here to file a report. Even if Donovan is telling the truth, we need to go through the motions on this or it'll seem weird. We didn't see the vehicle. There probably won't be prints on the brick, so they don't have much to go on anyway. At school tomorrow, I want you to play scared around Donovan, okay? Let him think that he's got the upper hand."

"So far, it seems like he does, Garrett."

"I know that, but you need to let him know that you know it, too."

I could feel the fury rising up in me at the thought of giving him exactly what he wanted. Few things bothered me more than giving in to "the man," regardless of who "the man" was. At Jasperville High, Donovan Shipman was just that. And letting him beat me just wasn't an acceptable option. I wanted to rage against the hand that tried to hold me down.

Actually, I wanted to chop it off and shove it up Donovan's ass.

"I don't know if I can." The words tumbled out of my mouth absentmindedly, a reflex I couldn't shake.

"Kylene," Garrett said, kneeling down in front of me. That look of fear was in his eyes again, and I hated seeing it there. It looked so wrong. "I don't give a shit about your pride right now. I do, however, give a shit about you not getting hurt. Understand?"

"There's got to be another way. . . ."

"If you have suggestions, I'm all ears, but I can't think of any." I thought for a second, then shook my head. "Let me go board this thing up," he said. "I'll be right back."

He smiled, then gave me a hug before making his way to the back door off the kitchen. He was on a mission to secure the broken window. I, however, was left plotting how I was going to get to the bottom of the photo scandal and the Donovan steroid mess without pissing off everyone in town. Possibly without much help from the cops. I was smart, but even I had my doubts about my ability to pull it all off. I needed advice. I needed wisdom. I needed my father. He'd know how to navigate the situation.

While I figured out how to break the news to him, I saw the brick lying in a pile of broken glass, and went over to pick it up. In the light of the moon, it looked like something was written on it. I bent down to see, not wanting to touch it, and found my suspicion to be true. One word was written on it in black marker, the letters angry slashes across the hard clay.

LEAVE

Adrenaline shot through my veins as doubt flashed through my mind. Why would Donovan have written that on the brick, especially if I posed no threat to him? If he was above the law like he insinuated, then there was nothing I could do to stop him. Whoever heaved that brick through Gramps' window wanted me gone for another reason altogether.

While Garrett was outside in the shed, looking for plywood, I snatched the brick up with my sleeve-covered hand and ran down the hall to my room. I stashed it under the bed for safe-keeping. At the time, I wasn't even sure why. Maybe it was Donovan's declaration combined with my general distrust of the police, but something in my gut said not to turn over that evidence. That I might need it one day.

My dad's blind trust in the justice system was what had landed him behind bars.

And I wondered if my reckless attitude might one day land me somewhere even worse.

SIXTEEN

One of the deputies came that night and took our statements about what had happened. When it came to how the window broke, I cut Garrett off and said that we hadn't found what did it. The officer made a confused face, and I shrugged. Garrett didn't say a word but shot me a sideward glance.

Once all the questions were answered, which weren't many, the deputy came to the conclusion that it was likely a random act—but Garrett and I knew better. We kept that tidbit to ourselves.

The cruiser pulled away, and I turned to head back inside but ran in to Garrett instead. He looked down at me with demanding eyes. I sighed before I explained.

"I just thought that maybe it would be best not to hand the brick over. I know," I said, throwing my hands up in defense, "it was probably stupid. We can always take it in and say we found it somewhere in the house later. But I just—"

"I'm glad you kept it," he replied, cutting me off. "I just wish you'd told me the plan. I don't like feeling blindsided."

"Sorry about that."

He gave a nod, then made his way down the hall and grabbed the vacuum cleaner.

"Guess I should clean up my bed for the night."

After he vacuumed the glass off the couch, Garrett made

himself comfortable. He seemed unwilling to leave me alone. It was almost midnight by that point and we were both exhausted. I gave him a hug and said good night, then made my way down the hall to my bedroom.

I closed the door and collapsed onto my bed. I fell asleep not long after. I didn't remember sleeping for long when a rather upset Gramps stormed into my room and flipped on the light.

"You wanna explain why I've got a sheet of plywood the size of Texas boardin' up the front picture window?"

I glanced at my phone to find it was already six in the morning. With a heavy sigh, I hauled my butt off the cot and walked over to Gramps. I could see that he was trying to control his anger, but he was pissed. I'm sure that was quite a sight to come home to.

"I meant to call you last night—"

"And why is Garrett Higgins sleepin' in my living room? I was unaware that I sanctioned opposite-sex sleepovers."

"Gramps, it is soooooo not what you think. I promise."

"Then best you start explainin' it to me."

I took a deep breath and walked over to him, wrapping my arms around his surprisingly fit midsection. Hugs always were his Kryptonite.

"Garrett came over last night to study. While we were doing our homework, some jerk in a truck chucked a brick through the window, then sped off."

Gramps' expression turned grim. I prayed he wouldn't start interrogating me. I never could lie to him. And the truth would have knocked the world right out from under him.

"I was afraid somethin' like this might happen eventually. People 'round here . . . some of them ain't real happy to have you back in town. Think you and your daddy reflect poorly on Jasperville."

That was so not where I was expecting the conversation to go, but I was ecstatic about it nonetheless.

"We filed a report with the sheriff's office. I don't think they have much to go on, though. It was dark. I didn't get a plate number. We couldn't even make out the color or model of the truck."

"That's okay," he said, hugging me back. "My insurance should cover gettin' it fixed up. I'm just glad you all are okay."

"Garrett wouldn't leave me by myself. That's why he's sleeping on the couch."

"I'm up," Garrett called from the far end of the hall, heading for the bathroom. "Morning, Mr. Johnson."

"Good morning to you, too, Mr. Higgins. Thanks for watchin' over my girl last night. And I presume I have you to thank for coverin' that window up with plywood."

"Happy to do it, sir."

"You're a good egg, Higgins. Stick close to my Kylene, will ya? I'm worried 'bout her."

The look Garrett flashed me said *I am, too*, but he kept that to himself. Instead, he nodded at Gramps, then pushed open the door to the bathroom and closed it behind him.

"I should get ready for school," I told Gramps, turning away from him.

"The warden told me you'd been down to see your dad a couple times now." I stopped dead in my tracks. There was something in Gramps' voice that was unsettling. Something serious. A hint of warning.

"Yeah," I said, looking over my shoulder at him. "I miss him."

"Course you do, Kylene. But, in light of what happened here last night, I don't know that you should be goin' there on your own."

"You think someone is trying to hurt me specifically?" I tried to sound surprised.

"Nothin' like that. I just think 'til the sheriff knows more 'bout what happened last night, you should be careful. Not sure the prison is the best place to find people of high moral character."

I bit my lip to keep the words "neither is school" from coming out.

"Okay, Gramps. I'll bring Garrett with me next time."

"Good idea. Now go get yourself cleaned up. You got them damn raccoon eyes your mama used to have when she didn't take her makeup off."

I laughed.

"Not a good look for me?"

"That ain't a good look on nobody," he replied, heading back down the hall to the kitchen. "Go get ready. I'm gonna fix you two somethin' to eat."

I smiled to myself as he walked away. He was old but strong. Hard yet soft. And I loved him completely.

If anyone hurt one hair on that man's head in order to get to me, I'd skin him alive.

Garrett drove to his house so he could change his clothes, then we were off to school. It was supposed to be unseasonably hot, so I was grateful for his operational air conditioner. I was also extremely grateful for him, too. As much as I liked to think I was tough, a brick through the window in the middle of the night might have made me crap my pants for a second. I didn't like being caught off guard.

He parked his truck at the front of the lot and hopped out. I joined him around the front of the vehicle, and we walked into school together. We got plenty of looks on the way: riding together in a car appeared to mean something far more than just needing a lift or trying to reduce your carbon footprint. I was pretty certain that by the end of the day, the rumor mill would have Garrett and me sleeping together. Hell, he might have even been my baby daddy. Only time would tell. I was morbidly curious to see just how ridiculous the gossip would get.

"You remember what I said last night?" he asked, opening the door for me.

"I do, indeed."

"Good. Try your best to give Donovan what he wants. It'll buy us time."

"My soul will likely die in the process, but I'll do it. For you."

Garrett ran past me on the stairs, flashing a mischievous grin over his shoulder.

"What soul?"

His laughter rang through the stairwell, drawing even more attention to us as we raced to the third-floor physics room.

"Ouch. That hurt, Higgins."

"Truth cuts deep, Danners."

I joined in his laughter as I chased after him up the steps. I didn't care who stared at us. What people were saying. For the first time since my father was incarcerated, I had a moment of not giving a shit. Since I knew it would be fleeting, I tried to hold on to it as long as possible.

Then I crested the final stair to find Mr. Callahan glaring at me, and that moment faded. I had no idea why that man had it in for me so badly, but it was clear that he had his thoughts on my father, and, because of them, had particular thoughts about me as well.

I looked over at Garrett, who shared my *Who ran over his dog this morning?* expression. Together, we walked past Mr. Callahan to enter the classroom.

"Ms. Danners. A word—in the hall."

Garrett looked concerned but went in without me.

"What can I do for you, Mr. Callahan?" I asked, staring up

at him with the same disdain he showed me. When the moment became awkward enough, he spoke.

"Have you finished your assignments yet?"

"Um, no. Because I have until the end of next week to do it. . . ."

"They're due by the end of today, or you can be expecting a failing grade this term."

I could feel the blood rushing to my cheeks in anger, but I managed to curb it so I didn't say something to make the situation worse.

"I believe Mr. Thompson—you know, the principal—said that I had two full weeks to get caught up without penalty. If you don't care for his policy, I'm sure he'd be happy to discuss it with you." Callahan's expression soured, but he remained silent. "Should I go down there now and get him? Have him clear this whole thing up for you?"

The bell rang while we stood outside the classroom, neither one of us willing to make the first move. Like with any good standoff, the first to flinch is the loser. And I had no intention of losing that particular showdown. Callahan was way out of line, and I'd had too long and stressful a night to put up with his shit.

"I don't think that will be necessary," he replied, his expression so sour he looked like he was in physical pain.

"Great. Then I'll have those to you as per Principal Thompson's instructions and not a day before."

With no other power card to play, he told me I was late and ordered me to take my seat. I entered the room with a smug smile on my face. Garrett gave a quick nod, acknowledging what he correctly assumed was my win, and my smile widened to a grin. I'd managed to put one enemy in his place, and we both knew it. If only it were so easy to take all the rest of them down.

SEVENTEEN

My morning classes went by without any Donovan sightings. He wasn't in gym, which was both a relief and also unnerving. I wanted to just get it over with—show him how terrifying I thought he was so he could think he was getting the better of me. I still wasn't convinced that was the best plan of action— letting a bully know he was winning—but I'd agreed to do it. I trusted that Garrett knew him well enough to know how to best navigate the situation.

I had to stop by my locker on the way to lunch, so I sent Tabby ahead to nab a seat. In the interest of speed, I unlocked it and just started tossing in books that I was done with for the rest of the day. I found the notebook I needed after lunch and stuffed it into my bag. When I closed the door, the metal echoing through the nearly empty hall, I looked over to find Maribel Chavez storming toward me, her brown eyes shooting daggers at me.

By the look on her face, you'd never have known we'd once been close.

"Tell me what you said to Jaime the other day," she demanded. Her hands were firmly planted on her hips, which meant she had no intention of walking away without answers. She threw her long black hair over her shoulder for effect, cocking her head at me. She was already losing her patience.

"Good to see you too, Maribel."

"Cut the shit, Kylene. What did you say to him?"

"Nothing. I poked fun at him for taking Spanish class. That's it." Her eyes narrowed. "What? You don't think it's ironic that he's in there? Your parents speak Spanish at home. . . ."

"That's not what I'm talking about, and you know it. You said something to him that got him all worked up."

"If he got worked up about anything I said, then that's on him and his conscience," I replied, turning away from her. She snatched my arm and wheeled me around to face her.

"He didn't do it. I don't care how ashamed you were of those pictures; blaming him and the others was wrong."

I ripped my arm from her grasp and leaned in closer to her.

"I'll let that slide because he's your brother and I can appreciate the need to protect your family, but if he's so innocent, then he shouldn't be upset about anything I say. They all got away with it anyway. He should be thrilled."

She muttered something under her breath in Spanish.

"I know he wasn't involved," she replied—in English this time to be sure I understood.

"Really? Could you account for his whereabouts that night when it all happened?" Her expression darkened and she shook her head. "Well, then, Maribel, you shouldn't speak in absolutes. Tends to bite you in the ass when you find out you're wrong. Because the truth is that whether or not he actively had anything to do with it, he tightened ranks with the others and rode it out. Lying by omission is just as bad—so is withholding the truth."

Her hard features softened for a second. It was as though she'd never really contemplated Jaime's involvement in their alibi, that his account of that night had been a part of The Six's freedom in some way. The realization twisted her features into an ugly expression.

"See you around, Maribel," I said, walking away. This time, she didn't try to stop me.

Tabby waved me over to the table where she and Garrett were already seated. I sat down next to her, and she slid my lunch over. It was an à la carte buffet of awesomeness.

"Did you get what you needed?" she asked before taking a bite of her french fry.

"That and then some." My dry response wasn't lost on her or Garrett. Their silence demanded I explain. "I ran into Maribel Chavez. . . ." Garrett winced at the mention of her name.

"Not a warm welcome, huh?" Garrett asked.

"Nope. She told me to lay off her brother."

Garrett scoffed. Tabby, however, looked confused as hell.

"Jaime seems like a nice enough kid. He's always really quiet in the classes I have with him. Why would you mess with him?"

"Remember that thing about AJ we need to fill you in on that requires a lot of tequila?" Garrett asked. She nodded in response, straightening up like she was about to get the lowdown. "Jaime was involved, too."

"Did Garrett tell you about the excitement we had last night?" I asked, hoping she'd take the bait. My photo scandal, or Boobgate, as I'd come to call the incident over the years—my attempt to deflect the seriousness of the situation in order to cope—was not something I really wanted to get into at school.

"He did! Right before you got here. How scary. . . ."

"But not entirely surprising. I mean, let's face it. I'm not exactly welcome in this town. It was bound to happen eventually."

"Do you think it was Donovan?"

I shrugged.

"Probably, but—"

Before I could say any more, an underclassman walked up with a note from the office.

"Oh, boy," Garrett muttered to himself.

"I didn't do anything! I swear!" I said.

"Better go see what you're in for this time," he replied, stealing a fry off my tray.

"Don't let him eat all my food while I'm gone," I told Tabby. She nodded, then slapped Garrett's hand as he reached for another one. The intensity of the slap made me laugh. "Don't break him, Tabby. We might need him one day."

By the time I made it to Mrs. Baber's desk, I was starting to wonder exactly what I'd been sent for. I hadn't done anything wrong—at least not *that* day. Donovan wasn't around, so it wasn't likely related to him. My anxiety about it grew as I waited for her to get off the phone.

"Ms. Danners," she said, not bothering to look up at me. "You're needed up in Mr. Callahan's office. Something about your homework."

"Son of a bitch," I mumbled to myself before snapping a smile onto my face. "I'll head right up there. Thanks."

I stormed up the stairs to room 333, ready for a war, but when I opened the door, I found the classroom empty—with the exception of someone, who was definitely not Mr. Callahan, sitting at the desk.

"Hey," AJ said, standing to greet me like we were meeting for a date. Ambush would have been a far more appropriate description.

"Mrs. Baber said I needed to come up here."

"Yeah . . . I needed to talk to you and figured you couldn't refuse an invitation from the front office, so . . ."

"How'd you pull that off?" I asked.

"I'm Callahan's teaching assistant this period. Instead of

going to study hall, I hang out up here and do menial tasks for him. I may or may not have abused my position to get you up here." Sneaky bastard. "Before you freak out, you should know I didn't do it because I wanted to talk about us."

"So, just to be clear, this summons has nothing to do with me needing to argue with Callahan right now?" He shook his head. "Great! Then I'm going back to lunch—"

"Ky!" AJ called. Against my better judgment, I hesitated. "Regardless of how you feel about me, you need to listen." I turned to look at him, giving him my very best *the fuck I do* expression. He ignored it entirely. "I heard someone talking today about the window at Gramps' house. It was fine when I left last night. . . . Tell me what happened."

"Someone threw a brick through it with a welcome-back message attached."

I swear the color drained from his face in an instant.

"Are you okay?"

I splayed my arms out to the side to show I was fine. "Never been better. Now, if we're done here—"

"I know you're starting shit with the *others*." The way he said "others" made it clear who he meant. The other five.

"I didn't start anything. They did—you all did—the second your camera started snapping photos. And I intend to prove what happened that night. If I were you, I'd be worried."

"Worried?" he scoffed. "You proving who did it would be the best thing that ever happened to me!" His confidence gave me pause. "You go right ahead and figure out who took those pictures. The second you know, you can pass that information along. I've got a couple years' worth of anger to let loose on him."

I opened my mouth to cut him off at the knees, but the fire behind those green eyes stopped me. I'd never seen such thinly veiled rage from him. If I hadn't seen it staring at me from across the room, I wouldn't have believed it.

"I'll keep you posted," I said, turning to leave. I needed to get out of there before he saw my resolve falter. With every step I took, doubt started to creep into my mind, but I locked it away for another day. I needed to stay focused. I had too many things going on around me to let sentiment make me sloppy.

When I reached the cafeteria, I only had five minutes left to eat. I sat down and started to inhale my food as quickly as decent table manners would allow. Tabby looked horrified at my behavior, while Garrett just laughed.

"This reminds me of the eating competition you entered at Marco's Pizzeria freshman year. . . ."

I shrugged.

"I won, didn't I?" I replied through a mouthful of food.

"What did you have to go to the office for?" Tabby asked.

"Callahan wanted to see me," I said as I shoved another fry in. It helped cover up my lie.

"He's such a dick," Garrett replied.

"Whatever. I just have to survive a year of him. I'll be fine."

The two of them talked while I ate, until the bell broke us up.

I walked into Spanish on a clear mission. If I'd ruffled Jaime's feathers the day before, then I would keep at it until he broke. Dad had warned me that there likely wouldn't be much evidence in the sheriff's file—that the statements all read the same—but since I wasn't a cop and no lawyers were there for them to hide behind anymore, all I needed to do was break one of them. If their stories were built on a foundation of lies, one crack and their collective defenses would fall.

In the rubble, the truth would be found.

Jaime groaned when I walked in the room, then looked away,

choosing to take a sudden interest in the weather outside. Cloudy with a chance of thunderstorm—kind of like my mood.

"Hey, Jaime," I said, feigning happiness to see him. "I had the best talk with Maribel today. Any guess as to what it was about?" He didn't bother to respond. Instead, he just stared out the window and ignored me entirely. "She seems to be pissed that I was all up in your face yesterday. What's the matter? Was it easier to stand what you did to me when I wasn't around—a walking reminder that I'm an actual person with feelings . . . well, arguably, anyway. Is that an inconvenience for you? Should I transfer out of here so you don't have to suffer anymore? Would that make you and your sister happy?"

"You don't know what you're taking about," he muttered, just as the final bell rang. Mrs. Stewart rushed in to start class, but, as far as I was concerned, Jaime and I were continuing our conversation.

"Okay. Maybe I don't. Let's pretend that I'm totally wrong about all of this. Care to share some truth? Enlighten me, maybe?"

He turned to stare me down, but something was missing from his glare. Hatred, maybe? I'd expected to see it, but it wasn't there. Instead, his eyes burned with a frustration I understood. One that ate you up from the inside out until you could barely contain it. One that kept you up in the dark of night, never letting sleep find you.

"You need to drop it, Ky," he said under his breath.

"Ky? Are we back on that level?" I whispered as Mrs. Stewart rattled off verb conjugations.

He shrunk down in his seat and tapped his pen against his notebook.

"Just leave me alone."

"I'm afraid I can't do that, Jaime. Not until I get what I want."

"Then I hope what you want is trouble, because you'll find

it if you keep asking people about that night—starting shit with the others."

"Great!" I whisper-shouted. "The threats just keep on coming. . . ."

He turned to look at me, concern burning in his warm brown eyes. It quickly became apparent that he really did think I was in trouble. That my threat comment had struck a nerve. It was then that I realized that, of all the guys involved, he would be the egg that cracked if I kept leaning on him. I'd have bet on it.

I damn near smiled with satisfaction.

He bolted from class when the bell rang, bumping into anyone in his way. I wondered if he was going to run off to the others and fill them in; if I was going to have more bricks thrown through my windows with love letters attached. Then I wondered if maybe Donovan hadn't been the one to vandalize Gramps' house at all. If I'd gotten to some of the others like I had with Jaime.

Getting to the bottom of my scandal would certainly give me peace of mind, but I wondered at what price. Losing any of those guys from the football team would do nothing for my reputation in the town's eyes. They'd be the boys whose lives were ruined by an unfortunate event. And I'd be the meddlesome little slut who brought them down.

The hometown antihero.

I walked out to the parking lot, my steps uncertain. For the first time since I resolved to find the truth about what happened that night, I wondered if it would all be worth it in the end. But then I walked by two underclassman girls, who were staring and whispering as I passed them on the stairs, the judgment in their eyes plain, and I knew I had to bring The Six down. The town could hate me all they wanted for ruining their perfect football season. Those consequences I could take. The whore stares, I could not.

When I arrived at Garrett's truck, he was leaning against the front of it, arms folded over his chest.

"Sorry I'm late, Dad," I said with a wink.

"Don't make a habit of it."

We jumped into his truck and drove away, the wind whipping through the open windows. I cranked the radio and we sang cheesy eighties songs until our voices nearly gave out. It felt like old times in so many ways—carefree and simple. I wished it could have gone on forever. But eventually Gramps' house came into view—the plywood bandage covering the front window—and my mind snapped back to reality.

The hits would just keep coming until I shut the fight down.

EIGHTEEN

I made my way over to Meg's office to start my official first day. Even though it was only for a couple of hours, it was better than nothing. That was a shift's worth of pay that my wallet desperately needed.

"Hi, Marcy," I said as I walked in the front door. She raised a finger to me while she held the phone receiver in her other hand. Then she waved me past to Meg's office. I read her loud and clear and made my way back there.

After I knocked on the door, Meg called me in. I found her poring over organized chaos, files strewn all about her desk and sideboard. I located a chair not covered in file boxes and took a seat.

"Tell me my first job isn't to clean your office, because I might quit."

She laughed.

"No. Marcy is going to go over the file room and teach you how to answer the phone, which is an art form in and of itself."

"Whatever, politely brushing people off is totally in my skill set."

She shot me a dubious look over the reading glasses perched on the tip of her nose. "I'm sure. Now, before you get started, I obtained the information you texted me about." She pulled a manila folder from the clutter on her desk and handed it to me. "I gave it a look through, but there's really not much in there, Ky. And, I'm worried that your reading it is only going to pick at an old wound."

"You're right. It will, but no more so than going to school every day does."

She nodded. "Point taken. So, tell me how I can help."

"You can't. Not yet, anyway. There's this kid at school—one of the boys. I think seeing me is really getting to him."

"You think you can break him. . . ."

"Yep."

"Well, if you can, that would be amazing, but make sure you get any confession recorded on your phone somehow so he can't recant later."

"Way ahead of you."

She smiled with pride.

"You sure you don't want to go to law school? You always turned your nose up at the idea, but you'd make a damn fine lawyer."

I shook my head dramatically.

"Nope. Hard pass. Too many rules."

"Well, yes. There are those."

I stood up to leave, tucking the file under my arm.

"I'm going to go see if Marcy is ready for me now."

"Okay." When I reached for the doorknob, Meg stopped me. "Ky, I need to tell you something else—something I just learned." I turned to face her. "Luke represented a couple of those boys. . . ."

"I know," I said, cringing a little. "Dad told me."

She let out a loud exhale.

"Is that going to be a problem for you? I totally understand if it is."

"I don't think so," I replied, doing my best to sound convincing. "My mind understands that it's his job. The rest of me is trying to settle with that fact."

"If it makes you at all uncomfortable—"

"Meg, if he thought what happened that night was my fault, we'd have a problem, but . . ."

She cracked a wry smile.

"He wouldn't work here if he thought it was. And you'd have to get in line to punch him in the face."

"Then I think we're good."

I returned her smile, then opened the door and made my way back to the front of the office. It was time to get to work. Right after I had a peek at that file.

By five o'clock, I finally had the hang of the file room. Marcy left me alone to practice sorting through various case boxes and would be back later to check on how I did. The second I heard her footsteps disappear down the hall, I pulled out the folder Meg had given me and opened it.

Because there were never official charges pressed against any of The Six, I knew the file would consist primarily of interviews and copies of the photos from the internet. I found transcripts of interviews in there, including mine. I set it aside, not wanting to see it. Instead, I grabbed Eric Stanton's and started scanning through his account of that night.

At first, it read like a play-by-play of the evening. He'd been drinking, partying, and was in the hot tub with me and a bunch of others that night. He meticulously named every single person there. Somehow he managed to sound superior even through a piece of paper.

The interview eventually turned toward his whereabouts at the time the photos were taken. The story I expected to read was there. He was in the basement playing cards with Scooter,

Donovan, and Mark, while Jaime and AJ were hanging out over near the booze. I rolled my eyes and pressed forward to material I hadn't expected to see. I don't know why I didn't expect to read how my character came into question—how the sheriff got their take on my behavior that night—but seeing it spelled out before me was a whole new level of violation that I wasn't prepared for.

I read on as bile rose in my throat and a cold sweat rolled down my back. Account after account all said the same thing. That I was flirting with everyone that night. Throwing myself on anyone in a five-foot radius. That I was drunk, but not pass-out drunk. That when they left me alone in the hot tub, that I was totally coherent. Eric, Scooter . . . Donovan. They all said the same. It made me start to question my account of that night.

Maybe it wasn't as accurate as I had thought.

With that possibility racking my body with a numbing sensation I hadn't felt since the morning I woke up to find my boobs all over social media, I grabbed the next interview from the pile and read the name at the top: AJ MILLER. I swallowed hard and tried to calm my shaky hands. Fear that I couldn't fully explain coursed through me, tightening my chest. There was something terrifying about reading his story. Something paralyzing about reading his account of what happened that night. A part of my mind begged me not to read it—to just cling to my belief of his guilt.

The other told that part to suck it up.

I scanned through the sheriff's comments about him. How distraught he looked. How he seemed unfocused and easily distracted—all signs of guilt. But then I continued on, and the part of my mind that had wanted to leave well enough alone cringed. For the better part of AJ's interview, he kept saying the same thing over and over again, until the sheriff put the interview on hold until his mother could get there. I read those two lines until I couldn't see straight any longer, my vision slowly blurring. Whether they were tears of anger or frustration or something else I didn't want to contemplate, I didn't know. What I did know was I never wanted to read those lines again.

I threw the file across the room, breathing hard as I worked to contain the scream that wanted to escape. I couldn't unsee what I'd seen, nor could I shake it from my mind: *"I should have been with her. I never should have left her alone. . . ."* I'd been right about his feeling guilty, but not the why behind it.

A knock on the open door ripped me from my downward spiral. I turned to find Luke standing there, a tentative smile on his face. His timing really could have been better.

"Hey, I just spoke to Meg. Can we talk for a minute?"

"Of course," I said, standing up. I tried to wipe my eyes without him noticing. If he'd seen me do it, he had the good form not to mention it. "Listen, I know what you're going to say—about representing some of those guys—"

"I'm sorry about what happened to you," he blurted out, cutting me off. "Sorry—I just had to get that out. Also, I don't want this to be super awkward, but I feel like you need to hear this, too, so you're not worrying about it later." I folded my arms across my stomach, trying to hold it together a bit longer. Standing there before him, knowing what he'd heard and seen about that night, was almost too much to bear, especially after everything I'd just read. Luke, seeing my distress, softened his expression. He looked away from me and ran his hand through his hair. The gesture reminded me of Garrett. Somehow, that tiny similarity helped set me more at ease. "Kylene, I don't know how else to say this, so I'll just say it: I never saw the pictures from that night. When the sheriff briefed me on the evidence, he offered to show them to me, and I declined. No charges had been made, and I had all the pertinent information regarding the phone and social-media distribution of the photos.

Had push come to shove, I would have had to look them over, but at the time I saw no need to do that. I knew your father through mutual friends. Out of respect for him, I decided to wait until seeing the evidence firsthand was absolutely necessary."

I let out a loud exhale. "Thanks for that."

He nodded.

"If there had been more evidence, the sheriff might have been able to file charges and have the charges stick, but there just wasn't."

I let out a mirthless laugh.

"Yeah, maybe."

"Not a lot of faith in the local police, huh?"

"You could say that. . . ."

"Well, I hope you find whatever it is you're looking for in that file, but I'm not sure you will," he said, trying to land that blow as gently as possible.

I dropped my arms from my stomach and shrugged.

"Gotta start somewhere, right?"

He nodded again, a slight smile tugging at the corner of his mouth. "Good luck with it."

"Thanks. I'll probably need it."

He shook his head.

"I'm not so sure about that. If I were a betting man, I'd be inclined to put my money on you."

With that, he disappeared back down the hall, leaving me to my boxes of files and the determination to prove him right. I walked across the room to where the file in question had fallen and I tucked the stray papers back inside. If I had to walk through fire to get out of hell, then I would. My past didn't get to own me forever.

NINETEEN

Meg and Luke both stayed late that night and offered to give me more hours if I wanted to continue filing. Marcy had given her nod of approval, so as long as I stuck to what I'd learned. Nobody seemed too worried about me screwing up.

Two hours later, Meg said they were shutting it down for the night soon and told me to head home. I slid the box of files I'd been working on up on the shelf and grabbed my bag.

"See ya, Meg," I said before heading for the front door. I stepped out into the near dark of night and made my way to my car. With every step I took, I felt like someone was watching me. But every time I turned to search the area, there was no one there.

I jumped into my car after doing a quick scan of the back seat. Even then, I still couldn't shake that feeling. My gut was rarely wrong.

Wasting no time, I fired Heidi up and pulled out of the parking lot. Traffic was light at that time of night, so I easily made my way onto the main road, headed home. As I drove, I passed a familiar truck. Donovan rolled by while I stopped at a four-way. He sneered at me while his passenger, Mark Sinclair, did his best to avoid eye contact. I did my best to remember Garrett's words and look like Donovan was winning—I was backing down. That basically translated to me looking away without doing something to antagonize him.

It was the best I could do.

I turned right at the stop and drove along through town, the sun rapidly falling from the sky. Streetlights were sparse on that side of town, so I drove in the darkness. Only the occasional set of headlights passed by. Just as I made a right onto the main road leading to Gramps' street, a truck pulled in behind me, riding my bumper so hard it looked like he was in my back seat.

"Asshole," I muttered, speeding up enough to put some distance between us. But that was eaten up in a hurry. Whatever I did to gain some space, the truck countered seconds later.

Doing forty-five in a twenty, I sped toward Gramps' street, banking a tight left without signaling first. I hoped the dickhead wasn't following me, but the screech of brakes followed by lights in my rearview and the roar of an engine shot that fantasy down in a hurry.

"Shit!" I shouted, slamming my hand on the wheel. Was Gramps home? Could I get to Garrett's with this guy trying to run me down? Could I park and get into the house before he could get to me? All I could do was drive down the winding street and hope that an idea came to me.

As I neared Gramps' house, I could see lights on inside. Daring to push my speed to fifty, I raced toward the driveway, slamming on the brakes so I could make the turn. I threw it in park and ripped the keys from the ignition before bolting for the house. I heard the squealing tires of the truck as it came to a stop and the slamming of doors.

"C'mon," I said, fumbling with the keys in the lock. I opened the door, then shut and locked it, running over to Gramps' landline to call the cops. My cell was in the car and I didn't dare go out to get it.

"Nine-one-one. What is your emergency?"

"Someone just tried to run me off the road," I said, my voice shaky. I provided the dispatcher with all the details, and he told me to remain inside until the sheriff arrived. What seemed like an hour later, a cruiser slowed to a stop out front. I hung up and raced out there, stopping by my car to see if they'd taken my stuff. To my surprise, my backpack was there, my phone still lying on the passenger seat in plain view. What was missing, however, was the thin manila folder that Meg had given me—the one with all the evidence from my photo scandal.

"Son of a bitch . . ."

"Kylene," a voice called. A voice I knew well. I climbed out of the car and found Sheriff Higgins standing there, looking all kinds of official. No greeting beyond my name.

"Some dickhead just chased me halfway through town."

"We got some complaints about speeding in this neighborhood. I imagine that was you?"

"Me and the aforementioned dickhead trying to run me down."

He took a deep breath.

"You get a plate number?"

I looked around at the two nearest streetlamps—both lights were dead—then back to him.

"No."

"Make and model of the vehicle?"

"Big truck. Loud engine."

"Do you have anything at all I can use to actually find this person?"

My growing rage was about to spill over when something dawned on me. *Fingerprints.* Nails in the coffin for criminal rookies.

"You got a print kit on you?" I asked, cocking my head.

"No. But I can call for one."

"Then you might want to do that, Sheriff, because whoever did it was dumb enough to ransack my vehicle for something."

He looked surprised for a moment, then gave me a nod as he radioed back to the station for a deputy to bring the print kit. I stepped back onto my porch when my phone started ringing.

Garrett.

That boy never could turn the police scanner off.

"I'm fine," I said by way of greeting.

"What happened?" The concern in his tone was plain.

"Somebody wanted to play NASCAR in my hood. When I pulled off into the driveway and ran for the house, the asshole stole something from my car." The sheriff shot me an irritated look while I filled his son in. "I think I should go. Your dad's giving me the hairy eyeball right now." I said those words loud enough for Garrett's dad to hear me.

"Do you want me to come by?"

"No. I'm fine."

"Okay. Call me when my dad leaves."

I said goodbye and hung up just as the deputy pulled up. He was out of the car and gloved up in a heartbeat. He probably didn't get to do it often. His eagerness to play CSI was obvious.

The sheriff and I hovered while the younger man dusted Heidi's handle, the door, and various places inside. Once he finished, he climbed out and informed Sheriff Higgins that he had all he needed. He walked away, leaving Garrett's dad and me in awkward silence.

"So . . . you need anything else from me? Prints to rule mine out?"

He shook his head.

"That won't be necessary. I'm pretty sure we still have them on file. You remember the tractor incident, I'm sure. The one where you, AJ, and my son thought it would be cute to steal Mrs. Flanagan's tractor and take it for a spin."

"The keys were in it—"

"Opportunity is not synonymous with permission, Kylene."

My hair bristled at his words. I was well aware how true they were. Funny how no one else in town seemed to grasp that.

"She never pressed charges," I argued, focusing on the subject at hand.

"No, but only because your father and I paid for the damages." I cringed, remembering how the three of us were made to pay that money back. The words "backbreaking labor" came to mind.

"Okay, well . . . if you don't need anything else from me, I'm going to go," I said and turned to walk away, but Sheriff Higgins' words stopped me cold.

"I need you to tread lightly, Kylene." I looked back at him, the surprise I felt undoubtedly written all over my face. "You've got enemies in this town." His eyes darted over to the plywood on Gramps' house, then back to me. "I suspect you already know that."

I eyed him tightly.

"Are you one of them? Should I be worried that your deputy isn't going to come up with anything conclusive?"

His chest rose and fell, his jaw working hard to suppress his anger.

"I can't manufacture evidence to suit your claims, young lady."

"No," I said, shaking my head. "But I wonder if you can make it go away if need be. . . ."

His eyes went wide at my thinly veiled accusation. Maybe he was offended, or maybe I'd hit a nerve. I didn't really care either way.

"You don't know what you're talking about," he said, leaning toward me. "And if I were you, I'd heed my warning, Kylene Danners. This town don't want you here. They'll keep making that point until you get it through your head."

"Guess I'm lucky to have cops like you here to protect me then," I deadpanned before walking back to Gramps' house. "You be sure to let me know if you find anything conclusive, Sheriff."

I closed the door behind me and locked it. The night's events had me rattled for more reasons than I could count. Not the least of which being Sheriff Higgins' warning. The town didn't want me back—not really news to me. But to assume they'd resort to scare tactics seemed a bit extreme, even for a football-obsessed town like Jasperville. And that also didn't explain the file missing from my car. That car chase was no random incident. Neither was the disappearance of the file inside. Whoever chased me down knew that I had a copy of the sheriff's notes.

I whipped out my cell and dialed Meg, quickly bombarding her with the details of what had happened. She was silent for a second, absorbing all I'd said, then told me she'd call me back in a minute. I sat in Gram's recliner and waited for Meg's call. When my phone finally rang, I scrambled to answer it.

"Meg! What's up? What did you find out?"

Silence.

"I called the sheriff's office demanding another copy of the file."

A pause.

"Yeah? And . . . ?"

"It's gone, Ky."

I felt all the blood drain from my face.

"Gone? What do you mean 'gone'?"

"I mean I had three deputies tear that place apart, and not

one of them can find the file your copies came from earlier today. They can't find the digital copy, either. They said they'd call me as soon as they tracked it down, but you know as well as I do that they're not going to—"

"Because someone made it disappear. . . ."

I could hear Meg talking in the background. Something about seeing what she could scrape together but not to get my hopes up. My mind couldn't quite wrap around her words; it was too busy trying to piece together my own thoughts. In that moment, I knew that the sheriff wouldn't be calling me with any news. That all those fingerprints pulled would lead nowhere.

It was no coincidence that the file had gone missing that night. I was closing in on a scandal of a different sort—one involving dirty cops and football heroes and those who didn't want a nuisance case to get in the way of a football legacy. Because that just couldn't be allowed to happen. The Badgers had nearly made it to the state finals my freshman year, and everyone was convinced we were a shoo-in for next season. But my inconvenient accusation that someone had taken those pictures against my will would have put quite a dent in that goal: the removal of any one of those players could have paralyzed the team. And this year would be no different.

Whoever wanted to make Boobgate disappear had a vested interest in either keeping the players safe from the law or making sure we made the state finals. I could think of one individual in particular who wanted both. One who'd boasted that he was above the law in our town. One who'd driven by me earlier that night in his hulking truck.

Was Donovan Shipman really immune from the cops in Jasperville?

All signs pointed to yes.

TWENTY

Back when Boobgate actually happened, I just wanted it to all go away. One sit-down with the sheriff and his deputies had made certain of that. With my father at my side, I weathered all sorts of questions that I never had expected to. Had I ever had sexual relations with any of the accused? How many drinks did I have? What was I wearing? Did I tell them to stop? After each one, I could see Sheriff Higgins' expression change. That he was starting to see me—and the case—in a different light. The rest of the town wasn't far behind. I was young and still naïve enough to believe that the law would be on my side.

How wrong I'd been.

My father, seeing that the kids were going to walk because of "insufficient evidence," told me that he would keep investigating until he could prove that this wasn't a case of postpicture remorse, which I'd quickly become accused of by virtually everyone around—including the boys. That, in fact, I had been an active participant in the whole thing until the repercussions came down upon me. Only then did I cry foul. As much as my need for justice remained, I couldn't bring myself to fight for it any longer. I told him to let it go.

All I really wanted was to escape the ridicule I faced on a daily basis. Escape the town determined to put the victim on trial.

I sat in my room and stared at the stack of files Striker had given me to investigate my father's case. But the longer I stared at them, the more I realized that I was useless to Dad until I put to rest the demons still haunting me. One way or another, I needed to prove what happened that night.

With a heavy sigh, I closed my eyes and sorted through what bits I remembered from the aftermath. It was all jumbled together in my mind, but I knew that every one of those guys alibied another until there was no one left standing capable of having committed the crime. How terribly convenient for them. But what if someone could poke holes into their stories? Someone who remembered that night a little differently. Someone who never came forward or whose account was dismissed. If Sheriff Higgins was shady back then, it seemed totally plausible, if not probable.

I grabbed a pen and paper and started to jot down the names of everyone I knew was there that night. With no list of names from the file to cross-reference, I had no way of knowing whether or not they'd been questioned. But I could figure that out pretty easily with an ambush in the hallway at school.

I was so not above that.

As I listed off names, Meg called me to check up.

"Are you sure you're okay? I mean, I know you're an independent kid and all, but . . ."

"Totally fine, Meg. Frustrated, but fine otherwise."

She let out a breath.

"I'm so angry with myself for not making another copy just in case."

"Why would you, though? You should have been able to just get another one from the sheriff's office if you were 'representing' me in a civil suit. That was the cover you used, right?"

"It was. And, yes, you're right."

"I wish I'd read the whole thing when I was supposed to be

in the back office filing," I said, trying to lighten the mood. Meg totally took the bait.

"I'm sure your boss would have loved that if you'd gotten caught."

"Not so much, I don't think."

She paused for a moment, creating a looming silence on the line.

"Ky, I know the subject isn't your father's favorite, but have you asked him about his investigation of what happened?"

His investigation?

"No, because he didn't really do any. He started to, and I asked him to stop—that I just wanted to ride out the rest of the year, then leave."

Meg hesitated.

"Listen, kiddo. I'm invoking the cone of silence on what I'm about to tell you, got it?"

"Okay . . ."

"Your father did investigate your case as much as he could off the books. More specifically, he reached out to one of his friends at FBI headquarters in Columbus—one of the cyber-crime guys. He had him look into the photos and how they were shared, posted, et cetera. From what I gleaned from your mother, there might have been something there, but I never heard anything after that. I wondered if you'd found out and pitched a fit or something."

"Are you saying that you think that guy might have evidence that could help prove what happened?"

"I'm not saying that. I'm saying that if it were me, I'd be paying FBI headquarters a visit."

"Do you have a name?"

More silence.

"I'm trying to remember. It was something super basic—like John or Jim. Definitely a J-name."

I scribbled that down on my notepad.

"Awesome. I'll see what I can find out with that."

"I'm really sorry about the file, kid. I'll keep putting pressure on the sheriff, but I just don't think it'll matter."

"I know, but thanks anyway."

"'Night."

I hung up the phone feeling somewhat guilty. A part of me wanted to tell Meg that I already suspected the sheriff was dirty. The other part—the part tired of being dubbed the girl who cried wolf—didn't want to say a word until I could prove it.

Exhausted and in need of sleep, I turned off the light and lay down on my bed, clothes still on, and let my mind wander. Facts swirled around in my brain, just out of reach, but they were getting closer. All I needed was one good lead and I could crack Boobgate wide open.

I fell asleep hoping tomorrow would bring exactly that.

I spent the better part of physics trying to figure out who to interrogate first. I had the list narrowed down to about four names, all of whom were decent kids with great families. Maribel was on that list, though I wasn't looking forward to poking that particular bear with a short stick. It seemed unlikely that she'd be willing to help.

When the bell rang, I hauled ass to where I knew she'd be. I'd spent a lot of time that week observing everything around me, and one thing I'd learned was that she loved to stop by the girls' room before second period. How lucky for me.

I slid through the door to find her reapplying her lipstick in the mirror.

"Maribel—got a question for you." She shot me a sideward glance, then kept applying. "Where were you the night those pictures were taken?"

That seemed to get her attention.

"Nowhere near you," she said with disdain.

"I gathered that, given that your boobs weren't in those pictures, but that really isn't an answer."

"I was inside the house."

"Good. Getting better . . . Where in the house?"

She dropped her hand away from her face and turned to pin irritated eyes on me.

"In a bedroom, okay? You happy now? I didn't see anything."

"Interesting . . . Can anyone corroborate that story, or . . . ?"

"No."

"Then how can you be so sure your brother didn't do it?"

"Because he didn't." Her words were little more than a growl.

"He was seen near the hot tub around the time the pictures were taken, Maribel. Explain that."

"I can't, but I know him and I know he wouldn't do that. And so do you."

"I don't know anything like that, but if you're so convinced he wasn't the one to actually commit the crime, then I'll bet he knows who did. He listens to you, Maribel. Make him drop his bullshit story and stop covering up for everyone else."

She clenched her teeth while inhaling deeply. One loud exhale later, she seemed to have calmed down.

"Jaime didn't do it. He doesn't know who did."

I shook my head.

"I wish I could believe that," I replied, turning to leave. I stormed out of the bathroom, mentally scratching her off my list. My entire interaction with her had been a bust. Though I wasn't derailed by the setback, I wasn't excited about facing a bunch more conversations like that one.

Study hall was quiet since Mrs. Summers moved Tabby away from me. I really wanted to talk to my friend. I really needed her help.

I settled for info-dumping on her between classes, which was an impressive feat given how short our trip to the locker room was. By the time we arrived she knew everything about my wild chase through Gramps' neighborhood—minus all details revolving around Boobgate. I knew I needed to fill her in on all that sooner than later. I made a mental note to make time to do that on the weekend.

We were actually early to class for once, so we hovered around the perimeter of the gym like everyone else. But the second I saw Donovan walk in, I made a beeline for him, leaving Tabby behind to wonder what in the hell I was doing.

"Hey, Shipman!"

He turned slowly to face me.

"Something got you all worked up, Danners?"

"You and Mark have a fun night together? Do anything interesting like, oh, I don't know . . . maybe try to run me off the road on my way home?"

My accusation garnered the attention of everyone around us. Before I knew it, we were encircled by students desperate for some drama. Which was basically the whole class.

"Danners, I'm starting to feel sorry for you. Your imagination is becoming more delusional by the minute."

"Right . . . just like I imagined you about to beat your girlfriend up in the parking lot the other day?"

"What you saw in the parking lot was what you wanted to see. This whatever the hell it is you're talking about now—this batshit story about running you off the road—that's something else entirely."

Some of the kids in the mob gathering around us started to laugh.

"I want my file back," I said, ignoring his deflection.

His laughter stopped and his amused expression fell. He

looked like I'd said something that genuinely surprised him. Like he really had no idea what I was talking about.

"Danners, I don't know how to make this clear to you, but I have no clue what you're talking about."

Though I really wanted to believe he was lying, I didn't think he was.

"Stay away from my house," I said, turning to walk away.

"You mean your grandpa's house, don't you? Because you don't have one anymore. You don't have anything."

"She's got me," Tabby said, stepping up beside me.

More laughter from the kids in class.

"Okay, everyone," Ms. Davies shouted, blowing her whistle to break it up. "I can see you'll be keeping this class interesting today." She pushed her way through to the center of the circle to find Donovan, Tabby, and me standing there. "Boys on that end of the gym. Girls, over there." She indicated where she wanted us to go, and everyone dispersed, gossiping to one another as they did. "Danners, is there a problem here?"

"No, Ms. Davies."

"Good. Then you and Tabby head over there for me. Mr. Shipman, I have a special job for you today," she said, ushering him toward the boys' side of the room.

"What was all that about?" Tabby asked quietly as we walked. "You left out the fact that you thought Donovan was the one who chased you."

"Oops . . ."

"And what file were you talking about?"

"One of the files for my dad's case," I said—or rather, lied.

"Oh. That's weird. And scary." She looked at me as though she expected further explanation, but I had no intention of giving it to her. I could fill her in on the truth later. Indoor field hockey wasn't really conducive to meaningful conversation.

By the time gym was over, Tabby was less focused on what

had happened, but I could tell that wouldn't last long. I needed a buffer. I needed Garrett.

We walked into lunch to find him waiting for us at our regular table. With trays in hand, we made our way over to him and sat down.

"What's up, Tabby?" he asked, looking at her with a furrowed brow.

"Ky filled me in on last night's chaos. I hate feeling like I'm always a step behind."

Garrett shot me an accusing look.

I let out a sigh.

"So, what's the plan for tonight?" I asked, rerouting the conversation.

"Only one thing to do around here on Friday night," he replied, taking a bite of his pizza.

"No," I whined shaking my head. "Not the game . . ."

"What game?" Tabby asked, not understanding the *Friday Night Lights* routine of the rural Midwest.

"The football game."

"Oh!" Tabby exclaimed. "I've never been to an American football game before! You guys have different rules down here. It'll be so fun!"

"You actually like football?" Garrett asked, unable to hide the surprise in his voice.

"Yes. My dad is friends with the owner of the Canadian Football League team in Calgary. We always had box seats. It was awesome."

"Sweet Jesus . . . tell me we're not actually going to go," I groaned. "Someone. Please. I'm begging you. . . ."

"Oh, I think we have to go now, Ky. It would be un-American to not take her."

"I'm okay with that. You can take her if you want to, but leave me out of it."

"Nope. I can't allow that. We're all going."

"Dammit, Garrett! Why do you choose this moment to pull rank?"

"Because I can."

"So we're going?" Tabby asked for clarification.

"Looks that way." I exhaled heavily as I slumped forward onto the table. Football was so not how I'd planned to spend my evening. I wondered if I could somehow come up with a bad case of food poisoning after school. There had been some dodgy-looking leftovers in the fridge from a couple of days ago. Maybe a mouthful or two would take care of my *Varsity Blues*. "Now, somebody give me some good news because I'm desperately in need of some."

"We have an assembly this afternoon," Garrett said, the amusement in his tone telling me just how much he enjoyed torturing me.

"Tell me I'm sleeping and this is all a bad dream."

"It's a pep rally–inspirational speaker combo," Tabby added.

"What am I being inspired to do?"

Garrett choked on a laugh. "To not do drugs . . ."

I shot up straight in my seat. "You're shitting me—"

"Definitely not shitting you." Garrett and Tabby laughed at my reaction while I plotted my escape. No way was I going to be able to sit through that BS. No way in hell. Not with my mouth shut, anyway. "Looks like it's about time to feel that Badger spirit," he mocked, cleaning up his spot at the table. I cringed at his words.

I wasn't ready for the afternoon yet.

Being ambushed by one of my least favorite things did little to bring out my finer qualities. When Principal Thompson announced that it was time to head down to the auditorium,

I audibly groaned. Cheerleaders and school spirit and someone telling me to "just say no" was likely to be the death of me.

It looked like a total free-for-all in the auditorium, so I stood
in the middle of the aisle, looking for Garrett and Tabby. A
stiff shoulder to my back knocked me forward, and I looked
up to see Scooter Brown smiling back at me.

"Twatwaffle," I muttered under my breath.

"Ky!" Garrett called, waving me over. I walked back up two
rows to sit beside him near the farthest aisle—the easiest way
to sneak out.

"Good thinking, Higgins. We'll be out of here in no time,"
I said, sliding into my seat. Then I looked back at the exit to find
Mr. Callahan standing in front of it, staring back at me. "What
is it with that man . . . ?"

"He's got your number. But don't worry; the singing should
cheer you up."

"There's singing?" I couldn't hide the horror I felt at the
thought. He simply nodded and smiled in response. "Do me a
favor. When that starts, just render me unconscious somehow.
It would be an act of mercy."

"If I do that, who's going to knock me out?"

"That's your problem. I called it first."

"Fine. I'll just do something to get kicked out instead."

"See? You're more resourceful than you give yourself credit
for."

While everyone took a seat, I located Tabby's red hair a few
rows in front of us. She looked over her shoulder and spotted
us, waving frantically when she did. Garrett and I waved back
with equal enthusiasm and then laughed. A sharp glare from
Mr. Callahan quickly quieted us.

The cheerleaders and dance team filed onto the stage and
wasted no time diving right into their pom-pom-waving
schtick. Maribel was at the head of the squad, calling out chants

for us to follow along with. I hunkered down in my seat to weather all the pep.

Eventually, Principal Thompson came out to wish the team good luck and then introduce our speaker. He was a drug dealer turned pastor, who had a few words for us on the perils of substance abuse. It's not that I was against the message—I wasn't. Drugs were a great idea if you wanted to completely screw up your future and end up dead or in jail. On that, we agreed. But what I didn't agree with was the preachy way he tried to relay that message. Judgment wasn't going to keep kids off drugs. Viewing corpses, patients in withdrawal, and prison cells was what they needed—a big fucking dose of reality slapping them in the face. That would make them think twice about shooting up or snorting down whatever the high du jour was.

While the speech continued, I became increasingly irritated with it. All he talked about were street drugs, completely ignoring the abuse of prescription medications. Most families had a veritable pharmacy in their bathroom cabinet. How that was being overlooked was beyond me. Hell, our school was filled with class-one narcotics and mood-altering meds: the nurse's office was chock-full of them.

"Drug-free school zone, my ass," I said to Garrett. "This whole thing is a crock."

"Ms. Danners, be quiet." Mr. Callahan loomed over Garrett and me, standing right behind us.

"Sorry, Mr. Callahan. I just have a problem with hypocrisy. I was sharing that with Garrett."

"I'm sure that your family has . . . different views on all things illegal, Ms. Danners, but some of us don't share those views, and I'd much prefer you keep them to yourself."

"So, you don't find it at all strange that I have to be subjected to this diatribe when Nurse Henry is handing out Ritalin and

Adderall like candy all day long? Those aren't addictive drugs? Those don't have life-altering side effects?"

"Those are properly prescribed medications. Not crack bought in a back alley."

Not if they're prescribed by Dr. Carle. . . .

"It all cooks up the same, Mr. Callahan. Snorts the same too . . ."

"That's it, Danners. Out. Now."

"Mr. Callahan, I'm just pointing out—"

"NOW, DANNERS!"

Mr. Callahan was loud enough to draw the attention of most of the student body. I could feel the anger pooling in my cheeks. He was a dick and was way out of line. I had big plans to tell him exactly that once we were out in the hall.

I slid past Garrett, who shot me a look that said *Keep your mouth in check, Ky.* I gave him one that said *When I'm cold and dead.* He didn't seem pleased by my nonverbal reply.

By the time I was out of the auditorium, Mr. Callahan had already started in on me. I was a bad egg from a bad family. I'd never amount to anything if I kept it up. And my attitude was going to take me nowhere good. All things I'd heard before.

When he finally shut up and just stared down at me, clearly awaiting some sort of repentant reply, I smiled up at him like I hadn't heard a damn thing he'd just said.

"So, should I just head to the principal's office now, or . . . ?"

"Go back to your classroom and wait for the bell. Principal Thompson has better things to do with his day than try to get through to you. You're a lost cause."

"Sounds good. Thanks."

Without another word, I hitched my backpack up on my shoulder and made my way to the staircase. Mr. Callahan had just given me exactly what I'd wanted. A free ticket out of that shit show. It also gave me time to figure out whose cage I was going to rattle next. I still had a lot of names on my list.

I planned to check a few more off before the day was done.

I walked into the house and dialed Striker's number.

"Tell me I don't need to send bail money," he said by way of a greeting.

"Not yet, but you might want to set some aside just in case."

"Way ahead of you," he replied with a laugh. "So, to what do I owe the honor of this call? You did get the papers I sent Dawson over with, right?"

"Yep. Thanks so much for those."

"Well, if it's not about that, then do you want to fill me in, or should I keep guessing?" He paused for a moment, then blurted out something that nearly made me spit out the sip of water I'd just taken. "Tell me you're not pregnant—"

"Jesus, Striker! No. I'm not knocked up. I may live in the pregnancy capital of Ohio, but that doesn't mean I'm trying to help them keep that dubious title."

He breathed a sigh of genuine relief. "Okay. Good. I just wanted to make sure. Now, let's hear it."

"It's really nothing ominous. I was just hoping we could meet up tomorrow for lunch. Maybe start those monthly get-togethers that you suggested we have before I moved away. Possibly talk a little business . . ."

"How's your investigation going, by the way? Come up with anything helpful?"

I exhaled hard, flopping down onto the couch.

"Not really. I've been a bit distracted."

"By . . . ?"

"By the unfinished business I have in this town."

"I see," he said, his tone suddenly all business. "You been digging into that?"

"I have."

Silence.

"And? Find anything good?"

"Good? No. Interesting . . . yes."

"Lay it on me, kiddo."

So I did. I told him about him about the car chase and my stolen original file and the fact that the sheriff's department couldn't seem to find it now. That any trace of it—digital or otherwise—was gone.

He was quiet for a moment, absorbing the details I'd shared.

"Sounds like you're onto something, Kylene, but it also sounds like you've stepped on some toes in the process. Any idea who stole the file?"

"I thought maybe it was that asshole football player who's gunning for me, but I'm not sure. He has all but told me he's above the law in our town, but when I accused him of doing it, he looked genuinely confused. Like he had no idea what I was talking about."

"Was he part of that case?" Striker asked, having switched to full-on detective mode.

"Yes. He was one of The Six. But, again, if he thinks he's so above the law, he wouldn't care. If he got away with it once, he'd get away with it again, right?"

"Maybe," he replied, his voice trailing off. "Listen, I have to run. I'm getting another call that I have to take. Meet me at my office at noon. We can go out from there."

"See you then."

"Sounds good. And Kylene? . . . Be careful, okay? I can't have anything happen to you."

"I'll be fine. I promise."

We said goodbye and hung up. I rushed around the kitchen to make dinner enough for Gramps and me both, even if I wouldn't be home to eat it with him. While I ate, I scribbled in my notepad, trying to work through everything I knew about Boobgate and what had happened that night. I'd always remembered flashes of the evening after a certain point but never fully clear moments. At the time it had happened, I'd been so drunk I could barely function. Not one of my prouder moments, but I was young and invincible, right? What could possibly go wrong?

Apparently, a lot.

Frustrated, I cleaned up my dishes, then got dressed. I still had about twenty minutes before Garrett was due to pick me up, so I lay down on the couch and tried to clear my mind. I'd never really tried that hard to draw forth my memories of the party. I was so traumatized when it all came out, I couldn't have focused on it if my life had depended on it. But now, I thought maybe it was time to give it another shot.

Inhaling deep into my belly, I tried to slow my heart rate and center my thoughts. Considering those things were usually running around like toddlers on coke, it was no easy task. But eventually I could feel myself being lulled into a meditative state. I could see the earlier parts of the night. The ones with me in AJ's lap and Garrett handing us beers. The ones with us laughing the way only carefree kids can.

The deeper into the night I delved, the spottier the memories got. I remembered a group of us getting into the hot tub—AJ, Garrett, Maribel, and Jaime all part of that crowd. The other faces were fuzzy. The heat of the hot tub must have made the alcohol's effect on me even stronger. I remembered feeling sleepy.

A bunch of the group got out at the same time, wrapping up in towels. Garrett was one of them—or at least it looked like he was. I couldn't be sure. Maybe Maribel, too. AJ was still there, his arm around my shoulders. I remembered him saying something to me—words I couldn't grab to pull closer—but I distinctly remembered him getting out at some point, too. I was left with Jaime and the other faceless partygoers.

Then I remembered being alone.

Then darkness.

I focused harder, trying to scrape through the opaque barrier in my mind that wouldn't let me see the truth, wouldn't let me see the events as they played out that night. I wondered if my mind had erected the roadblock because I'd already been completely dead to the world when it all went down, or if it did so to protect me from the truth.

Either way, it wouldn't yield.

"Dammit!" I yelled, shooting up off the couch. Just as I did, I heard a noise outside the house. I ran to the front door and looked through the peephole but saw nobody there. Still certain I'd heard something, I unlocked the door and eased it open a crack. I looked down on the front porch to see a manila folder lying there. The one that had been stolen from my car!

Without thinking, I lunged for it, snatching it up and hurrying back into the house, locking the door behind me. I stood in the foyer and slowly opened it up. Then I dropped it.

I felt sick to my stomach and choked back the bile rising up my throat. Breathing hard, I stared down at the copies of the photos from that night—hundreds of them—each with a simple note on them.

NEXT TIME WILL BE WORSE. . . .

I ran to my bag and ripped my phone out, dialing Garrett.

"Get over here now!" I shouted before hanging up. It was hard to contain the fear I felt, the present mixing with the past to create a debilitating cocktail. I crashed to the ground a few feet away from the file I couldn't bring myself to touch and waited for Garrett to come.

TWENTY-ONE

Garrett nearly tore the door off the hinges trying to get inside. I unlatched the dead bolt to let him in. He burst through the door, looking ready to throw down against a threat that wasn't there.

"What happened?" he asked, searching the room. Then he took a step forward and heard the crinkle of paper beneath his feet. He looked down at the evidence there and cringed. Then he pulled me into his arms and held me tight. "I'm so sorry, Ky."

"Whoever stole the file did this," I said, trying to focus on the mystery at hand rather than my rising emotions and the fear snaking its way up my spine.

He let me go so he could assess my expression. I'd told him about the stolen file earlier that day, so he knew about that. What he didn't know—what I'd withheld at the time—was what that file had contained.

And it hadn't been a slew of topless pics.

"Meg got me a copy of your dad's notes from the boob scandal. That's the file that was stolen from my car. And that," I said, pointing at the manila folder, "is the exact folder she gave me, present contents excluded." He glanced down at the evidence strewn across the floor, then quickly looked back to me. "They all say the same thing: 'Next time will be worse.'"

"This is getting out of control, Ky," he said, stepping off the pile of photos to pace around the room. He raked his fingers through his hair—something he'd always done when he couldn't work through a problem in his head. Or when he knew the answer and didn't want to acknowledge it.

"I need to call your dad. I just . . . I wanted you to be here. My last meeting with him was strained, to say the least. I thought maybe your being here might help."

He let out a mirthless laugh.

"Help? Yeah . . . I don't think me being here will help at all, not that it matters."

He wouldn't look at me—not a good sign. So I stepped into his path, moving into his way whenever he tried to side-step me.

"Spill it, Higgins. You're not telling me something. If this is about what's happening, then I need to know."

"It's about my dad," he started, looking past me to the ply-wood window in the living room.

I felt my hackles slowly rise.

"What about your dad?"

"I don't think there's any point in showing him those," he said, pointing to the mess of photos. "Just like I don't think there was any point in you reporting your car break-in . . . or Gramps' broken window, for that matter." He hesitated for a second, finally looking down at me with guilt-ridden eyes. The longer he waited, the more I felt like I'd explode if he didn't speak. "And I'm starting to think there was never any point in you reporting what happened to you freshman year. . . ."

I looked up at Garrett's worried face, my mouth agape. I could hardly believe what I was hearing. That night, standing inside Gramps' living room, littered with half-naked pictures of me, my best friend in the whole world shed light on a truth that I didn't want to believe.

His dad wasn't going to do a damn thing to help me.

TWENTY-TWO

I don't know how long I stood there, begging my mind to come up with something coherent to say, but it didn't. Garrett looked far too embarrassed to say anything more. Whether he was ashamed of his father or bothered by the reality that we were without reinforcements, I couldn't tell.

Probably a bit of both.

"Garrett . . . do you have proof of this? That your dad is dirty?"

He sighed heavily and stepped closer to me, lowering his voice.

"Things have been weird between us for a while now—since around the time your pictures surfaced."

"Weird how? Because it's a big leap from 'things being weird' to 'my dad is a shady bastard.'"

"At first, I couldn't make sense of it. You know how you are just a walking barometer for things that don't feel right? That don't add up?"

"Yeah."

"Well, with him, I'm like that, too, and I'm telling you, I knew something was up. I just couldn't put my finger on it. He looked . . . *guilty*. Like he felt bad about what happened to you. I didn't think anything of that at the time, because, I mean, he should have. He'd known you since you were little. Half your childhood was spent at my house. I chalked it up to him feeling terrible that he wasn't able to find any evidence that could really stick against AJ and those guys. Other than the pictures, he had nothing to go on—no way to ultimately tie them to AJ, since his phone had been spotted by the pool when he was inside. I know you think my dad is a jerk when it comes to the way he treats women—hell, I do too—but I couldn't imagine that he was really willing to blow off your case because he thought you'd brought it on yourself."

"That makes one of us," I muttered under my breath. "Your point?"

"My point is that after you moved, and I was left trying to figure out how to navigate high school without you or AJ or anyone else I used to give a shit about, my thoughts on why my dad looked guilty started to sour." Garrett stood there in the darkened foyer, staring at me with a fire in his eyes that I'd never seen in relation to his father. AJ? Yes. Donovan? Absolutely. But never his dad. "I realized his guilt was never about you. In actuality, it was never really guilt. It was fear. He was afraid of something."

"You think someone is behind him pulling the strings. . . ." I said, more pieces of the puzzle falling into place.

His eyes narrowed as he held my gaze and he nodded once.

"After Mom died, Dad was strapped with all her unpaid medical bills. They didn't have life insurance. No final arrangements planned. Nothing. I mean . . . she was so young. . . ."

The sudden strain in his voice when he spoke of his dead mother drew me to him, and, angry or not, I wrapped my arms around his waist, giving him the support he needed in that moment. He'd loved his mother fiercely. So fiercely that he'd thought he could love her back to health after her accident. But that didn't happen.

And that damned near broke his spirit.

"I'm good, Ky," he said, gently pushing me away so he could see my face again. This time, there was no anger in his stare. Only grief. "The point is, all that stress he'd been under—all those extra hours he put in on the job to make a dent in that debt—suddenly went away one day. It was so abrupt that I couldn't help but notice. Hell, a complete idiot would have."

"Is it possible that he negotiated a payoff with the hospital? I mean, don't get me wrong, I don't have faith in many people, but your dad? Really? He could be a chauvinistic dick sometimes, but . . . he used to take us for ice cream after our T-ball games. Tell us scary stories when we camped in your backyard—"

"And that was all before Mom died, Kylene." Garrett's tone was suddenly stern and cold, and it shut me up in a hurry. "Do you think I want to believe he's been bought, Ky? That's like you wanting to believe your dad is guilty."

Point made.

"I'm sorry, I didn't mean it like that. It's just so hard to swallow." In truth, it really wasn't. Between my interaction with his dad the prior evening, my file going missing at the sheriff's department, and Garrett's observation, it didn't seem hard at all.

But that didn't make it any easier to accept.

"I checked with the hospital—to see if they'd made an arrangement with him. The lady told me that my mother's bills had all been paid—in *full*."

"Holy shit, Garrett . . ."

"And since neither of us won the lottery—"

"Someone else paid it for him. A bribe." He nodded. "This is crazy, Garrett. Like totally messed up."

"I don't think we should tell him about this. In fact, that might be the worst idea."

"Okay," I said, nodding to myself as my mind worked overtime trying to figure out what to do. I grabbed my phone and dialed Meg, hoping she'd know how to handle our epic cluster-fuck.

"Ky?"

"Meg. I need you to come over to the house right now."

"What's wrong—"

"The stolen file has made a reappearance of sorts—with a few nifty new additions." My acerbic tone told her everything she needed to know.

"I'll be right there," she said. "And Ky? Don't call the cops. Not until I see what's going on."

"No worries there," I replied, shooting Garrett a cautious glance. "I don't think they'd be any help."

"I'll be there in five," she said, then hung up.

Meg didn't bother knocking. Instead, she came barging in like the cavalry she was—or at least the one we hoped she'd be. After a quick reintroduction to Garrett, who she hadn't seen in years, we got right down to business.

"Where was this left for you?" she asked, scooping the evidence off the floor and carrying it over to the kitchen table. Much to my dismay, she began spreading it around, looking for anything that could be of use. She made sure she put gloves on before doing it.

"On the front step. I didn't see anyone come or go, not that it's easy to with our new opaque window." I gestured to the plywood, and she frowned.

"Related incident?"

"I'm starting to think so," I replied, running to my bedroom to grab the brick that sailed through the picture window. I handed it to her when I returned, and she eyed it carefully.

"You didn't give this to the cops when they came?" she asked, her eyes narrowing at me.

I shrugged.

"Maybe I'm psychic. Or maybe I just don't trust the fuzz."

Meg's gaze darted to Garrett. I could practically see her picking him apart in her mind.

"You're the sheriff's kid, aren't you?" He nodded. "Did you know about this? Because you should know better than to withhold evidence." He nodded again. A wry smile stretched across her face. "Guess it's a good thing for me you don't." She stacked the photos up and stuffed them back into the folder. Garrett looked relieved to have them put away. "Now, I don't mean to offend you when I say this, Garrett, but I don't trust your father's department at this point in time, so I'm going to keep these locked up at my office until I can get to the bottom of this."

"How?" I asked, thinking it was the million-dollar question that had no answer.

She cocked her head at me, flashing a look of disappointment.

"I told you I have resources, Ky. I'll have my private investigator do a little digging for me. In the meantime, I'm going to have someone install a discreet camera to watch the front of the house. Maybe one for the back, too. And I don't want you staying home alone anymore, got it? You can come stay with me if you need to—whatever. But no more home alone for you."

"I'll make sure she isn't," Garrett said.

Meg quirked a brow at him.

"He's just a friend, Meg," I explained before she could put him on the stand and cross-examine him.

"Okay. That should cover it for now. But in the meantime, I need you two to act as normal as possible, which I realize is asking a lot under the circumstances. Someone is keeping a close eye on you, Kylene. You've stirred up a hornet's nest with your return home and your digging around in matters put to rest a long time ago. I need you to do your best to lay low. Act normal. Can you do that?"

"Yeah," I said, sounding unconvincing at best. "I think I can."

"You too, Sheriff's Kid. I need you both to keep your noses clean—for your sakes as well as mine." She tucked the file under her arm and made her way to the front door. "There's a football game tonight, right?" Neither of us bothered answering her rhetorical question. It was Friday. Of course there was a game. "You should go. Public places are good. Safe."

"We were planning to go when all this happened," Garrett said.

"Good. Then stick with that. I'll call you if I find anything out. And if anything else goes down, I'm the first call you make from now on, Ky. Understand?"

"Yes ma'am," I replied, forcing a smile.

"No more 'ma'ams,' please. They make me feel old."

She gave us a wink before slipping through the front door and closing it behind her.

"Are you sure you're up for all this?" Garrett asked, looking concerned.

I took a deep breath.

"Someone is just trying to scare me, Garrett. And I don't scare that easily. So let's stick our middle fingers high in the sky by going to the game tonight and acting like everything is right with the world."

"It's clearly not, if *you're* at a football game," he replied before cracking a little smile.

"Yeah, but . . . it's Jasperville. It's expected—practically mandatory. I can pull it off."

"Then we should head out. We're already late to get Tabby."

I grabbed a sweatshirt and stopped in the kitchen to leave Gramps a quick note. I let him know I went to the game and that we'd be home later. Then I told him I loved him.

Wiping a rogue tear from my cheek before Garrett could see it, I picked up my keys and headed out the door with Garrett on my heels.

We rode in silence, neither one of us really in the talking mood. But that would have to change before Tabby jumped in with us, and Garrett was the first to realize that fact.

"You know, I thought I'd have to drag you from Gramps' tonight to get you to go."

I looked over to see him smiling at the thought.

"Like you could! You know I have crazy monkey grip, Higgins. Once I latch these babies on to something, there's no prying them off." I held my hands up in front of him and turned them back and forth. "I didn't want to wound your mannish pride by making you look like a wimp."

He choked on a laugh. "I think I can handle you."

"Really? Because I recall you and Craig Warrens having a damn hard time trying to throw me into Sadie Turner's pool freshman year. You two tried to pull me off their retaining wall for a solid five minutes—until you finally gave up."

"I gave up because Sadie wanted to go make out in the basement."

"A convenient excuse."

We picked up Tabby and drove the short distance to the school. Once we parked and made our way through the ticket line, we found a place to sit on the bleachers and waited for the game to start. Garrett offered to get us some drinks and quickly disappeared into the horde of people near the concession stand.

Neither one of us mentioned what had happened that night.

I added it to the list of subjects I needed to brief Tabby on that weekend.

"There are so many people here."

"Football is a way of life in this town, and, really, the better part of the state. People who don't have kids in school come to watch the game. It's their idea of a fun night out."

"But not yours . . ."

"I feel this is more torture than anything." And that night, it really was. Keeping up the facade of normalcy was more complicating and exhausting than ever.

"Thanks for humoring me."

"That I did, and I would do it again, my fair Canadian." I slapped my hand down on her knee and gave it a shake for effect, earning me a smile.

"You're so weird. I love it."

Tabby and I waited a solid ten minutes for Garrett to return. I tried my best to scan the crowd for anyone suspicious staring me down. But really, that could have happened for any number of reasons not related to the incident that night. By the time he got back, I already had to pee.

"But you haven't even had anything to drink yet!" he exclaimed. Apparently, he'd forgotten about my tiny-bladder syndrome.

"I'll be right back. Keep your pants on."

He shot me a look that said *Are you sure you should go alone?* I gave him one that said *I don't think you can come with me.*

I made my way down the metal seats to the sound of Tabby giggling at something Garrett had said. The girl had a laugh that forced you to smile, even in light of all that had happened. It was infectious. Loud and bordering on annoying, but infectious nonetheless.

By the time I reached the far end of the concession stand, where the bathroom facilities were, I was in full-on pee-dance mode. If I'd been five years old, the crotch grab would have been inevitable.

"Excuse me," I said as I slid past the group of girls clogging up the small room trying to look in the mirrors. My good manners earned me some dirty looks—or maybe that was my day-after-regret reputation—but I didn't care. I had to go too badly. Once I was locked away in my stall, they started talking again.

"So where did Kaleb go? Didn't you come in with him?"

"Ugh . . . he's talking to Jackson about something. Something too important for me to overhear, apparently."

"He is like sooo ridiculous, Anna. You can't let him treat you like that. He can't keep shutting you out."

"Oh, my God . . ." I mumbled under my breath. I needed to pee faster so I could escape the Mensa rejects playing dime-store psychologists. Listening to them made me question if feminism was really and truly dead, replaced by the arguments of girls who worshipped the Kardashians and thought they were the embodiment of girl power.

"We should just go sit somewhere else. Let him and his 'bruh' hang out for the night."

"Yes. That sure will show him," I said as the flushing toilet drowned out my words.

I opened the stall door to find the mob gone. With a sigh, I washed my hands and fixed my hair, then made my way out, heading back to my seat. I saw the two boys in question, Kaleb and Jackson, having a very close conversation while they stood under the edge of the bleachers. Judging by the way Jackson kept looking around like a paranoid addict, I couldn't help but want to know what was so important that they had to pull themselves away from their harem.

I made my way to a small storage shed next to the end of the bleachers and pressed against the edge of it out of sight. It was a bit difficult to make out their conversation at first, but it wasn't long before I heard a name that made my ears perk up.

"Dude. Seriously. I need to get hooked up with your girl's doctor," Kaleb said. I could hear him pause as if he were afraid someone was eavesdropping. Jackson choked on a laugh.

"Yeah. Good luck with that. Dr. Carle doesn't take referrals from just anyone. You can't get in with him unless he wants you to."

"So how do I make that happen?" Kaleb asked.

I rounded the corner, then, startling them both. Jackson's "girl" was Kaley Smelser, the soon-to-be valedictorian of our class. And, apparently, a patient of Dr. Carle's.

"Yeah. I'd like to know the answer to that, too, because I'm dying to get in to see him," I said.

Jackson looked me up and down once before his expression curled into a sneer.

"You? That's never gonna happen, Danners."

"Why not?" The two boys exchanged a look, then laughed at me. "Did I miss the punch line?"

"You *are* the punch line, Kylene. Let's just say that you're not really the right demographic for Dr. Carle."

I stared at him, practically boring holes into his skull with my glare.

"Is he not into blondes, either? Dammit! I have the worst luck with men. . . ."

"Oh, I'm sure he likes blondes, but he likes *green* a whole lot more." Jackson elbowed Kaleb in the arm, and the two walked away, looking back at me as they did. I had no doubt that they were talking all kinds of trash, but I couldn't have cared less about that. I was too fixated on what Jackson had just divulged. Dr. Carle's part-time work schedule—his referral-based practice—had nothing to do with his near-retirement age or his specialty. It had everything to do with money.

TWENTY-THREE

With an evil grin on my face, I rounded the bleachers, ready to brave the cacophony of fans. As I made my way up, I bumped into my football-loving boss, Luke. Literally.

"Well, don't you look pleased with yourself," he said, smiling down at me. "I thought you didn't like football. What did you call it . . . 'Satan's favorite pastime'?"

"I did indeed," I replied with a laugh. "But my friends—and the rest of the town—seem to disagree with me, so here I am. Go Badgers. The more pressing question is, why are you here? Don't you live in Wilton? Shouldn't you be at their game tonight?"

He gave me an ambivalent shrug.

"Our team is terrible. Yours, however, is headed for the state championship if they keep it up. Seems like an easy decision."

"Wow, you really take this seriously."

"And you couldn't possibly look more underwhelmed."

"Oh, no. I could. I just don't know you well enough to show you the depths of my despair at this moment."

"You're quick on your feet, Kylene. You ever thought about being a lawyer?"

Yeah. Every time I picked up the transcripts from my father's case.

"Did Meg put you up to that? She asked me the same thing last night at work."

"It's a fair question."

"I'd be thrown out for contempt of court on my first case. It seems I'm not very good at keeping my mouth shut. Or following the rules. Or waiting my turn . . ."

"Okay. Point made, counselor. See you at the office next week?"

"Yep. Sure will."

"Can't wait."

"You'll probably want to take that sentiment back once you know me better."

"Hey, don't let this nice-guy front of mine fool you. I'm just buttering you up so you don't spit in my coffee when I work you like a dog."

"I'll keep that in mind."

He shook his head as he laughed at me. I had a feeling Luke could dish it out just as well as he took it. It promised to keep my time at the firm interesting, to say the least.

"See you around, Kylene."

I gave him a wave, then turned to head over to where Garrett and Tabby sat. She was cheering like a maniac while he just stared over at her, clearly uncertain what to do with her. It was good to know that I wasn't the only one who could leave Garrett Higgins speechless.

The game was a complete shutout. The other team didn't stand a chance against our defensive line. Donovan hit the opponent's QB so hard at one point that I wasn't certain the kid was going to get back up. It was a healthy reminder that I didn't want to get into a fistfight with him.

Not even with a full set of pads on.

"That was really fun!" Tabby said as we exited the stadium area. "They played so well. And AJ . . . geez, that kid's got an arm on him!"

"Among other things," I muttered under my breath.

"Are we going to go to the bonfire, too?"

"Bonfire . . ." The word felt like poison on my tongue. Judging by Tabby's reaction to my reply, it must have sounded like it, too.

"Yeah. I heard there's some big party afterward. I don't know where, but—"

"McIntosh's Farm," Garrett and I replied in unison. We'd both been there before. We knew the bonfire routine.

"Great! So you know where we're going."

Garrett looked at me and shrugged.

"I'm game if you are. It's your call, Ky."

"Ugggh . . . now I'm going to be the bad guy if I say no." Tabby looked so earnest—so certain that it was going to be a blast—that it felt like kicking a puppy if I told her no. I needed some of her guilting ability. "Fine. Let's go."

"It'll be so much fun! I promise." Tabby's enthusiasm was admirable, but clearly misdirected. Maybe they didn't have bonfires in Canada or something, but she was in for a world of disappointment when she realized it was basically a big fire with drunk people hanging out around it.

Or maybe that was how they partied in Canada and she enjoyed it.

"Don't make promises you can't keep, Ginger McHappy-pants. And you're riding in the back. It's your penance for encouraging this ridiculous idea." Without argument, Tabby ran ahead to the truck and hopped into the back seat. "I'm seriously rethinking our friendship right now. I want you to know that," I yelled at her.

"Oh, stop. You love me."

"Clearly, because only that or a lobotomy would make me do this."

Garrett walked beside me slowly while Tabby waited for us in the truck.

"You sure you're good with this?" he asked, doing little to hide his concern.

"Honestly, the game was a great distraction. I forgot about earlier for a while, and that's something I can live with."

He gave me a smile before jogging toward his truck and climbing in.

Just as I got in he fired up the beast, and we rolled out of the parking lot, headed to the south side of town, where McIntosh's Farm was. It had a lower clearing that was perfect for holding illegal parties. McIntosh hadn't actually farmed on the property for years, and he was senile at best back in my freshman year. There was no way that he was aware of what was going on at the clearing. The downside to the place was the terrain. If you had a car like mine and the weather had been even remotely inclement for a day or two prior, you weren't going to be able to get where you needed to go.

Garrett's truck, however, could get through anything. It was a tank.

It didn't take long to reach the property. We took the worn-out road for a mile or two before we reached our destination. Judging by the roaring fire, we arrived later than most.

"Behold the ninth wonder of Jasperville!"

"Oh, this is going to be so much fun!" Tabby exclaimed, leaning forward between the front seats.

"She is a bit too keen on this, isn't she?" Garrett asked me. I simply nodded in response.

"Are you two drinking tonight?" Her question caught me off guard.

"Are you?" I replied. I looked over my shoulder to find her shrugging at me.

"Why not? I'm eighteen. That's the legal drinking age where I'm from."

"You do know it's twenty-one down below the forty-ninth parallel, right?"

She shot me a scathing look.

"I'm well aware of that. We make fun of you guys for that all the time. You're old enough to decide the fate of your nation either by defending your country or going to the polls, but you can't drink. Seems awfully backward to me."

"The Canuck makes a valid argument," Garrett said, parking the truck among the sea of 4x4s already peppering the field.

"One that I'm sure your dad will take into consideration if she ever gets caught."

I shot him a sideward glance, and he stiffened at the subtext.

"You sweat the small stuff too much," she said, jumping out the side door. "Let's go!"

"Why do I get the sinking feeling that I'm going to be baby-sitting tonight?" I muttered to myself.

"I've babysat you for years. Turnabout is fair play, Danners."

I groaned at the truth to Garrett's statement; I wished he'd babysat me a little more that night our freshman year.

I followed Tabby's lead and got out of the truck. Garrett joined us, and together we all made our way toward the massive crowd of people gathered around the fire. The football players had yet to arrive, but that was normal. I knew they'd be there soon enough, which meant I'd have the pleasure of being surrounded by The Six all evening. Scooter and Eric would leer at me. Jaime would avoid me like the plague. Mark would look indifferent, and Donovan, if provoked, would likely try to throw me into the fire and burn me like the witch they all thought I was. At least then I wouldn't have had to deal with AJ.

Maybe third-degree burns would be worth it.

Garrett and I watched as Tabby practically skipped toward the crowd, delighted at the prospect of a fun-filled night. There was a part of me that remembered what it was like to enjoy those things—to get caught up in the carefree vibe of everyone there. But I'd done that once and paid the price for it. I hadn't had a drink since then. I didn't think I'd be starting tonight.

"I'm going to go rein her in before she gets carried away," Garrett said, pausing before he fought his way through the crowd to retrieve the fun-loving redhead. "You sure you're going to be okay with this?"

"Yeah, I'm fine. Don't worry about me. I'm not the one about to shotgun a beer," I replied, pointing at Tabby, who already had a can of some cheap beer in her hand.

"I'll be right back." He stormed off, grumbling to himself about the new girl being a pain in the ass like me. It made me laugh. There was a time when he was that pain in the ass, too. He was so the pot calling the kettle black.

I felt a bit naked without Garrett and Tabby at my side, and my anxiety from earlier that night started to amp up again. It was like all eyes were on me when they walked away. Like the vultures had all found their prey. My shield of invisibility seemed to disappear in their absence, leaving me vulnerable.

But not paralyzed.

Instead of cowering away, I took a cleansing breath and lifted my chin a bit higher before I navigated my way through the mob of high schoolers. It took about five seconds before I was wearing someone's beer, a nasty side effect of lightweights wearing high heels in a grassy field. I wanted to be a bitch about it—my nerves were frayed enough already—but the girl started puking right after, so I was just thankful I didn't end up with *that* all over me.

Though it would have been a fabulous reason to leave early.

By the time I made it into the interior of the circle, I was starting to rethink my no-drinking policy. I was going to need a good buzz if I was going to be forced to tolerate these people and their judgment-filled stares. I spotted Garrett with Tabby on the other side of the fire. They were laughing at the kid next to them, who tried to crush a can against his forehead and failed terribly in his attempt. I could see the red ring on his forehead from where I stood. I couldn't help but chuckle myself.

I started to walk around the fire to get to them, but I got derailed by a name in conversation: Dr. Carle. Two girls in the senior class were standing close together, whispering to one another. Kaley Smelser—the girlfriend of Jackson and topic of his shady conversation under the bleachers that night—leaned in and handed the other girl a tiny package of something. It could have been nothing, but my suspicion of Dr. Carle and the discretion used in the handoff made me wonder. . . .

Wanting to eavesdrop, I made my way over to them, doing my best not to be obvious. I could hear them talking as I slowly passed by them.

"They'll keep you up for *days* if you take enough. And your mind is so clear."

"Can I get more?"

"I have an unlimited supply of them. I'm not supposed to share, but I will for you."

Interesting . . .

I kept walking, not wanting to linger nearby. Instead, I went and got a beer that I had no intention of drinking, then headed back toward them. By the time I got there, only the future valedictorian was there. She caught me looking at her and shot me a dirty look before disappearing into the swarm of kids around her.

"Is that a beer in your hands?" Tabby asked as she and Garrett approached me.

"Holy crap! How did that get there?"

"That's a good question," Garrett said, plucking it from my hand. "I think I'll hold on to that for safekeeping."

I gaped at him, feigning shock.

"So Captain Canada gets a beer and I don't? I call shenanigans."

"Beer is like the fifth food group up north. Her parents probably put it in her bottle when she was a baby. I'm not too worried about her."

Tabby nodded enthusiastically.

"It's true. I'm virtually immune to its effects. Besides, this is American beer. It's basically water."

"Oh, that's perfect then. I'm parched." I grabbed the can back from Garrett and cracked it open, taking a huge swig of the skunked beer. It took every ounce of facial control I possessed not to twist my features into the look of disgust they begged to show. "Mmmm . . . yummy."

"What happened to your no-drinking policy?"

I gave them an ambivalent shrug. "You tried to enforce it and failed. End of story."

After the night I'd had, a drink seemed like the best idea ever.

"You rebel!" Tabby exclaimed, clinking her can against mine. Apparently, she wasn't against my push-back-when-pushed attitude.

"Two sassy peas in a pod, that's what you two are."

"Which makes you screwed," I added.

"Completely."

I laughed at Garrett's resignation and handed him the can. He nodded and took a swig of it.

"Dear God that tastes like it's been festering in the sun for days."

"It probably was."

I looked over to Tabby, expecting her to chime in, but found her staring off in the distance, concern worrying her brow. I turned to see what she was staring at and found a mob of football players approaching. Donovan was leading the pack—like the alpha wolf he'd become. The usual suspects followed not far behind.

"Maybe this wasn't such a great idea," Tabby said, taking my hand in hers. "Do you want to go?"

"Why? I can't run every time I see him—or the rest of them, for that matter. And even Donovan's not dumb enough to do something here with all these witnesses."

"Damn right he won't," Garrett said, squaring his shoulders.

"Whoa! Down boy. Try to keep your testosterone in check. That is not a fight you want."

"Why not? Afraid I'd lose? I'm not exactly tiny, Ky."

"Right, but you're not fueled by chemical strength enhancers, either, like 'roid-boy over there. It'd be like going to battle against Juggernaut. Unless you have superpowers I'm unaware of, I wouldn't suggest it."

"That would be so cool if you did have superpowers," Tabby said, tossing her empty can into a nearby bucket. "I wonder what they'd be. . . ."

"Okay, she is officially cut off, and you are not picking a fight with Donovan."

"I'm not looking to start something, Ky, but if he goes after you, I'm sure as hell not going to stand by and watch."

"Fair enough. I appreciate your unwillingness to watch me get my ass kicked."

I smiled wide, trying to ease the tension coiling in Garrett's body.

"I need another one," Tabby announced, scooping her arms around Garrett's and my waists. She ushered us away from the incoming football players and toward the coolers of beer.

"Do you not understand what cut off means?" I asked with a laugh. Garrett joined in, teasing Tabby as we let her escort us toward the far side of the party.

I looked over my shoulder as we walked, wanting to see if we'd been spotted. The narrow eyes of Donovan staring at me let me know we had. I maintained eye contact, unwilling to flinch first, but when he puckered up and blew me a kiss in a menacing way, I did. I started to look away before catching myself.

I wouldn't let him intimidate me.

Without thinking, I stopped and turned to face him. Raising two middle fingers in the air, I waved them around like sparklers on the Fourth of July. So much for the looking-afraid/laying-low game plan. By the time Garrett realized what I was doing and intervened, it was too late. Donovan was a bull seeing red. He was all but scraping the ground with his hooves and snorting. Actually, he might have been snorting, but I was too far away to tell.

Looked like someone had taken a few too many pills that night.

Right before he charged, AJ stepped in front of him, grabbing him by his shirt. Donovan wrapped his hand around AJ's throat and pulled him in closer. For a second, my heart dropped into my shoes. I was pretty certain AJ was about to die.

But then suddenly Donovan let him go with a shove for good measure. AJ stood his ground like the fearless kid I'd once known him to be. The good guy. The white knight. Not the opportunistic pornographer he'd turned into.

"I think maybe it's time to go," Garrett said, pulling me away toward the edge of the crowd. As he dragged Tabby and me toward the truck, I couldn't help but stare at AJ. He hadn't moved. He just stood there in front of Donovan, silently baiting him. I had no doubt that he had reiterated his earlier threat. The question was *why*? He'd told me that he would have intervened for anyone that day in the locker room, but that was because I was alone there. There was nobody else to help me. That wasn't the case tonight. He stood nothing to gain from doing what he'd done, which made me question his motives the whole way to the truck.

"Have you lost your damn mind?" Garrett asked, snapping my attention back to our fleeing group.

"I'm sorry. I don't know why I did that."

"You know exactly why you did it. You just can't let shit go, Ky. It's like a disease to you. Your temper is going to be the death of you one day."

"I know. I'm sorry guys, I just—"

"How about you *just* don't do it again? Maybe try thinking before acting when you're pissed off?"

"I was fine until he smiled that smug, victorious smile and kissed the air at me. Then I just lost it, and—"

"Started a war?" Tabby said. She'd said it without judgment, but it was clear in her tone that she was worried.

"I started that the day I helped Amy. I couldn't really make things worse."

"Yeah," Garrett scoffed. "That move totally made everything better."

"I said I was sorry!"

"I heard you. But sorry doesn't make everything okay, Ky. You should know that better than anyone." Ouch. I visibly flinched at his words as I stood by the open cab of his truck. He was referring to AJ's pleas after the photo incident. No matter how many times he said he was sorry that it happened, it didn't make it better.

As much as I hated to admit it, Garrett was right.

"I was wrong," I said softly, trying not to choke on my guilt. "I need to get control over my temper. I know that. It's just— it's really hard, and there's just so much shit going on that I wanted to punch that look off of Donovan's face so much it physically hurt."

Garrett stood there holding the passenger door and sighed. He let it go and closed the distance between us to give me a hug.

"It's okay, Ky. Just try to direct your wrath a little more carefully, would you? Maybe keep your eye on the prize?"

I nodded in agreement, then wiggled out of Garrett's embrace to climb into the truck, closing the door behind me. As I buckled my seat belt, I saw Garrett walking away from the truck back toward the party. A jolt of panic shot through my body, until I realized that he wasn't going back there to go after Donovan. He was going after the person approaching the truck.

AJ Miller.

For a second, I couldn't move. I just stared out the windshield watching Garrett physically stop AJ from coming closer to his truck. The two stood inches from one another, Garrett's hand on AJ's chest. Finally, my brain kicked in and I threw the door open, trying to jump out, only to be thwarted by the seat belt.

"Stupid safety device," I grumbled, unbuckling it.

"Maybe you should—"

"Not now, Tabby."

I launched myself out of the truck and started running toward the boys. It looked like a standoff that had been a long time coming, and I wanted no part of witnessing it.

"Garrett! It's time to go."

"Yep. Be there in a sec."

"No. Now!"

"Ky," AJ started, "I told you to be careful with Donovan."

"She knows that, asshole. She doesn't need your lecture."

"Really? Does she need yours? Are you choosing sides again?" AJ's tone was laced with hurt and anger. Tabby came to stand beside me, holding on to my arm. She'd wanted to know the history between Garrett, AJ, and me, and it seemed like she was about to find out before the weekend.

"I chose a long time ago, AJ," said Garrett. "I don't need to choose again, because unlike you, I don't betray the people I care about."

"That's exactly what you did, Garrett. You turned your back on me! We were like brothers. We grew up together." AJ's face with flushed with anger and frustration. "How could you just flip on me like that?"

"How could I *not* after what you did?"

"I DIDN'T DO IT!" he shouted, getting all up in Garrett's face. "You know me—you know that I'd never do anything like that to anyone, let alone Ky. She's the last person in the world I'd want to hurt!"

"So she lied about the whole thing? Is that what you're saying?" Garrett punctuated his question by shoving AJ.

"I always understood why Kylene thought what she thought, Garrett. She was scared and violated, and the evidence was damning. I get that. Never once did I blame her for feeling how she felt. But you? How could you not even give me a chance? How could you not hear my side?"

"I did hear your side!"

"Guys, let's just drop this—" I said.

"Holy shit . . ." AJ's face went slack with shock—genuine shock. "It all makes so much sense now."

"What does?" Garrett asked, clearly irritated.

"Why you went AWOL after she left. Why you cut ties with your old friends—your old life."

"What in the hell are you talking about, AJ?"

"I was always the third wheel in your mind, wasn't I?" AJ stared at Garrett, silently demanding an answer. He got nothing. "I can't believe this. I knew you loved her, Garrett, but not like that." I couldn't help but pry my gaze from AJ to look up at Garrett. His fists were clenched at his sides, while his body coiled, ready to pounce on AJ at any moment. AJ was getting to him, which made me question if there wasn't a kernel of truth to the accusation. "You didn't want to really hear my side because you wanted it to be true. If it was, it gave you the opportunity you'd been waiting for to swoop in and claim what you thought should be yours."

"Shut your fu—"

"Tell me I'm wrong!" AJ shouted. "Tell me you didn't pine for her while she was gone, wallowing in your new bad-boy-rocker persona. That you thought you'd missed your shot to be with her." Garrett remained silent. "And then her life goes to shit, driving her back to this godforsaken town, and all is right with the world. You just take up your rightful place at her side like nothing ever happened. How convenient for you, Garrett."

"You asshole!" Garrett snapped, grabbing AJ by his shirt. "You want to know why I turned my back on you? Because as much as you said you didn't do it, and as much as I wanted to believe that, your actions told another story. You stood right alongside the others and held strong while she was balled up in the corner of her room, crying. You didn't do anything to stop the whispers about her in the halls or the laughter that followed her wherever she went. You didn't step up when someone said she deserved it or asked for it or felt guilty for being a whore and was trying to make herself a victim when really she'd wanted it all along." Garrett shook AJ for a second, tossing him back a step or two. When he lunged to grab him again, I caught his arm and held him back. "This town turned on her and you did nothing, AJ. NOTHING! You sat back and kept quiet and gladly slipped into the quarterback position when I quit the team because I couldn't stand to be near any of those assholes. Not after the things I'd heard them say. But you? You were all too happy to fill those shoes, weren't you? So don't turn this around on me and make it into something it isn't. I love Kylene the way I always have—as a *friend*. And that's why I did what I did. Because I know what it's like to be loyal, unlike your shady ass."

"You have no idea what loyalty is," AJ growled under his breath.

"Fine! Maybe I don't. But what I do know is this: I heard the guys that were there that night talking about what happened when you weren't around—when they didn't know I was in the locker room with them. I heard all about how you fed Ky booze all night until she was good and drunk and ready to pass out. How you bragged about how memorable the night was going to be. I guess memorable to you means taking pics of your topless girlfriend when she's passed out in a hot tub. The only comfort I find when I think about that night is that you didn't do anything else, because then I would have had to kill you."

"You sick bastard," Tabby gasped, clapping her hand over her mouth. Then she shocked the hell out of all of us. She took three determined steps forward and slapped AJ Miller square across his face. She caught him just right, creating a snapping sound that seemed to echo forever. "Get out of here. Now." Her shocked tone had left, replaced with an icy snarl.

AJ's sad eyes fell on me.

"I just wanted to make sure you were okay, and to remind you not to mess with Donovan. That's all. I'm sorry I dredged all this up, Ky." I said nothing in response. "Just remember that my story has never changed. I'm not sure Garrett can say the same—not if he tells you the real truth about that night." He turned and walked back to the party, disappearing into the crowd that had all taken an interest in what was going down.

"Let's go," Garrett said, heading back to the truck. I could hear the anger still lingering in his tone. With my mind reeling, I looked over at Tabby, who was wincing as she shook her hand. I knew that slap had hurt her almost as much as it had AJ.

"I'm going to have to teach you some moves if you plan on pulling stunts like that more often."

"I just—I just got so mad!"

"Yeah. I know the feeling."

"Did he—did AJ really do what Garrett said?"

I shrugged.

"That's partly why I left town just over two years ago. We said it was because my dad got a promotion—and he did—but we would have left regardless."

"No wonder you hate it here so much. I'm sorry I made you come tonight."

"Nobody can make me do anything, Tabby."

"Okay." She hesitated, looking at me with a thoughtfulness I was unfamiliar with. Then, without warning, she threw her arms around my neck and hugged me fiercely. She hugged me with the understanding that only another female could have. Someone who understands what it is like to live under the threat of sexual exploitation. Someone who knows what it is like to have society view you all too often as an object and not a person.

Garrett honked the horn at us. Tabby released me and wiped the corners of her eyes, then walked back to the truck and climbed in. She was far more complicated than I gave her credit for. She was sunshine and unicorns and Einstein all rolled up into one lanky redheaded package. But there was a fierceness in her that was easy to overlook, even if you had borne witness to it. She was a fighter. A force to be reckoned with.

And one hell of a friend to have in your corner.

I jogged back to the truck to join the other two, trying to process everything that had happened that night. It was a lot to ask of my brain. My head started to hurt minutes later as the three of us drove home in relative silence. Garrett dropped Tabby off, then brought me back to Gramps'. I was halfway to the house when he killed the engine and jumped out.

"What?" he said, as though I'd already begun my interrogation. "Meg was very clear: you are not to be alone at home, so . . . I don't see Gramps home. I'm staying." I shook my head and laughed as I walked up onto the porch. Thankfully there were no little presents waiting for me there. I already knew that I wouldn't be getting much sleep that night. My unanswered questions would never allow that to happen. But who needed sleep anyway? I could sleep when I was dead.

And if I couldn't find a way to shut down the escalating situations around me, I wondered if that eventuality would be far sooner than later.

TWENTY-FOUR

I slept in late that morning, exhaustion having kicked in. I came out to find Garrett gone and Gramps' truck in the driveway. He seemed to have gotten home from work later than usual—and he still had to go back in for overtime that day. I felt guilty when I thought about how hard he had to work at his age. He was getting ready to retire when everything went south for my dad. Once Gramps saw the writing on the wall, he knew he'd have at least one extra in his home sooner or later, and he kept his job. Knowing that I was a strain on his finances made me feel horrible, so I tried not to think about it any more than necessary. I hoped my job at Meg's would be enough to help out.

Once I was cleaned up, I headed to Columbus to meet with Striker.

I was a few minutes early, which was fine by me. I was hoping I could track down the cybercrime guy Meg had mentioned to me—the John or Jim who had looked into my case two and a half years earlier. With any luck, he still worked there. With a miracle, he'd remember something about the investigation.

I pushed through the glass double doors and walked up to the security desk. The officer working there smiled at me. He clearly had no idea who I was.

"Hi, I'm supposed to meet Agent Striker in a few minutes,

but I was hoping you might be able to help me with something while I wait."

"What can I do for you?"

"I'm trying to get in contact with someone from cyber-crime—he has a J name. Like John . . . or Jim . . ."

"It's Jim," a familiar voice said. I cringed before turning to confirm what I already knew. Agent Dawson was headed my way. Again.

"Great. Thanks for clearing that up." I returned my attention to the man at the security stop. "Could I get his number, please?"

"I've got this, Bill," Dawson said, taking me by the arm to usher me away. I didn't want to cause a scene by yanking out of his grip, but damn was it hard not to. When he put a few yards between us and anyone else in the sizeable lobby, he started in on me. "What do you want to talk to Jim about?"

"Not really any of your business," I replied, checking my phone to see what time it was. "I just need to talk to him about something personal. That's all."

He shook his head in disbelief at me. "And you think you're going to solve your daddy's case? It's just sad, really. . . ."

"Don't you have some asses to kiss this morning? I'm sure that's why you're here, isn't it? Someone is bound to need a coffee refill any minute now." I turned to look at Bill, the security officer, and smiled. "Hey Bill! Could you use some coffee? Dawson here is buying—"

"It's called hard work, Ms. Danners. Not something your family knows much about, I'm sure. That's why I'm here—to work hard and get ahead."

"I know more about hard work than you can possibly imagine. That's why I'm here and why I want to talk to Jim. So, if you don't mind," I said, turning to walk away. But Dawson's grip on my arm halted me. In a flash, his voice was low and threatening and his body was way too close.

"Jim from cybercrime can't help you with whatever it is you need help with—your father made sure of that." He let me go and I wheeled around to see his implication plain in his hateful stare.

"Jim Reider . . ." I whispered before realizing the words had escaped. Throughout the trial, he'd always been referred to as Agent Reider. I'd never met him before and had no way of knowing that they were one and the same. The fact that I didn't seemed to please Agent Kiss-ass more than words could say.

"Dawson," Striker called from the far side of the room. I jumped at the sound of his voice, moving away from Dawson a bit. "Don't make me tell you this again: she's only seventeen."

I looked up to find Agent Dawson smiling at his superior in an apologetic way.

"It was completely innocent, sir. I swear."

Striker stared him down before cracking a smile in return.

"Better be." Striker gave me a hug. "You ready to go to lunch?"

"Yeah. Let's go. See you around, Agent Dawson."

"Goodbye, Ms. Danners."

Striker and I walked down the street to his usual haunt, making small talk. But as we did, my brain was working overtime. Agent Reider, the man responsible for Dawson becoming an FBI agent and the reason for my father's incarceration, had been the one to review the circumstances of my case two and a half years earlier. Something about that was unnerving, if not beyond coincidence. I couldn't believe that there wasn't a connection of some kind. That the man who had helped get my father transferred to the FBI in Columbus, then later launched an investigation into him also happened to have been the one to look into whether or not those pictures could be conclusively linked to AJ—or any of the rest of them, for that matter.

Nope. My brain just wasn't having it.

"Kylene? Are you all right? You seem distracted."

"I just . . . There's just a lot going on."

"Your father said that to me once," Striker said, pinning dark brown eyes on me. "I wonder if he had confided in me if he wouldn't be in prison right now. So spill it, kid. What's going on?"

Well when you put it like that . . .

"So, I'm still digging around in my case, trying to find the truth behind that night so I can clear my name."

'Yeah . . ."

"Well . . . I got another threat delivered to my door last night." I explained all the details about the file and the car chase and the copies of my naked pics with the threat written all over them. By the time I was done, Striker looked like he was ready to turn green and Hulk smash the shit out of the restaurant.

"What does the sheriff have to say about it all?" he asked, doing his best to calm himself. He defaulted to fact mode when he needed to bring it down a notch. Unfortunately for him, answering his question wasn't likely to help.

"There hasn't been any real evidence to help tie anyone to the crime."

"This is the same asshole that botched your investigation in the first place, right?"

"Yeah. My mom's friend Meg—the lawyer—she's got some PI looking into things for me. I don't think she trusts the sheriff to handle this with any amount of competence."

"I like her already. Now, about these threats—any potential suspects?"

"I thought so for a second, but not anymore. I've definitely been pushing some buttons with kids at school when I ask about that night. Could be a parent of The Six."

"Maybe, but that seems risky."

"Not if you think the sheriff can't make charges stick."

"True. What else?"

"Honestly? Nothing. Oh wait, there was the message written on the brick thrown through Gramps' window, but—"

His sharp stare cut me off, demanding the details of that event. I filled him in on that and where it fit into the timeline. I threw in Donovan and the steroids and the sketchy town-doctor-turned-potential-drug-dealer to boot, just for the sake of transparency. By the time I finished, he looked baffled.

"And you've only been back for one week, right?" he asked, disbelief in his tone. I nodded. "I don't even know what to say about that."

"Say you can help me," I replied. His expression sobered at my words.

"I can't do anything on-book, but off-book . . ." I leaned forward, excited to hear what he had planned. "We're investigating something down in your neck of the woods right now. I'm going to call in a favor and see if I can get one of the agents to do some sniffing around on his own time."

"That would be amazing!"

"But you have to keep me in the loop."

"Of course."

"And you need to let Meg and her guy do the rest, okay? I know you want that vindication—hell, I want it for you—but these threats . . . they might not just be a scare tactic, Kylene. We need to take them seriously."

"I know."

"Good."

We ate our lunch, peppering our serious conversation with

stories of better times. By the time I left, I felt no closer to find-ing the answers I needed, but I felt lighter. Happier. Maybe just being somewhere other than Jasperville was enough for that, but I was pretty sure Striker was the reason. He was like the uncle I never had. I missed having him around.

He gave me a hug goodbye and left me to my long drive home and careening thoughts. So many separate mysteries running in parallel were starting to jumble my mind. I needed to clear at least one of them off my plate so I could focus on the others. If I didn't, I'd never have the time or mental fortitude to solve my father's case.

TWENTY-FIVE

I was halfway home when my cell phone started ringing. I hated to pick it up while driving, but it was Garrett, and I knew he'd want to know how things went. With a sigh, I grabbed it and hit TALK, immediately starting in before he could chew me out.

"—Striker knows everything now—except about your dad. I left that out for obvious reasons."

"Your ability to tell almost the whole truth has come in handy yet again."

"I'm gifted. Deal with it, Higgins."

He laughed.

"Can you stop by my place on the way home? Give me the details?"

"Yep. I'll see you in about forty-five minutes, providing you let me off the phone so I can drive."

He hung up immediately.

"You could have at least said goodbye," I said to myself, tossing my phone onto the passenger seat.

The rest of the ride to Jasperville, I couldn't stop playing my conversation with Agent Dawson over in my mind, trying to figure out how Reider factored into everything. Of course, I'd never get to know because he was dead. That fact raised the hairs on the back of my neck. My father had been convicted of killing Reider—of luring him to an abandoned building down-town and shooting him in cold blood. When Dad was arrested and charged, they claimed he'd done it to get rid of Reider because he was about to blow the whistle on some alleged criminal activity of my father's. Embezzlement, tampering with evidence—the list went on and on. To the feds, it was the ultimate betrayal—an abuse of power that led to the death of a fellow agent.

They said killing Reider was a convenient way to silence the man about to bring my father down. To me, though, his death wasn't convenient at all—unless someone had wanted to frame my father. Then Reider's death was the perfect tool.

My mind wandered as I drove, meandering through possi-bilities and far-fetched ideas until something struck me. If Reider had been the only one to investigate my father to that degree, then it was plausible that *he* had been the one doing sketchy things—not my father. It was clearly a matter of he said/he said, which I was all too familiar with. A standoff had been created between the two men that knew the truth, and now one of them was dead. Could Reider have manufactured all that evidence against my dad? Could he have been as dirty as Sheriff Higgins? If so, Reider's death could have been just as manufactured—a way to kill two birds with one stone. But not by Reider himself, of course. Had he been a pawn in someone else's game, like Garrett's dad? If so, the question was why?

And why would someone want to frame my father that badly?

Something about it all didn't sit well with me. I needed to write it down and start brainstorming motives with Meg. She'd know what to do with that information. Maybe Luke would help us. He was a defense attorney. Surely he'd know how to flesh it out.

I pulled into town, trying to focus my mind on something

other than Agent Douchecanoe and his mentor. I had other things that needed to be dealt with first, one of which was the fallout of the bonfire showdown. I drove another mile or so to the far side of town, where the houses were more spread out and properties were surrounded by trees instead of open land. Garrett's place was tucked back into a heavily wooded area, high up on top of a hill. It was a gorgeous piece of land, one that I'd spent so much of my childhood running around on. The smell of pine trees assaulted my senses as I pulled up the steep gravel driveway, the crunch of the rocks underneath Heidi announcing our arrival. Garrett was waiting on the front porch for me when I reached the top and parked the car.

"You hungry?" he asked, arms folded over his chest while he leaned against the front door.

"Always."

"I made lunch."

"Then I'll have more lunch." I winked at him and he smiled. "Where's your dad?"

"At work."

"Busy questionably upholding the law?"

"Something like that . . ."

I climbed the porch steps to join him and head inside. But instead of going in, he just stood in front of me, blocking the way.

"So . . . are we eating that invisible lunch out here?"

"No," he said with a shake of his head. His hair fell into his eyes slightly, hiding them from me. "I want to talk to you about last night."

"Garrett, I understand why you went after AJ—"

"He wasn't entirely wrong in what he said."

I felt my heart plummet into my stomach. The last thing I was prepared for that morning was for Garrett Higgins to tell me he loved me.

"Which part was he not wrong about, Garrett?"

He took a deep breath, raking his hair back away from his face. He stood up straighter, looking as though he were ready to face the music—whatever music that was.

"I did pine for you when you left. I had no idea how large a hole your absence would cause in my life. I tried to play that off last night, but he was right. I was a mess. . . ."

"Was he right about anything else?" I cautiously asked, not certain I wanted to know the answer.

He looked at me for a moment, his expression unchanging.

"If you're asking about the love accusation, the answer is no. I don't love you like he did—or still does. I've told you a million times, Danners: I don't do blondes."

"There's something else though, isn't there? AJ acted like you weren't honest about where you'd been or done or something."

Garrett exhaled hard and stuffed his hands in his pockets.

"Because I wasn't." My heart stopped for a moment. "I didn't tell the truth that night because I didn't want to get someone in trouble. But that lie in no way affected your case. I was alone with someone else. I didn't see anything—and, God, I wish I had, Ky. I wish I hadn't left you out there. I thought you were okay with the others. If I'd known—"

I took a deep breath.

"You couldn't have known, Garrett. It's not your fault any more than it's mine. But why didn't you tell me this before I left?" I asked, my tone soft and beseeching.

He looked down at me through that shaggy veil of hair, his eyes full of sadness.

"I just couldn't, Ky. Whenever I thought maybe the time was right, I'd see you flinch if I startled you by accident, or cringe if I reached out to touch you. Then I remembered the first time

I saw you after that night, all curled up in the corner of your room crying, and I knew I could never tell you if it brought back an ounce of that pain. That I couldn't be selfish and absolve myself of my guilt at your expense. So I kept my mouth shut." He looked away from me and dragged his arm across his face. "I'm sorry, Ky. You know I'd never intentionally hurt you."

"I know that," I said, wrapping my arms around his waist. "Except for that time you chucked an iceball at my head in sixth grade. I'm pretty sure you did mean to hurt me that day. . . ."

He laughed, and his chest shook beneath my cheek. It made me smile.

"You told Laura Jones I liked her. You broke bro code hardcore on that one."

". . . Because I'm a girl, Garrett."

"Yeah, well, sixth-grade me didn't understand that at the time."

We stood there for a moment in silence. The niggling sensation at the back of my mind finally broke when the realization struck me. Garrett's reason for lying about that night became clear.

"You were with Maribel that night," I whispered against his chest.

"Yeah . . ."

"Afraid your dad wouldn't approve?"

"I'm sure he wouldn't, but no. That's not why. I didn't want her name dragged through the mud, too. She had such a hard time fitting in at school when they moved—Jaime too. I just . . . it seemed pointless admitting what we were doing when it wasn't going to help your case, you know?"

"I do. I'm glad you didn't say anything about it." I looked up at him to see his face. "What happened to you two after that?"

"Nothing," he replied. He opened the door to his house and stepped back to let me in. "That was over before it began, really. Once it was clear that I was on your side and she was on Jaime's, it just died."

"I'm sorry, Garrett."

He forced a playful smile.

"Don't feel too bad about it. I told you the rocker look has paid off with the ladies. I wasn't kidding."

I shook my head and laughed as I walked past him.

"Really, because I don't see girls falling all over you now."

"You're kinda cockblocking me, Ky."

"What? Do not blame this on me, Higgins. You're the one clinging to Tabby and me like a sad puppy."

He simply shrugged and led the way to the kitchen as though I'd forgotten where it was. It looked exactly how I remembered it.

"So," he said, grabbing two plates from the counter, "tell me about your meeting today."

I quickly filled him in on the basics and explained that Striker was going to have one of his buddies look into the threats for me. He looked relieved at that and leaned back in his seat, chewing his mouthful of food.

"There's something else," I said, trying to figure out how best to explain the Reider situation when I wasn't even sure there was one to explain. But in order to do that, I needed to introduce Agent Dawson into the story. My expression soured at the thought.

By the time I was done rehashing both our first and second encounters, minus the Reider bomb drop, Garrett's brow was furrowed with anger. He remained silent for a moment, as though he wasn't sure exactly what to say. He really just looked like he wanted to punch something rather than talk.

"He's a total douche, right?" I asked, trying to coax a response from him.

"Total douche," he agreed. "You should tell Striker about what he said. If he's still tight with your dad, like you say he is, I'm sure he won't take that well. Agent Kiss-ass won't get too far with him once he learns that little detail."

"Speaking of little details, Kiss-ass dumped one on me before Striker saved me today."

"How so?" he asked before taking another bite.

"Meg told me that someone in cybercrimes had looked into the photos that AJ took—how they were distributed and all that mess—to see if they could find anything conclusive to press charges with. I asked if I could speak to this John or Jim guy when I went there this morning, but Agent Dawson intercepted me and, long story short, informed me that the man is Agent Jim Reider—the man my dad shot."

Garrett stopped chewing.

"Holy shit. That's one hell of a coincidence. . . ."

"I'm not sure it is one."

"How do you figure?"

"I don't know yet. . . . Call it one of my gut feelings."

"Did you tell Striker about it?"

"No. I want him focused on the threats. I'll talk to Meg about it and see what she wants to do with that information."

"And this dipshit rookie? What about him? You think you could make him useful somehow?"

"Dawson?" I asked, choking on my food. "Yeah, no. Definitely not. He might be easy on the eyes, but that's about all he's good for, as far as I'm concerned."

"You think he's good-looking?"

"I did. For about one minute—the minute before he found out who I was. I did think he was pretty damn hot. But as much as I enjoy a little eye candy, he ruins that the moment he opens his mouth."

"You do have impossibly high standards, Ky," he said, baiting me.

"Yes, it is a lot to expect a man not to sexually exploit you at a party or insult both you and your family the second you meet him. I should probably start collecting a menagerie of cats now for my later years."

"I'll make you a deal. If we're each not married by forty, we marry each other."

"Are you trying to save me from my crazy cat-lady future?"

"Yep."

"So selfless, you are, Garrett Higgins. Willing to marry a blonde to save her from her relationship downward spiral."

"What can I say? I'm a philanthropist."

"I literally have no comeback for that one."

I stood up to leave, putting my half-eaten lunch up on the counter.

"You're heading out?"

"Yeah. I need to get some homework done today—maybe pick through my dad's case a bit to see what I can find out about Reider in there."

He got up and cleaned off the table, then walked into the living room to grab his backpack.

"Let me get some clothes for later," he said, running down the hall to his room. "I'm coming with you. Meg's orders."

"Okay. But why a change of clothes?"

He reappeared with a mischievous grin.

"Because we're going to take the Canadian to the drive-in tonight."

He shooed me out the front door and walked over to his truck, his baggy sweatpants dragging in the gravel. As I climbed into Heidi, I wondered why I didn't love Garrett the way I'd loved AJ. It would have made my life so much simpler. He was gorgeous, smart, funny, and kind. Everything a girl could want. But we'd never been like that, and I doubted we ever could be.

Not even at forty.

TWENTY-SIX

Garrett took his don't-leave-me-alone assignment seriously. From the time I returned from Columbus, he wasn't willing to leave my side. I acted like he was being ridiculous, but, in truth, having him around was comforting—even if he was a total TV nazi.

"There's nothing good on," he said, turning the TV off and throwing the remote aside. He flopped back onto the couch, his feet dangling off the end. He just didn't fit on it like he used to.

"We have basic cable and no Netflix, Garrett," I said. "How high could your expectations have been?"

He sat up enough to peek at me over the back of the couch. His scowl was duly noted.

"Did you call Tabby about the drive-in?" he asked.

"I'm not so sure about going. I mean, another public appearance? Really? Are you trying to syphon my will to live?"

"It's better than sitting around here waiting for the other shoe to drop."

"I was kinda hoping there'd be no more shoes, but . . ."

"You know what I mean."

"I do," I sighed, walking over to the couch. He moved so I could sit down beside him. "I'll call her. I need to fill her in on everything anyway. That's as good a place as any to do it."

"Get the Canadian on the phone," he said, standing up to stretch. "Tell her it's a rite of passage in this town. She couldn't say no to that if she tried."

I laughed as he disappeared down the hall to the bathroom, leaving me alone in the living room. It seemed so much darker in there with the plywood covering the picture window. It made it eerier than usual. Or maybe that was just my growing paranoia that something bad was headed for me. The unknowns were mounting around me, hemming me in. Claustrophobia was one of my greatest weaknesses, and it certainly wasn't helping my unease.

I tried to shake it off and called Tabby to invite her to the movies. Not surprisingly, she accepted with a squeal and quick lecture on how drive-ins were a dying breed and we were so lucky to have one. She said she'd be ready in ten minutes and hung up. I could practically see her excitement through the phone.

"Is she in?" Garrett asked as he strolled back into the living room.

"Yep. Ready in ten."

"Perfect."

Fifteen minutes later, we acquired the Canadian and were on our way.

The drive-in was about ten minutes out of town, just off the main highway running west toward Cincinnati. Saturday nights were always packed there, but as long as you were early enough, you could get a good spot. Garrett rolled up to the entrance and paid for all of us, then maneuvered his way through the rows, finally finding what he deemed to be the perfect place to park. He backed into it so we could spread out in the truck bed to watch whatever movie was playing. We hadn't even bothered to check before we left.

There was only a hint of dusk remaining in the sky, which

meant the movie would be starting soon. Tabby announced that she had to pee, so I took her to the concession area, which had bathrooms around the back. Unlike the other drive-in a few towns away, it was located at the very back of the grounds, which was a total pain in the ass if you wanted snacks or had to pee really badly. It was a long walk if you were parked near the front.

"I'll wait for you out here," I told her, knowing it was pretty tight in the ladies' room. I took that opportunity to scan the lot for cars I recognized, looking for one massive truck in particular. Thankfully, I didn't see Donovan anywhere.

Tabby emerged from the bathroom, and the two of us headed back to Garrett's truck.

"Oh! We should get snacks."

Before I could argue, she bolted to the counter and ordered one of nearly everything they had.

"You think you got enough there, champ?"

She looked a little sheepish for a second, clutching a tub of popcorn to her chest.

"My parents don't have sugar in the house. I get a little crazy when I'm somewhere I can have it."

I looked down at her handful of candy and nodded, taking the pop from her hand, and we headed back to meet Garrett. He had the sleeping bags all spread out and ready to go.

"Tabby bought the whole concession stand," I announced as we walked up.

"Licorice Twisties! Nice . . ."

Tabby grinned. "They're so good, right?"

Garrett helped us into the back, catching the popcorn Tabby nearly dropped, and the three of us got settled against the back of the cab. The previews had just begun, but people were still rolling into their spots and getting set up for the feature. I noticed Eric Stanton pull into the row in front of us, a few spots over. His silver BMW was hard to miss. Scooter, Jaime, and Mark all stepped out of it and set up lawn chairs in front of the car.

Jaime looked over toward us and froze for a second before putting his chair with the others.

"Ignore them, Ky," Garrett said, shooting me a look. I grabbed a handful of Tabby's popcorn and shoved it in my mouth.

"Ignore who?" I asked, shooting popcorn everywhere. Tabby laughed like crazy, and Garrett just shook his head.

"Should we tell her now? Before the movie starts?" Garrett pressed, now turned to face me.

"Tell me what? I already know about the AJ thing. Is that what you wanted to talk to me about?"

"It's a bit more complicated than that," I said before filling her in on everything we'd been withholding. From Gramps' house to the stolen file to the anonymous threats that likely weren't connected to Donovan at all. By the time we'd finished, Tabby looked like her eyes would bug out of her head. "Oh, look, the movie's starting," I said, stealing the drink from Garrett.

"Ky . . . why didn't you tell me this before? This is *dangerous*. Like really dangerous. You need to call the police."

Oops . . . I'd forgotten that minor detail.

"About that," I started before Garrett ribbed me with his elbow. "Ow!"

"About what?" Tabby asked, looking past me to Garrett.

"It seems as though the sheriff's department may or may not be a wee bit tainted."

"*Tainted?*" It took a second for that to settle in before she fully got my meaning. "Oh, my God—you think they're dirty?

But Garrett's dad—" She cut herself off, staring at him with wide eyes.

"We can't prove he is," I said quickly. "There's just a lot of suspicious behavior surrounding my case and a few other things," I explained. "Something doesn't add up with it all, but I can't figure it out. Not yet anyway."

"Ky," she said, her note of warning plain.

"Tabby, I can't just let it go."

"She really can't," Garrett interjected. "It's against her religion."

"But I've got some outside help—one of my dad's friends from the FBI. He's doing what he can from his end."

"Okay . . ." She sounded anything but satisfied with my response.

"My boss, Meg, knows about it, too. She's my mom's best friend and a kick-ass lawyer. She's already working on things from her end. I'm confident that this situation will get cleared up in no time. She even said something about putting a camera up at Gramps' house to catch anyone in the act next time."

"I'd rather there not be a next time," Tabby said before taking a big bite of her Licorice Twisty.

"I don't think there will be. But if it makes you feel better, I seem to have a personal bodyguard to watch out for me." Tabby's eyes drifted over to Garrett then back to me.

She shrugged and nestled back against the cab.

"What the hell is that supposed to mean?" Garrett asked, mimicking Tabby's gesture before stealing a piece of licorice from her bag.

"Nothing. I'm just not sure you're bodyguard material."

Garrett chucked the candy at her head, and she laughed.

"It's clearly going to be a long night," I sighed, crawling forward until I had enough space to lie down on my belly. I balled the blanket up to make myself a pillow and hunkered down for the movie to start. I could hear the two of them behind me, still giving each other shit. It made me smile. I was so lucky to have the two of them in my life.

I hoped neither one got caught up in its chaos.

TWENTY-SEVEN

Forty-five minutes into the movie, the curse of my tiny bladder struck.

I climbed out of the truck bed to Garrett's mocking. Tabby started to follow me, but I called her off. If I couldn't go to the bathroom in a crowded drive-in, I couldn't go anywhere alone. And that wasn't a reality I was willing to entertain—at least not yet.

The lone concession worker smiled at me as I walked by—a clear sign that he had no idea who I was. It was refreshing to say the least.

I made my way around the back, which was well lit but still a little desolate. Woods bordered the back of the property, but they started at least fifty feet back from the building. If anyone were about to dart out of there, I'd have more than enough time to make a run for it.

I went to the bathroom in record time and emerged from the building just as the men's room door closed. I started to walk past it, but someone rounded the corner of the building, cutting me off. Jaime Chavez kept heading toward me, looking back over his shoulder like he was nervous. My adrenaline shot through the roof as my mind decided if fight or flight was the best response.

When he saw my wide eyes, he slowed.

"I need to talk to you," he whispered at me. "But not here. Not where we can be seen."

When I didn't reply, he walked past me, giving me a wide berth, and continued on to the far side of the concession stand. The side nobody ever went around. After a moment of hesitation, I followed him, making sure I kept a healthy amount of space between us. I brought my cell phone out for good measure too, ready to snap pics or call Garrett if I needed to.

"They all know what you're doing, Kylene," he said, his voice still hushed but harsh. "You need to stop."

"Stop what?" I asked, playing dumb.

"Looking into what happened that night. You asked Maribel those questions, and you've been all over me. But beyond that, I've heard the others talking about it. How you're picking fights with us in class—like with Eric and Scooter, and what happened last night with AJ at the bonfire. . . ."

"As far as I'm concerned, Jaime, you're all guilty in one way or another, and I intend to prove it."

"No!" he said, lunging closer to me. Out of reflex, my leg shot forward in a front kick, driving him back.

"Come at me again and I'll drop you where you stand," I said, turning to walk away.

"I didn't do it," Jaime said between jagged breaths. He was bent over, clutching his stomach, but his eyes were still on me. "But you're right. I lied about what I saw that night—I am guilty of that."

I turned back around.

"What did you say?" I asked, disbelief in my tone, though it shouldn't have been. Somehow, him confirming what I'd long believed shocked the shit out of me.

He stood up, his features still twisted in pain, and took a cautious step toward me.

"I said I lied about what I saw."

I quickly closed the distance between us, cramming my face in his.

"What did you see?" I asked. Disbelief had turned to anger. It was clear in my tone and my actions as I grabbed him by the collar of his shirt and pulled him closer still.

He wrestled his way out of my grip but didn't retreat.

"I saw Mark, Eric, and Scooter walk out to the hot tub just about the time the sheriff said the pictures were taken. AJ was nowhere near there. I know that because I was with him, just like he said."

"And Donovan? Where was he?"

"I remember him being in the basement near the beer. That's where AJ and I were headed when the other three went outside."

"Are you saying that you know for certain that AJ didn't do it?"

He nodded.

"He was with me from then until we came back upstairs together and found you passed out in the hot tub. We had no idea what happened until the next day. . . ."

"Then tell me why, Jaime? Why would you lie and let those three get away with something that disgusting? Why would you let them do that to me? You have a sister," I said, cutting myself off before my emotions spilled over. I let anger override me again so I could speak without giving myself away. "What if they'd done that to Maribel? Would you have told the truth then?"

Even in the darkness, I could see the harsh angle of his jaw working hard as he clenched his teeth in frustration. I was getting to him and I knew it. Then he shook his head, and my mind broke.

"I couldn't," he said, disgust in his voice.

"You would let someone do that to your sister? Let them get away with it—"

"You don't understand!" he all but growled at me, turning to walk deeper into the dark. When he returned, there was fear in his eyes. Real wrath-of-God fear. "The day after it happened—when it became clear that the six of us would be questioned—I got a call, telling me that we'd all be rewarded if I only told part of my story. If we all stuck together, nobody would have charges filed against them. I told whoever it was that I couldn't do that. That I wouldn't lie to the police. . . ."

"So why did you, Jaime? What made you change your mind?"

His fear faded, leaving a moment of silence in its wake.

"My mother didn't come to this country legally. . . . " he said softly. Realization slammed into me with brutal force. Whoever had contacted him knew that fact and leveraged it against him. No fourteen-year-old kid wanted to lose his mother, let alone to deportation. I knew what it was like to live without a mother. My heart ached for the choice he'd been forced to make.

"So you played along to keep her safe. . . ."

He nodded in response. "I'm so sorry, Kylene. I never wanted for this to happen to you."

He stepped closer to me, his hand reaching out for mine. Just as I was about to take it, voices from behind us made me jump.

"What are you two doing back here?" Eric asked, stepping around the corner. Scooter wasn't far behind him.

"Go away," Jaime said, stepping closer to me.

He viewed them as a threat, which spoke volumes about what he'd told me. He thought they were the guilty ones.

"Looks like the cat's out of the bag. . . . " I said, looking up to Jaime, silently begging him to play along—for both our sakes.

"Whatever," Scooter said, stepping closer. "I heard all about you getting him kicked out of class the other day. You hate him as much as you hate the rest of us."

I gave him a patronizing smile.

"Oh, Scooter. You're really not the brains of the crew, are you? You see, *sometimes*, especially if you're trying to have a secret love affair, you do things to throw people off the truth. Like, when everyone's watching, pretend as though you detest that person with every fiber of your being."

"Does that mean you're secretly in love with AJ Miller, too? You sure seem to act like you hate him," Eric added. "Or maybe you have some sick obsession with screwing all of us."

"Oh, no. Not you two. I genuinely hate you both. No act necessary."

"Is this why you kept looking back at Higgins's truck the whole time?" Scooter asked Jaime. "Worried she was hooking up with him, too? Once a slut, always a slut . . ."

"Let's go," Jaime said, taking my hand in his to lead me away. Scooter moved to let him pass, but Eric didn't budge. He blocked his path, the two of them standing nearly nose to nose.

"Don't forget how this works, Jaime. Don't let a tight piece of ass cloud your judgment."

"I'm not," he replied before shoving Eric out of the way. I walked past the two intruders, Jaime still leading me by the hand for effect. I assessed their glares as I did.

Scooter's was full of disbelief and confusion. Eric's was full of something else entirely. Rage.

Jaime dragged me almost halfway back to the truck before letting go of me.

"Why did you say that?" he asked, leaning in close to my ear.

"Because you put a lot at risk to tell me what you did, Jaime. I don't want to be the reason your mother gets deported."

"So you're not going to tell anyone what I said?" I shook my head no, and he let out the breath he'd been holding. "Thank you. And I'm sorry, Kylene. For everything."

"I understand why you did it," I replied, wondering if the others had been motivated somehow to comply or if they'd been just as leveraged into things as Jaime had been. Then my eyes fell on Eric's BMW and I stopped wondering about him. "Monday, we go back to hating each other, though—to keep up appearances."

He nodded, then walked off. I yelled something obscene at him as he did, garnering me the attention of a few people around us—including Garrett, who was headed toward where I stood. He looked at Jaime as he walked away and then back to me.

"You okay? I got worried and decided to make sure you were all right."

"I think that bike's already been ridden tonight, Garrett," Scooter yelled from a few cars down the row. "Might want to try the redhead instead."

I thought Garrett would kill him for sure.

Then Tabby saved the day—again.

"I don't do Americans. Sorry," she said, walking up to join us. Her delivery was so deadpan and perfect that I wished I had an award to give her. I couldn't have done it better myself.

Eric and Scooter stared at her as if she were crazy, then returned to their car. The three of us walked to the back of Garrett's truck and climbed in. The second we did, the questions began.

"What was all that about?" Garrett asked, staring Scooter down from across the row.

I explained that Jaime had wanted to talk to me—to apologize for everything that happened—when Scooter and Eric walked up on us. I told them how I'd covered for him and everything that followed. Then I prepared myself for the question I knew was coming.

"Why would you cover for Jaime at all?" Garrett asked.

"Because he told me something about the case—something I swore I wouldn't repeat because of how sensitive it is—but trust me when I tell you, not everything that happened is what it seems."

"How so?"

"He told me that he lied about what he saw. That he was with AJ that night and saw Donovan in the basement. But the other three? He saw them head out to the hot tub. . . ."

"And if he's fucking with you?"

"I don't think he is, Garrett. Not after what he told me."

"But you can't tell us why?" His irritation was obvious.

"I can't tell you what he said for the same reasons I can't tell Striker what you told me about your dad. The consequences would be . . ." I hesitated for a second and left it hanging. "But I can tell you that someone tried to bribe him into telling the story he told. When he turned their offer down, they blackmailed him instead."

Suddenly Garrett seemed far more willing to trust my judgment.

"So is there anything else weird going on in this town I should know about?" Tabby asked. She looked a bit overwhelmed by all she'd learned that evening. "Like, is your Gramps a secret agent?" She turned quickly to Garrett. "Are you really a superhero with powers? Please say yes, please say yes—"

"Sorry, Tabby. No dice."

"Dammit!"

She cracked a shy smile at us, and we took the bait, laughing so hard our stomachs hurt. With Tabby relatively in the know, we spent the rest of the movie scheming in the back of Garrett's truck about how to bring down The Three. Eric would be impossible to crack. Mark too. But Scooter? Scooter was little more than a yappy sidekick, and not a very smart one at that. If we could get him alone, I had no doubt we could get him to slip up somehow.

Maybe find out what the price was for his part in the cover-up.

TWENTY-EIGHT

Garrett wanted to accompany me inside, quoting, for the millionth time, Meg's direct order to never leave me alone. But Gramps was due home in twenty minutes, so I waved him off. I said I'd take the heat from Meg if she came down on him. At some point, I was going to have to be alone.

I turned the key in the knob to unlock the door, then I looked over my shoulder to see if Garrett was still there. Once the door was ajar, he rolled off. I didn't want to give him a panic attack by chasing him down the road, so I calmed my nerves with a deep breath and went inside—turning on every light I passed.

Everything looked fine. No ominous files were waiting for me on the kitchen table. No bricks with foreboding messages were lying in the middle of the floor. I let out a sigh as I stepped beyond the foyer, trying to calm my overactive imagination.

"Try to hold it together, Danners," I muttered to myself. I tossed my things on the kitchen table, then turned to head down the hallway. My tiny bladder was up to its usual routine. The hall was dark, and for a second it gave me pause. Something in my gut stirred as I looked down the shadowed space.

Irrational thoughts raced through my mind. Everything from serial killers in masks to werewolves and glittery vampires. Even though I knew I was being ridiculous, I couldn't get my feet to move. I pulled out my phone, ready to dial Garrett, but I stopped myself. Sooner or later, I was going to have to learn to deal with what was happening to me. The harassment. The warnings. Living in fear was something I had no intention of doing.

"Okay . . . here we go," I said, psyching myself up. I grabbed a baseball bat from the hall closet and made my way down the hall. The bathroom was clear—no vampires in there. Same with Gramps' bedroom. My room was closed, so I threw the door open, jumping back a step so I had room to swing the bat. When nothing jumped out at me, I leaned in and flipped the light switch on.

It became clear in a second that my room was empty—but someone had been in there. My window was open a crack, which would have been proof enough, given that I never opened it. But far more damning than that was the picture lying on my bed—a single modified photo with its not-so-cryptic message written in marker. My topless pic had Tabby's face where mine should have been. I didn't really need to read what it said. The message was already quite clear.

YOU CAN'T KEEP THEM SAFE. . . .

I bolted from my room, dialing the police as I ran. At the end of the hall, I hung up before anyone answered. We'd already established that Sheriff Higgins was useless to me. There was no point in wasting my breath.

I sat in the kitchen, baseball bat in hand, and tried to think of what to do. I didn't want to get Gramps involved in it. The worry alone could have killed him. Doing nothing wasn't an option, either. With shaky fingers, I dialed Meg, but she didn't answer. Not knowing what else to do, I called Striker.

"Kylene? Everything okay—?"

"Someone was in my room tonight. They broke in through my window."

"I want you to get out of there and call the sheriff right now."

"I can't call him," I said, wishing I could take it back immediately. He started in on me until I cut him off. "Trust me when I tell you this: the sheriff isn't an option. I can't say why. You have to trust me."

"You still need to get out of there, Kylene. I'm going to make a call. You get in your car and wait for me to get back to you. Got it?"

"I got it."

The line went dead.

I grabbed the evidence and my keys, then went outside to my car. It was hardly Fort Knox, with its busted-out windows, but I turned it on, ready to tear out of there as fast as Heidi could take me if need be.

Exactly one minute later, Striker called me back.

"Agent Dawson is going to be there in five. Don't go anywhere or do anything until he arrives, okay? In the meantime, you'll stay on the line with me."

I filled him in on everything that happened at the drive-in, including the admission Jaime had made. I told him about the mysterious call and the bribe and how Jaime had turned it down—and about the blackmail that followed. I left the details of how they leveraged him into lying out of the story, which seemed to piss Striker off. When I told him it would have involved U.S. Immigration and Customs Enforcement, he didn't ask any more questions.

Plausible deniability is a beautiful thing.

"You're getting close, Ky," he said, pausing to think. "If you were your father, I'd tell you to keep going, but . . . I know you want justice, and I basically told you to go for it, but this is getting out of hand, Kylene. I would never have guessed it would go this far."

"Nobody has done anything directly to me," I reminded him.

"These pictures seem like a way to intimidate me, and nothing more." I hoped he'd believe my bravado through the phone. If he'd been in the car with me, he'd have seen right through my act.

Headlights cut through the dark neighborhood and came to a stop in front of my house.

"Dawson's here," I said, getting out of the car. "I'll talk to you soon, okay? And please try not to worry. I'm probably blowing this all out of proportion."

"B and E isn't a prank, Kylene. Don't treat it like one. And tell Dawson to call me as soon as he's gone."

He abruptly hung up on me for the second time that night.

I climbed out of my car to find Dawson, looking irritated as always, storming up my driveway.

"Striker didn't brief me," he said, walking up to my car as I got out. "What happened now? You need me to deliver something to him this time?"

"Like this?" I asked, flipping him the bird. "Oops, that's for you, not him." I reached into the car and pulled out the photo. I hesitated for a second, not wanting to hand over the scandalous picture. Even with my identity hidden under Tabby's face, I was embarrassed. "Here," I said, reaching it toward him.

He snatched it out of my hand, his frustration plain. Then it fell from his expression, leaving wide, disbelieving eyes in its wake.

"Who is this person?"

"My friend Tabby."

"And the note?"

"That's for me."

He looked up to me, his game face intact.

"Why don't you walk me through exactly what happened here tonight."

So I did. I explained the previous threats, the town's dislike for me, and The Six (which were now The Three), though I did so without divulging the why behind it all. I knew I couldn't hide that fully, but I also had no intention of sharing that bit of my past with someone who loathed me like Dawson did.

"And you said your window had been shut when you left?" he asked. I nodded in response. "Was it locked?"

An excellent question—one I didn't have an answer for.

"I haven't been living here that long. I never bothered checking. Probably because I didn't expect someone to be climbing through my window to drop off creepy photos with my friend's face photoshopped onto it."

"These guys—the football players—why would they have motive to do something like this?"

"Let's just say they did something to me a couple years ago and almost got into trouble over it."

"Almost?"

"Yeah—charges were never filed."

He stared at me for a minute, his mind working hard behind his harsh hazel eyes.

"Does this have something to do with why you wanted to talk to Jim in cybercrimes?" The edge to his tone was notable when he referenced his dead mentor.

"Not important."

"I think it is."

"Well, I can see this is going to be an epic waste of time," I sighed, stepping away from him.

"Believe it or not, Ms. Danners, I'm trying to help, but that's impossible to do when you withhold relevant information."

"The *why* isn't relevant. The *who* is."

He let out a hard exhale.

"Show me your room," he said, heading into the house. I looked at my phone and cringed. Gramps would be home any minute. If Dawson was still there when he arrived, there would be no hiding what happened from him.

"Okay, but you have to hurry."

"Why? Got a hot date?" he asked as he stepped into the foyer. I let my silence be answer enough and led him down the hall to my room. I pointed to the only window it boasted, and he wasted no time looking it over inside and out for any signs of tampering. "I hate to tell you this, but it looks like it was unlocked. I can do a makeshift dusting for prints if you have what I need, but other than that, there isn't much to be done. I'll do a pass outside to see if any footprints were left by the window."

Without another word, he rushed out of my room and out the front door. Moments later, his head popped up in my window. Even though I expected it, I still jumped a little. Maybe the way he highlighted his face with his flashlight was to blame for my scare.

Asshole.

I made my way down the hall just in time to see Gramps pulling into the driveway. Panic shot through me, and I tried to think of what to do next, but nothing came to mind. I ran outside to greet him, welcoming him home loudly so that Dawson could hear me. I didn't know if he'd stay put until we were inside, but I didn't have a lot of faith. He seemed to live to torture me.

"How was work, Gramps?" I asked, walking with him up the porch steps.

"It was good, darlin'. How was your night?"

I looked back over my shoulder as we walked in. Dawson stood beside my car, staring at me. I gestured for him to stay put for a second, then closed the front door behind me.

"It was good. Went to the movies with Garrett and Tabby."

"That sounds fun. Do you—"

"Oh, shoot! I left something in my car. I'll be right back."

Gramps laughed at my outburst but didn't say anything as I bolted out the front door to my car.

Dawson leaned against it looking more put-upon than usual. Somehow he made irritated look good, which was annoying. I buried that thought as quickly as it popped up in favor of finding out if he had any information for me.

"Not going to invite me in to meet your grandfather?"

"Hell no. That man would eat you alive. Now, what did you find?"

He shook his head.

"Nothing we can cast."

"Great," I replied, my voice distant as my mind wandered. "Thanks anyway."

I turned to walk away, but Dawson stepped in front of me cutting off my path.

"Listen, Kylene. Whatever is going on—whoever is doing this—I don't think they intend to stop. From what you told me, these threats are escalating."

"It'll be fine. I'll talk to my friend Meg. She knows a guy. We'll figure it out."

"She 'knows a guy'? Is he in the mob?"

"He's a PI, smart-ass. She's got him looking into the last threat."

"Tell me something, Ms. Danners. Why not just take this all to the cops? Why all this cloak-and-dagger routine?"

"Because I can't. . . ."

"Does it have to do with those football players—the ones that got into trouble over something that happened to you?"

"They didn't actually get into trouble at all," I replied. "But if I say yes, will you drop it?"

"If that's the truth, then yes."

I nodded once, then looked away. "I need to go before Gramps comes out. Thanks for coming."

"I have a feeling I'll be seeing you soon, Kylene," Dawson said as he walked away. "Be careful."

I ran inside the house with a forced smile on my face.

"Friend of yours?" Gramps asked, looking at me with parental curiosity. Apparently he'd taken a peek when I didn't come back right away.

"Just a boy, Gramps. Just a boy. . . ."

"Well, if that boy wants to be sneakin' around my house at night, he'd damn well better have the nerve to introduce himself properly next time."

I stifled a laugh, thinking if Gramps only knew who Dawson was, he wouldn't be concerned.

"I don't think you have to worry about him. He won't be coming around anymore."

I walked over and gave Gramps a kiss on the cheek before heading to my room. I wanted to be truthful when I told him that, but something inside me told me that wasn't the case. Like it or not, Agent Dawson was now involved in whatever was going on with me and those threats.

TWENTY-NINE

Early the next morning, I called Meg again but couldn't reach her. Throughout the day, I kept trying her to no avail. Gramps noticed my frustration at some point, so I tried to let it go for a while, but I needed to talk to her. Her MIA status was starting to make me nervous.

Later that night, my unease was put to rest when she called to tell me her PI had been in contact and she wanted to discuss what he'd found. I told her I had news for her as well—that something else had happened. I told her the gist and she managed to keep most of the concern from her voice when she told me to meet her at the office right after school the next day. That we'd need to discuss some things before I started my shift. After she hung up, I realized I never asked what her PI had told her.

I was tempted to call her back, but I just didn't have it in me.

Instead, I grabbed some leftovers out of the fridge, gave Gramps a kiss on the cheek, and holed up in my room. With food in hand, I plopped down onto my cot and stared at the stack of papers on my desk—the transcripts from my father's trial. It was high time I really dug into those. It gave me something to do while Meg's PI tracked down a lead on the threats. I needed to find something in there that could prove that Reider might not have been on the up-and-up. Something that could cast enough doubt for someone like Luke to reopen my dad's case. I hadn't broached that subject with him, but he was young and ambitious, and getting my father acquitted could make his career. As soon as I found something concrete, I'd bring it to him.

But first, I had to find a nugget of truth buried in all the lies.

I slept late Monday morning and ended up racing out of the house at the last minute, praying I wouldn't be late for Callahan's class. As much as I wanted to go toe-to-toe with him, I needed to pass physics. Continually pissing him off wasn't likely to help me with that endeavor.

By the time I reached the parking lot, I had five minutes to find a place to park, and haul ass up to the third floor of the school. My odds weren't looking too great. I finally found a spot near the back of the lot, where Donovan's crew liked to congregate, and slid into it. Thankfully Heidi was small enough that I could manage it without a problem.

I was in a flat-out sprint by the time I reached the front steps to the school, taking two with each stride to save time. There was no time to go to my locker once I entered the building, so I continued up to room 333 at a rapid pace. Just as the bell rang, I slid through the door, closing it behind me. I flashed Mr. Callahan a smile, then made my way to my seat.

The morning announcements echoed through the room while I pulled out whatever notebook I had with me. As long as it had paper in it, I was good to go. I could hear Garrett trying to get my attention from two rows over, but I waved him off, knowing that Callahan was likely waiting for me to do something wrong so he could send me out of the room. I think he regretted not sending me to the principal's office during the school assembly.

Talk about an opportunity wasted.

Like a good little schoolgirl, I sat at attention all through class, even answering some of Callahan's questions. He thought I wasn't bright enough to make it in the world. I thought acing his class would make him look like the stupid one. I was on a mission.

Forty-five minutes later, the bell rang. Before I could even finish packing up my stuff, Garrett was at my side.

"What's up with the goody-two-shoes routine?"

I shrugged and threw on my backpack. "I like physics?"

"You like making Callahan look bad."

"Wrong. I *love* making him look bad."

He laughed and shook his head as we walked out of the room.

Before I went to the cafeteria for lunch, I carelessly threw my morning books into my locker, slammed the door closed, and jumped when I found a face lurking behind it. AJ had always loved to scare me like that. The smile he wore as he leaned his head against the wall of lockers told me he still did.

"And my day just keeps getting better," I said, turning to walk away from him.

"Ky! Wait!" He gently grabbed my elbow to keep me from leaving. "I just want to talk to you for a minute. That's all."

"You keep saying that, AJ, but these minutes are adding up. I'm going to start billing you for my time."

"Great. Address is still the same. Send me an invoice whenever."

He threw in a wink for good measure, then smiled. I felt my heart soften a bit at the sight. I needed to get out of there before it started to melt.

"What do you want, AJ? I'm hungry. I want to go eat before hungry turns to hangry." I leaned in closer to him, whispering in a conspiratorial way. "You should want me to eat before that happens, too."

"I'm well aware of what you're like when your blood sugar drops. You think I forgot the picnic incident? I thought you were going to drown Garrett after he ate all the food."

"I would have if he hadn't been clinging to his paddleboard like a big baby."

"He's scared of you when you're angry."

"That's because he's smart," I replied. "Smarter than you, apparently."

"I don't remember you dating me for my mind, Ky," he said, leaning in closer to me. "Although, I'm pretty sure you told me once that my intelligence turned you on." I stared at him in the hallway, paralyzed by the turn of our conversation. "So anyway, homecoming is this weekend. . . ."

Finally, my brain caught up.

"Your point?"

"You have a date yet?"

"Now why would I need a date when I have no intention of going?"

He frowned a little. "You should go, Ky."

"I should do a lot of things, AJ, like walk away from this conversation before it takes a turn for the worse—as if that were possible—and yet here I am, my morbid curiosity not allowing that to happen."

"Go with me."

He stood there before me, his expression so earnest. For a brief second, he broke through my defenses and made me feel something for him. Whether it was pity for being blamed for a crime that Jaime said he couldn't have committed, or guilt for assuming he had, I couldn't tell, but I felt it all the same. It hurt to realize that I could have been wrong—that I'd turned on him without really giving him a chance. Emotions I didn't want to feel welled up inside me and started to seep out.

Then I welded the breach closed and shut them down.

"AJ, that's never going to happen," I replied, my tone notably softer. "Whatever you're trying to do—whatever game you're playing—I'm not interested."

"It's not a game, Ky," he said, looking as wounded as he sounded. "And if you think you can make me give up on you this easily, then you never knew me at all."

"Okay, AJ. You say it's not a game, then prove it."

His expression brightened.

"How?"

"Tell me if you were paid off to change your story about what happened to me that night."

He couldn't have looked more horrified.

"What in the hell are you talking about? Like a *bribe*?"

"Did someone blackmail you into saying what you said?"

"Blackmail? Jesus, no. Why would you even ask that?" I studied him for a minute, looking for any signs he was lying. Not a single one was visible. "You don't think I did it anymore, do you?" he asked, his horror slowly morphing into hope.

"I'm still not going to homecoming with you," I said, evading his question.

"Oh, you're going. You know I'm the most stubborn ass you'll ever meet, besides you, of course." He flashed me a mischievous grin that reminded me of so many good times we'd had together. But those times were gone. Right or wrong, things had changed.

"Then you know you might as well give up, because I'll outlast you on this. I can guarantee that."

"We'll see," he replied, still smiling. Then he looked past

me at something down the hall and frowned. "I'll see you around, Ky."

With that, he turned and disappeared into the mob of people rushing to get to their next class.

"What did he want?" Garrett asked from behind me. I turned to answer him.

"He asked me to homecoming."

Garrett literally stopped dead in the middle of the hallway, causing some poor freshman boy to bounce off of his back then fall to the floor. It was comical, unlike the look on Garrett's face. I couldn't quite tell if he was contemplating AJ's mental state or mine, since I was so blasé about the whole thing. My money would have been on the latter, but I had been known to be wrong on the rare occasion.

Tabby came bounding up to us, smiling from ear to ear until she saw Garrett, apparently frozen in his speechless stupor.

"What's wrong with him? He looks like he's having a stroke or something."

"Give him a sec. He still might."

"Tell me you said no," Garrett said. "I don't care what Jaime told you. I still don't trust any of them."

"Garrett . . . I haven't completely taken leave of my senses. I might be blonde, but I don't suffer from the stereotypical deficits."

"Wait! Is that really your natural color?" Tabby asked, confusion in her tone. I turned my head slowly to look at her. "Oh. It is." She had the good form to at least look apologetic. "It suits you."

Without replying, I returned my attention to Garrett.

"To be clear, yes, this is my natural hair color, and, no, I did not agree to go with him. What Jaime said may or may not change things, but that chapter of my life is shut. I have zero intention of reopening it," I said. His expression sobered. "And just like that, I've killed the mood yet again. Why don't they have a class for that in high school? I'd nail the crap out of that one. . . ."

"I'm going to go grab some lunch. Do you want me to get something for you guys?" Tabby asked. "You look like you need a minute."

"That'd be great, Tabs. Thanks."

She smiled and gave us a quick nod before making her way into the cafeteria, leaving Garrett and me alone.

"Sorry, Ky," Garrett said, turning to me. "I just . . . the AJ thing really threw me for a loop. I think I'm a bit on edge these days with everything going on."

"That, my friend, makes two of us." I flashed a grin at him that earned me one in return. He threw his arm around my shoulders and walked us into the cafeteria. Our presence together seemed to cause a scene. I was becoming convinced that was exactly why Garrett did it.

"So, are you going to go to the dance at all then?" he asked.

"Um, no."

"Why not?"

"Because!"

"Because why?"

"Reasons."

"Like?"

"All the obvious ones."

Garrett laughed. "I think you should go."

"Seriously, I think you're losing it, Garrett."

"Hear me out, would ya?" He pushed open the door to the patio eating area and let me walk through before him. "It would make a statement if you went—your middle finger to everyone here. The whole town for that matter."

"Yes, I can totally see how me in a cocktail dress and heels says 'fight the power.'"

"Those would just show everyone how fabulous you are. Your presence there is what matters. It says you don't care."

"So does me not going."

"But not in the same way. Think about it: if we walk in together—two of the most once-popular kids in this school—it says we don't play by their rules."

"Wait, was that your attempt at asking me to go?"

He shrugged. "I figured that was a given."

"Wow . . . that level of hubris is impressive, Garrett Higgins."

"Relax, Ky. I thought we could get Tabby to go, too. God knows she's stuck with us for good now."

Our collective gaze fell upon our gawky friend in the lunch line, swallowed up by the commotion around her. With us, she'd found her place. Alone, she still floundered.

"Garrett," I said, leveling my gaze on him as he sat down across from me at the table. "She hangs out with us. Her social-climbing days are over."

"Fair point, and all the more reason to bring her along."

"Bring who where?" Tabby asked, setting a tray of assorted lunchroom items down in front of us.

"You to homecoming."

Tabby looked at Garrett like he'd spoken a foreign language. "What's that?"

"The foreigner comes from a strange, faraway place that doesn't worship football like we do. This will require explanation," I said, pulling a bag of chips off the tray. "It's a dance. A formal dance where girls get all gussied up in dresses and boys spend all night trying to figure out how to get them out of those gowns."

"Oh! The homecoming *dance*. Got it. Sounds super fun. Are you two going?"

"Yep. And you're coming with us," I replied.

Tabby clapped her hands as she bounced up and down in her seat. Apparently, homecoming was right up her alley.

"When is it?"

"Have you not seen the gazillion posters in the hallway about it?" I did nothing to hide my disbelief.

"I didn't notice them," she said plainly.

"Really? They haunt my dreams. . . ."

"It's this Saturday," Garrett said. "Starts at seven."

Tabby's elation fell flat in an instant. "I'm out of town. We won't be back until at least seven thirty."

"So you can meet us there. It'll be fine," he told her, trying to cheer her up.

Her smile returned. "I'll check with my parents, but I'm sure they'll be okay with it, especially since it's not a date."

"Definitely not a date," I said, popping a chip into my mouth and munching it loudly. "I'm not into threesomes."

"Dream killer," Garrett muttered to himself before his facade of disappointment fell and he laughed.

"That's me, kids: Crusher of Souls. Purveyor of Disappointment."

"You probably kick puppies, too," Tabby added with a giggle.

"And punch babies," Garrett added.

"No way. I love puppies," I said with a wink.

We all laughed, drawing attention to ourselves. That seemed to be our lunchtime MO. And I didn't care one bit. I loved how I felt when I was around those two. How they both challenged me to see the value in things I balked at. Maybe homecoming wasn't my thing anymore, but maybe it wasn't going to be the torture I assumed it would. Either way, one thing was for sure. The three of us were about to make homecoming a lot more interesting.

THIRTY

I walked through the law office entrance to be greeted by an empty front desk. Marcy must have been in the back room, so I rushed there to help her out. As I walked down the hall, I heard an angry male voice. Luke's office door was opened slightly, and I could see a hand still holding the knob through the small opening. The displeasure in the owner's voice was plain.

"No, I don't think you heard *me* correctly. You will have it by next week without excuses, understand? If you think for one second that you're going to tie me up with your bullshit, you've got another think coming."

Luke emerged from his office, cell phone pressed to his ear as he stormed toward the front desk. He was enraged, judging by the flush in his face, but, like a pro, he managed to keep that from his tone. The sight of him was intimidating. If I was in trouble, I'd have wanted him as my attorney.

"Just make sure that it happens. No excuses."

He hung up on whoever was on the line and tucked his phone in his pocket.

"Remind me not to get on your bad side," I told him, braving a small smile. It earned me one in return.

"Sorry about that," he said, sounding much more himself. "Being a defense attorney isn't very glamorous."

"Or stress-free by the sound of it."

"Not at all."

"Oh, good! You're here," Meg called out from the far end of the hall. "Come on back." She waved for me to follow her.

"Secret meeting?" Luke asked.

"Yes, but I'm afraid you have to know the handshake to get in, so . . ." Then I shrugged at him and he laughed.

"Have fun," he said as he walked out front.

I laughed as I entered Meg's office, taking a seat across from her.

"Okay, here's the short of it," she said, propping her elbows on the desk. "There were some partial fingerprints on those photos you gave me, Ky, but the owner isn't in the system. He—or she—is clean."

"Not helpful."

"No. But, what is helpful is that those prints are the same as the ones we were able to pull from the brick you withheld from the sheriff. The one telling you to leave town."

Holy. Shit.

"Wait—you're saying those events are related then?" My Donovan theory was officially dead. Or was it? "I was sure Donovan Shipman had thrown that brick through Gramps' window. Can we get him printed?"

Meg gave me a sympathetic look.

"I'm way ahead of you, kiddo. His prints were on file from the photo incident—to see who'd touched AJ's phone. It's not him."

"Okay . . . I guess that's comforting in one regard."

"The threats can't be coming from any of those boys. They were all fingerprinted when they were brought in for questioning two years ago," she added. "I don't think the threats you've received are related to that case. At least not directly."

"Maybe there will a different set on the photo left at my

house last night while I was out." I dropped an envelope containing the photo on her desk. "Open it later," I said. She gave me an understanding nod.

"Got it. I will. I'll have my guy test it, too. Maybe we'll get lucky with this one." She tucked the envelope in a desk drawer. "In the meantime, can you think of anyone else that would want to leverage you out of town?"

About a hundred names flashed through my mind.

"Too many to count."

"Think, Kylene," Meg urged. "Anyone who pops into your head?"

"No. Not outside of The Six."

"That's okay. We'll keep digging. In the meantime, why don't you get to work? Poor Marcy could really use your help today."

"Consider it done," I said, heading for the door. "Maybe I can help Luke out, too. He seems a bit stressed. . . ."

"That's the life of a defense attorney," Meg replied with a laugh. "Never a dull moment."

THIRTY-ONE

From the moment I walked into JHS the next morning until the time I left, nothing went wrong. Mr. Callahan wasn't a complete prick. I didn't hear anyone talking crap about me when they thought I couldn't hear them. And lunch was actually identifiable. *This is what high school should be like*, I thought to myself.

Maybe one day, it would be.

After school, I tried my best to weave through the parking lot to avoid Donovan, Scooter, and Mark, who stood next to their vehicles in the back row. Unfortunately, there was a lack of SUVs and pickups to hide behind, which left me in clear view. With a deep breath, I made my way to my car—one row in front of where they stood. Their laughter echoed through the parking lot. I was pretty certain it had to do with me.

"Hey, Danners! Scooter was just telling us about you and Jaime," Donovan shouted, pushing off his truck to walk toward me. "Gotta give it to you; I didn't see that one coming."

"I'm sneaky like that," I said, continuing to my car. I could hear Striker and Meg—even Dawson—in my mind, telling me to back off. To lay low. For once, I really wanted to follow their advice.

But I just couldn't.

"You'd like to think so, wouldn't you?" he asked, sounding haughty.

"We know what you and Jaime were talking about that night," Scooter said, his tall-but-toned frame headed my way.

"Do you, now? Because, let's be honest here, Scooter. Your ability to accurately recall events is directly related to how badly you want to impress the guys—or save your own ass. So I'm not really sure you heard anything at all."

"If he told you anything, he's dead. You both are," Scooter said, lunging toward me. The other two had followed him, and Mark caught Scooter by the arm and shot me a look that encouraged me to leave before things got ugly.

"That sounds a lot like a threat, Scooter. I seem to be getting a lot of those these days. I think my attorney will be super interested to hear about this one."

"Won't matter if he does," Donovan said.

"*She*," I corrected. "If *she* does. And I assure you, it will."

"You really don't get it, do you? Nobody is going to believe you. Your credibility is shot in this town. All you're going to do is embarrass yourself even more than you already have."

"If that's even possible," Scooter said with a laugh.

"I've been wondering something for a while now, Scooter. Maybe you can clear this up for me. Your story about the night of the party: you said you were with Eric and you both saw the others in the basement. In fact, you all said some version of that story—except for AJ. Why do you think that is?"

"I don't know," he said, looking confused. "And I don't really care."

"It's strange that so many of you gave the same story—almost word-for-word."

"Because it was true," Scooter said, stepping toward me.

"Maybe. Or maybe you were all coached on what to say."

"Who would do that, Danners?"

"Who, indeed? You didn't all share representation, so it wasn't your lawyer. It makes me wonder if you know exactly who did it and you're covering for him—that you all are. I know it's not AJ—his story is the only one that differed from the rest of yours. Did the others lie to cover for you, Scooter? I wonder what could have motivated them to do that." I dared to take a step nearer to him. "Part of me thinks you're too stupid to have pulled off a stunt like that on your own, but the other is starting to think it was that stupidity that drove you to do it in the first place."

Scooter's face turned red, his eyes, murderous. Stammering in half sentences punctuated by four-letter words, he made another play for me. This time, Donovan shut him down with a straight arm across his chest. Scooter fell backward like he'd been drilled with a two-by-four. Donovan, however, hadn't even broken his stride.

"I think it's time for you to go." Donovan hovered over me like the tower of muscle he was, glaring down at me.

"What about you?" I asked as I stared up at him. "What made you lie? Was it a coveted referral to see Dr. Carle and his never-ending prescription pad? A football scholarship would be a cushy pass out of this town—one you're not getting with academics."

Donovan didn't say a word. Instead, his right hand shot out to strike my face. I slipped to the left, dodging the blow, then followed it up with a kick. My shin landed perfectly, slamming the sharpest part of it in the middle of his thigh. The force of the blow made his knee buckle and he staggered back. Mark caught him before he hit the ground.

"My knee!" Donovan screamed, struggling to stand. "You fucking bitch!"

There was something paralyzing about the roar of his voice. It should have sent me running, but instead, I stood there and watched as the beast prepared to come for me. It was clear in that moment how deeply the steroids controlled him.

Just how dangerous they made him.

"Go!" Mark shouted at me as Donovan regained his footing. I didn't need to be told twice.

I ran to Heidi and fired her up as fast as I could. Gravel shot everywhere as I peeled out of the parking lot. By the time my adrenaline wore off, I was stopped at a light on Main Street, resting my head against my worn-out steering wheel.

"Why, why, why . . . ?" I asked myself as I bumped my forehead against the plastic wheel. "Why can't I just keep my mouth shut?"

I'd stepped in it big-time with Donovan, and I knew there'd be no turning back.

Once I got home, I spent a solid hour in my room, pretending to do homework while Gramps made dinner. But in reality, I was brainstorming how I could possibly use what I knew about Donovan's shady prescription to leverage him into leaving me alone. Just as I was about to give up and start my homework, I thought of something else. Something that could potentially shut him down for good.

A few years back, Ohio had a drug scandal that not only rocked the state but the entire nation as well. A young teenager had tried to report her father for illegally distributing medications at his pharmacy, but the state board didn't listen. Months later, after a thorough Drug Enforcement Agency investigation, thirty-five pharmacists around the state were arrested. The media shit storm that rained down on the State of Ohio Board of Pharmacy as a result was brutal.

If they were smart, they wouldn't let that happen again.

So I quickly devised a plan that all but recreated the circumstances of the previous case, then I dialed the contact number for the board and waited.

"State of Ohio Board of Pharmacy; how can I direct your call?"

"Who would I need to speak to about filing a report of abuse?"

"I'll connect you right away."

It certainly looked like they'd learned their lesson.

"Complaints; this is Dana; how can I help you?"

"Hi, Dana. My name is Gigi Smith, and I'm calling in regards to an article my high school newspaper is running on prescription abuse in my town and the professionals making this possible. I wondered if the state board would like to comment on how something like this can happen."

"What kind of prescription abuse?"

"Bogus prescriptions being written and filled. Pharmacies automatically refilling scripts for controlled substances. That sort of thing."

"Those are pretty bold accusations."

"That doesn't make them any less true."

"Do you have proof?"

"I do, but I won't reveal my sources. If you think I'm lying, maybe you guys should head down and investigate for yourselves. The Williamson Pharmacy in Jasperville, Ohio. I think you'll find the trip worth your while."

"Who is this again?"

I hung up the phone, not wanting to get pulled into an on-the-record reporting of a crime. My bogus ID would do little to help support my claim of fraud. All I could do was wait and see if they'd follow up, but I was fairly confident they would. They didn't want another media nightmare on their hands.

With any luck, the DEA would be shutting down Donovan's drug shack soon.

Then maybe the boy could overcome the beast.

THIRTY-TWO

The next day after school, Tabby begged me to bring her over so that she could see what I planned to wear to homecoming. Given I had very few options, I knew it wouldn't take up much of my night. At least I hoped not. I could only be excited about dresses for so long.

We drove to Gramps' house after school, the wind blowing our hair around like crazy through the open windows. I felt so carefree it was ridiculous. It reminded me of freshman year before everything went wrong.

"So you and Garrett—you've been friends since you were little?"

"Yep."

"And you never dated?"

"Nope."

"Ever? Not even for like five seconds?"

"Not even one."

"Huh . . ."

"Huh what?" I asked, looking over at her as we sat at a red light. "Just ask what you want to really ask me, Tabby."

"It's just that . . . you seem like you'd be such a great couple."

"We would, if we were eighty."

"I think you two would be great together." A pause. "Have you ever kissed him?"

I inhaled deeply, wishing that I could just lie and tell her no, but I couldn't. Lying to Tabby was like cutting the horn off a unicorn. It was a desecration somehow. Like I was tainting one of the only purely magical beings left in existence. I just couldn't do that.

But man did I want to.

"Yes. Once. It's a long story that I'm not going to rehash, but yes. I've kissed Garrett Higgins."

She honest to God started giggling like an eleven-year-old, hands covering her mouth and all.

"So . . . how was it?"

"I don't know. Wet? Awkward?"

"How old were you?"

"What is this? The Spanish Inquisition?"

She hesitated for a second, scrunching her features up into a confused expression.

"No. And the Spanish Inquisition wasn't really an inquisition, per se. It was a tribune of—"

"Oh, my God, Tabby. I know what the Spanish Inquisition was."

"Okay, but you just used it incorrectly."

"Please turn green. Please turn green. Please—"

"Just tell me how old you were and I'll drop it. I promise."

"Twelve, okay? I was twelve. We were at summer camp. Someone dared us to do it. We did it. The end."

"I bet it was good. He has nice lips."

"Well, maybe you can plant one on him at homecoming. Draw a little attention away from me for once. You can tell me if it was worth it afterward."

We spent most of the night trying on the few dresses I owned, laughing until we nearly peed, and doing all sorts of girly things

that I hadn't done for a long time. She almost made me excited
to get dressed up and attend the dance that only days earlier I
dreaded.

I was getting dressed when I saw Tabby staring at the stack
of files on my desk. She walked over and flipped one open,
scanning the contents.

"What's this?" she asked. I zipped up my pants and walked
over to her.

"Transcripts from my dad's trial. I'm trying to figure out a
way to get him acquitted or pardoned or something. Even if
he shot the other agent, I don't believe for one second that it
was intentional. Something happened there between them that
night—something that forced his hand. My father isn't a killer,
Tabby."

She turned to me and forced a sad smile.

"I'm a whiz at fact-checking . . . and I'm pretty good at finding small discrepancies in things. Maybe I could help you
wade through this stack . . . ?"

I felt my throat tighten.

"Yeah, Tabs. That'd be great."

She looked at me for a moment before plucking a file off the
pile and plopping down on my bed.

"We should probably start a whiteboard or something—like
they have on all those cop shows—so we can keep track of the
facts and highlight anything we think looks shaky. Do you
have any copies of your dad's attorney's paperwork?"

"No."

"That would be helpful. I think you need an attorney to request it—or your father."

"I can ask my boss about that. She'll do it if she can."

She gave me a nod, then went back to speed-reading the
transcripts. She was three files deep before I finished my first.
By then it was time to take her home.

"I think it's interesting that Agent Reider would have agreed to meet your father at the building, alone, without any backup, if he for one second suspected your father knew of his investigation. I mean, even if he didn't, isn't it kind of odd? Like, why meet out there to talk?"

"Unless Reider thought it would be more suspicious to my dad if he didn't agree. If my dad had suspected he was investigating, Reider's refusal to meet with him would have thrown up red flags, right?"

"Yeah . . . I guess. It just seems like Reider had everything to lose by going to meet him there, that's all. It doesn't seem like something a seasoned detective would do. Not without a backup plan of some sort."

"You're right. He could have easily told my father he'd meet him there and then set up a sting or whatever they call it. So why didn't he? Why didn't he have backup?"

"If you can figure out the answer to that, my guess is you'll have cause to reopen your father's case," Tabby said, heading down the hall.

It sounded so simple. Poke holes in Reider's motivation to meet my father that night. But I doubted it was simple at all.

If it was, my dad wouldn't have been convicted.

THIRTY-THREE

Since Tabby and I spent the night playing dress-up and junior detective, I didn't get the last of my makeup work finished. Every class I had on Thursday was used to cram in as much homework as possible without getting busted in the process—not an easy task, but one I accomplished. By the end of the day, I had only two assignments left to go before I'd dug myself out of the two-week hole I was in.

Tabby asked if I wanted to read through more of my dad's transcripts, but I told her I couldn't, even though I wanted to. I really had to get the last of my work done—especially because everything I had left to do was either math or physics. No way was I coming up short for Callahan's class.

I raced home so I could get started, parking in the empty driveway. As I made my way up the front walkway, a familiar voice called to me from the street. I didn't need to turn around to see who it was. His voice was seared into my brain.

"Ms. Danners." I looked over my shoulder to find Agent Douchecanoe sitting in a sedan parked in front of the house.

"Agent Dawson." I did little to hide the contempt in my voice. "I was hoping to not see you for a while. Have you come of your own volition, or did Striker send you again?"

I watched as he climbed out of his shiny new car, his smug

smile firmly intact. He strolled up the driveway like he didn't have a care in the world.

"I'm here to talk to you about your situation. Striker asked me to keep an eye on you while I'm down here on another matter."

I inwardly groaned.

"You don't strike me as the babysitting sort."

"Because I'm not. I followed up with him about the threats you've been receiving. He said if I wanted any chance of earning favor with him, I'd keep you safe."

I cringed.

"Good luck with that. . . . I'm not really a safety kind of girl."

"Or one who follows the law, I'm sure, but that doesn't change anything."

"I think Striker and I need to have a little chat."

"If you think you're going to leverage me out of this by telling him what I said about your father, don't bother. He already knows how I feel. Why do you think he sent me? He's got a sick sense of humor. . . ."

I wanted to call him a liar, but when I thought about it long enough, it was exactly what Striker would have done, just to stick it to the kid.

"He really does. So, got any news for me other than the bad news you already dumped on me, Agent Dawson?"

"Not much yet. Unfortunately. I don't have a whole lot to go on."

"Because there isn't much." I thought about the new information I'd gotten from Jaime and Meg, but kept that to myself. Striker, I would tell. Dawson? Not a chance.

"Maybe I'd have more if you'd tell me about this prior incident—the one from your past," Dawson said.

"Maybe. Maybe not. Either way, you don't get to know about that. And since any record of it seems to be conveniently miss-

ing from the sheriff's office, you can't dig anything up." That
got his attention. "At any rate, thanks for checking up, Agent
Kiss-ass. I'll be sure to tell Striker you've been totally helpful."

I turned to leave, but he caught my elbow, halting me.

"Not so fast, Ms. Danners. I'm not finished yet."

I looked down at his hand then back to him.

"Yeah. I think we are."

He let me go and I started to walk away.

"What's with the little showdown after school the other
day?" he asked. I stopped dead in my tracks and turned to silently face him. "Yeah. I've been watching you, Danners. Like
I said, Striker said to keep an eye on you. I can't help but wonder
if you're not creating some of the chaos you go running to him
about. If you're not—"

". . . Bringing it on myself?" I replied, my voice low and full
of warning. I knew if he said those words I'd lay him out flat,
cop or not.

"If you're not nearly as clever as you think you are. I watched
you practically pick a fight with those three. It looked personal,
and I couldn't help but wonder if it somehow tied back into all
this. If you're meddling in something you shouldn't be."

My jaw nearly hung open. I couldn't believe what I was hearing. Instead of coming down to really investigate, Agent Dawson was keeping tabs on me. He didn't seem to believe I was
in trouble.

He thought I *was* trouble.

"You think I'm lying." It wasn't a question.

"I think that your family name doesn't give me a lot of confidence in your story."

"Did you miss the part where Donovan took a swing at me?
Did I ask for that?"

His expression soured.

"I didn't see that. I saw you baiting the skinny one. I saw his friend hold him back, and then the big one knocked him aside to keep him from going after you again. Then I got a call."

"Then I guess you missed the best part. But please, feel free to judge me on only part of the story. You seem pretty good at that."

"Your dad is guilty. Get over it."

"Just like you're over your mentor's death?" His eye flared with rage. "Yeah. I didn't think so."

He took a step closer to me, leaning his face into mine.

"If you think I'm going to stand here and listen to your tantrum, you're high. I don't give a shit about you or whatever high school drama you've manufactured. I'm here to help Striker help you and further my career. If you don't like me or my methods, too bad. You're stuck with me either way."

I could feel my fist clenching at my side, and I forced myself to close my eyes and take a deep breath. If I hit him, I'd be arrested for sure. I also didn't want to prove him right about me.

When I opened my eyes, I found him staring at me with an amused expression. It was clear that he knew he was getting to me, and he enjoyed every second of it. But before I could reply, I heard the rumble of a truck echoing through the neighborhood. Garrett's truck. His timing couldn't have been any worse.

"Time for you to go, Agent Dawson," I said. He looked over his shoulder at the massive truck pulling up in front of the house.

"Your boyfriend?"

"Best friend."

"The sheriff's kid?"

Guess he'd done a little homework after all.

"That'd be the one."

"Then this should be really interesting." His smile brightened before he wove his arm around my shoulders and bent his head down to my ear. "Time for you to play along, Ms. Danners." I opened my mouth to argue about whatever it was he thought he was doing, but he shut me up with one quietly spoken sentence. "I don't need the son of the sheriff knowing who I am, so be a good girl and follow my lead." While I fumed internally, Dawson turned to face Garrett as he approached. To Garrett's credit, he didn't falter at the sight of us, but I knew he was confused as hell.

"Hey, Ky. Who's your friend?"

"This is—"

"Alex. Alex Cedrics. Ky's boyfriend."

"Ex-boyfriend," I said without skipping a beat. It was all that I could do, though, to keep the disgust off my face.

"Oh. Ky never mentioned you. I'm Garrett." He reached out his hand to shake Dawson's, and the special agent accepted it.

"Well, you know Ky. She's a bit tight-lipped about some things."

"Yeah," I said with a laugh. "You know me. . . ."

"So you're from Columbus?"

"Worthington, actually. Just outside the city."

"Did you guys go to school together?"

"Oh, no. Alex went to *private* school. Hence the old-man outfit he's sporting."

Garrett laughed. Dawson, however, squeezed me in response. A little too tightly.

"We met through friends. I took one look at her and knew she was the girl for me."

"Then we broke up when I left," I added, flashing a smile.

"Which is why I came down here. To talk some sense into her."

"Good luck with that," Garrett said, his eyes bouncing back and forth between me and Dawson. "She's a stubborn ass."

"So I've noticed."

"Okay, Alex. Garrett and I have some homework we need to do. It was great seeing you. We can talk more about this another time. . . ."

"You can count on it," he replied, looking down at me. For a second I was afraid he would try to kiss me goodbye to sell our routine to Garrett, but he didn't. Instead, he pulled me into a hug and pecked me on my cheek.

I fought the urge to rub it right after.

"Call me later?"

"Absolutely." He let me go and turned to Garrett, shaking his hand again. "Nice to meet you, Garrett. Maybe I'll see you soon."

"Nice to meet you, too."

Dawson walked to his car and got in. with a wave through his sunroof, he headed out of the neighborhood, leaving me behind to field the barrage of questions headed my way from my best friend.

"Sooo . . . ex-boyfriend, huh?"

"Please. Not now."

"Why didn't you mention him before?"

"Because he's my ex? I didn't think it was important. And besides, we've been up to our eyeballs in catching up and deal-ing with Donovan. Alex kinda fell to the wayside in light of those things."

"Fair enough."

"Can we just go do some math homework? That sounds way better than rehashing my love life."

"Yeah," he replied with a laugh. "It really does."

Just as I cleaned up my books, needing a break from the home-work marathon, Gramps walked in the front door.

"Hey there, Kylene. Did I just pass young Mr. Higgins on the road?"

"You did. He just left. He was helping me get caught up."

He walked over and gave me a kiss on my cheek, then stood there for a moment, looking down at me in the longing way that adults often did. There was always something distant in their eyes, like they were reliving something that you couldn't understand because they never told you about it later when they snapped out of it.

"Something wrong, Gramps?"

"Wrong? No, darlin'. Just thinkin'."

"About what?"

"You growin' up and leavin' me here. I saw your dress layin' out in your room the other day. Got me to thinkin' about all kinds of stuff. Graduation. College. Your weddin' day. I sure do hope the good Lord lets me live long enough to see it all."

"Aw, Gramps," I said, throwing my arms around his waist. "You will. You're too ornery to die."

"That might just be true, Kylene," he replied with a laugh. "Now, I'm fixin' burgers for dinner. How many do ya want?"

"Two! No, one. I have to fit into that dress from two years ago. It's a bit on the tight side. Best not to tempt fate, right?"

"You girls . . . Boys like a little meat on them bones."

"Yes, well, my size-too-small-for-me-now dress does not."

"You got a date for this dance?"

"Garrett and Tabby are coming with me."

"That's a real good plan, Kylene. Boys may come and go. Your friends will always stick by you."

"Agreed." I let him go and grabbed my book bag off the table. "I'm going to go put this away, then come help you cook."

"I sure would like that."

"I would too, Gramps."

I walked to my room, thinking that Gramps was right. None of us were guaranteed any time on earth, but the older you got, the more that rule seemed to apply. And though Gramps wasn't ancient, he wasn't a spring chicken, either. I needed to make the most of my time with him while I still lived in Jasperville. When Gramps was around, everything seemed a little bit better. A little bit easier. A little bit brighter. To know that one day he'd no longer be around was a thought I pushed far out of my mind.

But it was still a fact that couldn't be ignored.

THIRTY-FOUR

Mr. Callahan actually looked disappointed when I dropped a file of homework on his desk Friday morning. He'd clearly wanted to fail me, but I was confident he'd find one way or another to try to screw up my GPA. He was reliable like that.

I felt like a homework fairy the rest of the day, handing in assignments like a good little student. With homecoming weekend coming up, the teachers went easy on us—except for Callahan, of course. The thought of a virtually homework-free weekend was a dream come true.

At the end of the day Tabby stopped by my locker to let me know that she didn't need a ride home, so I decided I'd take a little drive around the outskirts of town. Refamiliarize myself with the place I'd once called home. It would kill time and get me up to speed on the state of the place. All in all, it seemed like a solid plan.

Unfortunately for me, the plan had to be executed in a less-than-solid vehicle.

After about fifteen minutes of meandering my way down some of the lesser-traveled roads around the perimeter of town, Heidi started to act up. At first it didn't seem like much. Just a slight burning smell. Nothing she hadn't done before. But it quickly escalated until she rolled to a stop, sputtered, then died. Copious amounts of smoke billowed from under her hood. It wasn't looking good for my car. She'd never pulled a stunt like that before.

"You're killin' me, Heidi," I muttered as I opened the driver's side door. The car protested with a loud creak as always.

I reached down and popped the hood before walking around to the front of the car. After a few attempts, I managed to get it open without choking to death. As the smoke cleared, I stared down at the traitorous engine and wondered how in the hell I was going to figure out what was wrong.

Cars were so not my thing.

"C'mon, girl. What's gotten into you today?" Unfortunately, the car didn't respond. With a sigh, I pulled my cell phone out of my pocket and dialed Garrett's number, hoping he'd be finished with whatever errand it was he had to run. The phone rang repeatedly, eventually going to voice mail. I tried texting him next, just in case he was somewhere he couldn't talk, but received nothing in return. "Great . . ."

I was stalled out in front of the old Goodman Tire plant. It had been shut down a few years earlier and now just stood vacant and decaying—a reminder of why Jasperville's economy had plummeted even further. Though the road was still used, it was far from busy. It was a shortcut if you didn't want to take the highway, but not many people bothered anymore. The empty plant was still a sore spot for most.

With Gramps still at work and Tabby without a car until her dad got home, I was pretty much out of options. I looked up a towing company and put a call in. Then I waited.

I'd been sitting in the grass away from the road for at least five minutes before anyone drove by. Unfortunately for me, no one even batted an eye at my car. Chivalry was officially dead.

With a sigh, I stood up and brushed off my pants before heading back to my car. My phone was starting to die and I needed to plug it in. As I leaned in through the open passenger side door, I heard a vehicle roll up behind me. I quickly plugged my phone in and turned the key in the ignition half-way to see if the battery worked. When it did, I did a little happy dance, then backed out of the Honda.

"Well, isn't this convenient." I turned to find Donovan's massive form blocking out the setting sun.

Panic shot through me before I shut it down.

"It sure would be if you'd happened to be the tow truck I called for. The one that will be here momentarily."

"You're not that lucky."

"Apparently not."

He took a step closer to me.

"You know, a girl like you should be careful where she drives in a car that unreliable. You're not too popular in this town. People talk. . . ."

The way he let the comment hang in the air gave me the chills. But instead of retreating like my body begged me to, I held my ground. We may have been relatively isolated where we were, but cars were bound to come by soon enough. I just needed to buy myself time.

"The pharmacy I go to got raided by the DEA today," he said, continuing his slow, methodical approach. "But somehow I bet you already knew that, didn't you?"

"Nope. Didn't have a clue—" He smiled down at me right before he grabbed my wrist in his hand and began to squeeze it. The pain was immediate. His grip was like a vise, and it only worsened when I tried to pull away.

"You think you can shut me down that easily, Danners, but you can't. And you won't. Ever. All you're doing is making me more and more angry." He wrenched my wrist backward, making me roll up to my tiptoes. Then he leaned closer to me, whispering like all clichéd bad guys do. "And reckless."

In the distance, I could hear the thrum of an approaching

engine. Donovan, too busy terrorizing me, didn't notice. I took that moment to capitalize on his oversight.

I drew my left knee back and drove it into his balls as hard as I could. He let me go, collapsing to the ground at my feet. With him no longer blocking my view, I could see the car pulling up behind Donovan's truck. I'd hoped it would be the tow truck I'd called for. Instead, it was Agent Dawson.

Hardly the cavalry I had dreamed of.

I watched as he got out of his car and walked toward us, his aura of arrogance reaching me long before he did. I couldn't see his expression well as he approached, but his aviator sunglasses undoubtedly hid the contempt in his eyes. The second he reached where we were, he took one look at me and Donovan (writhing on the ground at my feet), then started in.

"So, Danners, would you care to tell me what's going on here?"

I wanted to tell him what had happened, but I didn't for two good reasons: One, there were no witnesses, which left me in another he said/she said situation. Two, I still didn't trust the prick.

"My car broke down." Short, simple, and to the point. That was how you answered questions in an interrogation. And I had no doubt that I was in for one hell of one.

"I can see that," he replied, his sharp gaze penetrating through his reflective lenses as it drifted down to Donovan, then back to me. "Did it break down on his balls?"

"No."

"Would you care to tell me why he looks like he might never be able to reproduce one day?"

"Not really."

"I pulled over to help her, and the crazy bitch kicked me in the nuts."

"*Kneed* you," I corrected. "I *kneed* you in the nuts. Let's try to keep the facts straight, okay?"

Donovan tried, but he couldn't stifle the hatred in his eyes when he looked up at me. I wondered if Agent Dawson saw it—saw the beast behind the boy. Once he was finally able to stand, he turned to address the Fed.

"She's completely insane. She needs to be put away—just like her dad."

"Her father is in prison, not a mental-health facility, and though your point might be valid, she's not getting put away. Not today, anyway." Dawson shot me a sideward glance. "So, if you and your balls are good to go, I suggest you head out."

"Who the hell are you?" Donovan asked, stepping up to Dawson like he was about to throw down.

Dawson didn't even flinch.

"Who I am is irrelevant."

"I asked you a fucking question," Donovan said, leaning in closer. After my kick to the groin, it was clear that Donovan was in no mood for Dawson's shit—which made me wonder why Dawson wasn't flashing his badge and cowing him with his FBI trump card.

I sure as hell would have.

"And I told you it's time to go," Dawson said, his voice unwavering. Donovan's jaw flexed while he decided his next move.

Then a sly smile spread across his face, and he started to laugh.

"I see what's going on here," he said, his eyes darting back and forth between Dawson and me. "I'll let this go because it's clear you're thinking with your dick and not your brain, but let me give you a little piece of advice, bro: this town bike has had a lot of miles put on it already. Might wanna try riding something else instead."

Dawson smiled back at him, but it was full of malice.

"Keep it up and I'll let her make it so *you* never ride again."

Somehow, those simple words came out in such a dark and cold and threatening manner that I took a step back from the guys, chills running up my arms. Donovan was scary in a brutish, thug sort of way. But Dawson? He had that eerie calm about him that was totally unnerving.

"Have it your way," Donovan said before walking away. I let loose a sigh of relief as he did, thinking it was all over. But Dawson rained on my parade as soon as Donovan's truck pulled away.

He removed his glasses to pin angry eyes on me.

"You want to tell me what that was about?"

"Is not telling you an option?"

"You know I'm not actually down here to babysit you, right?"

"If you are, you're really bad at it."

"Don't get cute with me."

"You sound like an old man sometimes, you know that?"

"Only because you act like a child. Listen, I keep seeing you mess with this kid. You need to back off. I don't think he's a fight you want."

"And yet he's one of the many I have, so . . ."

"So maybe you should stop sticking your nose where it doesn't belong and let me do my job."

"Do you think I somehow manufactured this scenario? That I broke down on purpose to lure him out here so I could kick him in the nuts? He's the one harassing me, Dawson, not the other way around."

He shrugged. "Maybe. Maybe not. All I know is that, based on what I've witnessed up to now, you're just as likely to have started it as he is."

I stared at him blankly.

"How are you some hotshot rookie at the FBI when your head is planted so far up your ass?"

That question earned me a nasty look.

"Get in the car," he said, pointing at his generic black sedan. When I didn't move, he took me by the arm and started walking me in that direction. I pulled away from him, yanking my arm out of his grip, but as I did, my damaged wrist slid through his hand, causing me to cry out. I pulled it into my chest and rubbed it for a second before releasing it.

"Don't you dare try to make me look like I abused you, Danners, because there's no evidence—"

When he grabbed my hand, his words cut off. Now silent, he stared at the striped red marks on my wrist that were already starting to bruise. He gently turned it over in his hand, assessing the damage. Then his scrutinizing eyes fell on mine.

"You're an asshole, you know that?" I said, taking my hand away. This time, he let me.

"What happened to your wrist?"

"I hurt it."

"Hurt it *how?*"

I could feel my teeth grinding together as my anger grew. I didn't want to tell Agent Dawson what happened. He didn't get to know. He thought I was young and stupid. The daughter of a felon. A meddlesome piece of trash. I didn't want his help or his sympathy. He could shove both up his ass, for all I cared.

"You're a detective," I said coldly. "Figure it out."

With that, I walked toward his car just as the tow truck pulled up. After talking to the truck operator, I climbed into the cab and slammed the door shut on Dawson, who'd been impatiently waiting. He looked like he wanted to follow, but instead he walked to his car and drove off. I breathed a sigh of relief, knowing I didn't have to ride into town with him. The last thing I wanted was to be stuck listening to whatever lecture he deemed necessary that I hear. I didn't really want to go to jail for assaulting an officer of the law. But I knew I would just to shut him up.

THIRTY-FIVE

The tow truck driver took me and Heidi back to Gramps' house. There was no point in dropping my car off somewhere to be fixed. I didn't have the money for that. Thankfully Gramps was a whiz with engines, so I hoped he'd have some time to give it a look. Being without Heidi was like losing a limb. She was my freedom.

After my car was backed into the driveway, I got an invoice from the driver and he pulled back out onto the street and drove off. I breathed a sigh of relief. I was petrified that I'd have to pay him right then and there. And that just wasn't going to happen.

With that bullet dodged, I grabbed my book bag out of the front seat and headed for the house. I'd almost made it through the door when a bad omen arrived. Agent Dawson rolled up and parked out front. He started in on me from the second his car door opened.

"I'm not finished talking to you, Ms. Danners."

"Conversation is a two-way street, hotshot. And this lane is closed."

I slammed the front door in his face—just as he stepped onto the porch. Most people would have taken the hint, but not Dawson. He was a dog after a bone.

He pounded on the door repeatedly. I stood just on the other side of it, smiling. I knew he was probably turning red with anger.

I peeked through the peephole. Yep. Red as a beet.

The banging ceased for a minute and he leaned closer to the door.

"I know you're standing right there, Ms. Danners. I'm going to give you about five seconds before I whip out my badge and start yelling loud enough for the whole neighborhood to hear: 'FBI; I have a warrant.' Would you prefer that?"

My smirk turned to a frown. I knew he wasn't bluffing. Something about Agent Dawson told me he never bluffed. Ever. Just as he began counting down, I opened the door. Apparently, I was a toddler in his eyes.

"So you *can* see reason. That's good to know," he said as he pushed his way past me into the house. "Is anyone else here?"

"Nope. It's just you and me. Want me to pop some popcorn and throw on a movie? It'll be super cozy. I promise."

My tone was so laced with sarcasm that I nearly choked on it. Dawson seemed unamused. In truth, he seemed unamused by most everything.

"What happened to your arm?"

"Why didn't you flash your badge at Donovan to make him go away?"

He looked at me for a moment, then answered.

"I wanted to see how violent he was. See if your claims about him were true."

"And? What's the verdict?"

"Not until you tell me what happened to your arm."

His no-nonsense stance and arms folded across his chest told me he wasn't messing around. He would withhold his answer until I gave him mine.

"You don't want to know."

"Why don't I?"

"Because it would make you wrong about me. And something tells me you don't like being wrong very much."

"You're right. I hate it."

"Then allow me to spare you your self-hatred. Nothing happened. The door's that way," I said, indicating the one he'd just entered.

Instead of leaving, he stepped closer to me, once again taking my hurt wrist gently in his hand to inspect it.

"Donovan did this to you, didn't he?" With a clenched jaw and anger blazing in my eyes, I nodded. His expression devolved further to one of rage. Agent Dawson appeared to be about as much a fan of women beaters as I was. "You should have told me."

"So you could do what? Arrest him? You have no jurisdiction for that, and it was my word against his. I know how well that pans out. Trust me." With a quirk of his brow, I could see him lining up his interrogation in his mind. "Let me stop you before you get going, hotshot. You don't get to know my story. You haven't earned that kind of trust, and I highly doubt you ever could. So don't bother asking."

His features hardened. "Wouldn't dream of it."

"Well, now you got what you came for. . . . Door's still that way."

He hesitated for a second, staring at me like I was a puzzle he just couldn't quite figure out but was determined to. Then, just as he turned to leave, his phone rang. He picked it up and walked toward the front door, answering it as he grabbed the knob.

"Agent Dawson." He was silent for a moment before he turned back to look at me, his eyes wide with disbelief. "I see. Not sure how that involves me. . . ." More silence. "Really? Okay. Where is he now? Yeah. Keep me posted."

He hung up the phone without another word and walked toward me.

"You really don't need to say goodbye. You can just go."

"I'm sorry," he said, shocking the pants off me. "I was wrong about Donovan. I let my prejudice about your family cloud my judgment."

I couldn't even put a sentence together. Instead, I just stared at him, my mouth slightly ajar. When I said nothing, he continued talking. "So that was a buddy of mine from the DEA. Any idea why he might have been calling?"

"Drugs . . . ?"

"Apparently he was called in to aid with an investigation at a local pharmacy here in town."

"Oh?"

"Yes. It seems there was an anonymous call from some high school newspaper regarding fraudulent prescriptions being filled at this particular place. Prescriptions found to be written by a single physician." He eyed me tightly, waiting for a reaction from me.

"Dr. Carle?" He nodded. "And did they find anything?"

"Seems that way. You wouldn't know anything about that phone call, would you?" I just stared at him in silence. "That's what I thought."

I clasped my hands together behind my back to prevent him from seeing them shake. He slowly walked toward me, and I started to wonder if somehow I was in trouble. Big trouble. The kind that might involve bail money.

He came to a stop right in front of me, looking down at me with a harsh, assessing gaze. I tried to steady my breath and calm the tension in my face, but that was hard with Agent Dawson breathing down my neck. Every fiber of my being wanted to bolt out of that room. Instead, I stood there and waited.

"I have to follow up on something one of the guys they brought in said," he told me, his voice serious and low. "My buddy at the DEA seems to think this guy has information related to the case I'm currently investigating. Information that might break it wide open." I stared up at him with bated breath. He paused for a beat. "All because of you. . . ."

I swallowed hard. "Just doing my civic duty."

He said nothing but continued to scrutinize my reaction. It was clear that he saw something in it that fascinated him. I just couldn't for the life of me figure out what that was.

"You're a loose cannon, Kylene Danners. Loose cannons are dangerous."

"Danger's my middle name . . . ?"

His hard hazel eyes brightened for a split second as a wry smile turned up the corners of his mouth.

"I'm sure it is." With that, he turned and walked toward the front door. But before he exited Gramps' house, he looked back at me one last time. "Try to stay out of trouble while I'm gone."

Then he closed the door behind him.

I let out the breath I'd been holding for far too long and collapsed forward, propping myself up with my hands on my knees.

"Holy shit . . ."

While I wanted to celebrate, a part of me—the paranoid one—was freaking out. Donovan suspected it was me that got the DEA involved. Even if he couldn't prove it, that wouldn't matter. I would get the blame. My only hope was that his stash would quickly dwindle and he'd become a quasi-reasonable human being again. Not a solid plan, but the only one I had at the moment.

Suddenly, being home alone seemed like a terrible idea.

THIRTY-SIX

I awoke the next morning to the sound of my phone vibrating violently on the bookshelf next to my head. My eyes were still heavy with sleep as I tried to reach for it, my hand fumbling along the wood surface until I located the phone. I blinked my eyes repeatedly, trying my best to focus them enough to find the talk button. When I finally did, I pressed it and put the phone to my ear.

"Hello?" The word came out in a sleepy slur.

"Guess where I am at the moment," a curt voice replied.

"Who is this?"

"Agent Dawson. Striker gave me your number. Why are you still asleep? It's ten—"

"Because it's Saturday. That's what you do on Saturdays. Apparently you've forgotten." I thought I heard him laugh on the other end, but I couldn't be sure. Maybe I was still sleep-drunk. "What do you want, hotshot?"

"I thought you might be interested to know that Dr. Carle is in with my DEA friend now."

"Holy shit! I so wish I could see how that goes down."

"Yeah, well, that's not how it works. I just wanted to let you know that—" He cut off and started talking to someone in the background. I could hear two muffled voices. A couple of minutes later, he came back to our call. "I have to go. Carle just gave up a lead in my case."

He hung up without another word.

I sat there for a minute, my mind still waking up to the reality that this was really happening. That I'd brought down an illegal prescription drug ring in town. And I wouldn't get to see the man behind it all squirm.

Or would I?

I scrambled out of bed and rifled through my room, grabbing the clothes I'd worn the day before off the floor. After I threw them on, I ran to the bathroom and brushed my teeth while I peed. I barely had time to do either, so I figured multitasking— however gross it might have been—was required. I ran to the kitchen, pulled my hair into a low ponytail, and grabbed a bagel out of the fridge. I was out the door exactly two minutes after I'd hung up the phone, ready to drive to the sheriff's department.

Then I realized I didn't have a car.

I ran back in and grabbed Gramps' keys from the hook by the door and jumped into his truck. I knew he wouldn't need to be at work until two, so I had time. I hoped he didn't need it for anything else before that. But this was just too important to miss.

I took the stance that the speed limit was more of a suggestion rather than an absolute, and really applied that theory on my way to the sheriff's office. I arrived there in seven minutes, hoping Dawson hadn't already started his interrogation.

Then I nearly ran him over in the lobby.

He eyed me curiously when I walked in, looking me up and down. He'd undoubtedly put together that he'd seen me in those clothes the day before. I simply shrugged and walked up to him, unconcerned.

"Did I miss the part of the conversation when I told you to come down here?" Dawson said, sounding incredibly formal.

"You didn't directly tell me not to. . . ."

"You need to go," he said, ushering me toward the door.

"Come on! You wouldn't even be here if it wasn't for me and my genius!"

As annoyed as he looked, he couldn't deny that truth.

"What do you want to know?"

"Did he admit to writing bogus scripts?"

"He did. He essentially admitted that, for the right price, he could diagnose you with whatever you needed to obtain a script for otherwise highly controlled substances." I couldn't help but smile in response.

"I knew it!"

"Not bad, Ms. Danners. Not bad at all. Now, it's time for you to go."

"But I want the gory details!"

"I don't have them, and even if I did, I couldn't share them with you." I stared at him with wide eyes and prayed they'd work on him. I didn't want to blow his case, but man did I want to know how Dr. Carle sweated it out. How he tried to argue his way out of what the DEA already knew. Dawson looked at me, then let out a put-upon sigh. "Sit over there and wait," he said, pointing to a chair in the waiting room. "I don't think this will take too long. Dr. Carle is pretty worn out."

"Want to bet on that?"

He looked over his shoulder at me and I wiggled my brows.

"What's the bet?" he replied.

"Um . . . no clue."

"Fine," he said, sounding put out by having to set the terms. "If you lose, you wash my car."

"Deal," I agreed. "And if you lose?"

He flashed me a devious smile. "Then Alex Cedrics gets to dance with you at your stupid homecoming."

"How is that a win for me? That sounds way more like a threat . . . or punishment."

He laughed at my horror.

"It is. That's why I suggested it."

"Bet's off. Now, get in there and do your job."

"Afraid I might embarrass you?" he asked, quirking a brow. Before I could come up with a retort, he walked away.

I watched him disappear down the hall to where the only interrogation room in the building was. I'd spent more time in there than I'd ever hoped to two and a half years earlier. Shaking that thought from my mind, I sneaked down the hall to the bathroom and ducked in when one of the deputies walked by. Once he was gone, I peeked up and down the corridor to make sure the coast was clear and then ran to the room adjacent to the interrogation room, the one I really hoped no one was waiting in to observe the interrogation. One calming breath later, I grabbed the doorknob and opened the door.

Nobody was in sight.

I let out a sigh of relief as I quietly closed the door behind me and tiptoed over to the one-way mirror. Dawson was standing, leaning forward with his hands braced against the table that separated him and Dr. Carle. The elderly doctor looked scared and exhausted, and I couldn't help but wonder why he hadn't lawyered up yet, especially given the severity of his crimes. I hoped his arresting officer hadn't forgotten to read him his rights. We didn't need another criminal in Jasperville being let off due to police incompetence.

"I'm going to level with you, Doc, for two reasons. One, I'm not in the mood to play games. And two, because you already admitted to having information for me. I don't like being jerked around. For your sake, I hope that's not what you're doing." He paused for a second and rolled up his shirt sleeves in a methodical manner. For whatever reason, he made the act look intimidating—menacing even. "So here's the one-time deal I'm willing to make with you: tell me what you know, and the DEA and the FBI will go easy on you. It's really that simple. We're not after you—we're after the guy behind the curtain. The only downside is that my offer expires in exactly sixty seconds. So what will it be, Doc? Multiple felony charges or leniency?"

I could practically see him weighing out his options. Dawson had strong-armed him, and it was impressive, to say the least. The factor I couldn't quite account for was whether or not he was completely bullshitting the good doctor, or if he'd meant what he'd said.

Or maybe some gray area in between.

"Thirty seconds left," Dawson said, checking the clock on the wall.

"I . . . I need proof that you're not pulling one over on me," Dr. Carle said, trying his best to sound like he had the upper hand in the situation, even though he clearly didn't.

"I'll show you the paperwork now if you need to see it," he said, handing it over to the doctor. He scanned it quickly before asking for a pen.

Once he finished signing, he slid it over to Dawson, and leaned back into his chair with a sigh.

"Where do you want to start?"

"Based on the statement your pharmacist buddy made to the DEA, it seems you were blackmailed into doing this. What I want to know is the specifics as to how." The doctor adjusted himself around in the chair. "Give me something I don't already know, or I'll burn that signed piece of paper and you'll be doing time for multiple counts of prescription fraud. So if you don't want to spend the rest of your life in a penitentiary, I suggest you start earning your keep."

That rattled Dr. Carle's cage.

"I don't know who the blackmailer is. But before you start threatening me, let me explain." I could see the tension in Dawson's back through his shirt. He was coiled for another outburst. Restraint was not his strong suit.

We had that in common.

"I'm listening. . . ."

"All our correspondence was done on paper. No phones. No computers. Just hand delivered, typewritten letters."

"When did you start receiving them?"

"About a year ago. I found a letter waiting for me on my desk at work. Nobody seemed to know who had dropped it off. When I opened it, I was horrified by what it said. In it was a detailed account of something I had done. Something I didn't want anyone to know about.

"I had no idea how this individual came to know about . . . that event, but he did and was more than happy to expose me. It would have been the end of my career, my marriage. . . .

"Then a few months ago, I received another note, outlining that he wanted me to creatively prescribe certain medications for certain patients."

"He wanted you to commit fraud?"

"Yes."

"Tell me why you didn't go to the authorities with the letters."

The doctor gave Dawson an incredulous look.

"I think you and I both know why. To do that would have meant confessing to crimes. So I rolled the dice. And it was a moot point anyway. I burnt the letters as per instructions. I wasn't about to tempt fate and keep one." The doctor fidgeted again in his seat.

"At the bottom of every letter, it was always addressed the same way: 'Advocatus Diaboli.'"

My hair stood on end at those words. Something about them was so familiar. My brain raced to try to place them to no avail, leaving me irritated, but I knew that phrase had meaning to me.

"The Devil's Advocate," Dawson said from the other side of the glass divide. I could see the strain in Dawson's profile. He didn't like this information for some reason or another. Or maybe he just didn't like what it implied. Serial killers and psychopaths loved to hide behind cryptic aliases.

Any way I sliced it, it wasn't a good omen.

Dawson started to pace the room. He came to stand before the mirror—right in front of where I stood on the other side. He stared at it like he could see me. Then he abruptly turned back to Dr. Carle.

"Tell me about the prostitute, Dr. Carle. That's the information I'm here for."

The old man looked like he was about to keel over right there.

"I—I didn't mean for it to happen. I had no idea how old she was. . . ."

"The prostitute? How old was she?"

". . . Sixteen."

"Doctor, are you admitting to me that you had sex with a minor for money?"

He nodded his head.

"Say it out loud."

"Yes, I had sex with a minor for money—but I didn't know!"

Holy. Shit.

"When?"

"Two years ago." His eyes slammed shut as his features tightened. He looked like he was trying not to cry. "I swear I didn't know she was underage!"

"I don't believe you," Dawson roared, slamming his fists down on the counter. "What you've just told me is enough to get a warrant to dissect your life piece by piece, Doctor. Tell me I won't find other incriminating evidence somewhere. Kiddie porn on your home computer? Dubious internet searches? Give us enough time and we will find it."

"NO!" the doctor yelled. "Don't. My wife will find out."

"I think your wife will be the least of your concerns by the time I'm done."

"I'm a pediatrician! I love children. I swore an oath to take care of them. I would never hurt them intentionally!"

"But that's exactly what you did, isn't it? You gave them medications knowing that they had every intention of abusing them, and you sexually victimized another. You're a disgrace to your profession. But you'll have a long time to think about that—in prison."

"No. you can't! You said you'd—"

"The DEA will go easy on you for the fraud. I'm a man of my word and I'll keep that. But you haven't given me enough on who's behind the prostitution ring to reduce your charges. You'll be arrested for soliciting and for sexual assault of a minor. And I'll see to it that you do time. Believe that."

I lunged away from the window, needing to get out of there before Dawson left his interrogation. I stepped out into the hall and took off running—until I slammed right into a disheveled-looking attorney headed toward the interrogation that had just ended.

"Sorry! I didn't see you." When I looked up to apologize, I realized it was Luke.

"Ky, what are you doing here? Are you okay? Did something else happen?"

"No! Nothing like that."

"Did you get arrested?"

"Oh, my God, no! I was just . . . hoping to track down that missing file."

His lips pressed to a thin line. "Okay. Good. I'm glad you're all right. Now if you'll excuse me, I have a client waiting."

"Dr. Carle?" I asked, unable to hide the surprise in my tone.

He looked over his shoulder, eyes narrowed. "Yes. Why?"

I shrugged, hoping to play it off.

"I saw them bring him in and I put two and two together."

His features tightened, marring his normally jovial expression.

"I've got to go. I'll see you later, Kylene."

I waved, then watched him walk into the room that held his guilty client. He was not going to be happy when he found out that Dr. Carle had spoken before he arrived. As I walked toward the main area of the building, I wondered how awful it would be to have to represent someone who'd done what Dr. Carle had done. Luke's love of constitutional rights must have been as strong as his love of football.

I made my way toward the main entrance, almost back to my seat, when someone caught my arm. I turned to find Dawson staring at me. His expression was a blend of emotions—a mix of disbelief, anger, and awe. The urge to smile at him in victory was hard to contain.

"Where were you just now, Danners?"

"The bathroom. Why?" He looked unconvinced but couldn't prove otherwise, so he let it go. "Did you get what you were hoping to? For your case?"

"Yeah. I did."

We stared at each other for a second in silence before he opened his mouth to say something. Just as he started to speak, a guy I didn't recognize rounded the corner and called him over.

"I guess you better go get ready for your big dance now, Danners," Dawson said. "Try to keep your nose clean while you're there. I don't want to get any frantic calls tonight, requiring me to come bail you out."

Prick.

"Don't worry, Dawson. If I wanted someone capable of rescuing me, I wouldn't call you. Your track record is a bit shoddy. And since I seem to have lost the bet, I won't be seeing you there. Let me know when you need that old-man car of yours washed."

THIRTY-SEVEN

Gramps was working on my car when I came home. It was as good as new—windows and all—and ready to take me to the dance. It wasn't sexy, but it was working, which was good enough for me. Gramps started to go into what had happened to Heidi, but I stopped him with a big hug and kiss. I didn't really care what had happened to it. I cared that it was working.

"I'll pay you back when I get my first check," I said, pulling away from him.

"You will not. I got the parts from the salvage yard. Cheaper than filing a claim. You just keep your money for yourself, Kylene. You earned it." I smiled up at him, then hugged him again. Gramps truly was the best. "I left you some money on the kitchen table for tonight, too—in case you kids are goin' out for pizza after."

"Thanks, Gramps."

"I just want you to have a fun night."

"I will."

"Now I gotta go get cleaned up for work. Won't be home tonight, but the rules still apply. Don't be out too late. And no boys at the house, except for Garrett."

"I know, Gramps. I'll be home without issue. Promise."

He gave me his famous side-eye glance, then headed for the

house, wiping his hands on a rag along the way. I followed behind him and made my way to the kitchen to fix him some lunch. I hadn't seen him for a while. I thought a little family time was overdue.

A couple of hours after Gramps left, it was time to get ready for the dance. As I laid everything out in preparation, I realized I needed some things from the store, so I rushed into town to get them. When I got there, I all but ran to the makeup section and stared at a wall of lipsticks until my eyes hurt. After a few minutes, I just grabbed a shade of red I thought would work with my dress, then headed for deodorant.

That was a must.

There was someone in the aisle when I turned down it. His back was to me, but I recognized him right away. Mark Sinclair. Yay for me.

"Mark," I said dryly, reaching for whatever brand of deodorant was cheapest. He turned to look at me. On his forehead was a bruise, and his lip had clearly been split. "Yikes . . . what happened? Kru Tyson go hard on you this morning, or did you get jumped in aisle seven?"

He scoffed and shook his head. "I don't understand you, Kylene. You're a smart girl. Tough. Pretty. But you don't know when to walk away. For whatever reason, you just have to hang around and poke the cooling corpse."

"Are you the cooling corpse in this analogy?" I asked. His expression soured. "I just want to be clear. . . ."

After making his selection, Mark started past where I stood, stopping to whisper something in my ear as he did.

"You need to leave what happened back then alone, understand?"

My blood ran cold.

"Or what, Mark?"

He looked at me, his eyes filled with a mix of frustration, anger, and something else I couldn't quite place in the harsh fluorescent lighting.

"Something really terrible is going to happen to you. . . ."

I drove home with Mark's words echoing through my mind. Something about it just didn't sit well with me, and I couldn't shake that feeling. When I got home, I tried to focus on getting ready for the dance instead, but my home-alone status made me edgy. I watched some ridiculous romantic comedy while I got ready to help ease my anxiety about what he'd said. By the time I'd finally managed to pull up the zipper of my dress, I felt calm.

Before I walked out the door, I looked in the mirror at my reflection and smiled. Mom always said that the right shade of red lipstick on a blonde was a sight to behold. She would have approved of my choice. She would have told me how beautiful I was. She would have cleaned up any rogue makeup and checked my teeth for lipstick before I left. But she wasn't there to tell me those things. She was gone.

Instead, I did all those things by myself, alone in my room.

Then I wiped away the tear forming in the corner of my eye and walked out.

"Well, well, well," Garrett said, standing outside the school, waiting for me. "You're making me rethink my stance on blondes, Kylene Danners."

"Who are you kidding? You're way too stubborn to admit you've been wrong all these years!"

I smiled as I walked up to him and wrapped my arm around his waist. He pulled me into a hug and kissed the top of my head.

"So, you ready for this?"

"Kids dressed in rented tuxes and cheap satin dresses, dry-humping each other on a dance floor? Garrett, this is what dreams are made of."

We laughed as we made our way around to the back of the school, where the gymnasium entrance was. Mobs of students dressed in formal wear were posing outside, getting pictures taken by family and friends as quickly as they could. Given the forecast and the ominous clouds brewing above, it wouldn't be long before it started to pour.

Garrett and I sneaked past them and made our way into the dance. It was just as tacky as I'd expected. Maybe even more so. Streamers hung from every available surface like someone had TP-ed them with rainbow-colored toilet paper. Tables lined the perimeter of the room, each decorated with a barrage of metallic paraphernalia. I was pretty sure the shelves of the party store in town had been raided.

"Sweet Jesus. This place is a train wreck."

"C'mon, Grumpy. Let's get you some punch. Sounds like your blood sugar is dropping." Garrett smiled, pleased with his dig.

"Lead the way."

We made our way over to a refreshment area at the back of the dance. The one that would surely be spiked with some cheap liquor before the night was through. Garrett poured us each a glass and then headed toward a table not far away. We sat and watched as more kids started to come in.

"Let the games begin," I said, raising my glass to Garrett. He clinked his against it and we both took a big sip. If it hadn't gone so poorly for me the last time I drank, I might have been open to doing a shot or two just to get through the night. I really needed something to perk me up a bit.

I needed Tabby.

"When's the eager beaver getting here?" I asked.

"I think she said she'd be an hour late. Her dad's dropping her off."

"I could use some of her sunshine right about now."

"Or you could just witness the awesomeness going on in the corner over there and enjoy." He pointed to a dark corner near the entrance to the gym, where two obviously drunk freshmen were going at it. Apparently the chaperones were asleep at the wheel, because her dress was almost pushed up over her hips before Ms. Davies came flying out of nowhere and accosted the two of them, dragging them out of the room. I was half tempted to go eavesdrop on that conversation. I doubted Ms. Davies would disappoint.

"That was entertaining, but we need something that'll last longer than five minutes."

Garrett laughed. "So, do you want to dance?" I looked at him like he'd been possessed by demons. "I'll take that as a no. . . ."

"Listen, I'll let Tabby drag me out there because her enthusiasm is hard to deny at times. But you I can say no to."

"You're a crappy date." He winked at me and downed the rest of his drink, but my attention was pulled somewhere across the gym.

AJ strolled into the room, looking like he owned the place. He'd always had such natural confidence. It was one of the things that I was initially attracted to. I remembered his swagger the day he walked up to me in the cafeteria and, in front of everyone there, asked me out. It was as if he never doubted

I'd say yes. Not because he was cocky, but because there was an assuredness to him. It made it impossible to say no.

Even for me.

I snapped out of that memory. Occasionally my mind would forget everything that had happened between us—disconnect the AJ I'd once known from the one I thought he'd become.

"Ky, are you listening to me?"

"Huh? What? Oh, sorry. My mind just wandered off. It's been a long day."

"C'mon. We're dancing, and that's final. No thinking tonight. Just fun. Can you handle that?"

"You fight dirty, Garrett Higgins."

We got up and made our way to the mob of students on the dance floor and survived our Tabby-less homecoming time by making each other laugh with nineties-themed battles and quirky moves.

"Hey!" he yelled at me over the music. "Did you hear they shut the Williamson Pharmacy down? Rumor is they were filling bogus scripts."

"You don't say. . . ."

He looked at me, realization dawning in his eyes.

"I don't know how you pulled that one off, Ky, but your dad would be proud."

"Yeah . . . I can't wait to tell him."

Just about the time I was ready to take a break, I caught sight of a redheaded beanpole in a midnight-blue cocktail dress, standing at the entrance to the circus.

"It looks like our special snowflake has arrived," I said, turning Garrett around to see Tabby on the far side of the room. He reached up to wave her over, a smile on his face as he did so. She lit up the second she saw him and came darting across the room toward us.

"This place is amazing!" she squealed. She practically tackled me, wrapping her thin arms around my neck to hug me. Then she disentangled herself and did the same to Garrett. "The decorations are so pretty! And the music . . . I love this song! Why aren't you dancing?"

Garrett shot me a sidelong glance.

"Tabby," I started, giving her my most serious look, "did you drink some happy juice before you got here?"

She blushed. "I snuck a sip or two when my mom and dad were upstairs . . . right before we left the house."

"Okay then, Gingerpants. Let's go see what those skinny legs of yours can do."

As if she'd been waiting for permission, Tabby started dancing, nearly knocking over anyone in her way. Those bony elbows of hers cleared a path for us, and the three of us soon found ourselves having a good time. But just as soon as we'd gotten started, the DJ played a slow song—one I had no intention of dancing to. Garrett looked at me, and I jerked my head at Tabby.

"Don't make Americans look bad," I said, and gave him a pat on the shoulder. "Tabby, go easy on him."

She smiled.

I made my way back to my table while the two of them danced. As I stared out into the crowd, letting my eyes jump from couple to couple without focus, I could sense someone approaching. When I looked over, I found AJ standing a few feet away from me wearing a tentative smile.

"I know what you're probably going to say to this, but—"

"AJ, don't. Please. I'm begging you. Don't—"

"Kylene Danners, will you dance with me?" He reached his hand out to me, and I stared at it. I remembered how much I used to love to hold that hand. How safe and warm it felt when it was wrapped around mine. How, at one point in my life, I'd have let the hand guide me just about anywhere.

But in that moment, I just wanted it to go away.

"I don't want to keep you in suspense, so I'll be blunt. No, I don't want to dance with you. I don't really want to dance with anyone, for that matter. I hate dances. I'm literally here because Garrett and Tabby guilted me into coming."

"Of course. Garrett. Guess I should have known."

"Yes, Garrett. The guy out there dancing with Tabby. Not me. Because Garrett doesn't want me and never has, remember? We've been through all this already. He was your best friend, AJ. You know him better than that. And besides, you know he doesn't go for blondes. Never will."

"Some exceptions are worth making."

The weight of those words and the sadness he clearly felt when he spoke them could not be ignored. AJ Miller was still heartbroken about how things ended between us. He didn't hide it nearly as well as I did.

"Where's your date? Maybe you should try dancing with her. That's kinda how these things work, ya know?"

"I didn't bring one."

"Ah, I see. Going stag so you can pick off the solo chicks. It's a good strategy, though it seems to be slim pickin's."

Intense eyes met mine.

"The pickin's look just fine to me."

"AJ, can we just not do this? I need you to give up. It'll be better for us both."

"I disagree."

"Of course you do. . . ." I sighed, wishing the DJ would play something else so I could go join Garrett and Tabby. As it was, I was considering that option anyway. "Is your plan to just wear me down?"

"Nope."

"Then why must you be such a pain in my ass? I forgive you. Really. Cross my heart and hope to die and stuff. I absolve you of your guilt—again. Now, go, fly away, my unburdened dove. Be free!"

I shooed him with my hand to little effect. Instead, he pulled up a chair right in front of me and sat down. He leaned forward, propping his elbows on his knees as his bright green eyes stared at me.

"Prove it, Ky. Prove you forgive me."

I eyed him dubiously. "Prove it how?"

He reached his hand out for me again. "Dance with me."

"And fuel this delusion of yours—that things can just go back to how they were? Nope. Not doing it."

"One dance. That's all. One dance and I leave you alone."

My eyes narrowed. "One dance and you leave me alone? For good?"

"I won't bother you again."

"For tonight or in general?"

He smiled. "In general."

I sat there and once again stared at his hand as if it belonged to the devil. And I knew how deals with him went.

"One dance. One song. Then you leave me alone for the rest of the year."

"Deal," he said, taking my hand in his and leading me onto the dance floor.

"And the summer, too."

"Of course."

As AJ and I walked to the middle of the floor, I realized that almost everyone there was rubbernecking, trying to see what in the hell was about to happen between us. It made me want to run, so, just to spite them, I didn't. I stayed and held up my end of the bargain.

For a moment, we just stood there and stared at one another. At first, it couldn't have been more awkward. But then he took my hands and looped them around his neck, letting his fingers glide along them as he dropped his to the small of my back. Blood rushed to my face at the contact, my body betraying my mind yet again, and I stepped closer to him so he couldn't see the flush of my cheeks. With my face so close, I could smell the cologne he'd always worn. The one I used to smell on my clothes after our dates. Without thinking, I closed my eyes and breathed it in.

It smelled how love should feel. Warm and sweet, with an edge of something you just can't quite place. Something that keeps you coming back for more.

"Kylene . . ." he whispered in my ear. His hands tightened against my back, pulling me against him, and, for a second, I wanted to stay—wanted to sink into him and let the sway of his body lull me into a state of peace I hadn't known for years. But my mind finally beat down my heart and took control. I withdrew from him enough to put some space between us. Enough that I could think clearly. Enough that I could remember the present and not the past.

"Let's just get this over with," I said softly, unable to meet his gaze.

"How you flatter me," he replied with a laugh.

"This is strictly business for me," I said, not sounding nearly as convincing as I'd have liked. "A means to an end."

"Are you sure about that?" he asked, his tone confident and alluring.

I knew what he was doing—baiting me into a playful argument—but I had no intention of falling for it. I needed to suck it up for one song, and then he would be gone. I needed to keep my eyes on the prize.

"Do you remember homecoming freshman year?" I said nothing in reply. "You and Garrett thought it would be an amazing idea to go to Matthew's Ice Cream Shop afterward to try to eat the Super Sundae Special. I'm pretty sure I warned you both, but you were convinced that with your combined eating power, you could take it down." He kept talking like I wanted to take his trip down memory lane. "Fast-forward thirty minutes, and the two of you were bent over puking in Mrs. Pomodoro's front lawn. I'd never seen more vomit in my life."

"You really know how to charm a girl, AJ. . . ."

"Do you ever think about those times?"

"Against my will? Yes. But then I just see flashes of my girls plastered on the internet, and my mind gets with the program and blocks out that year of my life."

He paused for a second, and I looked up at him, wondering what his deal was. His expression was pained, like what had happened to me still haunted him as it did me.

"Ky, I feel like I did everything wrong back then. I was young and freaked out, and I fumbled every ball I could have in the aftermath. I was scared that I was going to go to jail, and that fear clouded my judgment. Garrett was right: my actions didn't support my words."

"AJ—"

"What Garrett didn't know was why. That my dad left my mom with nothing when he bailed on her. How there wasn't going to be any money for college. I'm smart, but not like you are. I would never have gotten a full ride on academics alone. Football was my chance to get a free education. But if you think I haven't hated every moment I've spent with those assholes— that I cringe when I listen to them in the locker room—you're wrong. I keep my head down and I do what I need to. That's all. Those guys aren't my friends. Christ, how could they be? One of them did that to you, and if I ever find out who it was—"

"AJ!" I said, cutting him off. "Enough. Just leave it alone."

"I can't," he said, leaning down so close I could feel his breath on my cheek. "I still love you, Ky. . . ."

"No," I said, shaking my head as I pushed away from him.

"I need you to know that."

"I didn't sign up for this," I said, finally freeing myself. "I have to go."

Before he could argue, I stormed away from him, shoving my way through the forest of coupled bodies. I needed to get some air, or at least get away from the emotional mess that AJ was about to make of me.

I'd almost made it to the periphery of dancing students—was almost free—when I saw someone who stopped me dead in my tracks. Standing before me, clean-shaven in a sleek black suit that was anything but old man–ish, was Dawson. The smug, satisfied look on his face snapped me from my utter disbelief. I quickly replaced it with hostility.

"Dawson," I said with a sigh. "What are you doing here? I'm so not washing your car right now. . . ."

"I didn't break Dr. Carle as fast as I'd wanted to."

"So you got all dressed up and came over here to tell me that?"

"I lost the bet, Danners. And I'm a man of my word. I take that very, very seriously."

"This is adorable, really, but I don't think you can afford to have Donovan see you here," I said sternly.

He shot me a look of utter incredulity.

"He's not here. I checked."

"Tell me this is all a joke. *Please*," I said. His silence was not encouraging. "I can't take much more tonight. I feel like it's raining nightmares in here. . . ."

"Am I really that awful?" he asked, his expression giving nothing away.

I hesitated. "I literally don't know how to answer that question."

"Then how about you shut up and dance with me so I can feel as though I've fulfilled my end of the deal, okay?"

I looked back over my shoulder to see AJ staring at me, a mix of emotions I couldn't read flaring in his eyes. Then I turned back to find Dawson glaring over me in AJ's direction.

"What were you in such a hurry to get away from when you nearly ran me over?" he asked, still looking past me to where AJ stood.

"Take your pick. This music. These people. These horrendous decorations—"

"Okay. Have it your way." His enigmatic reply gave nothing away, but the intensity of his gaze when it returned to me meant something. I just wasn't sure what, exactly. "But we're dancing."

I sighed as yet another torturous slow song began.

Before I could begin to argue, he took my hand in his, then looped his free arm around my back. I placed mine on his shoulder and took a cleansing breath.

"You clean up pretty nicely there, Danners."

"Shhh," I scolded. "No talking. Just dancing—"

"Dresses suit you."

"Silence suits you."

"So tell me something, what did you do to that poor kid, anyway?" he said, ignoring my jab entirely. "He did not look happy to see me."

"Yes, yes, Dawson. You're sooooo big and scary. I'm sure everyone here is absolutely petrified of the big bad federal agent who's come to make me miserable."

"Oh no, Danners. Tonight, I'm just Alex, your questionably ex-boyfriend."

"I fail to see the questionable part, but . . ."

He only laughed in response. The all-knowing tone of it didn't sit well with me. I pulled away from him enough to see his amused expression highlighted by the twinkling lights that hung from the ceiling.

"What's so funny?"

"Nothing, Danners. Maybe you should take your own advice and be quiet so you can hear the music."

While I fumed, the DJ switched gears and put on something a little too peppy to dance the way we were. The second the tempo increased, I pulled out of Dawson's arms.

"Thanks for the dance, hotshot. Next time, remind me to refrain from making bets with you."

I started for the door to the hallway. Dawson didn't follow. The urge to look back at him grew, if for no other reason than to see if he was as excited to get out of there as I was.

In my attempt to escape him, I slammed into Amy, who was walking into the gym just as I was leaving.

"Sorry!" I said, spinning around to see if she was okay. Her wide eyes and pale face stared back at me for a moment. Then she grabbed me by the arm and dragged me down the hall to the far set of double doors, where we were alone. "Amy, what's going on?"

She looked around before pulling me into the water-fountain nook.

"I don't know who else to turn to about this," she said, her hands fidgeting with every sequin on her black dress.

"Is it Donovan again?" I asked, keeping my voice as gentle as I could and still be heard over the bass resonating through the hall. She shook her head.

"Those pictures that were taken of you," she started, looking embarrassed. "Someone did the same to me. I don't even know when or how, but I've seen them, and I'm scared he's going to post them."

"Who, Amy? Who took them?"

"Mark Sinclair . . ."

I felt my heart drop to my stomach, then slam back into my chest.

"When did you see them?"

"Donovan and I were over at his house yesterday. They went outside to do something, and I stayed in. I just wanted to put some music on, so I opened up his laptop . . . and they were right there, like he'd just been looking at them before we came over." My stomach roiled at the thought. What a sick bastard. "I didn't know what to do, so I ran outside and told Donovan I wasn't feeling good. He took me home, but it didn't take him long to figure out I was lying. I was terrified to tell him, thinking he'd blame me."

"But you told him anyway?"

She nodded.

"He threatened to go over there; he was so angry I thought he'd kill him, Kylene. I really did. He eventually left and came back thirty minutes later. He wouldn't tell me what happened, and I knew better than to push too hard."

"Is Mark here now?"

"Yeah. He's got a cut on his lip and a bruise on his forehead, but he's here." She cringed, folding her arms over her stomach. "Who does something like that?" she asked, hoping I'd have an answer. But I clearly didn't. "How can he act like nothing is wrong?"

"I don't know, Amy. But I'm damn well going to find out." I started to walk away, but she stopped me, jumping right in my path.

"Please don't do anything here. I don't want a scene. . . ."

"I need you to go back in there and act like everything's normal, okay? Can you do that?" She nodded frantically. "Good. I'm going to go get proof of Mark's sick little pastime."

I hurried down the hall and back into the gym. Garrett was talking to Dawson while Tabby's head popped up every now and then from the center of the dance floor. I finally caught Garrett's attention and he came over. With utmost efficiency,

I filled him in on everything Amy had just told me. His head whipped around to search the crowd for Mark, but we didn't have time for that. He and I were about to go get the evidence we needed.

Tabby spotted us as we slipped out of the gym and was soon at our sides, asking what was up.

"Tabby," I said, using my most serious voice. "Garrett and I are going to go get proof that Mark Sinclair took those pictures of me. We need you to stay here and make sure that neither Mark nor his parents leave, okay? You know who Mr. Sinclair is, right?"

"Yeah . . . he teaches my AP chemistry class."

"Perfect. His wife is here chaperoning. She's wearing a short purple dress and I just saw her circling the perimeter of the room. I need you to call me if any of them leaves, okay? Can you do that for us?"

"I feel like I should come, too," she argued.

"Listen, North of the Border, Garrett and I don't want to get caught in the middle of a B and E; we need you to make sure that doesn't happen." She looked at me, clearly torn. "Besides . . . I think committing that crime is a gray area for possible deportation, and I can't afford to have you shipped back to Canada. I need you here."

I shot Garrett a look, and he nodded in agreement.

"We both do."

After a moment's contemplation, Tabby finally nodded, accepting her role in the plan.

"What about Alex—your ex? You're just bailing on him?" Garrett asked. Tabby shot me a confused look, and I shook my head. We had no time for that discussion.

"He'll be fine. He wasn't supposed to come anyway. He'll figure it out." I turned and took Tabby's hands. "Remember. If any of those three leaves, you're on the phone with me the next second, got it? His parents live at the end of a private road. We need time to get out of there."

"I've got it," she replied with a nod. Then she gave us each a crushing hug and told us to be careful before she disappeared back into the gym.

"So, what's the plan?" Garrett asked as the two of us made our way to the main exit.

"I'm going to grab my gym stuff out of my car, and then we can take your truck out to Mark's." His serious expression broke for a second, allowing a smile to spread across his face.

"You've always wanted to get naked in the back of a truck, haven't you, Danners?"

"Yes. And I've manufactured this entire plan just to make that happen, so if you'd be so kind . . ." I pointed to his truck in the parking lot, and he shook his head.

"Don't make me regret doing this," he said as he stepped out into the rain and ran toward his truck. I ran to Heidi and grabbed my gym bag from the car. By the time Garrett pulled up in front of me and I climbed in, I was practically drenched.

I wiggled my shorts up over my wet legs while Garrett drove, then slipped my sneakers on. Was I certain about what we were doing? No. But we were going to do it nonetheless.

We were about to embark on a potentially felonious adventure. One that would prove once and for all who had violated me—and others, apparently. With my resolve intact, I stared out at the storm as Garrett raced through town. In next to no time at all, I would have the evidence needed to help bring down Mark Sinclair.

The One.

THIRTY-EIGHT

The drive should have only taken about twenty minutes in good weather. However, the downpour had made the winding dirt roads more treacherous to drive on. Before long, they would start to wash out if the storm kept up. Because Jasperville was in a valley, nestled in the foothills of the Appalachian Mountains, flash flooding happened. I just hoped it wouldn't that night.

It was pitch-black when we reached the outskirts of town. With the storm looming, I saw few cars on the road. No headlights cut through the darkness but Garrett's. The low-lying clouds and the heavy veil of rain created an eerie haze in front of us—a thick, glowing aura of creepy that reminded me of a bad horror movie. Garrett dimmed his lights to decrease the effect and turned left onto Mayfield Road, headed toward the Sinclairs'.

We finally came upon the one-lane bridge that crossed Midler Creek. The one knocked out by water during the last big flood a few years back. Though the storm was nothing like that one, I got a nervous feeling in my stomach as Garrett drove over it. Getting trapped on the other side with no means of escape was so not what I needed. I cast a dubious glance at the dark sky above me and exhaled.

I hoped luck would be on our side.

He rolled across the bridge at a moderate pace. It was difficult to see the railings with the thick fall of rain around us. Halfway across it, I could hear the roar of the water underneath.

I sighed as the truck's wheels gripped the dirt road on the far side of the bridge.

With the storm threatening to ruin our plans, Garrett drove as quickly as he could on the bumpy dirt road. It quickly began to turn to mud, and I wondered how long it would be before the whole thing started to run like a river. At least I knew Garrett's truck could get through it. That we wouldn't be stuck there—providing the creek didn't flood.

Unfortunately for me, the creek was the least of my worries that night.

A couple of minutes after we crossed the bridge, we turned up the Sinclairs' private road. We drove for a while until Garrett turned the truck into an overgrown path of sorts. He said it led to some old fishing spot deep in the property, and that we'd be wise to hide the truck there, just in case someone came home.

"It's not far to the house from here. We're already wet. A little rain isn't going to hurt us at this point," he argued, slipping out of his suit coat. He jumped out of the truck, and I did the same, rounding the back of it to meet him. Together, we walked up the packed dirt road toward the top of the hill where Mark's house stood. I filled Garrett in on my plan as we made the trip.

"So Tabby is going to call if any of them leave, right?" Garrett asked, fishing his phone out of his pants. He stared at it for a moment with a look of concern.

"What is it?"

"I don't have any service here. Do you?"

I made a move to grab my phone, then realized it was still in Garrett's truck. That I'd forgotten to grab it.

"Shit! It's in the truck."

"Not helpful, Ky."

"I know that, Garrett. It's not like I have a lot of places to put it," I said, lifting my pocketless skirt for effect. "I'm going to run back and get it. You go ahead and see if you can find an open window or something. Hell, maybe the front door is unlocked." He looked like he was going to argue with me, but I shut him down. "We don't have time to waste. You go. I'll catch up in a minute."

"All right. Just hurry, okay?"

"I'll be right behind you."

I turned and took off at a jog. It was dark, but I could make out the road and stuck to the middle of it to avoid washed-out spots along the edge. As soon as I had my phone, I'd be good to go. The flashlight on it was really powerful.

It took longer than I'd expected to get back to the truck. The road deteriorated the farther from the house I got, forcing me to walk. By the time I got there, I figured Garrett would have panicked and doubled back. I opened the door, grabbed my phone and his coat so I had somewhere to put it, then shut the door.

I looked down at my phone; it was almost eleven o'clock, which meant it was even later than I'd hoped. I checked to see if I had any service, only to find out I didn't. Whether it was the storm or the patchy service in the woods around Jasperville, I didn't know. I just hoped it got better as I neared the house.

Just as I was about to round the back of the truck and head back up toward the house, I heard the heavy fall of feet approaching. They grew louder as they neared. Garrett, being the reliable kid he was, had indeed doubled back to see what the holdup was.

"I'm coming!" I shouted as I started toward him. "The road was shit." Garrett said nothing in response. "Aw, c'mon . . . don't be pissy. I didn't keep you waiting that long."

"Long enough," a man replied.

By the time my mind registered whose voice it was, a blinding pain shot through the side of my head and I crashed to the ground. A ringing sound distorted his voice as he hovered over me, his massive silhouette shrouded in darkness. I turned my phone's flashlight up toward him while I struggled to make my vision focus. As the two blurred forms converged, my fear was confirmed.

Donovan Shipman was about to get his revenge.

THIRTY-NINE

"You really shouldn't keep a man waiting. We don't like it."

I said nothing while I tried to get my bearings, my head still ringing.

"What's that? Nothing clever to say, Danners? Finally at a loss for words?" Donovan taunted me as he loomed above me, a threat far greater than the storm raging down on us. "Maybe if you'd learn how to butt out, you wouldn't find yourself in this position. But you can't do that, can you, Danners?"

As I tried to roll onto my forearms and push up onto my hands and knees, I opened my mouth to respond. But before I could, I was met with a crushing kick to my ribs, knocking me onto my back. I screamed in pain and instantly regretted it. He'd broken ribs with that blow. Breathing was officially a challenge.

"I have to say, this is going to be a lot less fun than I expected if you're just going to lay there and take the beating." I clutched my side and tried to calm my breathing. My diaphragm was in spasm, and if I didn't get it to chill out in a hot hurry, I was screwed. I'd have no shot at getting away from him. As it was, it wasn't looking good for me. Garrett was my only hope of escape. "C'mon, Danners. Make me work for it," he taunted, pushing at my limp legs with the toe of his boot. "At least Garrett put up a fight. I really expected more from you. Looks like you're all bark and no bite."

Fear crept through my pain-racked body, dulling the effects of Donovan's punishment. He'd already gotten to Garrett. God only knew how badly he'd hurt him. I needed to get away and get help. I needed to save Garrett and myself.

With a clearer mind, I let my training take over. When Donovan took a step closer to me, I saw my chance. I back-swung my leg toward him, clipping his legs out from under him. He fell like a massive tree cut down at the base. The second I saw that he was headed for the ground, I scrambled to my feet—wincing in pain—and grabbed my phone. Then I was running up the road toward the Sinclair house and Garrett.

"You bitch!" Donovan screamed after me. I hadn't really hurt him, only bought myself some time. If I didn't find a way to put more distance between us, I'd be in real trouble. Knowing he was after me, I crashed through the brush into the woods, hoping to lose him in there. My flashlight function was off, making it harder for me to navigate through the trees, but it kept him from easily knowing where I was.

I slipped on the wet ground, almost falling several times. The pain in my ribs stabbed through me with every breath, but I continued to barrel my way through the woods, heading in the direction I thought I needed to. With every step I took, I could hear Donovan not far in the distance, closing in on me.

"I'm going to kill you, Danners, just like I killed your little friend."

His words were indigestible. My mind refused to let them in, not allowing the weight of them to be processed. Garrett was dead? Nope. My brain wasn't having any of that.

Instead of letting Donovan's claim paralyze me, like he'd intended, I let it drive me forward through the pain and the overgrown brush and the fear that if he caught me, I was screwed. My head was swimming from a mild concussion, which made navigating the woods more challenging than it already was. The only advantage I had over Donovan was my size. I could fit through things that he had to bulldoze his way through. I knew that if I could choose my path wisely, I would keep precious distance between us. Distance I needed to get to the house, cell reception, and Garrett.

Hopefully, I'd find him alive.

"There's no way out of this one, Danners." I bit my lip to keep from responding. He was baiting me and I knew it, but that knowledge didn't make it much easier to keep my mouth shut.

Thunder clapped around us following a bolt of lightning that must have struck the ground not far away. Maybe a mile or two at best. It seemed Donovan Shipman wasn't the only deadly thing chasing me.

I dared to slip my phone out of my pocket during the almost constant flash of lightning that refused to cease. I needed to see if I had reception yet. I needed to call for help. Unfortunately for me, that wasn't the case.

"Dammit!" I cursed under my breath.

My side was seizing up with the injury to my ribs, making it almost impossible to run anymore. Hiding behind a massive tree trunk, I searched my surroundings as the sky erupted with more flashes of light. I could see a mound of rocks in the distance, and I decided that hiding there might be my best bet. With any luck, Donovan would pass me before he realized I had hidden from him. The storm was loud, the wind rustling the dying leaves in the trees. It was possible he wouldn't notice the absence of my footsteps.

It was possible that he would, too.

I rolled the dice and took my chances, deciding that if I didn't get a minute to rest, he'd catch me sooner rather than later. And even if he did find where I had chosen to hide away, at least I'd have the upper hand for a few seconds. I clutched a big rock in my hand; if I got a good swing at his head, it'd do some damage. The kind I needed to impair him enough to get away.

Tucked down against the far side of the big rock jutting out of the ground, I tried to slow my breathing. In the nose, out the mouth, and repeat. I could practically hear Kru Tyson telling me that over and over again, just as he had when I trained under him—especially when we were sparring. "If you can't control your breathing, you can't control the fight," he'd say while making me do burnout-punching rounds on the heavy bag until I could barely feel my shoulders or lift my arms. "Your opponent isn't going to stop coming at you because you're tired, Kylene. Work. Dig deeper. Try harder." The memory of his tough love was just what I needed in that moment. Donovan wasn't going to stop coming for me. I needed to dig deeper. Try harder.

Live longer.

Just then, I heard Donovan calling for me off in the distance—much farther away than he had been before. My plan had worked. He'd lost my trail. With determination coursing through me, I slipped around the rock and started back toward the road, cutting a new path along the way. One that aimed toward Mark's house, or at least the direction I thought it was.

I eventually reached a clearing of sorts, one that likely delineated the edge of the property. It was a welcome sight, but it left me without any cover. I decided to chance it, and ran across the field of knee-high grass as fast as I could. Lightning still cut through the sky around me, a jagged reminder of just how exposed I was. I was easily the tallest thing out there—a beacon for the lightning to strike. I reminded myself that at least a bolt of lightning would be a quick way to go. Donovan's methods would be far less humanitarian.

The land started to take a turn uphill, forcing me to bear-crawl up it. It was far too wet and unstable to climb it any other way. By the time I crested the top of it, I was caked in mud and grass. I must have looked like a nightmare, which only seemed fitting given that I was living one.

And that's when I saw it. Somewhere off in the distance, a building whose exterior was brightly lit. I was almost there.

With renewed strength, I held my broken ribs in place and ran, pumping my good arm wildly. I knew that Donovan had likely figured out that I'd tricked him, and that if he had, he'd be heading back here to cut me off. Time still wasn't my friend.

Cell service, however, would be, once I reached the house.

It seemed like an eternity, but I eventually found myself standing in the long gravel driveway. I could see Donovan's truck parked down at the bottom of it, where he'd tried to hide it behind a cluster of bushes. I ran there, hoping to find Garrett nearby—alive. Unfortunately, he was nowhere to be seen. I opened the door to Donovan's truck to find his keys dangling in the ignition. I snatched them, not trusting that Donovan wouldn't do the same when he returned. A part of my brain was screaming for me to steal the truck and escape, but I couldn't. Even if I had been willing to leave Garrett there, I wasn't certain I'd return with help in time to save him.

So I went to find Garrett.

With my cell phone in hand, I headed toward the house, dialing Agent Dawson. He may have been a pain in my ass, but he was nearby and reliable, and not a big fan of Donovan. He was my best bet if I wanted to get out of this alive. I heard it ringing as I pressed it to my face like the lifeline it was. It rang and rang, and my heart raced with anticipation, awaiting his voice on the other end of the line. But that voice never came. Instead, a digital recording sent me to his voice mail.

I nearly screamed in frustration.

I left a message—a frantic, rambling message telling him where I was, who was after me, and that Garrett had been hurt, was possibly dead. I choked on those final words, then hung up. Wondering if I should dare call the sheriff. He may have been dirty, but dirty enough to let his own son fall victim to the people he was in bed with? I found that hard to swallow. With phone in hand, I ran toward the house, seeking shelter from the glow of the outside lights. I needed somewhere to hide and call the sheriff.

Then I needed to find Garrett.

I ducked in behind the far side of the front entry stairs. They were wide and flanked by evergreen shrubs of all sorts, which would hide me away from Donovan. As I dialed the phone, my heartbeat hammering in my ears, I heard something off in the distance. A cry of some sort. It was drowned out by the howling winds, but I could hear it nonetheless. It sounded like a wounded animal.

"Sheriff's department—"

"My name is Kylene Danners. I'm up at the Sinclair residence with Garrett Higgins. We've been assaulted by Donovan Shipman; he's at large. I think he's coming back for us."

Again, while the dispatcher was firing questions at me, I heard that same cry in the distance, but stronger this time. More familiar. And clearly human.

Garrett.

Without thinking, I bolted from my hiding place out into the storm, headed in the direction I thought I'd heard his voice. I wanted to scream his name but couldn't risk it. With the lightning still dancing across the sky above, I dared to turn on my flashlight for a short time, aiming it along the tree line on the back side of the property. At first, I saw nothing and was discouraged, knowing my friend was out there, possibly dying, and I couldn't see him. But just as my frustration threatened to overtake me, I saw a flash of white.

A white undershirt stained with blood.

I took off in a sprint, turning off the light to remain as inconspicuous as possible. He wasn't that far away, but it seemed to take ages to reach him. When I finally did, I slid on my knees to his side, rolling him over to face me.

I gasped at the sight.

His face had been beaten—badly. His eyes were so swollen they could barely open. His cheeks already bruising. And that's just what I could see in the dark of night. Needing to know what other injuries he'd sustained, I turned on the flashlight and began searching his body. He moaned as I lifted his shirt, and I shushed him gently, trying to soothe him.

His torso was one large mass of purple and black.

Whatever Donovan had done to him, he'd done it well and thoroughly. He hadn't left an inch of flesh unmarred. How Garrett wasn't dead from internal bleeding was beyond me.

"Garrett?" I cried, choking back a sob. He simply groaned in response. "I'm going to get you out of here, okay? You're going to be all right. Do you hear me? You're going to be fine."

I could feel my fear bleed to anger.

Fear paralyzed.

Anger motivated.

The dispatcher was still talking to me on the line, but I ignored him, tucking my phone away in my jacket pocket, but I left the call going just in case. I looked down at my friend, who was most likely dying, and tried to figure out how to carry his massive body to Donovan's truck. Then reason won out. There was no way I could get him to it, but I sure as hell could drive it to him. It was a hopped-up 4x4, with off-roading capabilities, not unlike Garrett's. A soggy lawn wouldn't stop it.

"Listen to me. I'm going to get the truck. I need you to hang on for me. Okay? Just hang on. I'll get you out of here."

He didn't respond, which only heightened my anxiety about his condition. I took off running back around the front of the house to the driveway where Donovan's truck was parked behind the bushes. I didn't bother looking for him. I had a one-track mind in that moment, and it involved getting behind the wheel. I knew I'd use the truck as a weapon if I had to. Running Donovan over with it seemed an appealing idea, especially after seeing what he'd done to Garrett.

I wouldn't have thought twice, given the opportunity.

Only feet away from the truck, I fumbled with the keys in my jacket pocket, trying to fish them out without breaking my stride. I managed to hold on to them while I pulled them out and hit the automatic start button. The truck roared to life, and I felt the tiny butterflies of victory flutter inside me. With it, I could get Garrett and get the hell out of there. Providing the bridge was intact, the truck would likely be able to cross it. And I was willing to take that chance either way.

Staying trapped on this side of it with a psychotic Donovan Shipman just wasn't an option.

I ran up to the truck, yanking the door open to jump in. A boot to my chest welcomed me, knocking me back onto my ass on the wet lawn. I slid a few feet back, trying hard to force air back into my lungs. While I did, Donovan hopped out. He stalked toward me like a lion ready to pounce on his kill.

Or soon-to-be kill.

"It's over, Donovan," I wheezed, scrambling backward. "I called the sheriff's office. They know we're up here. They know you're after me."

He looked down at me for a moment, then laughed. It was loud and booming, and illustrated exactly how unhinged he'd become.

"You still don't get it, do you, Danners? You don't see that none of that matters."

"You think the sheriff isn't going to rat you out when he sees what you've done to his son?"

He shook his head no.

"I'm not going to be here when they find the bodies."

My heart dropped into my stomach.

"They already know it's you that attacked us, Donovan. I told them. It's on record."

"Really?" he replied, feigning surprise. "Because I have a feeling that when they go looking for this alleged call, they won't find a thing."

"Bullshit!" I yelled, regretting it the second my diaphragm pulled on my ribs.

"'Fraid not, Danners. The sheriff's department will make this look however they need it to. That's what they did when your tits ended up all over the internet."

His words settled on my addled brain, clearing it completely.

"It wasn't Mark. . . ."

At that, he laughed.

"You're so predictable, Danners. You and Higgins both. At the slightest whiff of a lead, you act first and think later. Setting Mark up didn't take a whole lot of work. I thought using Amy would be a nice touch, though, since you two have something in common now. . . ."

"You took those pictures of her."

His wicked smile widened.

"I thought I might need leverage one day."

"But Jaime said you were in the basement that night . . . that it was the other three that went to the hot tub."

"Oh, they did . . . right after I finished taking those pictures of you on AJ's camera." His smile gleamed in the light of the moon. I watched helplessly as it came closer. "And you've blamed AJ for it all along."

I tried to sit up as he neared me, my ribs screaming in protest. I needed to look him in the eyes, even if it would be the last thing I ever saw.

"Why? Why would you do it?"

He shook his head, then reached for my face, running his finger along my jaw.

"It's a shame you don't remember. You brought this on yourself, really. I tried to kiss you that night, and you pushed me away. You looked so repulsed by me. . . . Nobody disrespects me like that. Not ever." He grabbed a fistful of my hair and yanked my head back. "So I'm going to get that kiss now, Danners. And then I'm going to make you disappear."

His lips crashed into mine, and I struggled against him to no avail. His grip was like iron. Then, as quickly as it started, it was over. He shoved me down to the ground and got up, walking back to his truck.

"How you feeling about your detective skills now?"

"I may have failed to figure out what happened that night, but I shut your little drug operation down, didn't I?"

"For now . . ."

My eyes went wide with realization.

He nodded in response.

"Who's got that kind of power, Donovan? Nobody around here does."

He laughed again.

"She can be taught!" He shouted those words at the pretend audience he apparently wished was witnessing our showdown.

"Why would anyone go to these lengths to help you, though?

Help any of you. Yeah, you can play football, but that's it. I highly doubt whoever is behind this is backing you so you can play college ball. . . ."

"You don't get to know the why, Danners. And even if I told you, it wouldn't matter. You won't be able to talk once I'm done with you."

He pulled a baseball bat out from the cab of his truck and my body went stiff. The devastation to Garrett's body made a whole lot more sense. He hadn't just beaten him up. He'd nearly bludgeoned him to death.

Twirling it around on the palm of his hand, he approached me, making a spectacle of what he was about to do. I crab-walked backward, trying to get away from him, but I knew my efforts were futile. I couldn't outrun him. I couldn't effectively stand and face him. All I could do was dodge the blows for as long as possible before the inevitable occurred—they started landing.

Holding the bat with both hands, he raised it over his head, prepared to slam it down on me. I stared up at him with fear in my eyes—the fear that racked my body. I'd always thought I'd go down with a fight. Thought I'd never give up. But as I looked up at his hate-filled expression, I knew it was over.

So I screamed.

I screamed so loud that I thought my eardrums would rupture. Even Donovan winced at the shrill sound of it. It was enough to buy me a precious few seconds. The seconds I needed to save my life.

"Drop the weapon!" I heard off to my left. Donovan's gaze fell to the far side of the truck, where Agent Dawson stood, gun drawn and pointed right at him. "I said, drop your weapon. NOW!" Donovan did no such thing. Instead, he looked back down at me and smiled—a twisted, ugly smile that illustrated just how far he had devolved. "Last warning, Shipman. Drop it and back away from the girl, or bullets start flying. Do you understand me?"

"I just need to finish up here first," he replied, coiling to hit me with the bat. In utter disbelief, I watched him swing it down toward me with unimaginable force. I closed my eyes, poised for the killing blow. But it never came. Instead, an ear-splitting sound rang out through the clearing. I rolled to my side, covering my head. Moments later, a limp body collapsed to the ground beside me, arms and legs akimbo. Donovan's empty eyes stared at me unblinking, and I could not force myself to look away.

I started to scream once again.

"Kylene?" a voice called. I could barely hear it over my hysterics. "Kylene? Are you okay? Look at me! Look. At. Me!" Agent Dawson grabbed my face and turned it away from the body lying next to me. Instead of a cold, dead stare, I found one filled with anger and concern. The combination was strange on him. Irritation and indifference seemed more natural. "Are you okay?"

"Yeah." My reply was weak and shaky, and the perfect representation of how I felt in that moment. "Is he . . . ?"

"No, he's not dead. He's unconscious. I shot him in the leg, then pistol-whipped him. He'll live. For now. Let me see where you're injured."

He reached for my arm to guide me up, and I yelped from the pain. Realizing that I wasn't as okay as I'd claimed, he gingerly scooped me up in his arms and placed me in the driver's seat of Donovan's truck.

"Garrett! We have to get him to a hospital right away. Donovan beat him so badly—he must have internal bleeding."

"Where is he?" Dawson asked, his tight expression all business.

"Over that way. Get in. I'll drive us there. It'll be easier."

Without the argument I'd anticipated, he got in the passenger side, and the two of us sped to Garrett. The storm had let up slightly, but the yard was still a muddy mess. I had to slow to a roll as we approached for fear I wouldn't be able to stop and would run him over.

Dawson shot out of the passenger side and ran to Garrett. He assessed him quickly, then picked him up as best he could and brought him to the truck. I hopped out and opened the door to the back seat. Dawson and I worked together to ease Garrett on the bench. I climbed in with him and sat so his head could rest in my lap. Dawson drove us back around to the front of the house, where flashing red and blue lights met us.

"Sheriff's department is here," he announced.

"I called them."

"What about me?"

"I did! You didn't answer!"

"No," he shouted before regaining his composure. "I mean you should have told me what you were doing before you even came out here."

"You wanted me to tell you that I intended to break a few laws in order to obtain information I needed to figure out who is behind the scandal I refused to tell you about? That seems totally legit. I'm sure you would have been all-in on that one."

"No. I wouldn't have. I would have told you to sit your ass at home and leave these things to the professionals."

"Yeah, well . . . my dad did that, and it didn't turn out so well for him."

"So now you're a vigilante? Taking the law into your own hands? Because that didn't seem to turn out so well for you, either."

With no clever comeback, I kept my mouth shut and focused my attention on Garrett. He was breathing, but it was shallow and labored. I was worried about him. And I had good reason to be.

"We need to get him to a hospital."

"I'll take him, but I've got to talk to the sheriff before I leave. I'll be quick."

"No, Dawson. He needs a doctor now. If you're not taking him, then I am."

"And how do you propose to do that? The bridge is flooded and almost impassable."

"How did you get here, then? Fly?"

He was quiet for a moment.

"I crossed it."

"Then if your car could get across, I can get this beast across, too."

Dawson put the truck in park next to the two hopped-up sheriff's department SUVs. Instead of getting out, he gripped the wheel and took a deep breath. He looked at me in the rearview mirror, his eyes sharp and narrowed.

"I didn't drive over it," he said. His voice was low and cold, and it made my heart stop for just a second. If he didn't drive across it then . . .

"Oh my God—"

"I don't suggest you try throwing Garrett over your shoulder and walking along the railing, like I did. The current is nasty and the water's cold. It's probably too high now to even attempt it. You'd get washed away for sure. And I really don't feel like launching a search-and-rescue party for you tonight. I think you've made things eventful enough already."

I stared at him in the dark of the truck's cab, trying to make sense of what he was telling me. His car hadn't been able to get over the bridge, so he braved the growing water to get to me. To come to my aid.

The look of surprise on my face made him laugh.

"Close your mouth, Ms. Danners. You look like a cartoon."

With that, he jumped out of the truck and made his way over to the deputies that were attending to Donovan. Sheriff Higgins himself was nowhere to be seen. There were no ambulances there, which told me the water really was dangerously high, but I figured if the sheriff's SUVs could make it, then Donovan's truck could too.

I crawled into the driver's seat and threw on my seat belt. Then I said a little prayer to the God I no longer believed in, and put the truck in gear. I could see the flash of anger in Dawson's face when I spun the tires in the mud, peeling out until I hit the firm ground of the driveway. He yelled something at me—something I couldn't make out—but I saw him run after me as I pulled out onto the road and sped away.

Committing grand theft auto in the process.

"It'll be okay, Garrett. I'll get you to the hospital."

It seemed to take forever to navigate my way down to the overflowing creek, but once there, I knew I could make it. I swallowed down my fear and revved the engine, thinking my best bet was to gun it and hope the weight of the truck and its momentum would carry us across the short span before the water affected us too badly.

Gripping the wheel, I hammered the gas, and we sped toward the creek-turned-river. The splash when we hit it was tremendous, launching up around the sides of the vehicle, temporarily blinding me. But I kept my foot on the gas and powered through. I could hear the metal grinding along the guardrail—the one I was glad was still in place. Donovan's truck wasn't going to make it out of my stunt unscathed, but I didn't care. I just needed Garrett to make it.

I felt the front wheels grip the edge of the road on the far side, and I squealed with delight. I knew we were in the clear. Once the truck was fully out, I hammered the gas yet again and raced off toward the hospital.

Fifteen minutes later, I was standing at the nurses' station, yelling for someone to bring a gurney to the truck I'd illegally parked in the emergency drop-off lane reserved for ambulances. As far as I was concerned, in that moment, I was one.

A flood of scrub-wearing staff came out with the requested gurney and loaded Garrett onto it. I moved the truck, then hurried back into the hospital. Because I wasn't family, I wasn't allowed back to the examination room. Relegated to the waiting room, I plopped myself down in a corner chair and immediately grabbed my ribs.

Then I remembered the phone in my back pocket. I took it out to find that my call with dispatch had been disconnected. I tried to see when the call had ended, but my touch screen was cracked and behaving erratically—probably from getting soaked. I was amazed the damn thing was working at all.

It was functional enough, however, to call and leave a message for Gramps, telling him that Garrett had been hurt and that I was at the hospital, waiting to learn more. I'd be there as long as I needed to be. Then I called Tabby. I'd explain what happened later, but, for now, I just wanted to let her know that we were okay.

Or at least I hoped we would be.

I stood up to go outside and make the call, wincing at the pain in my ribs. A nurse at the front desk noticed my pain and came out to me.

"You need to be seen," she said matter-of-factly, shoving a clipboard into my hands. "You can fill these out in the exam room. Follow me."

She stormed off past the intake desk down a hall to the left. Not wanting to pick a fight with her after everything I'd been through, I let her lead me to a run-of-the-mill exam room, fully equipped with light-green-curtain surround. She drew it back and pointed to the bed, indicating she wanted me to sit on it, so I did. I hitched a hip up on there carefully, holding my ribs as I did.

As she walked away, I asked for directions to the bathroom. She rattled them off while I gingerly climbed down from the bed. The second my feet hit the cool concrete floor, a flash of cold shot through my body, and I broke out in a sweat. My head felt like it was going to explode. Either my adrenaline just crashed or I'd been hurt far worse than I'd imagined. Before the darker implications of my potential shocklike symptoms could fully settle in, I made my way down the hall as the nurse had instructed. There was a rush of hospital staff hurrying about, making me feel dizzy with their movements. The place was busier than I'd expected. I wondered if there'd been a bunch of accidents with the storm.

The pain abated slightly, and I could see the first hall on my left coming up, so I carefully maneuvered around the wheelchairs and gurneys lining the corridor, ready to turn and get out of the chaos of the main hallway. My body swayed hard in the direction—a little too hard—but before I crashed into the wall, I felt a hand on my elbow, stabilizing me.

"Kylene," Luke said, pulling me into his body. "You don't look well. You need to sit down."

He ushered me down the hall to the right, away from the bathroom, and into a private room. It appeared unoccupied, which really didn't matter to me in that moment. I just wanted to sit down and catch my breath. I felt weak and clammy, and I started to let the worry about potential injuries seep through to my conscious mind.

"I need to call the nurse," I said, my voice thin and thready like my racing pulse. I reached toward the call button, but Luke intercepted my hand. He held it in his as he looked down at me. The dark scrutiny in his eyes pulled me from my deteriorating state.

"You just had to get involved, didn't you? Too much like your father, I imagine." I tried to wrench my arm from his grip but I couldn't. He was too strong for me.

"You knew," I wheezed, the pain in my chest making it harder to catch my breath.

"Knew? Ah, c'mon, kiddo. Give me a little more credit than that. I engineered the whole thing. You know how much I like football. I especially like betting on it. I saw an opportunity and I took it. Thanks for giving me the perfect chance, by the way. Couldn't have done it without you."

My eyes went wide.

"You're the one that bought them off—that threatened Jaime!"

"Correct."

"Did you send those threats, too?" I asked, disbelief in my tone. How could I have been so wrong about him?

"C'mon. That's beneath me and you know it. I don't do grunt work. I pay others to do it for me."

Realization slapped me hard.

"You're the Advocatus Diaboli. . . ."

At that, he laughed.

"Hardly. He's a few steps higher up the food chain than me."

I coughed and collapsed in on myself, clutching my ribs as best I could as my strength waned. My traitorous eyes darted over to the nurses' call button once again, but Luke stepped to my side, making it impossible to reach.

"You knew Donovan took those pictures, didn't you?" I said.

He gave me an ambivalent shrug.

"I did. There was evidence enough to prove it. Evidence that never saw the light of day. As for the others, I did what I needed to in order to make sure they all got off. I knew in a year or two, they'd make it worth my while. With that many players under my thumb, I could dictate whether we won or lost—maybe throw a game or two here and there when it suited my purposes."

"You're Donovan's get-out-of-jail-free card—not the sheriff."

"If you want to call it that. . . ."

I craned my neck to look up at him as he loomed above me, a harbinger of doom.

"Why would you admit that?" I asked, though the cold sensation crawling up my back had already answered that question for me. He told me because he could. Because I wouldn't be a liability. I wouldn't be leaving that hospital alive.

The fear that shone in my eyes must have given me away. All he did was smile down at me with a wickedness that made my blood run cold.

"Looks like Donovan might have punctured your lung, Ky. You've got to be careful with injuries like that. You could throw a clot . . . get an embolism. . . ." He withdrew a syringe from his pocket and flicked at it several times with his finger. "I had this ready just in case Donovan didn't finish the job for me. He's a bit unreliable at times—but he sure did a number on your friend. He'll be lucky to make it out of surgery alive." His grin widened. "And if he does . . ." He shook the needle in the air in warning.

I took as deep a breath as possible, mustering what little bit of energy I could, and shot off the bed to the door, hoping I could get there before he stopped me. I didn't have the capacity to scream—nobody would have heard me through the door—but if I could have opened it, I would have had a chance. Unfortunately, I didn't make it more than three steps before Luke hooked an arm around my chest—crushing my injury further—and pulled me against him. I could see the door—my means of escape—but I couldn't reach it. I couldn't even cry out in agony as he squeezed me harder. I just felt the tears run down my face as my mouth flew open, my silent scream unheard.

"This will all be over soon," he said in my ear, holding me with one arm while he flipped the cap off the needle with his free hand. I watched, helpless, as the sharp tip of it came toward my arm. "It'll be over for your dad soon, too. . . ."

My eyes went wide at his words. While my brain absorbed his threat, I saw a familiar face pass by the narrow window in the door. It came back into view, peering in the room. Before I realized what was happening, Sheriff Higgins threw the door open, his gun drawn and trained on Luke.

"I'm gonna need you to put that down, Luke," Sheriff Higgins said. There was a fearful determination in his eyes as he stared down my would-be murderer.

"Let's not give the girl a false sense of hope now, Sheriff. We both know how this is going to end. How it has to end. . . ."

Higgins' grip on his gun twitched before it clamped down even tighter.

"She's too high profile," the sheriff said. "You kill her and it'll come out. *He* won't be happy about that. We'll all go down."

"Not if you do your job. She's troubled. Girls her age disappear all the time around these parts. . . ."

The sheriff's expression went slack.

"And my son . . . ?"

"I think you know the answer to that question already, Jack."

"Shoot him," I said weakly, drawing Sheriff Higgins' attention to me.

"He knows he can't do that," Luke said, condescension dripping from his tone.

I looked down at the needle looming dangerously near my arm. All I needed was a distraction—just a little time to get away from him.

"Whatever they have on you," I started, pinning my stare on Garrett's dad, "it can't be worth your son's life. You already lost your wife. What's left for you if you lose him, too?"

Sheriff Higgins' eyes darted from me to Luke and back to me again. Then he took a step closer, his gun aimed at Luke's head.

"You shoot and you'll end up taking her out, too," Luke said. "And nobody will be coming to your aid. You'll find yourself in the cell next to her father."

He took another step.

"My aim is pretty damn good."

"You'd better hope so."

I could feel Luke's heart racing against my back, and I knew that time was running out. I looked up at the sheriff, begging him to focus on me. When his eyes met mine, I mouthed the words "on three." Then I silently counted down.

One . . .

Two . . .

Three!

The sheriff lunged for Luke's arm while I used every ounce of energy I had to push it away from me. The second the sheriff grabbed a hold of it, I ducked underneath, despite the screaming pain in my chest, and staggered out of harm's way. I scrambled on all fours to the door, looking back over my shoulder to the struggle behind me. Luke had wrestled the sheriff's gun away from him and had him pinned to the ground. Sheriff Higgins was fighting for control of it, and it didn't look promising for him. I knew if I'd called for help, it would be too late. Luke was younger and stronger, and he was going to win. If he did, I was dead, plain and simple.

I saw the syringe lying on the floor, and I quietly made my way over to it. I snatched it up and hesitated for a second. Only one.

Then I slammed it into Luke's neck, dispensing the deadly liquid inside.

He wheeled around, arms flailing up to where I'd just withdrawn the syringe.

"You bitch!" he seethed. He shot himself at me, knocking me to the ground. He climbed on top of me and wrapped his hands around my throat. "If I go, you go with me."

He continued to choke me until his grip started to weaken— his face growing pale. Then he collapsed. Sheriff Higgins pulled me gently to my feet. Luke lay on the floor, stone cold dead. Whatever had been in that needle was highly effective.

"We need to get you a doctor," he said, ignoring the dead man, the problem he'd have to clean up.

"You need to go," I said, my voice rough and harsh.

He ignored me entirely.

"Here," he said, reaching out to help me walk.

I looked up to find Sheriff Higgins' stern expression staring down at me while he escorted me toward the door. I could see determination twisting his features, but there was something else in his gaze as he ushered me away from the dead body.

Fear.

"Sheriff Higgins, I'm so sorry about—"

"Not a word, Kylene," he said, shutting me up in a hurry. "Garrett's in surgery. He's gonna be fine. He has to be. . . ." His tone was softer—far less gruff than it had been. He lingered there for a moment, silent, and I wanted him to say something— anything, really. Yell at me if he wanted to. It was my fault his son was hurt. If he wanted to take that out on me, I could hardly blame him.

"Donovan beat him with a baseball bat."

"I know." Judging by the strain in his features, he was working hard to control whatever mix of emotions was swirling within him. "From what I've heard, you came close to suffering the same fate as my boy." I didn't dare speak, afraid the tears I was fighting back would spill forth, so I nodded instead. "Kylene, I need you to hear me and hear me well, girl. You don't know what you're messing with. You've stumbled onto something bigger than you can even begin to imagine. You need to walk away, or I can assure you, you won't like what happens. A beating with a baseball bat will be the least of your worries."

I wanted to be angry with him—to yell at him for being a coward. A liar. A disgrace to the badge. But behind his cop bravado, I could see what was driving him. There was a waver to his voice that I'd heard before. One I'd heard when my father sat me down in the basement of our old home and made me promise him I wouldn't lie on the stand. He understood the consequences of that action far more than I could have ever fathomed. I wasn't thinking clearly at the time. I had a singular focus—keeping him out of prison.

The parallels between that situation and the one I had found myself in were not lost on me. Sheriff Higgins was clearly aware of things that I was not. Things I probably couldn't have even begun to comprehend in that moment. My focus had once again been too singular for me to care. His hope was to broaden the scope so as to avoid unpleasant consequences. Consequences he appeared convinced I'd face.

"The people you're involved with—"

"Not now, Kylene. I need to deal with this," he said, looking back to Luke's body.

"No," I said softly as a grim realization dawned on me. "You

need to go. It's important that you look like you had no involvement in this. Get out. Go stand by the nurses' station. I'll
wait a couple of minutes and then call for help."

"You're just like your father, girl. You get something in your
head and you just can't let it go. You're gonna dig and dig until
you bury yourself alive in the wreckage of everything you've
torn apart to get to the truth." He leaned in close to me, pinning
stone cold eyes on mine. "Just like your father did. . . ." His
words permeated every pore in my body, leaving me paralyzed. "You think your father is in prison because he actually
committed that crime? That he shot that man in cold blood to
cover his ass?" My blank stare proved answer enough. Sheriff
Higgins looked around the room as though he might be overheard, then he lowered his voice and leaned in even closer still.
"Your father poked around just like you are now, and he pissed
off the wrong people. He's lucky prison was where he ended
up." While I stared at him, trying desperately to wrap my
head around what he'd just admitted, he continued: "Guilt and
innocence ain't black and white, Kylene. They're shades of
gray. Those people your father messed with painted him into
the verdict that they needed. You keep doing what you're
doing, and you will learn the hard way, too. Lady Justice is far
from blind."

He flashed me a look of warning before turning to leave.
Then he opened the door and disappeared through it without
another word. But really, what else was there to say? Sheriff
Higgins had just told me that he knew my father was innocent.

I just needed to prove it.

FORTY

I walked into the courthouse ready to face down the asshole that had ruined my life and nearly killed my best friend. It was only his arraignment, but I needed to be there, needed to see him shuffle into the courtroom, hands cuffed in front of him, feet shackled, wearing a bright orange county-issued jumpsuit. The satisfaction in that alone would take the edge off what he'd done to my life. But it was only the tip of the iceberg. Knowing he'd do hard time for how he'd beaten Garrett didn't seem punishment enough, but it would have to do.

Justice isn't always as satisfying as victims need it to be.

I made my way down the hall looking for Tabby, who'd insisted on being there. Instead of a gawky redhead waiting for me outside the courtroom, I found AJ Miller standing there, looking uncertain but resolved. Mark Sinclair stood at his side. He gave me a nod that said so much—that he was sorry, that he'd tried to warn me that afternoon at the store. That maybe he wasn't the criminal I'd thought him to be.

As my pace slowed, AJ pushed off the wall and came toward me. We met in the middle of the hall, adults rushing around us, and stood there awkward and silent for way too long.

"AJ—" He cut my words short with a gentle brush of his fingers along the bruise on my cheek.

"Don't say it. Please . . . I don't need you to say it."

"I'm so sorry."

He let out an exhale, dropping his hand to his side.

"You just can't help yourself, can you?" He smiled as he scolded me, but there was a weariness to his tone. A sadness and frustration he couldn't cover up. His words went so much deeper than the context of that conversation.

I opened my mouth to reply, but nothing came out. Because how do you even begin to really apologize for what I'd demonized him for? There was no Hallmark card for "sorry I blamed you for a crime you didn't commit." Sorry in general just seemed to fall short.

A flash of red in my periphery distracted me from the depths of AJ's green stare for a second. Tabby approached us cautiously, like if she made the wrong move, the moment would all fall apart. I gave her a nod, and she turned back around and went inside, leaving me with AJ in our never-ending moment of awkwardness.

"I have to go," I said finally, doing my best to sound normal and not let the emotions building up inside me show. I needed a stone face when I saw Donovan. To show him that he didn't beat me.

"Do you want me to come with you?"

I shook my head.

"I'll be fine."

Forcing a tight smile, I brushed past him, headed for the door Tabby had disappeared through. I didn't look back to see if AJ had followed. I could feel the weight of his stare as I walked away.

Because Donovan's case involved minors, the room was only open to victims, law enforcement, family, and friends. Meg was waiting in the front row of the gallery with Tabby seated next to her. They waved me over, and I slid past a couple of sheriff's deputies to sit down in between them. Tabby immediately took my hand in hers, giving it a little squeeze to tell me she was there for me. That she had my back.

I squeezed hers in return to let her know I was okay.

"He's up next," Meg whispered in my ear. "I don't want this to upset you, but he's pleading not guilty. I wanted to tell you so you weren't blindsided."

"I figured he would," I replied, my tone hushed so we didn't get kicked out.

"There's a mountain of evidence, and his attorney is the worst public defender ever to pass the bar. He's going down, Ky—for what he did to you and Garrett as well as the photos. Everyone will know you didn't lie about that night, I promise you that." Meg hesitated for a second, which drew my attention. The worry in her brow was plain. "As for Luke—"

"You couldn't have known, Meg. I would never have guessed, either. . . ."

She nodded in silence as the judge ordered the next case to begin. Once called, I watched Donovan, in his orange jumpsuit, ushered over to his attorney at the defendant's table. The fact that he had the world's shittiest attorney told me that whoever had been backing him had dropped him like the sack of shit he was. No more get-out-of-jail-free cards for the football god. Just prison—provided the court system didn't fail me, again.

The whole process was entirely anticlimactic, and over almost before it started. His bail was set at an astronomical number, the judge citing that the gruesome nature of Garrett's attack and the predatory nature Donovan had displayed when he sexually exploited me as his reasons. The judge wasn't a fool. He knew Donovan was dangerous.

With a whack of the gavel, Donovan was led off by the bailiff. He looked over his shoulder at the crowd, finding me easily among the few faces there. He hadn't lost any of the heat from his stare. I let a serpent's smile spread wide across my face in response. Then I blew him a kiss goodbye. His eyes went wide and murderous, but they soon disappeared around the corner. He and his murderous eyes were headed back to jail, where they belonged.

The judge announced that court was concluded for the morning, and one by one everyone left the room. Meg had work to do and headed back to her office. Tabby's dad was meeting her for lunch. She asked if I wanted to come along, but I was in no mood for that. When I declined, she hesitated, her desire to argue with me written all over her worried expression, but she didn't. Instead, she bent down and gave me a careful hug. Then she too walked out of the room, the door closing behind her echoing through the empty space.

I sat alone on the hard wood bench and stared at the defendant's table. I couldn't shake the sense of déjà vu coursing through my veins. With every beat of my heart, it grew stronger.

I had vowed to get justice for my father when I returned to town. That I wouldn't rest until I cleared my father's name. But even in my brief search for answers, it became abundantly clear that the conspiracy ran deep. That there were players so untouchable that I would need help in reaching them. As much as I hated to admit it, I couldn't do it alone.

I heard the door to the courtroom push open, followed by heavy, deliberate footsteps. They came all the way up to the front row before stopping. I didn't bother to look up. I knew the sound of that determined gait. That confident swagger.

"Mind if I sit?" Dawson asked. I barely nodded in reply.

He joined me on the bench, his shoulder brushing up against mine as we sat in silence. I shifted my gaze to the witness stand—the one from which I would find myself testifying against Donovan. I stared at it thinking of how I'd failed my father when I'd taken it before, and vowed not to fail Garrett the same way.

"It won't go to trial," Dawson said as if reading my mind. "He'll strike a deal for a reduced sentence. Sorry to be the bearer of that particular news, but it's true. No lawyer in their right mind would go to trial with his case."

"Okay . . ."

Silence.

"How are your ribs?"

"Sore . . ."

He hesitated before pursuing the conversation further.

"I'm sorry . . . about what happened to you—"

"It's not your fault—"

"Not that," he said, cutting me off. "I'm sorry about what those boys put you through."

Ah. That sorry.

"Not your fault, either, but thanks."

"And I'm sorry I pushed you to tell me about it."

"You couldn't have known."

"No," he replied, his voice distant, "but he's going to pay for all of it."

"And I get vindication." I damn near choked on the word. "It doesn't feel as great as I'd hoped it would."

"Vengeance isn't as satisfying as we'd like sometimes." He fell silent for a moment, his gaze dropping to the floor before he spoke. "Listen, Danners. I have to tell you something you're not going to like hearing." He took my lack of response as a go-ahead and continued. "We learned something else during Dr. Carle's interrogation. Something that indicates his involvement with an underage prostitution ring in southern Ohio." I could feel the weight of his stare on the side of my face. "But something tells me you already knew that." I didn't bother to respond. I could hear in his tone that he already knew about my observation of his interrogation. "This girl—we know she's from Jasperville. That there are others being prostituted here as well." My head turned slowly to face his. "I'm going to be going undercover to find out who's behind the sex ring."

"That's a career-making assignment," I replied, my voice neutral.

A pause.

"And you're my cover story."

I blinked repeatedly, trying to pull myself from my running thoughts to focus on what he'd just said.

"Excuse me?"

"I'm going to pose as your boyfriend from Columbus—Alex."

He continued to talk, but my brain shut out his words. Everything he said sounded fuzzy, like I was underwater. By the time he'd finished his brief explanation, he stood up, waiting for me to join him.

"We need to go," he said as though he'd been forced to repeat himself.

"Why?"

"Court is back in session," he said, looking at the few adults entering the room.

"I'll be right out," I said, turning to focus on the witness stand again. He hovered for a moment before walking away, leaving me alone with my careening thoughts.

I'd gotten vengeance for myself and put the photo scandal to rest—finally. And though there was immense satisfaction in that outcome, it wasn't enough. Until my dad was free to share in that victory, it seemed tarnished somehow. Tainted.

My resolve was renewed in that courtroom.

What I needed to do was buckle down and figure out exactly how his case, Agent Reider, the sheriff, and the Advocatus Diaboli all interrelated. That was the only lead of substance I'd

come across that could prove my father's innocence. But I couldn't make anything of it on my own. It was way above my skill level.

Not so of Agent Dawson.

If he needed my help to go undercover, then he could have it—at a price. In return for my assistance, he'd help me do the one thing he'd rather die than do. Dawson was going to help me prove my father's innocence.

Together, we'd bring down the Advocatus Diaboli.